MacAVITY'S PUB

A Mystery

by

Dan H. McLachlan

In the smoky mirror of fiction, this book reflects actual incidents that occurred forty years after the Vietnam War. Beyond that, it is a fabrication. Names, characters, places, and incidents either are products of the author's imagination or are used fictitiously, and any resemblance to actual events or persons, living or dead, is entirely coincidental.

Copyright © 2009 Dan H. McLachlan
First Edition
All rights reserved. No part of this book may be reproduced or transmitted in any form or by any electronic or mechanical means, including photocopying, recording or by any information storage and retrieval system, without the written permission of the publisher, except where permitted by law.

cover by Linda Scott
author photo by Liela E.R. McLachlan

Published by Aventine Press
750 State St. #319
San Diego CA, 92101

Library of Congress Control Number: 2009934724
Library of Congress Cataloging-in-Publication Data

ISBN: 1-59330-607-5

Printed in the United States of America.

Acknowledgments

The following people love challenges. They helped me with advice, information, stories, editing, and encouragement. They are Professor Howard McCord (ret.); Lieutenant Colonel Donald B. Kaag (ret.); Dr. Jay Hunter, M.D.; Mert Geltz; Randy and Dee Hall; Deputy Mike Neelon, Latah Sheriff's Department; Corporal Scott Mkolajczyk, Latah County Sheriff's Department; Detective Joshua Larson, Latah County Sheriff's Department; Bill Thompson, Prosecuting Attorney, Latah County; Sharon Taylor-Hall; Bill Hall; Captain Danny Danielson, who also helped edit; Colonel Bud Hall (ret.); Lieutenant Commander Ed Morken; Ed Baldus; Linda Scott; and my son, Peter S. McLachlan.

I am particularly indebted to my wife, Liela E.R. McLachlan, who did meticulous editings and gave valuable advice.

"So, whose idea was it to mess with those old shits, anyway?"

--Jerry Hobbs-Smith, Camas Tribe

Chapter
One

I worked the gears in Leap's Western Star semi headed into town to dump grain at the elevators. The cab was hot, and I was bored with the hauling of wheat. I let my mind drift over the treetops winding down the banks of Ryback Creek, wishing I could pull over and nap in the shade.

A CB conversation started to squawk from the radio bolted under the dash. It was Smoke. He sounded excited about something. It sounded like he was out towards the breaks above the Clearwater River.

There was a four inch lip where the town's pavement begins, and I jolted over it with the familiar whanging of haul gear that sounded like a drawer of scrap iron falling on concrete. I pulled over and turned up the volume to hear better.

The airways are usually pretty silent during harvest, the calls crisp. Voices low and calm. But not now.

"No. I don't see anyone now. Where's Hammersmith? Get hold of him!" Smoke said.

"He's walking over to his Gleaner now." Sounded like Mike, Hammersmith's foreman.

Nearly thirty of us, scattered over the Bench busy at the harvest, remained silent, listening.

"Can you get his attention, Mike?"

"Hang on."

A minute or two passed.

Finally, "Hammersmith. Pick up!"

Hammersmith came on loud and out of sorts. "What?"

"I'm above your place. A beat up car is in front. I saw two guys go in," Smoke told him.

Hammersmith's farm sat in a hollow above the breaks where our bench land dropped one-thousand, five-hundred feet down to the Clearwater.

"In *where*, Smoke? I'm busy here."

"I saw two guys go into your house, Eric! Listen to me! They parked out front and went up and through your front door!"

I could hear the static of the airways while Hammersmith considered this. "Can you see if Ruthie's home?" he asked.

"She took the car and left about two hours ago, Eric, when I was doing the ridge. She pulled by me."

Again things went silent. I pulled the brakes and waited.

"Jables! You there?" Hammersmith suddenly bellowed over the speaker.

"Yup," Jable's deep voice came back. It sounded like he was far out on the edge, over by his slopes at the foot of Cup Hand Ridge. His farm bordered Hammersmith's.

"Meet me at the house."

"Gotcha."

"I'm coming," Mike said.

Hammersmith barked, "I know you are. Pick me up."

Smoke came on again, "I'm going to park the combine on your back road, Hammersmith. They won't get by me."

"You have your .243?" Jables asked.

Smoke laughed. I could see him in my mind. He was always armed. He never removed his .243 from behind his truck seat, and he often packed a Kimber Ultra Carry .45. He had also been a Vietnam fighter pilot and was the only one I knew of who smoked long, thin cigars almost constantly, even while harvesting.

"I'll watch them though the scope, pardner, 'till you get here."

No one spoke. I waited, and then finally decided to release the brakes and drive the short distance to the scales. Hammersmith came back on. He sounded closer in, and I could tell he was in his truck now by the high RPM's whining in the background.

"Anyone out near the exits?" he asked, with a hitch in his voice as his truck took him over a water bar.

For the next few minutes we keyed in from all the edges of the fifteen by ten mile bench. Since I was at the elevators with about six other trucks, we were nearest the single north/south highway in Idaho, Highway 95, that was five miles due east of town. We told him. There are also three other exits from the Bench, two down narrow canyons to the river and one going north over Cup Hand Ridge and into the Bitterroots.

"You folks bottle up the exits," Hammersmith said.

Hammersmith had been a naval commander during the Vietnam war. And it crossed my mind as I jacked my semi across the paved road out of town that these two guys in his house were certain to have stumbled on Hammersmith's study by now. This dark, heavily draped room was where he kept his ribbons, his ship's colors, his American flag, the photo of him standing beside Kennedy, and photos of his ship's bridge, decks, turrets, crewmen, and friends. If I were these guys, I would run as fast as I could out of the house and the hell out of the state. It would have been like innocently looking into a closet and seeing a fifteen foot black mamba sleeping on a pile of laundry.

One by one over the next twenty minutes we let Hammersmith know we were in place.

And then we waited. We drank from our gallon jugs, took bites from sandwiches, and did what we old timers did best, enjoy the comfortable world of our thoughts.

My trailer holds sixty thousand pounds of wheat. It has two dumps and is about as long as can be possibly driven over the rolling dirt roads that twist among the dune-like hills of the Bench. On Hammersmith's instructions, I had the trailer running along the one and one half lane road with the tractor cab jogged sideways on the asphalt. There were three turnouts across the four foot deep ditches that ran beside the road, and we had blocked those too with one truck from the Baldus and two from the Cricket farms.

I decided to get out of the cab, stretch my legs, and then take a bottle of Windex and a couple sections of paper towels and see if I could get the dust and chaff off the windows for a change.

The air was still, and the elevators had shut down their lifts while everyone waited. The silence was nice. Ryback, population one-hundred and seventy, simmered quietly under its canopy of elms, sycamores and locusts. We didn't have the luxury of children's voices squealing at their games--they had all grown up and moved away. Even the birds were silent in the intense heat. The dog days of August.

Suddenly Smoke's garbled voice, shouted over the CB.

"...taking off...st..."

Three loud bangs thumped over the speakers.

Hammersmith keyed in, "They're coming your way Jake. Don with you?"

"He's here," she said. "We have the International just out of sight around the elbow."

"You'd better stand off," Hammersmith told them. "Smoke punched a couple .243 holes in their trunk and it's leaking gas."

"Got it." It was Don. He and Jake were the best married team on the bench, and the money rolled in for them.

Don came back on after a moment.

"Hammersmith. Better call someone. The way we're set up they'll hit the semi before they know its on the bend."

I understood what he was saying. The grade down Rattlesnake was ten feet wide, steep, graveled, and hung five hundred feet above the creek. The canyon was no more than a notch narrow and deep as an ax blow. These two guys, if they went off the road, were in for a nasty flight.

"We should wait," Jables came on with. "They might stop and start running on foot. No need to bother anyone."

Magnet was the nearest town of any size, and was a forty minute drive away. Everyone knew what Jables was saying, but it didn't really matter. No one could alter the fate these two had spun for themselves.

Now the CB started chattering like a swatted hive. Everyone in the fields had driven or climbed to the high points that looked over the entire Bench.

"They're still coming your way, Jake."

"They're moving hell bent for leather. Dust is rolling out behind them."

Sitting in my truck was like listening to old time adventure radio.

"Holy shit!" This BB Boyde, Leap's grandson. "They just went by below me sideways in the gravel! They must be going fucking eighty!"

"Language, BB," Leaps keyed.

"He's right! They're rolling thunder," someone said.

I found myself holding my breath, sitting on the edge of the seat, my feet out the door on the high step listening.

Then, "They're over the rim and coming at you two. Hang tight!" It was Huey, nicknamed for the Navy Huey helicopters he'd flown in Vietnam.

Don came on again. His voice was lower than usual and he spoke slowly and clearly.

"Hammersmith, they went off the road. They took to the air to miss the truck."

We could hear a stuttering meowing in the background, like a small, wounded animal. For the life of me I couldn't picture what it might be.

Finally Hammersmith asked carefully, "They all right?"

"Not so much," Don said. "They're down in the creek. I'll need some help plowing a firebreak on the east rim. The barley's not in yet."

At that point Lonnie, a towering man who was our mayor and grower's union manager cut in.

"I'll take it from here, men," he said. "Thanks for everyone's help. I suggest you either get back to work or help with the fire." He paused, measuring his words. "No need to hang around and interfere with the sheriff's business. I'll make the calls."

Almost as soon as he signed off the town's siren howled to life, and moments later the fire engine roared out of town, volunteers hanging off it like Keystone Cops.

"Paul. You there?" Don radioed.

Surprised, I unclipped the mike from the dash.

"I'm here, Don."

"Lana at home?"

"Yes, she is."

"I'm here, Don," Lana piped in from the house.

"Could you come out to Rattlesnake for a bit, Lana?"

"Jake?" Lana asked.

"A little. Yes," Don said.

Chapter Two

Most people don't understand how tedious working harvest is. It's hot, dusty, tiring, repetitive, and boring.

We were running behind, however, so Leaps kept us at it the rest of the day rather than letting us on the fire line. I did find some solace, however, in listening to the action over the truck's CB, visualizing everything as it played out.

By two that afternoon the heat was at its one-hundred plus worst, forty acres of Don's barley had burned and more was getting away from him by the minute, Hammersmith had been robbed, two guys had burned to death at the bottom of Rattlesnake, and Jake, one of the toughest gals out there, was sitting on her ranch house porch with Lana sipping iced tea laced with rum. In short, it hadn't been a good day for the town.

Smoke continued to shuffle back and forth in his bank-out wagon hauling grain back from Leap's combines to my semi. I continued to listen to the airways, my CB turned up over the rumble of our diesels.

Ryback's ambulance and fire truck were on the rim of the canyon. They had been joined by seven farms that showed up with their water trucks and their crews that arrived separately. The field hands came mounted on 4-wheelers and tore across the rolling fields from all directions at the sharp ends of dust clouds that streamed behind them. Their equipment racks bristled with shovels like lances held by mounted Sioux.

Overhead, the smoke towered like a nuclear cloud, dwarfing the scene and plunging everything into an orange and black darkness split by the flickering serpent of flame crawling through the barley.

By the time the three, big, off-road fire trucks made it down from Magnet, things were only beginning to get under control. Don had plowed a swath twenty feet wide as best he could around the rim, but still the barley burned, outrunning him. Rattlesnake was hopelessly ablaze in a firestorm that raced its length up to the shallow pinch where two water trucks had stopped to wait for it.

Watching all this from the grade, Charlie Rand, our sheriff, leaned against the door of his white Ford Expedition. He studied the roadbed and tumble marks the twisted car had made to where its blackened shell now lay on the scorched rocks far below.

Short, slender and powerful, Charlie had been raised with his three brothers and two sisters at the foot of the Bitterroots on his family's three thousand acre homestead ranch. He had been a fine cowboy, a moderate rodeo roper, and had finally left his crowd of siblings to study law enforcement in Denver. After ten years, he grew tired of being shot at by deep-fried teens, and came back home to work his way up in the sheriff's department.

As sheriff, Charlie could get out of his uniform. He said he never liked them. Felt more at home in his ranch duds, and now he stood with his weathered, gray felt Stetson pushed back on his thick, black hair. He wore faded Wranglers over the top of his boots, and had his badge hooked onto his belt next to his holstered Colt XSE .45 Commander.

Harvest fires are a common occurrence here on the Bench where it gets so hot and dry that simply spinning a combine wheel on the stubble could ignite one. And so the effectiveness and swiftness of the fire trucks was no surprise to anyone.

Within the half hour the top fires were out and Don was able to finish plowing the fire line. Then everyone walked to intercept Huey's Dodge pickup that came bounding towards them through the grain.

In moments beer cans were tossed out and opened, and everyone stood and watched the canyon burn clean. They drank and wiped sweat from their soot blackened faces, and cheered as eleven deer, two of them bucks, escaped the flames and ran out across the fields towards Cup Hand Ridge.

Now the upper canyon was bare of brush, the ground smoking here and there, and below the burned-out car, three sets of firemen, four to a group, were lowering themselves into the canyon on two-inch hoses. Soon they reached bottom and began putting out flames that crawled down against the updrafts.

The difficulty for the men was the steepness of the gravel and talus on the sides below the road. Still, they made short work of stopping the flames' march and hung on as the haul-backs assisted their returns. It was a slick operation, and the blackened fighters were greeted at Huey's truck with opened beers and handshakes all around.

The last transmission I listened to before calling it a day was that Sherman Vics, the coroner, had arrived in his ugly brown Suburban. Soon he was bitching about having to be lowered to the wreck ahead of the body recovery guys from the ambulance. Apparently he felt they would accidentally kick a rock down and kill him. He was a little guy, but feisty, and he rarely allowed anyone to push him around without getting an ear full.

Only Charlie and one fire truck remained to set the ropes, and it sounded like Don and a few curious stragglers were standing around waiting to see what came out. I reasoned Don felt he *had* to stay, it being his land, even though he was worried about Jake. But Jake and Lana were probably into their third rums and were doing just fine.

At that point I swung around and parked the big rig on top where we had left off, set the brakes, and got out into a blessed breeze. As usual, Smoke had taken off for MacAvity's Pub while I was making my last run. My guess was that nearly the entire Bench would be there ad hoc, and I headed in to take part.

Chapter
Three

From the air Ryback looks looks like an oasis in the middle of the Sahara. Or better still, a small, tree choked island on a rolling sea. To its north, shaped like a bent finger pointing to the Bitterroots, Cup Hand Ridge lifts heavily from the surge, pines swaying on its summit. In the spring, the ocean swells are emerald green, spotted with patches of bright yellow canola fields that float randomly out from its slopes. Now, in August, the deeps have turned a dark gold, weighed down with grain.

The Camas Tribe, living down on the shores of the Clearwater, say if you want to know who you are, look around--what you see is yourself. I understand that. That's how I feel.

I came into town and headed for my normal parking spot under an old locust across from MacAvity's Pub. There must have been thirty trucks and a smattering of cars parked around the building, so I drove the four blocks home and walked back.

Ryback's downtown is two streets wide and two blocks long. It sits at the bottom of a large city park that slopes up to the graveyard and Lutheran church. The church's tall, white steeple looks down on us all.

One of the town's streets holds the elevators, our Ryback Union Warehouse Company office, Black's Welding, and the Warehouse-owned store. Parallel to this street is Main Street, lined by a seamless row of abandoned one story brick buildings that had once been stores, the city hall, library, and jail.

Butte MacAvity's Pub rises two stories from the corner in a red brick tower of arched windows and intricate ledges. His grandfather, Coe MacAvity, had fled Scotland's depression and built MacAvity's Pub in 1886 from local clay he wagoned in and kilned against the slope. Butte's father and then Butte himself, now seventy-eight, had kept it humming ever since.

Grandpa Coe, homesick for Scotland and single malt whiskey, designed the interior to resemble his favorite watering hole in Glasgow. Bar in front, four booths down one side, tables in the back, Coe's living quarters above; this was as he remembered it. The finished structure, "Coe's Doom" as nay-sayers called it back then, stood alone in the prairie like a lighthouse, and Ryback grew up around it.

Nothing about MacAvity's has changed since. It is exactly the same now as then.

Butte reached for my bottle of Wiser's Whiskey the moment I stepped in. The place was packed, and I had to crane my neck before I saw Hammersmith, Leaps, Smoke, and Huey sitting in a booth. The crowd had displaced them from their usual stools at the bar. Smoke practically ripped a chair out from under a field hand and slid it over, motioning me to sit down.

"The elevator still open?" Leaps asked.

"I was the last, I think," I said. I turned to Hammersmith. "Anything missing from the house?"

"Nothing touched I could tell," he said, probably for the tenth time. "Well, except for in my study. They pushed a bunch of stuff around and been in my desk before they heard we were coming."

I raised my eyebrows.

"Ruthie left the CB on in the kitchen," he explained. "They musta heard Smoke talk about his .243. I think we would have got them, otherwise. I think Smoke wanted to sight-in before elk season." This drew a dry laugh from us.

"Were they looking for something?"

"I don't know for sure."

Butte placed my Wiser's ditch down in front of me, and Hammersmith slid a pile of money towards him, but Butte ignored it and worked back through the crowd.

I watched him go and realized we all, everyone in the bar, looked like a gathering of rest home residents high on steroids and ready to raise hell. I don't think a solitary person among us was under the age of fifty. And except for Smoke's cigarillos, there wasn't a cigarette in the place. Apparently all our smokers were dead now.

Huey was telling about his talk with the firemen.

"No," he was saying. "There was only *one* body in the car. Just one."

Practically the whole crowd had one ear on our table and the place went silent.

"But there were two!" someone said. "We all saw two, didn't we?"

Smoke tapped his ashes down the neck of an empty beer bottle. "Yes, we did."

"We sure did, indeed," Don said from the door.

We turned as he and Jake entered, followed by Lana and Charlie, the sheriff. Charlie had his hat off and wiped his forehead on his shirt sleeve.

Butte started pulling up glasses for them as they made their way though the throng over to our table.

Lana slid onto my knee and Charlie propped one arm on top of the booth behind Smoke, leaned over and shook a paper bag out onto the table. Hammersmith jerked his tall rum and soda out of harm's way.

The crowd pushed forward to have a look.

There, among the sweat rings from our drinks, lay a charred Zippo lighter and an odd looking pistol with a long, cylindrical barrel.

The place was dead silent except for the sound of clothes rubbing as people shifted to see better.

"This gun yours, Eric?" Charlie said.

"Charlie, I don't even know what kind of gun that is," Hammersmith said.

"All right." Charlie reached down and took up the lighter, "I got through to Erickson, and he said he hasn't taken up smoking, and he hasn't been burglarized today or any other day."

Erickson was our area's Game Warden.

"So, is *this* yours?" he asked. He placed the blackened metal lighter in Hammersmith's hand.

Hammersmith turned the lighter over and rubbed his gnarled thumb over it to read something that was engraved on its face. He then turned it so the ceiling light could hit it. He squinted. And then, as if dark shadow had passed over his face, he looked around at all of us, pushed back his glasses and pinched the bridge of his nose. Then he placed the lighter delicately on the table and sat back in his booth, his head against the leather. He folded his weathered, arthritic hands neatly on top of one another and shut his eyes.

Charlie didn't move a muscle.

Finally Smoke couldn't stand it any more and reached out, shutting one of his eyes as he picked up the lighter and looked at the inscription. I leaned away from Lana so I could see too.

The engraving said "Game Warden" in an arch below the lid. And below that was an engraving of a speed boat with a large wheel house and gear fore and aft.

"Holy shit," Smoke whispered, handing it off to Huey. "Recognize that, pardner?"

Huey took it from him and held it close to his round, Irish face.

"This isn't no game warden's, Charlie," Huey told him.

"That's what I figured," Charlie took the lighter from him and dropped it back into the bag. He came around beside me, reached over and placed the pistol in as well.

He then turned, rolling the top of the bag shut, and said, "Let's go up into your kitchen, Butte."

I turned. MacAvity was standing inches from my back. He nodded, turned and headed to a stairway door at the back of the building. People smoothly made room for him.

Charlie turned to us. "We're going to go get some privacy." He looked at our little group, "You here've seen it, so you're a part of this." He motioned for Jake, who was standing with some of the other women at the corner of the bar, to join us, then glanced and nodded OK to Leaps, who opted out with a shake of his head and walked out.

Butte MacAvity lived by himself in the upstairs quarters. He never married, he was an excellent cook and did most the cooking for the pub's counter meals. His quarters were tidy and rich in dark varnished wood, with walls overburdened by book shelves that lined every room save the kitchen. MacAvity lived quietly. He pretty much kept to himself and let rumors about him run their courses and fade away.

Smoke, Hammersmith and Huey knew their way around better than I, at least in the kitchen. In fact, Smoke went directly over to a cabinet, pulled it open, and took down a bottle of Laphroaig to refreshen his drink. Butte didn't pay him any mind.

In the center of the large kitchen was a dark eight foot plank Scottish farm table. Charlie again reached into the bag and carefully placed the remnants of the pistol in the table's center.

Butte pulled up two more chairs and motioned for us to be seated, but remained standing, himself. He took down a beautiful crystal two ounce tumbler and Smoke handed the scotch to him.

"This what I think it is, Butte?" Charlie asked, holding up the gun's burned remains.

"Absolutely," MacAvity said.

"Could you tell us?"

"It's called a hush puppy," he said.

Smoke, once our high school dare devil, smiled his thin smile, eyes keen like a border collie's.

"You know that too, Smoke?" Charlie asked, turning to him.

"Yup."

Then, "You, too, Huey?"

"Yes sir."

"Hammersmith?" he said, looking at Hammersmith for the first time since we sat down. "You *did* know what this was, didn't you?"

Hammersmith nodded, looking Charlie in the eye.

"You four are all Navy, right?" he asked, including Butte as he looked them over.

"Yup," Smoke said, sipping from his drink.

Charlie considered this as we all waited.

"Well then, with all due respect, let me ask you, Hammersmith, what the heck is this pistol--this 'hush puppy'--all about?"

Hammersmith pushed the long, cylindrical barrel of the automatic pistol around so that it was straight across in front of him. He refolded his hands on the edge of the table and leaned forward against them. "It's a silenced HiStandard HD Military Model .22LR. It was developed by the OSS."

Charlie nodded. "How'd these guys in the car get it?"

Hammersmith shook his head. "I couldn't tell you," he said. "Some of them were smuggled home after Vietnam. Maybe it's one of them."

Huey stretched his hand out and put it palm down on the table. "Look, Hammersmith, it's like..."

"I'll tell it, Huey," Smoke said. "Sit back and take a breath, OK?"

Huey blinked twice, then nodded and leaned back in his chair, his eyes returning to the tabletop.

I glanced over at Lana. She looked interested, but like she felt we shouldn't be here listening to this.

"So?" Charlie said, turning attention back to Smoke again.

MacAvity suddenly moved behind Smoke and put both his long-fingered hands on Smoke's shoulders.

"I'm Old Navy too, Charlie," Butte said. "You know that. Both Hammersmith and I, we go way back--you understand?"

He pointed to the pistol. "That pistol and that lighter are connected, and unless those two boys are a hell of a lot older than Smoke told me they looked, then there's no way in hell they could lay claim to those things as theirs. They had to get them from someone who was Special Ops in Vietnam."

I had to believe what he was saying because everyone in town knew he was a seven-gun-man, meaning he carried a different gun every day of the week. It was rumored he had a false wall in MacAvity's Pub where he stored nearly a hundred rifles, machine guns and pistols.

It was Charlie's turn to place his palm flat on the table in MacAvity's direction. "You said the lighter and the pistol are connected. You wanna explain?"

Hammersmith said, "The lighter belonged to someone who participated in the Mekong Delta's 'Game Warden' operation, Charlie. The pistol was the tool the Studies and Observation Group, or SOG, guys used. It was used for assassinations behind enemy lines. The SEALs carried them from time to time too."

No one said anything for some time.

Then, finally, Charlie got to his feet. He heaved a sigh, squared his Stetson on his head and walked over to the back door leading from the kitchen down the rear of MacAvity's Pub.

"Well, folks," he said, deliberating. "Thanks for your help. I don't know what the hell happened today, but it wasn't what I thought."

He put his hand on the door knob, looked at it a moment, then turned back to us. "I think I'm going to need you gentlemen's help on this one," he said flatly. Then he opened the door against the pink evening sky and clumped down the wood stairs and was gone.

Chapter
Four

Lana and I walked home down the alley with the sunset in our faces. We walked slowly, lost in our own thoughts about the day's events, holding hands as we often did.

Home, we dipped Mexican shredded pork out of the pressure cooker and slid it onto tortillas. We took them out onto the porch where it was growing cool and where a slight breeze was building. Lana went back in and brought out two glasses of shiraz, and we tucked in.

"You know," Lana mused, "Charley didn't ask anything about the missing guy."

I nodded and took the last bite of my burrito, chewing thoughtfully.

"That's weird, isn't it?" I said. "I haven't given him much thought either. I mean, we see two guys go over a five hundred foot embankment, their car explodes into flames, one of them vanishes, and only a slight mention of that fact is made. Is Charlie losing it?"

"I didn't see any of *us* pipe up either," Lana said.

"How could we not have found him?"

"Maybe Don and Jake didn't see him get thrown out. Maybe he got away down the canyon through the brush."

Smoke passed by in his black, modified GMC pickup and gave us a toot as he headed into the growing darkness out of town. After Smoke's military career, he came home to live on his family's homestead. But not enjoying farming, he leased the land to Cricket Farms. Always the fighter pilot and dare devil, Smoke's truck had an engine in it that mere mortals feared. I've driven it.

I drove it one night when he was too drunk, and when we left MacAvity's Pub for his ranch, he wanted me to "Open it up, man!"

So I did, as much as I felt was safe, and he said, "No, you pussy! I *said* open this fucker up!"

It was an eye bulging experience roaring down a narrow, paved road in the night with a drunk in the cab giving orders. The shaking dash registered one-hundred and twenty. I was so terrified I started to laugh and then howl with laughter, and Smoke did too. And after we reached his place alive, we sat in the truck under the ranch yard's mercury lamp totally spent.

He staggered through the back door of his white, two story farm house, and I eased the truck around in front of the barn and headed home. Shortly my hands were shaking with spent adrenaline and I wasn't laughing--not a bit.

Early the next morning Huey delivered him to my front steps to get his truck, and he was bright, showered, grinning and into his first cigarillo.

"Fast?" he asked.

"So so," I said.

"Yeah, right," he said, getting into his truck. "You wash your shorts out yet?"

When sitting on the porch with Lana I think about incidents like that night with Smoke. For that matter, I think about all of our pasts whenever time stands still for me long enough. I suppose all of us codgers here in Ryback do that now. Who knows?

Lana stood up, took my plate and went though the screen door into the kitchen. She returned with her glass refreshed and sat back down, putting her feet up on another folding chair.

I studied her, admiring her after all these years. Forty six years? Now how'd *that* happen?

She was looking out over the darkening fields, her face serene. Her hair was still a shiny buckskin that matched her slender arms and legs, and sitting there in her white tank top and faded jeans she looked about the same as she did when we were in high school together, when she was a sophomore and I was a senior. Smoke, Huey and I were classmates, and while they were at after school sports practice, Lana and I worked on the yearbook and the monthly school paper together. We were never apart after that year. And what a time we had!

"You wanna meet me at MacAvity's Pub tomorrow after we shut down?" I asked her.

"Not really," she said.

I nodded. "I want to talk to MacAvity. I want to get his take on this 'missing somebody.'"

"Not a bad idea. He always seems to know a bit more than all the rest of you put together."

"Well..."

"You gotta admit."

"I admit," I said. "When a guy comes back from the service, walks into his father's saloon and puts on a black flat brimmed Stetson, baggy white shirt with garters holding up the sleeves and braces holding up his pants, lets his hair and beard grow out as a model for Jerry Garcia to imitate, then puts a loaded .45 Colt Combat Commander down the back of his pants," I took a breath, "he's probably either crazy or he knows something the rest of us can only guess at."

Lana was staring at me. "Do you rehearse this shit?" She gave her short happy laugh. "Go talk to him. Have a beer. His buddy Hammersmith will be there anyway, so maybe you three can solve the mystery tomorrow."

She put her hand on my knee and stood up. "Finish your drink, sweetie. I'm going to my room and read in bed."

Eventually I gave up the porch after I had had two more glasses of wine and had lost the ability to cogitate with any rhyme or reason. I went in, latched the screen door, made it to my bedroom determined to make the last week of harvest as tolerable as possible. Peas and garbanzos. What a bunch of filthy, dusty, nasty things to have to breathe.

Chapter
Five

I woke up in the dark just before dawn choking on smoke. I jumped to my feet, threw on my bedroom light, and ran into the living room, calling out to Lana as I passed her bedroom. I went through the living room to the kitchen and into the utility porch, snapping on lights as I went.

There was no smoke coming up the stairwell from the basement, so I turned to go back into the kitchen where Lana had appeared. She was pulling her light cotton robe tight across her front and was wide eyed and alert.

"Where's all this smoke coming from?"

"I don't know," I said.

I went past her and back into the living room. No flames.

"Look out the window, Paul," she called after me.

Between the huge grain elevators across the street, the security lights were dim in a tan fog of smoke.

"I bet it's the Tucannon fire," she said. "The smoke's from it."

I unlatched the screen door and stepped out onto the porch with her where the smoke seemed less dense than inside the house. The Tucannon River's canyon fire had been burning wildly in the Blue Mountains for four days. Apparently a subtle flow of air was now carrying it towards us from the south, forty-five miles away. Like a billowing avalanche it was rolling up the Snake River gorge and over the lip of the grade onto the Bench. It flowed past the elevators towards us like a muddy stream wrapping around pilings.

It was 4:40.

I went back in and opened all the north windows and returned to the porch where we sat away from the smoke trapped inside. My room, particularly, was thick with it.

At 5:30 I phoned Leaps to confirm we were still working, and was on the road out of town by 6:00. At 6:19 the sun peeked over the horizon in a haunting ruby glow and materialized into an orange ball streaked with blood red bands and stripes. As it rose, the light increased until, by the time I reached the job site, the air was a dull tan, and the trucks and combines stood like copper cutouts on the rust colored ocean of stubble.

Mike was on the site. Mike was Hammersmith's sole hired man. In the old tradition, Mike lived in one of the homestead houses and maintained the farm year round. During harvest he drove truck when Eric was on the combine, and if Eric was busy, Mike would harvest and drive too, not uncommon on the smaller places.

I pulled in, the last to arrive, and they were standing around in the smoke talking, acting like they weren't waiting for me. As soon as I pulled to a stop, Smoke came over and opened my door. The others turned to their jobs of lubing the hundreds of points on the combines and dragging the compressor hose around blowing the chaff and dust out of the cabs and machinery.

"Well, pardner," he said, "Mike says they're going to try to take prints inside Hammersmith's study today. The Commander's pretty upset."

I got out. He followed me over to my semi.

"I'd be pissed too," I said.

"Yeah, and they sliced one of his pictures before they ran. They cut through that picture he has on his desktop of him in full dress. Broke the glass out to do it."

"Why the hell did they do that?"

Smoke was playing with his Zippo, twirling it between his thumb and index finger. "Makes you wonder who those two fucks were, doesn't it?"

"No kidding!"

He turned to go, but stopped.

"You know Kimmy Musselshell's place down at the mouth of Rattlesnake?"

I nodded.

"She phoned the tribal police last night just as it was getting dark whispering that a man was sneaking though her orchard all bloody and ragged."

"She phoned Josiah?"

"And Oscar. So they phoned Charlie and they all met her at the stock gate in the middle of the damn night. Only thing they got out of the deal was a sample of blood off the top rail."

He paused. "I guess they'll have it analyzed or something."

I nodded.

Then Smoke winked, went over and climbed up into his rig's cab.

"We might have some fun yet, pardner!" he yelled.

By noon the air was like thin milk and visibility was up to over a mile. But still my throat was sore and my eyes stung. I was glad to stop for lunch.

Smoke was sitting in the crushed stubble of our latest loading spot, leaning up against one of his combine's $3,000 tires, eating lunch from his Playmate cooler.

I pulled up, set the brakes, cut the engine and went over to join him. I could hear Leaps' combine working out of sight. Often he didn't stop for lunch, so Smoke and I were the lunch bunch. The two others on our crew usually sat off by themselves in their pickups listening to Paul Harvey.

Smoke handed me a cookie as I sat down. I opened my thermos, poured a cup of tea, and dug into an egg salad sandwich Lana had put together for me.

We ate in silence, and shortly Smoke slid down in the shade with his head resting on the lid of his cooler he always tipped over on its side. True to his lunchtime routine, he shut his eyes behind his wraparound shades and dozed, leaving me to rest against the other half of the tire and look out over the Bench from our high point.

I didn't get to MacAvity's Pub that night for beer as planned. The wind shifted around three that afternoon, the air cleared and the sky turned back to a brilliant blue, and Leaps got on the CB and said we were going to take advantage of the conditions and work until the elevators closed at eight. He said he'd use his cell phone to tell our wives. He told Mike to shut down at five and go pick up a bag of chicken he'd order from the pub and bring it out. We'd eat on the job.

But while we were out in the fields, Sheriff Charlie Rand had gone to Eric and Ruthie Hammersmith's to have lunch and to talk about their break-in. As a result of that discussion, Charlie had brought the FBI in on the case, and that afternoon the FBI dusted Eric and Ruthie's place for prints and left with the blood sample Charlie had at his office in Magnet. Apparently they found two prints on the broken frame of Eric's photo, but that was all. At least that's what Eric had phoned to tell Butte, and what Butte had told Jables and Huey who were at the bar when the call came in.

The question was why did Charlie call in the FBI for a simple burglary attempt that didn't take place on the reservation? It seemed unlikely they would be interested even if it was in their jurisdiction.

Lana had the answer to that.

I was home by 8:30, and was just getting into the shower when Lana came in from the garden. She sat on the toilet seat to talk with me as she often did after I got in from the fields and was showering.

"Jake and I decided it'd be nice if we two gals headed into town for supper since you guys were still harvesting, and we swung by to get Eric and Ruthie to followed us in," she said.

It was Friday night. MacAvity and Sheila, his help for the past thirty years, set up a salad bar and served meals every Friday and Saturday nights. Sheila was thin as a whippet, had a tongue on her like a razor, was quick to laugh, and, rumor had it, had an arrangement with Butte that had helped them survive their individual isolations all those years.

"So did they join you?"

"Yeah, they did."

"I'm listening," I said. The shower felt great so I just stood there letting it run over me.

"Ruthie told me and Jake that at the house Eric had instructed Charlie not to notify the FBI about the break-in. Eric was really concerned and explained he had been the commander of some base on the Mekong Navy SEALS worked out of. He said he was sure whoever had that gun and lighter had either been a SEAL or Special Forces. He said as CO he had made some enemies, and left it at that.

"Ruthie said after Eric told Charlie this, Charlie went out front and over to his parked Expedition. She saw him on his radio, and when he came back in he apologized and said he had to phone the FBI because the implications of the burned-up gun and lighter made it a federal matter too serious to ignore. Then Eric walked with Charlie back out to the Expedition and Charlie drove off.

"Ruthie said when Eric came back into the house he was mad as hornets at Charlie."

I pulled back the curtain and looked at her. "Ruthie told you all this?"

She nodded.

"Where was Hammersmith?"

"She told us after we'd eaten. Eric was acting pretty depressed and didn't say much during the meal, and when Butte came to clear our dinners and pour coffee, he nodded his head for Eric to follow him. They went upstairs and left the place to Sheila for almost twenty minutes."

She paused and handed me a towel. "That's when Ruthie told us. She's pretty scared, is my take."

When I was out of the shower I phoned Smoke and then Huey and told them what Lana had said. That's the way Ryback is. It's understood we keep no secrets. We care for each other and keep one another safe. That's why we've lived so damn long.

But Huey took what I told him in an odd way. He listened to what I told him without interrupting, and when I was done, he didn't ask or say anything. He just thanked me and hung up. Puzzling.

Chapter Six

I normally wake up a few moments before my alarm does, but the next morning it had to earn its keep--5:30 and ticking. Lana met me in the kitchen. I put on the tea kettle and wandered back to the living room leaving her at the cutting board putting me up a lunch.

I felt bone tired. I sat listening for the water to come to a boil and wondered if I should call Leaps and tell him I couldn't make it because I had misplaced my arms and couldn't find them.

Smoke, Huey and I were all sixty-six, having been classmates, but mornings didn't seem to bother them like they could me. I reasoned it was because they had spent their whole lives either being kicked around by the military or by their farm machinery, and I, on the other hand, had retired from the sedentary job of copy editor at the Confluence Tribune. Big difference.

Even Hammersmith and MacAvity were holding up, and they were seventy-eight and seventy-nine respectively.

The kitchen phone rang. Lana answered with a "'Morning," "Yup," and "I'll tell him."

She looked around the corner. "Leaps says too much dew this morning. You're to come out at 10:30."

Hooray!

She finished making lunch anyway and put it in the refrigerator. Things were looking good for a morning free of harvest, but oddly, nothing seemed to be getting lighter outside. Darkness persisted.

The Bench has some strange days, but usually in the winter. Two things can happen then, whiteouts and icebows.

We don't have any fences except at the farm yards, and trees only grow in town, in the draws, and on Cup Hand Ridge. So, when the January snows start piling up and filling in the roads, there are no landmarks, and the Bench looks like a brilliantly white sea. But when a winter land-fog settles in, or when we have a ground blizzard, the snow and the sky become indistinguishable from one another. A person can't tell what they are walking *on* or what they are walking *in*. It's very disorienting, causing vertigo.

Icebows, though, look like beautiful, often circular rainbows around the sun, only instead of the sunlight reflecting off water droplets in the air, they reflect off ice crystals. This happens when the temperatures fall below zero.

But I had never seen the sort of day I stepped out into that morning.

During the night smoke from the Tucannon fire had returned. With its return came a smooth lid of cloud that trapped it against the valley floor like mortar between bricks. The drive to the fields was like navigating through a coastal fog in the darkness of predawn. And here it was nearly noon! It was like a total eclipse of the sun.

Something else seemed strange about the morning because Smoke wasn't at his bank-out wagon, and Leaps, who was usually already cutting by the time I arrived on late-start mornings, was walking towards me even before I came to a stop. Something was wrong.

I rolled down my window.

"You have to go in to town," he said impatiently. "The sheriff wants to talk with you guys at MacAvity's, pronto."

"What for?" I said.

"I don't know, Paul. But I've got to pull Shay from his Gleaner to haul every time the Western Star is loaded." He turned and walked off saying over his shoulder, "Come back as soon as you can."

Leaps left me hanging with a feeling of dread and anxiety that rode in the cab with me the seven miles back into town. By the time I parked, I was undone.

I pulled in between Smoke's and Huey's pickups and got out. Rounding the corner to go in, I saw Charlie's Expedition and a black Suburban parallel parked in front.

I entered the pub and passed through the swinging saloon doors. Sheila looked out from the kitchen, obviously irritated.

"They're upstairs with the Feebs," she said. "If you don't mind, I'll just stay down here and prepare for the lunch rush by myself. Wouldn't want to impose on such an important meeting..." and she turned back out of sight.

Feebs?

Butte, Smoke and Huey were seated comfortably upstairs in Butte's deep leather chairs around his huge coffee table. Two men were on the couch, and Charlie was seated in one of two kitchen chairs that had been brought in. They stopped talking as I entered.

"There you are, Paul," Charlie said. He stood and nodded at the two dressed in tan chinos, sport jackets and ties. They looked tough.

"This is Special Agent Gibson and Special Agent Pfeffer," he said. "FBI."

They leaned forward and the couch leather creaked. I shook their hands.

Pfeffer looked at Charlie, "He doesn't need to be here," he said. "In fact, it'd be better if he wasn't."

Charlie looked down at him. "You wanted this meeting and I called it. Paul stays."

Charlie motioned for me to have the seat by him.

"What's going on?" I said.

It was Butte that answered. "Arson."

Pfeffer spoke calmly. "We think Commander Hammersmith might be a target," he said.

"An arsonist at Eric's?" I said.

"That's where we left off when you arrived," said Charlie.

"We've spent the morning with the Commander," Pfeffer said, addressing us all, now. "And after talking with him, we wanted to meet with you three, um four, as well. We think before you guys scared them off, the two men who broke into his house were planning to burn him down, and we don't know why. Maybe one of you can tell us. We suspect that they burned out the River Bend Mercantile down on the Tucannon that started the whole canyon fire, and then came up here."

Charlie read my mind. "The Bishops are OK. They sold the place about ten months ago, but the Cambodian couple that bought the store were found in the ashes." He looked at us briefly. "The Tribune is sitting on that fact, as I expect you will, too, Paul."

Pfeffer leaned forward with his elbows on his knees. I noticed Gibson take out a small, leather covered note pad and ball-point.

"Does the name Rojas Franzani mean anything to you men?"

After a pause Butte pursed his lips. "Nope," he said. Pfeffer looked to each of us and we shook our heads. He looked at Charlie questioningly, and Charlie shrugged his shoulders. Gibson slipped the note pad back into his jacket.

"Well," Pfeffer said, placing his hands on his knees, "we wanted to meet you and ask you to keep your eyes open."

He stood and Gibson scooted to the edge of the couch and waited, but Butte was having none of it.

"So tell us," he said, "was this Franzani guy one of the burglars?"

"No." This was Gibson. His voice was a lot larger than his body, and it startled me.

"Have you identified the burned body yet?" Butte asked.

"Yes. It wasn't Rojas," he said.

There was an impatient arrogance about Gibson and the way he was answering Butte. It dawned on me that he was the senior member of the two "Feebs," as Sheila called them, and he had somehow pushed one of Butte's buttons.

Gibson now stood and straightened out the back of his jacket, but Butte was now standing as well, facing him.

Apparently Gibson had decided we weren't worthy.

"Good day, gentlemen," he said.

"Well, then," Butte said in his low, dangerously gentle voice, "would you first mind sharing with us who *was* cooked in that heap, or are we here so you can model your clothes for us?"

That got me scanning the four of us for dress code violations. Outside of the fact we looked our usual feed-store-clothing-rack selves, Butte the exception, everything looked in order.

Charlie stood and intervened. "The victim was named Salas Valladores," he said. "His dental records look like he had once tried to bite a mule's hoof. He was a friend of Rojas Franzani's son. The son's name is Cano. The blood on Kimmy Musselshell's gate was Cano's, and the two prints were his."

Gibson was staring at him like he wanted to make him stop.

"See?" Butte said sweetly to Gibson, "That's how you should talk to old fucks like us."

Butte turned his back on him and went into the kitchen.

Gibson grew red in the face and didn't move until Butte was around the corner.

Charlie cleared his throat, "Well?"

Gibson didn't say a thing. He slapped imaginary dust from his chinos and went out. Pfeffer gave us a palms up what's-a-person-to-do and followed.

Charlie picked his hat up from where it hung over the edge of the coffee table and pushed it down on his head.

"And," he said, "when Cano and Salas were seventeen they were convicted as adults on two counts of arson and were given fifteen years for each count to be served consecutively."

Gibson's voice thundered up the stairwell, "You coming, Sheriff?"

Charlie ignored him. "They were paroled three years ago after serving twenty years, but they skipped and vanished."

He turned to leave, stopped at the stairway door and said, "They were convicted for burning down two Vietnamese restaurants, one in Provo and one in Ogden."

Charlie touched his brim, "See ya,"

We sat and listened to his cowboy boots clunk down the wooden stairs.

"That's a good boy, there," Butte said from the kitchen door behind us. "But we still don't know why those two shits were after Hammersmith, and I'd venture a guess that those FBI hotshots don't either."

Huey got to his feet, worked his way around the coffee table and went to the door without saying a word.

Astonished, I looked at Smoke for an explanation, to find him watching Huey with complaisance.

Huey opened the door and was gone.

"Smoke?" I asked.

"Vietnam changed him, Paul," he said.

He pulled out cigarillo, prepared to light it and said, "So what are we going to drink for lunch, kind sirs?"

"I'll tell you what, though," MacAvity added, heading for the liquor cabinet, "I bet ol' Hammersmith can set us straight, and I betcha Charlie didn't have a chance to tell him what he just told us."

He looked at me and grinned. "What do you think, Paul?"

"Don't have a clue, Butte. But I'll have some of that Wisers. Sometimes Huey makes me feel like shit."

Chapter
Seven

The semi was where I'd left it. In the cab the note pad clipped to the dash showed Shay had made two runs, one of 37,050 pounds, another of 41,660.

I could see Leaps' huge green John Deere leveled on the steep side of the ridge just south of me, and coming towards him on the lower side was Shay, tipped dangerously in his non-leveling Gleaner. Smoke wasn't back yet from MacAvity's Pub.

I took my cooler out and sat back against a front tire in a scant strip of noontime shade. I opened the cooler and took out an egg-hot sauce-mayonnaise sandwich Lana had made on thick slices of her rich homemade bread.

I bit into the sandwich and thought about our meeting with Charlie and the two agents. But mostly I thought about Butte's, Hammersmith's, Smoke's and Huey's mutual bond and my part in it. I have thought about that bond practically my whole life, and what I knew was both impressive and, at the same time, frightening.

Huey was the quiet one of our bunch. Unlike the rest of us, he not only said he believed in God like so many people, but he actually *did*. I don't think I know anyone else I can say that about. In fact, each year after harvest, he spent three weeks volunteering at a mission in Cambodia. He'd been doing that for more than twenty years.

But it was his idea, in 1954, that the three of us should go Navy like Hammersmith and MacAvity had. Mentions had been made in the editorial pages of the Trib. concerning the US's growing interest in Southeast Asia's affairs, and to us farm boys it sounded exciting.

Because I had not played sports with Smoke and Huey in high school, I had never felt they considered me 100%, and I saw our serving together as a great opportunity to amend that. The sorry part was that the Armed Forces welcomed them, but because I had been partially blind since birth in my left eye, I was ushered out, figuratively speaking. So while I languished at SEWU studying journalism, they went NROTC at the University of Idaho. We graduated in 1962, and I took a job at the Confluence Tribune while my pals Drew "Huey" Houston and Nick "Smoke" Cline, went off into the world wearing beautiful Navy uniforms.

Huey was to distinguish himself flying Bell UH-1B Huey "Seawolf" helicopters. And Smoke, still reckless, screamed off the decks of a huge carrier nicknamed "The Bonnie Dick" in his A-7 Corsair II fighter jet and surprised everyone by returning to Ryback still alive.

After their return from the Vietnam conflict, their humor had changed from pranksterish to cynical. Butte MacAvity and Eric Hammersmith, Ryback's revered warriors, two years later took Smoke and Huey under their wings and hammered their lives back into some semblance of inner peace. And in my opinion, just in time.

I took out my thermos and unscrewed the top. Lana had made me lemonade. This is a rare sort of treat since she makes a gallon of it from six lemons and two cups of sugar, and frowns on its health implications for me. But she knows I love the stuff.

Like Smoke and Huey, I have always held Butte and Hammersmith up as my heroes, which explained why Smoke and Huey had gone into the Navy in '58.

Hammersmith was in his early twenties when his father died. He and Ruthie had only been married two years, but within months of the funeral, Eric leased the family farm to Jables Weinman, his neighbor, and joined the Navy. Ruthie, the smartest, cutest student in their graduating class, was left to run the place. While the farm thrived under her supervision, Eric became Lieutenant Commander Eric "The Hammer" Hammersmith.

By the time Smoke and Huey reached Vietnam, Hammersmith was the CO in the "Brown Water Navy's" Task Force-116 in the Mekong Delta. His headquarters were aboard a refitted LST (Tank Landing Ship) that he anchored in the Bassac River off Can Tho, and a platoon of SEALs were attached. His command was given these fourteen highly trained warriors by the Atlantic Fleet's SEAL Team 2. He had Huey Houston transferred to his command, and Huey used the helipad located amidships on the LST for his Seawolf.

As for Smoke, he was aboard The Bonnie Dick, which was stationed off the mouths of the Mekong in the South China Sea. Smoke ended up flying support for Hammersmith's PBRs (River Support Boats) and SEALs. Huey found himself in his Huey Seawolf gun ship doing the same thing. Small world, thanks to Hammersmith's clout.

As for Butte MacAvity, he had been Special Forces in the '60s, and later an instructor of SEALs. As a Chief Petty Officer, Butte's love of weapons had drawn him though the Armed Services until he found himself instructing FNGs (fucking new guys) in the use of weapons deep in the Everglades at Mayport, Florida. These FNGs had survived the toughest, most Darwinian training ever devised by man in the Navy's Special Warfare Center (NSWC) at Coronado, California. But nothing had prepared them for being shipped to Chief MacAvity's crushing regimens.

Hammersmith had gone into the Navy when his father died. When MacAvity's father died, he came home.

When Smoke and Huey came home, Hammersmith and MacAvity became their fathers. That's the equation as I saw it.

I put the lid back on my empty Tupperware sandwich container, dropped it into the cooler, and drank the thermos cup empty of lemonade. I leaned back, shutting my eyes against the day's white glare, remembering the waves of depression that had washed over me during those days.

No more than an hour ago MacAvity had said, "What do you think, Paul, ol' pal?" But thinking about these guys, it was Smoke and Huey who had been adopted by our childhood heroes, not me. I had driven a desk and written articles about other people's lives, and cut and pasted copy during my own. And I spent years feeling sorry for myself no matter what these buddies said or did to make me feel differently. But that's one of the advantages of growing old with friends who never turn their backs on you--you eventually leave the stupid shit you have created for yourself behind at the side of the road. What I *didn't* know, sitting there, was that things were soon to unfold that would at last compel me to prove myself to them as well as to myself over a period of three long and dangerous years.

I was just beginning to doze when Smoke's GMC came bouncing up through the stubble. He tried to throw as much dust as he could over me as he swung his pickup to stop. He leaned out his window.

"Wake-up, you lazy fuck," he said happily. "Let's get this harvest done *today*. All of it. I'm drunk and I'm sick of this shit, and besides, you and I got a meeting to attend tonight."

"What meeting?" I said, closing the cooler against the dirt raining down on me.

"I'll pick you up at nine. Hammersmith is coming in to talk to us."

"At Butte's?"

"Where else?"

"I'll walk it and meet you there," I said.

"Suit yourself," and he trotted down the far side of the hill in search of his bank-out wagon.

At that moment, Shay came on the CB wanting to know where Smoke was.

I scrambled up into the cab and grabbed the mike. "Headed for his rig," I told him.

"You see me?" he said.

He was down on the flat below Leaps.

"I see you."

"I'll dump on you down here," meaning for me to swing the big rig down and around to meet up with him.

Leaps added, "Smoke, you there?"

No answer.

"Swing over by Smoke and tell him to get over here," Leaps said. "You stay down when you get here and make sure you're locked. We don't need another fire. Smoke will dump on you next. I'm not leaving this side hill. I'm slipping some."

Chapter
Eight

That night the wind shifted again, and I found myself walking to MacAvity's Pub under a canopy of stars that backlit the street's giant sycamores.

The town was dead quiet except for Smoke's truck coming off the hill and slowing to make the corner onto Main. He eased up beside me and kept pace five feet off my left shoulder, looking straight ahead as if he hadn't noticed me. The smooth rumble of the GMC's engine accompanied me the entire two blocks. Still Smoke stared ahead through the windshield, a cigarillo clamped tightly between his lips. He had his black Navy baseball cap pulled low over his eyes which shined wicked in the darkness.

When I stopped to cross the street to the pub's door, Smoke stopped too. I looked over at him again, and he was flipping me off and grinning. I busted out laughing.

It was 9:30 and there were eight or nine people still at the bar. Unusual for harvest, which left everyone exhausted. Jake and Sheila were in a booth talking over glasses of wine and the remains of their meals, and Don was volunteering as barkeep.

"Go on upstairs," he told us.

The room's furniture was exactly as we had left it that morning, and it was apparent from the debris and glasses that the two old warriors had been attacking a bottle of White Horse with determination.

Smoke dropped into the third chair, leaving the couch for me.

"Bring out the bottle," Butte said, and I went to the cabinet behind the couch and got the Wiser's, knowing Smoke would help on the White Horse.

I got two glasses, sat them on the coffee table, and eased down on the edge of the couch to make my drink.

"Men," MacAvity said, holding up his half empty glass, "here's to us."

We toasted.

Smoke looked around. "Where are Huey and Hammersmith?"

Butte said, "I've brought Eric up to speed this evening with what Charlie told us."

He put down his glass. "And then we phoned Charlie to ask him why those Cambodians didn't make it out of the store." Butte was looking into his glass. "And he said it was because they had each been shot twice in the head."

Smoke tapped a smoke out of its box to light. "And they were shot with .22LRs?" he ventured.

"Bingo," Butte said. "And there's little doubt that the FBI lab will match them to the HiStandard found in the wreck."

Butte looked at us, frowning.

"The Hammer was very upset," he said quietly. "I've only seen him this bad once, and that was when his daughter died of meningitis."

He paused. "He felt he needed to go home immediately, as if he was afraid of Ruthie being there by herself."

"What about Huey?" I said. "Where's he?"

"Eric didn't want to bother him with all this. Huey finished his wheat today, so he's free to leave for Cambodia and will be busy getting the details put together for that."

Smoke lit the cigarillo and put the Zippo on the coffee table by his glass and pulled the ashtray closer.

"I think it's strange that he doesn't want Huey here," he finally said.

"I understand, Smoke," Butte said. "When I told Eric that the FBI asked if the name Rojas Franzani meant anything to us, and when I added that one of the two men that were in his house was Franzani's son, I thought he was going to pass out."

He took a sip. "I'm dead serious. He was shaken by the news. Whatever Franzani means to him, he doesn't want Huey in on it."

"But Huey already knows," I reminded him.

"I know, Paul, and the way Huey left here tells me that he's familiar with the name too," MacAvity said.

"That's just the way Huey is," Smoke said. "He'd rather walk off by himself to deal with shit."

"It has something to do with what happened in Vietnam, doesn't it?" I asked.

"That was thirty-eight years ago, remember," Butte mused, "yet ghosts do come back sometimes. But that's not what I'm concerned about right now. I'm thinking we should protect Hammersmith. I think his life might be in danger."

Smoke wagged his lowered head back and forth like he had every time our high school coach told our student body that the team the school was to play that Friday was a tough bunch.

"You think someone wants to kill him?"

"I'm saying he acts like someone is going to try," Butte said.

If Hammersmith was frightened, I damn well could be too.

MacAvity saw it in my face. "Nothing serious," he said. "We're just going to watch his house each night from eleven to two AM. Those are the hours that if anything *is* going to happen, it *will* happen," he added. "Since it seems to concern Franzani's son, Cano, who is apparently still alive, and since Cano tried it once already during the day, nights are the obvious option."

"But all we know for sure," I said, "is that two Cambodians were murdered."

They looked at me.

"Is this a newspaper interview or are we having a drink here?" Smoke asked, a slight smile folding back his cheeks.

I felt my face redden.

"Paul's right," Butte said. "We don't know anything more than that for sure. But if the bullets match the "hush puppy," that means those same two shit heads killed the Cambodians and then came up here. They were walking around in Hammersmith's study and made it a point to cut though a picture of him. That tells us something."

He paused, his eyes taking on the shine of a man that is growing sinister.

He went on, "And Hammersmith recognizes, I assume, the name of the one guy's father and goes into shock. And what pisses me off is that those fucks from the FBI aren't telling us shit. They obviously know something about Franzani, and they seem to think Hammersmith and maybe even Huey know this guy too, but no one is telling us."

We remained silent, watching him warily.

"They know one thing, that's for damn sure," he hissed. "They know for a fact those guys were in Hammer's home, in the middle of the day, when they *knew* Ruthie and he were out, because they were *after* something. But those Feds don't know *what* they were after, and they aren't telling us what they suspect or what they *do* know."

"OK, we get your point, Butte," Smoke said.

"You OK with all this, Paul?" Butte asked, looking me over like I was coming out of anesthesia."

"I'm fine," I said.

"OK then, he said. "It's going to be eleven o'clock in an hour, so follow me."

He took up his glass and stood.

Smoke gave me a wicked wink.

"Lead on, Sarg," he said.

The bar was empty when we got downstairs, and Sheila was cleaning up.

Butte locked the door behind her as she left for home, and lead us to a door under the stairs. It opened into the cellar stairs. He switched on a light and we followed him down. At the bottom that he opened an ancient oak door with a dungeon key and swung it open. Behind it was another door, modern and made of sheet steel. He opened this by punching a code into a key box, and swung it inwards. Pressurized air came from inside in a rush.

MacAvity threw a switch and the room flooded with florescent lighting from plastic ceiling panels. It was a sixteen foot square concrete room that was painted white and was lined on one side with eight large Remington gun safes and one three-foot square standard AMSEC safe. Against the opposite wall were three large metal cabinets. In the middle of the room was a perfectly square, gray metal table, military issue, and the end wall was covered with photographs like Hammersmith had in his study. The pictures were of MacAvity in camo wearing a green beret, a black beret, in full dress uniform shaking officers' hands, accepting plaques, and the like. In the middle of it all was a framed poem. I went over to read it.

Smoke was standing surveying the scene. "You've been holding out on us, Butte!" he said. "Who all knows about your little secret here?"

"Hammersmith and Ruthie, among a few others. That AMSEC safe is his," he said, pointing down at it. "And

Sheila knows, but the rest of the folks have pretty much died off. Grandpa Coe built this room with the hotel, and the cement walls of this thing are two feet thick and not a cold pour anywhere. All I've done is put in environmental controls, the security door, and paint the walls white."

I read the poem which began:

Macavity's a Mystery Cat: he's called the Hidden Paw--
For he's the master criminal who can defy the Law.
He's the bafflement of Scotland Yard, the Flying Squad's despair:
For when they reach the scene of crime--MacAvity's not there!

There were six more stanzas and then it was signed T. S. Eliot.

Butte watched me read the poem. "A gift from my men," he said. "The name is a coincidence," he smiled, swinging open one of the Remington safes.

Smoke wasn't paying any attention to us; his eyes were surveying the contents of a gun safe approvingly.

I asked, "Why did he build this room in the first place, Butte?"

"He kept his whiskey, Salmon River gold, money, guns, and occasionally his sole prostitute in here to keep safe from drunken Lutherans, Catholics, and heathens," he said, adding, "He brought the prostitute with him from Nebraska. She was Sheila's grandma."

Again, small world.

He pulled two assault rifles from the first gun safe and put them on the table leaving the remaining ones. Smoke picked one of them up and sighted.

"Colt Match Competition HBAR .223. Nice!" he said, putting it back on the table.

Butte said. "You want to carry it?"

"Nope. I'm happy with my .243, Butte," he said.

MacAvity put one of them back in the safe, opened a second safe and took out a scoped sporting rifle.

"Here's a .270 Winchester 70 for you, Paul," handing it to me.

I took it dubiously, looked at the jeweled bolt and finely checkered stock and placed it on the table.

I hesitated. "You know, I'm not sure I should be doing this," I said.

Smoke looked over at me, not moving a muscle.

MacAvity picked up the rifle gently, put it back in the second safe, and swung the door shut.

He walked to the end of the line and opened a third safe, pulled out an automatic pistol and clip and placed them on the table beside the Colt AR-15.

"This is a Glock G-36 Slimline .45 ACP, Paul," he said. You can carry it for self defense." He paused. "You aren't opposed to defending yourself, are you?" he asked without rancor.

I shook my head. "But what will I be doing?"

"The same thing we'll all be doing. Keeping an eye on the Hammersmith's grounds," he said.

"Oh." That sounded much better than what I thought he might have up his sleeve.

MacAvity then opened one of the cabinets and started laying out what appeared to be monocular.

He took one of them and attached it to the Colt AR-15.

"This is my pride and joy," holding it up to admire. "A Newcon NVS 14 1x 2nd Generation Plus Waterproof Night Vision Monocular Goggle that set me back over three grand. This unit turns the darkest of nights into daylight. It's amazing," he said.

Smoke grinned. "That's a mouthful."

"These other two," which he handed to us, "are inexpensive Yukon Multi Task Night Vision Monocular Systems. Just push the button, and you have eyes."

I studied mine, turning it over in my hand. It was incredibly light, probably less than a pound, and fit comfortably in my hand. Now this was something I could do.

"OK," I said. "I'm game. Let me call Lana, and I'm ready to go."

Chapter
Nine

We were in my Tundra and coming in towards Hammersmith's by 10:50.

MacAvity told us Eric was not to know he was being protected. A matter of pride, I suppose. And Lana said she'd keep the secret but that I was embarking on something she felt was incredibly stupid, dangerous, and probably illegal. She felt I should have my head examined, that our taxes went to hire professionals, called *cops*, to do these sorts of things for us, and that if we killed someone out there in the dark, our lives would become irreparable. "I know," I had admitted. But what was I to do?

We pulled into an old wooden machine shed half a mile from Hammersmith's, parked and killed the lights. We let our eyes adjust to the darkness.

The shed was all that remained of one of the early homesteads, and it was buried in a stand of tall willows and apple trees gone wild.

MacAvity unzipped a large Navy duffle he had stowed on his side in the crew cab, and handed us our equipment. He had donned a pair of Russell Moccasins and led the way noiselessly through the rolling wheat stubble towards the tree covered ridge that overlooked the Hammersmith's house. The half moon was just beginning to show on the east horizon. It was ruby colored through the lingering smoke, and the fields showed up remarkably well, the yellow straw copper in the dim light.

Smoke had fallen in behind MacAvity, and the two of them set a rapid pace. I kept up easily, pushed along by adrenaline. I imagined these two were doing something they had once been very familiar with, but for me, I had never been more anxious in my life. Or excited. I had heightened awareness of my surroundings as never before.

We climbed up the back side of the ridge and slowly entered a dense stand of pines that sheltered the farm below. The timber was less than fifty feet deep but at least three hundred yards long.

MacAvity squatted behind an old logged-off stump and motioned for us to join him. We crouched down beside him and looked.

Two hundred yards below, the house, barn, machine shed and shop were bathed dimly by a mercury yard lamp. There was also a light on inside the house's living room, probably a night light, and luckily for us, Eric and Ruthie didn't own a dog to let them know we were spying on them.

MacAvity placed his Colt assault rifle on the flat top of the stump and swung his rucksack off his back. He pulled it open and took out three headsets and three Motorola radios. He attached the radios, turned them on, set the channels to eleven in the dim, green glow of their screens, and handed us each one.

"You stay here, Paul," he whispered very softly. "Smoke will be on your left clear out at the end of the timber where he can watch the farm track coming in from the back. I'm going to be on the far side of the buildings, close in."

He picked up his own radio. "If anyone comes along the road and parks, or if you see anything unusual, just tell us in the mike you'll be wearing," he said, taking up his own and putting it on.

He and Smoke rose into a crouch.

"And, Paul," he added, so quietly I could barely make out the words, "try not to move your body too much, and if you do, do it very slowly. And feel free to use your Night Vision all you want."

And then they were gone. Like ghosts. Vaporized.

I have hunted deer and elk most of my life with Smoke and Huey, so I was no stranger to the tedium and discomfort of a stand. To endure them was difficult because time stood still and ten minutes felt like an hour. But I had never been on a stand at night. I'd never been part of a perimeter of armed men, and I had never imagined I would be doing it now.

A couple things became apparent to me as I adjusted to a somewhat more comfortable sitting position behind the stump. For one, I felt a bit disembodied, as if I were whimsically watching myself sitting there in the dark wondering at my own thin grasp on reality.

And also, I had a creepy sensation that I had been deserted by Smoke and MacAvity--that they had set me up in an elaborate snipe hunt and had returned to their homes to have a nightcap and go to sleep.

So I dwelled on those ideas for some time, and then thought about Lana at home in bed and her recent admonitions of my night's activities. Those thoughts dominated my thinking for over an hour. I turned every word for hidden meanings, nuances, tones, you name it.

As MacAvity once admitted, being a sniper can be a total mind fuck when you're *not* surrounded by "dinks." It's the waiting in total isolation that turns the screws.

I tried to move my thinking into more positive channels, like planning next year's garden, or recalling pleasant mountaineering trips Lana and I had enjoyed together. Things like that.

And time crawled. The half moon rose slowly, casting shadows of pine needles over my arms and the backs of my hands.

I never saw Smoke or MacAvity once the entire night and had to convince myself they were out there. I had scanned for them using the Yukon monocular but didn't see a thing in the strange green light of the unit.

Finally, at two AM on the dot, I heard a twig drag on cloth and they were suddenly beside me.

"Having fun?" Smoke whispered. I could see his teeth flashing in the moonlight.

MacAvity motioned for us to exit the trees with him, and we made our way back to the machine shed. None of us said a word until we were back in the Tundra and heading back into Ryback. Then Smoke, who had lit up a cigarillo, sighed with pleasure and said, "Three hours without one of these is like going to hell."

"Chew." MacAvity told him crisply. He seemed in a dark, thoughtful mood.

"I hate that shit," Smoke said. "And that's literally what it is, *shit*."

No one said anything for the rest of the way in.

I pulled to a stop at the curb of the deserted street at the back of MacAvity's Pub, and MacAvity placed our equipment back in the Navy duffle bag and lugged it out after him. Smoke got out and gave him a hand.

Before shutting the truck's door, MacAvity said to me, "Not too bad, now, was it, Paul?"

"No," I told him.

"I'm thinking," he said, "that in four nights the moon will be gone and we might have a visitor or two then."

He nodded to Smoke, shut the cab's door and started for the back of MacAvity's Pub. Smoke, being the shit he is, looked back over his shoulder at me and threw me a kiss.

I turned the truck towards home, happy.

Chapter
Ten

I came in the back door as quietly as I could, took my shoes off in the utility room and was halfway through the living room when I noticed Lana, in her thin cotton robe, standing in the arched entrance to the bedrooms. Her arms were crossed under her small breasts, and her face was in shadow from the moonlight streaming through the front window. I stopped.

She didn't move. "You hungry?"

"No, I'm fine," I ventured.

"OK then," she said. She turned and went back into her room and shut the door.

Fatigue descended on me as I went to my own room, shut the door quietly, and slid out of my clothing and got into my bed.

I turned to my right and turned on the two-bladed window fan, turned off my reading light, and laid back on the cool sheets. The happiness I had temporarily felt outside the pub had slipped away, and in its place a heavy feeling of waste and personal error pressed down on me.

That was when my door opened quietly and Lana came in, pulled back my sheet, and climbed in naked with me. She settled in under my arm, her head on my shoulder and a hand on my chest. I pressed my cheek into her sweet smelling hair and soon we were asleep.

Hauling garbanzos continued. Huey had phoned his goodbyes and left for his yearly service in his Cambodia mission, and by Thursday harvest was over. I was on my own again, back into retirement with a check from Leaps for $6,800 on my desk.

The stump above Hammersmith's, however, continued to dominate my nights. To my credit, I had become proficient with the monocular and had enjoyed watching a group of eleven deer cross Hammersmith's upper pasture on their way to Cup Hand Ridge. On Tuesday night a large coyote, showing up nearly white in the unit's amplification, came up along side their house and sat less than thirty feet away staring at their kitchen window. I had also finally spotted MacAvity changing his position from behind the barn to an elevated perch behind the conical top of the concrete cistern on the hill opposite me. He opened his rucksack and pulled a out a sheet of some kind and pulled it over himself. From where I was, he became invisible.

Each night Lana packed me a thermos of tea, a half dozen of my favorite cookies, and a sandwich for my vigils. It made a huge difference in easing the strain. She had also removed the cup and stopper off the steel thermos and replaced them with a sport top so that I could sip tea without running the risk of making noise.

The morning after that first night we had talked about my involvement, and I explained how MacAvity was using me only as a lookout--an extra pair of eyes. I also emphasized that no matter what, he and Smoke intended to protect Eric and Ruthie's lives since he suspected someone was interested in harming them.

"But he's not positive?"

"No," I said. "It's more a precautionary thing. I'm in the trees above the road and Hammersmith's driveway. My job is to radio Butte and Smoke if anyone is coming. That's all. I don't even carry a rifle."

"Nothing else?" she said. "What if someone gets behind you or something? You could get hurt."

"Butte loans me a .45 pistol to carry each night."

This seemed to satisfy her, and from that moment on, she was in on it, made my midnight snacks and helped me keep my spirits up.

We were both very grateful when I could finally park the Western Star and come home for the year. Plus I was sleep deprived from the nights.

The moon's light was gone by Friday night. We were plunged into the kind of darkness that nights bring to the ocean, the desert, or here on the Bench. It's odd that at the edge of cities where the nights are illuminated by their dull glow, the skies seem much darker than in these remote places. Out here a person's eyes adjust to the starlight, and the landscape reveals itself as a mosaic of shadows.

It was on this Friday night that, as MacAvity had predicted, something finally happened.

I had taken up my position, Smoke and Butte were working around to theirs, and I took out the monocular and pushed the button on top to activate it. I wanted to see if I could detect MacAvity's movements as I had the night before. I found it fascinating the way he was able to ghost out of the trees and across the open area between our ridge and the buildings. He moved swiftly, bent over at the waist, and his moccasined feet seem to glide under him as if he were sliding on ice. I'd never seen anything like it. At the tender age of seventy nine, he moved like fluid.

He hadn't left the trees yet, so I swung the monocular across the ground he would be crossing, the buildings, the house, and then out along the road. As I scanned the road, I was jolted by the black shape of an SUV parked directly below me, less than a hundred yards away. It was pulled off the road into the stubble at the snout of the ridge. It was positioned so its passengers could just see around the timber and watch the Hammersmith's.

"Butte!" I whispered into the mike, "Stay hidden! There's someone below me watching."

"Where are they?" His voice was soft and slow.

"To my right peeking around the timber. They're in a black SUV."

"Gotcha."

Smoke whispered, "Should I hold?"

"Yes," Butte answered. "I'll check it out." Then, "No, forget that. Work your way over behind and below Paul. I'll go in low and come up on their back. Cover my ass."

"Gotcha."

I kept my monocular on the SUV. By adjusting its slight telephoto capability, I pulled in the image a fraction more, and the exposure adjusted in turn, brightening the image.

Resting the side of my hand on the stump, I stabilized the picture and studied the grill, hood, and front left wheel. After a few moments, I realized I was looking at a black Suburban. I also realized it was exactly like the FBI rig that Gibson and Pfeffer had driven to MacAvity's Pub.

"I think it might be the FBI," I radioed.

I didn't get a response. Smoke and Butte were maintaining total silence as they made their move.

Finally, after what must have been ten minutes, Butte came on.

"You in place?" he whispered so softly I could barely make out his words.

"Roger."

"Whatdaya think?"

"It's them," Smoke whispered.

Another long period of silence.

"Work your way back to Paul's Tundra. Drop your gear in the shed and wait for my signal. Then, drive up here with high beams and ask them if they need any help."

"I'm going."

"They're about to have a flat tire here. Find out what you can. We'll cover you."

"Where's the pickup point?" Smoke asked, movement in his voice.

"When it's done keep going. We'll work up the draw to Hammer's grain road at the back."

The night descended on me again as I lowered the monocular and turned it off. Ten more minutes dragged by. There was no sound. No movement. Nothing.

Then I heard two doors click open and the muted low voices of Gibson and Pfeffer as they got out of the Suburban.

At that moment MacAvity touched my shoulder, giving me a near heart attack. He was smiling, and he relaxed beside me, stretching his legs.

"I slid my Kersaw boot knife into their left rear tire just enough to give them a leak," he told me. "I think they just found out about it."

He massaged his right calf, then said into the radio, "Your turn, Smoke."

"I'm coming." His signal was surprisingly strong and clear.

Butte got back up onto his knees. "Stay here. I'm going to cover him, and knowing Smoke, this should be very interesting. These headsets are more sensitive than you'd guess, and I'll try to get close enough so you can pick out what's being said. You'll love it."

And he was gone, and not too soon. My Tundra's wildly bright high beams came swinging around the bend and flooded the ridge at my back. Smoke had the windows down and I could hear country music booming from the cab and across the field. Then he was out of my sight as he skidded to a grinding halt in the gravel beside the Suburban.

I could hear him bellowing, "Need any help there fellas?" All I could hear was Pfeffer mumbling something. Then I heard the Tundra's door slam with a mighty thud. Smoke was either being as obnoxious as possible, or laying down a screen of sound for Butte's benefit, or both.

Then, over my headset, their voices came in more clearly as Butte worked into place near them.

"Why if it ain't my two favorite gum shoes?" Smoke said in a drunken slur. "What the fuck you doing out here on Hammersmith's land? Making out?"

"Go fuck yourself," I heard Pfeffer say.

"Let me turn down this God fearing music so's I can hear exactly what you said." The radio was turned off. "Now what was that you said to me, you shit head?" Smoke said in a low, threatening voice.

Out of the corner of my eye Hammersmith's porch light came on, and he stepped out into its glare in his PJs. He had a powerful spotlight in his right hand and a pump shotgun in the other. The beam of his light swept the stubble and came to rest on the front of the Suburban.

"Nothing," Pfeffer grumbled, sidestepping Smoke's threat. It was obvious he was growing concerned at the turn of events. They probably didn't like being between a belligerent drunk and a man with a shotgun coming their way.

"Just changing a flat here, if it's all right with you," he said, but with a sneer in his voice.

Hammersmith had shifted the light to his left hand and now had his shotgun in his right by the grip, with his finger inside the trigger guard. He was half way across the field and coming fast.

"That's a damn shame!" Smoke slurred. "That happened to me once too when I was poking *my* girlfriend. Sure puts a damper on things, now, don't it?"

"Why don't you just get the hell out of here?" Pfeffer growled.

"Nah. I think I'd like to watch. See how the Federal Government does things. Might learn something." Then a pause. "'Sides, here comes my buddy Hammersmith. He might need some help cleaning this here land of all the shit that seems to be accumulating on it."

I looked down. Eric had reached the front of the Suburban and had stopped.

"You guys!" he said, astonished to see who it was. "What the hell you doing out here on my land?"

"That's what I've been asking them, Hammer," Smoke said. "Gibson's been real polite and not saying anything at all, but this here piece of shit is all bent outa shape because I stopped in a neighborly way to lend a hand."

Smoke came into view around to stand by Eric. His cigarillo was freshly lit and he was acting like he was way too drunk to be walking, much less driving.

Gibson spoke. "We were just looking over your place tonight, Mr. Hammersmith," he said politely.

Eric help up his hand to stop Smoke from saying anything. "You still haven't answered my question. Why are you out here on my land in the middle of the night? You have no business, as you say, checking out my place. You wanna check out my place, you come in broad daylight and knock at my door. A hell of a lot healthier that way too."

"I understand that, sir," Gibson said. "And that's what we were going to do tomorrow morning. It's just that we learned today the .22s are a match." He let this news settle in, and I saw Eric lower the barrel of his shotgun so it was pointing straight down.

Pfeffer seemed to have regained some semblance of calm after Smoke's verbal thrashing.

"Now we won't need to come here," he said. "But we would like for you to come to our office in Spokane tomorrow morning. We'd like to ask you some questions."

"I don't have that kind of time," Eric told them, turning slightly as he got ready to go back to the house. "You wanna talk to me, you come here. I'm not leaving Ruthie here by herself."

He took one step when Smoke said, "Climb in, Eric, I'll give you a lift."

"You're drunk, Smoke. I'd fear for my life."

Smoke blew a thin stream of smoke into the air. "I'm as sober as a judge," he said soberly. "I was just enjoying myself with these two pecker heads." He took a quick step backwards, holding up one hand to Pfeffer, "Whoa there, Tonto. Easy does it!" And then he laughed and Hammersmith and he got into the Tundra, drove the short distance down the road, and turned into the farmhouse.

"I'm going to kick that fucker's ass," Pfeffer told Gibson.

"You need to cool it with these vets, Bob. They'll surprise you."

"I ought to kick your ass, too," he growled.

"Why don't you help me change the..."

And their voices faded as Butte began making his way back to me.

"Paul," he whispered. "Can you work your way back down out of the timber without making any noise?"

"I'll try."

"I'll meet you there. Let's go get picked up."

Chapter
Eleven

I was home by one o'clock and fell into bed exhausted. I was sure Lana had heard me come in, but she didn't get up.

In the morning I told her everything that had happened. When I got to the end and told her how Gibson had warned Pfeffer to cool it with vets because they could surprise you, she cracked up.

"That's a hilarious understatement," she choked out. "If they had only known they were at that moment surrounded by a pack of you guys, armed to the teeth, teched-out, they'd have been wetting themselves." She got it under control, caught her breath and added, "There they were, all undercover and stuff, all alone out in the countryside in total blackness and all around them are guys with night scopes and assault rifles..." she started laughing again.

"I love Smoke," she said. "He's one of a kind."

"Me too," I said, grinning.

She got up from where we were sitting on the porch, went in, and came back out with our teapot refreshed. She refilled our two cups and sat back down.

She was serious now. "But it does tell us one thing, doesn't it?" she said. "It means that what you guys are doing is correct after all, right?"

"I think so."

"Are you going to tell Charlie?"

"I'm sure he'll be told this morning about the bullets matching," I said.

"No, I mean about your surveillance."

"I'd sure feel a lot better if Charlie and Hammersmith *both* knew," I said. "But it's Butte's call. I don't know anything about doing things like this."

Lana nodded.

"Are you going out there tonight?"

"As far as I know."

She nodded again over the rim of her cup, took a sip, and leaned back in silence.

"Have you noticed?" she asked.

"Noticed what?" I looked her over carefully to see what I might have missed.

"The smoke is gone."

It was true. The sky was pure blue, there were scattered puffs of clouds over the Bitterroots, and the air smelled of fields damp with dew. A lovely morning.

She said, "They feel it's under control. They'll be mopping it up now, I suppose. Let's hope the wind direction remains normal."

Lana already had the garlic pulled and hardened, and had one hundred and fifty pounds which the store contracted at four dollars a pound. That covered the costs of growing our entire garden and orchard, including the watering.

Now she was putting up the raspberries. The blueberries were in gallon ziplocs in one of our three freezers, and soon the potatoes would go into the root cellar along with carrots and apples. Pears, peaches, plums, apricots, and quinces would be canned, jammed and jellied. We would also go in with Smoke on a cut, wrapped and frozen elk he would surely get, our chickens would be giving us a few eggs a day all winter long, and generally, we'd be set.

While she worked the raspberries, I got the plank, step ladder, and two extension ladders out and carried them around to the west side of the house where the trailing edge of the shade was. I went into the basement, got the scraper, broad knife, four-inch sash brush, wire brush, two gallon paint bucket, and a new gallon of primer paint and carried them out onto the grass.

Today I would follow the sun clockwise around the house tending to any chipping, cracking or peeling paint areas that had developed over the year. Tomorrow I'd repeat the process with the barn, then come back and start over with paint. I'd be done in four or five days. But it was looking as if next year I would have to paint both our major buildings top to bottom. It had been ten years. Pays to buy quality materials.

Lana liked to run our Big Red Troybilt cultivator each fall and spring. She was a master at taking the corners and turnarounds and had learned how to use the engine's own balance and power to do those maneuvers for her.

My last job each fall was to disassemble our irrigation systems and store it, and to turn off the timers. And the final touch was when I uncapped the six inch tubes that went three feet into the ground, turned off the water and drained all systems.

By then the night temperatures would be dropping down below freezing, and by the end of December, the thermometer would read in the twenties and teens. Things would remain like that for the next two months with a few subzero snaps thrown in here and there.

Those cold snaps, that were known to reach minus fifty, added interest to the monotony of our winters. Plus, they freeze-dried the brilliantly blue skies and rolling fields of snow. On those days the snows squeaked under foot, and tires made it groan. Those were days of joyous walks and evenings of sitting before the gas log fireplace with good books and music.

I was done spot-priming the house by two o'clock that afternoon and was just moving the equipment over to the barn for an early start tomorrow when Smoke pulled up and came in through the gate.

Lana met him on the front porch, and soon I joined them to share in the lemonade.

"You'll find this interesting," Lana said as I took my seat.

Smoke told me, "Our two FBI boys came and took Hammersmith in an hour ago, pardner."

"You're shitting me!"

"Nope. Apparently just sitting down at his kitchen table wasn't good enough for them."

"How'd you find out?"

"Ruthie. She phoned Charlie and so forth."

"Did they arrest him," Lana asked.

"She said they wanted to show him some things and set some things straight, but they didn't arrest him." He paused and took a sip. "In fact, she said Pfeffer made a feeble apology for last night, and then kept his mouth shut as Gibson did all the talking."

"They take him clear to Spokane?" I asked.

Smoke shook his head. "Nope. Said they were going to Charlie's offices and would have him back home in time for supper."

"That's a relief," Lana said.

I agreed. "Charlie will make sure they treat him respectfully."

"And," Smoke added, "Charlie will be sure to fill us all in, if I'm not mistaken."

We were silent for a bit, mulling this news over.

"So," I said, "have you talked to Butte?"

"I just came from there. He's as puzzled as we are. I mean, I they wouldn't be so interested in Hammer if they didn't think there was a connection between him and that guy Rojas."

"It's still got to be because of that pistol and lighter," Lana said.

"I agree with you, Lana, and you want to know what I've been thinking?" Smoke said. "I think Rojas was the owner of both those items and that he was a SEAL. Wanna bet?"

We considered that.

"The question is, why would he give his son his hush puppy *and* lighter?" Smoke took out a cigarillo and held it up questioningly. Lana nodded, and he lit it. "I mean, I can understand him giving his boy the pistol, maybe, since that boy has got to be, what, forty years old?" He thought about this. "But why would he give him the lighter as well? You get a memento like that from someone who is either dying or *is* dead."

I was shaking my head.

"What?" Lana asked.

"I don't get it," I said. "If you were a Navy SEAL, which is a pretty amazing thing to be, would you give a pistol designed to assassinate people to your son who has just spent twenty years in prison and has skipped parole?"

Smoke and Lana thought about that a moment.

Lana said, "Maybe he ripped his dad off?"

"Well," Smoke said. "That would explain the lighter. Maybe--what's that kid's name?"

"Cano," I told him.

"Maybe Cano is a smoker and the lighter was, say, in the drawer with the pistol. He just lifted it for the shits and giggles. I mean, how much more pissed off could his dad be after seeing the gun was gone?"

"Maybe Rojas didn't make it back from Vietnam?" Lana said.

"So, I can see the lighter being sent to the son. That's fine. But the Navy wouldn't mail a highly illegal silenced assassin's pistol to a two year old as something to impress his enemies with in the pre-school's playground."

"Maybe a buddy brought it back with him, kept it all these years, and then turned it over to Cano when he got out of prison."

"Why would he want to do that? Like we said, Cano's an animal."

"Maybe he didn't know," I offered. "Maybe he was a home town buddy and was in the SEALs with Rojas, and Cano returned home still under parole and snookered him into giving it to him and then skipped with his buddy Salas--and there you go."

Smoke sat up straight at the mention of Salas.

"You notice anything similar about their names?"

This was directed at me. Forty years on the paper had taught me not to forget names. "What do you mean?"

"What are their full names?"

"Cano Franzani and Salas Valladores. You mean because they are both Hispanic?"

"So a Hispanic doesn't by nature seek out Lutherans to be friends with," Lana said. "Their whole neighborhood was probably Hispanic, Smoke."

"I know *that*!" he said testily. "But the SEALs were a pretty exclusive outfit. More than that, to become one of those guys you have to go through hell, and a Hispanic back in those days that would enjoy such a thing or be able to pull it off could have had some background training, say in his native country, and, say, by the CIA."

"Oh, God, Smoke, you've been watching too many movies," Lana said.

Smoke looked at his watch.

"Nice lemonade, Lana, but it's approaching o'beer-thirty."

"Sorry. I didn't mean to say that," Lana apologized.

Smoke laughed and tapped her on the shoulder with a finger as he stood. "No, no. What I meant was I'm dragging your asses to the pub to buy you a drink so we can have Butte explain all this shit for us."

And then his face twisted in thought.

"Franzani. Franzani. You know, I think I might have heard that name before." He paused. "If I'm right, and he was a SEAL, and I have heard his name, then he might have been one of Butte's fourteen SEALs."

"Well, shit man!" I said excitedly. "That would explain the FBI's interest in Hammersmith, now wouldn't it?"

"Let's go run this by MacAvity," Lana said.

She scampered from the porch for our Tundra, and Smoke and I raced to his truck so we could get rolling before she did.

Chapter
Twelve

It was close to three o'clock when we entered the cool interior of the pub. It was empty since the five o'clock crowd hadn't arrived yet--which usually included us.

MacAvity was behind the bar sitting on a stool and watching the History Channel. He clicked it off as soon as he heard us behind him.

"'Bout time," he said, reaching for glasses.

We slid onto our usual stools, leaving Huey's "missing man" stool vacant between Lana's and Smoke's at the corner.

MacAvity had on a cowboy's ribbon shirt with the usual arm garters, leather string tie, and his worn, flat rimmed Stetson.

He poured, and Smoke, taking out a cigarillo asked, "Anything new on Hammer?"

"Charlie's bringing him home," he said. Then, turning to Lana he said, "I phoned Ruthie."

"And?" Lana said.

"You know her. She wouldn't ask for a quarter if she needed a cup of soup."

"And?"

MacAvity was now thoughtfully wiping the counter with a clean white bar towel. "Do you think she would appreciate a visit from you and Jake today?"

Lana reached out and put her hand on his, stopping the towel.

"What are you doing, Butte, turning into an old softy on us?"

Before he could answer, she turned to go use the bar's phone. "Put that in a to-go, Pops," she ordered.

MacAvity wasn't done, though.

"Charlie and Hammersmith are stopping here for a minute on their way. Could you tell her?"

"Why are they stopping here first?"

"I figured they could both use a drink on the house," he said. "Nothing like having to spend some time with officious types to make you thirsty."

Lana nodded and dialed. When she returned there were two, twelve ounce lidded paper cups on the bar waiting for her.

Hefting them carefully, she smiled at Butte.

"So, which is Jake's?"

Charlie and Hammersmith came in on Sheila's heels. She nodded and went into the kitchen, and Eric took his usual seat around the corner of the counter at Smoke's elbow. Charlie sat on Eric's other side near the register.

Hammersmith looked a bit pale but otherwise just fine. He studied Smoke and me with narrowed eyes, and Charlie started scrutinizing the back of his right hand while Butte mixed Eric his rum and coke and got a Bud Light out for Charlie.

"You not getting enough sleep, Smoke? Paul?" Eric finally asked.

Butte acted as if he hadn't heard him.

"I'm OK," Smoke said.

"Me, too," I added.

He kept looking at us with those eyes, and I began to feel uncomfortable. But not Smoke.

"How's Pfeffer today?" he asked.

"He seemed OK too."

"And Gibson?"

"Him too."

MacAvity broke the tension by setting their drinks before them. Charlie took his up and swallowed deeply three times, then placed the chilled bottle on the counter and wiped his mouth with the white sleeve of his shirt.

"So, how's the stakeout going, men?" Charlie asked matter of factly.

Not missing a beat, MacAvity answered, "Pretty well, Charlie, but you missed the fun last night."

Charlie tapped a finger thoughtfully on the bar top a couple times.

"Now if you had sliced off the valve stem on their rig instead of making it look like a leak, you three might have had some issues to deal with concerning at least one pissed-off FBI Special Agent."

"Hard to tell what a guy will run over when he leaves the road and starts crossing people's farms," Butte said.

"That *was* a mistake on their part," Charlie admitted. "But they might not make another one."

Butte pulled up his stool.

"You going to stop us, Charlie?" he asked.

"That's up to Eric," he said.

But before Eric could answer, Smoke asked, "How long have you known?"

"You aren't the only one with toys, MacAvity," Hammersmith said tightly.

"I know that, Eric."

"What do you take me for?" Hammersmith said, his voice rising dangerously. "You think I'm going to let Ruth and myself be killed in our sleep? Don't you think I could and would watch your every move the minute you came into the trees?"

We didn't stir.

"You didn't think for a moment you could ask me if you could place a perimeter around my home? That I was an idiot that needed three nursemaids? Who the fuck do you think you're dealing with?"

Smoke and I looked nervously at each other. But not Butte.

"Answer me!" Eric thundered.

Butte folded his arms over his chest and stared back at him. I wanted to vanish.

"Tell you what, Hammer," Butte finally said, unlacing his arms and wiping his hands on the bar towel. "I get the feeling you would have done the same thing for any of us. Or, am I mistaken about you?"

After what seemed an eternity, Hammersmith broke their stare-down, shaking his head and taking up his drink. Charlie hadn't moved, still studying his hand.

"Rojas Franzani was under my command," Hammersmith finally said in an even voice.

Butte nodded.

"He was one of my SEALs. I had become concerned by reports dealing with his conduct in the field and had him put under arrest. I decided to have him flown to COMNAVFORV in Saigon to be questioned. I suspected he was possibly committing atrocities," he said, quietly.

After a moment, he continued, "Huey was transporting him. They took fire and began to smoke. Once they were in the clear..." he paused, "Huey put down in a paddy to see what could be done. But they were ambushed. In the confusion, Rojas struck his guard and jumped out, still cuffed. The VC gunned him down before Huey was able to lift to safety and return fire. Rojas was grabbed by the dinks and dragged off."

Hammersmith took another tiny sip. "Huey went down in the Bassac, and we pulled him, the guard and the crew out safely," he said.

After we digested this for a moment, Charlie looked up and said, "The FBI has come to believe that Rojas wasn't killed, probably because he was cuffed. They also suspect he is back in the states. And get this, the DEA is interested in Rojas as well."

He slide his beer bottle around in the tight wet circle on the bar before going on. "No one seems to know much more than that, but I want to tell you that I have a personal feeling of responsibility towards you men and everyone in the county. That feeling supersedes the demands these agencies are placing on me."

"What are you trying to tell us, Charlie?" Butte asked.

"What he's saying..." Hammersmith began, "Is that it's important that you have my permission if you guys are caught covertly on my property with the intent of protecting Ruth and my lives with automatic weapons."

"Are you saying you're willing to give that to us?" Smoke asked.

"I'll think it over," Hammersmith said, smiling for the first time since he came in.

We heard a truck pull up outside. It sounded like Jable's.

Charlie stood to go, and Hammersmith threw back his drink to join him, but Charlie stopped and pointed to each one of us.

"If any one of you ends up killing someone, things will become difficult for everyone, so don't do it. Take prisoners. But if it happens, I'm hoping you have a damn good reason. And make sure you can show in court that your victim would have killed one of you or one of the Hammersmiths." He headed to the door. "You better understand that, gentlemen. It's not an easy thing to prove to a jury."

They edged by Jables who was just coming in, greeting him briefly before leaving.

"What's that all about?" Jables asked, taking a seat at my left.

"A couple thirsty men," Butte said. "And I think another one just now walked in."

I turned back to Smoke.

"Well, Smoke, looks like we got our answer, doesn't it?"

Chapter
Thirteen

Lana came into the bar a little after six o'clock just as I was about to leave to meet her at the house for supper.

She came in briskly, gave me a quick kiss, and draped her arm around my neck as she addressed Butte.

"Hey, Softy, could you sell me a bottle of Bacardi and a quart of club soda?"

He reached under the counter to get unopened ones.

"How's Ruthie?" I asked.

"She's sitting outside in the Tundra with Jake," she said, accepting the bottle from Butte. She put a twenty on the bar and Butte pushed it back at her. "We're going to have a slumber party at Jake's tonight. You're on your own."

That got Smoke's attention, along with the handful of others who had trickled in. "We need to order some table dancers here, Softy," Smoke said.

Butte looked hard at him. "You ever call me that name again, and you're going to learn just how wrong you are, *Pardner*," he said. But it was in fun.

I turned back to Lana just as she pulled away and went out through the door.

Butte took my glass, but I shook my head.

"Tell you what," he said. "I've got some extra fine crab meat in the cooler, so if you two shits would like to have supper with me upstairs," he paused, looking at Smoke, "I'll phone Sheila to come in and we'll make an early night of it."

Smoke shrugged his shoulders. "Sure. Why not?"

Upstairs we filed in behind MacAvity, who proceeded to make us open-faced broiled crab on English muffin, with sharp cheddar melted on them. Nothing fancy, but they were large and the snow crab was fresh, delicious, and piled high.

It was pleasant eating in Butte's personal kitchen around the central table. He cooked on a large gas range. Hanging overhead from a copper hood and arranged on shelves were expensive culinary items he had picked up in his lifetime of travel. German and Chinese cleavers and knives, large sticky rice cookers with conical baskets, copper pots, stainless wire strainers, a beautiful Hawkins pressure cooker, bamboo spoons and ladles--the assortment was wonderful.

Afterwards, Smoke did the dishes in the deep porcelain sinks as I packed the extra sandwiches and made three thermoses of coffee as instructed. Butte, meanwhile, gathered our gear from the basement's "war room" and loaded it into Smoke's GMC.

Shortly we were on our way back out to Hammersmith's to begin an evening we had, until now, only suspected might occur.

Still dark and moonless, clouds strolled across the stars like prams in the park.

By now I had smoothed the floor of my nest behind the stump free of twigs and cones, and had lined it with a four inch thick layer of pine needles. I had come to almost enjoy my vigils. I was relatively comfortable, I had grown to enjoy playing with the night scope, and the eleven deer had grown used to our strange behaviors and ignored us as they passed by nightly on their way up Cup Hand.

Tonight, Hammersmith, alone in the house, had turned off all the lights, including the yard light, and the place was lost in the inky depths of the farm's small valley. Without the flare of the lights to confound our scopes, we had clear images of the entire area. However, to the naked eye it was darker than the inside of a cow, as Butte put it,.

If it hadn't been for this darkness, I wouldn't have noticed an orange glow that began to form five or more miles to the east toward the Bitterroots.

I spoke softly into my mike.

"Do you guys see a light towards the mountains?"

Smoke relied, "Not a thing. You drinking over there?"

Butte said, "Don't see it."

I studied the glow more carefully, not quite trusting my eyes. I came to see that the rise on the far side of Hammersmith's was blocking Butte and Smoke's views. I glanced at my watch, hitting the indiglo button. 1:40.

"I think it's a big fire," I finally said.

Just as I got that out, Ryback's sirens began howling the distant alarm in town. The sound carried out over the Bench eerily.

We waited.

Five minutes passed. Then we heard the growling of our fire truck's huge engine, and accompanying it, the whine of the ambulance. Shortly they came careening by us, sirens silent, but their lights whirling furiously off the sloping fields. Hammersmith's was momentarily ablaze in a swarm of blue, white and red puddles of color. And then they were gone.

Suddenly Eric came over our headphones. Apparently he had scanned onto our frequency with his own radio set and had been listening to us from the first night.

"Stay put, men," he growled. "It's Huey's. Jables phoned it in and has warned me just now."

"What's going on?" This was MacAvity.

"He said he heard a whumph, then two more, and got up to look down the valley at Huey's." He paused. "He says the house, barn and machine shop are engulfed in flames."

"Firebombed?" Butte asked.

"That's my guess."

They went silent and we waited.

During that time three pickups filled with volunteers came roaring past flashing blue dash beacons.

Ten minutes slid past.

I braced my elbows on the stump and watched the flames through my night scope. In the pale green amplification, they flared high, then died, then flared again. At one point a large burst of light filled the sky and I suspected one of Huey's five-hundred gallon fuel tanks had exploded.

Then I heard Smoke whisper over his radio, "See 'em?"

"Yup," MacAvity murmured.

I turned and scoped the draw behind the house. At first I couldn't see what they were talking about. Then, with sudden recognition, I saw the hood and windshield of a black older Ford Taurus slowly nosing through the deep grass down the overgrown, two-rut farm track. Its lights and engine were off, taking advantage of the slope to roll silently down past the barn and towards the house.

I had no idea where Butte had positioned himself, but if they kept coming they would pass within two hundred feet of Smoke.

"Let one of them in," Hammersmith whispered.

"Got it." It was said so softly I couldn't tell if it was Smoke or MacAvity.

Then, MacAvity, "Only back us up, Smoke."

The car came to a stop at the edge of the yard's gravel turnaround. Now I could easily see the faces of its occupants. There were two men, one of them blond, the other dark haired, and both white faced. They continued to sit. They were looking carefully at the house, and I could see they were talking quietly. They seemed to be of average, nondescript build.

FBI?

We waited. Five minutes. Ten.

Then both doors of the car opened smoothly, the dome light remaining off, and they slid out, leaving the doors open. They crouched, moving slowly until they were at the edge of the gravel. They were both wearing black jeans and black long sleeved T-shirts, and I could clearly see they held automatics. Glocks?

I held my breath, my ears rushing with each heart beat.

The driver then nodded to the other man and they both bolted across the gravel at a dead run. The gravel sounded like large dogs were running on it. The driver headed for the back door, and the other man headed around the side towards the front.

They hit the narrow band of lawn that surrounded the house, and the driver plunged through the back door, kicking it in as he went.

Instantly from inside came a fart-like sound similar to a high RPM motorbike revving its engine.

Simultaneously, the grass around the feet of the man running up the side started to jump and dance around as if alive. The man fell on his side screaming horribly again and again. His feet continued flopping and shaking like snared rabbits, and one shoe went skidding off on its own.

I could hear Butte's Colt futfutfutfutfut in three or four bursts from somewhere out of sight near the leading corner of the barn.

The man stopped screaming and said, "Oh my God. Oh my God," before he passed out.

"Hammer?" I heard MacAvity say in a loud voice.

"Yup. And you?"

"He's down and alive."

With that, the house lights and yard lights came on, and Butte appeared from where I thought he'd been and approached the downed man carefully just as Eric came out the back door and joined him.

Hammersmith was holding a tiny, stockless machine gun with a long clip extending down below it. He swung and crossed over to Butte's right as they approached the prostrate form at right angles. He kept the gun trained on the man's head as Butte reached down and turned him over onto his back. They didn't touch his gun, which lay several feet ahead.

Hammersmith reached into his back pocket and handed Butte four thick zip ties which Butte set about securing as two tourniquets just below the man's knees. He then rolled him back onto his face, took two more zip ties and connected them in a figure eight and cinched the man's hands together behind his back with them.

"You can come on in now, boys," Hammermith said.

I got unsteadily to my feet and stepped out of the trees and started down through the grass to the house. I saw Smoke doing the same a couple hundred feet to my left.

"Let's not touch anything until Charlie and his crew get here," Hammersmith said as Smoke and I came up.

He opened his cell phone and phoned Charlie's night dispatcher and asked to be patched through.

After a moment, "Morning, Charlie. We need the ambulance here at my house. Also, we have something for the coroner if you want to get him up. Yup."

He shut the phone and dropped it back into his front pocket.

I looked down at MacAvity's handiwork, and was shocked at what I saw. He had literally shot the man's feet off. They were still attached by strips of skin, but they had been turned into ragged bags of pink bone and red meat.

The grass under them was a deep puddle of blood that shined black in the bluish yard light.

Smoked look down as well. "Nice shooting, pardner," he said.

MacAvity nodded. "I aim to please, and Charlie wanted a prisoner. So here he is, all cut and wrapped."

I walked off a few yards. Smoke grinned at me, lit up a cigarillo, and shook his head.

"It's not pretty, is it, Paul?" he said soberly.

I shook my head, feeling cold and sweaty.

"I'll get some feed bags to cover this shit up," Eric said. "Looks like he's going into shock."

I saw that even unconscious the man was now trembling from head to foot.

"What was that noise I heard come from your house?" I managed.

"This," Hammersmith said, swinging up the odd looking machine pistol.

MacAvity explained. "That's an Ingram Mac10 .45. Shoots one-thousand, two hundred rounds a minute. That's twenty rounds a second," he said.

Smoke said, "Let's go see what it did, Hammer."

I didn't want to go in the house with them, but I felt morbidly compelled to at least have a look.

They led the way in, and I fell in behind them at a slight distance. A powerful, wet, coppery smell of blood and excrement overwhelmed me just inside the broken-in back door. The utility room leading to the kitchen was covered with broken pieces of sheet rock, and the wall just to my left was riddled with holes that shined with light from the kitchen.

They had stopped and were looking down at the floor beneath this wall as I entered.

I looked. And shouldn't have. I reeled back onto the gravel, leaned over hands on knees, until I began sweating profusely.

Then Smoke was beside me, his hand on the back of my neck.

"I'll go for the truck and get us home."

He led me to a bench on the lawn in front of the house under one of Hammersmith's locust trees. He eased me into it and headed down the driveway on foot, cigar smoke streaming behind him like a contrail.

I sat with my head in my hands, elbows on knees, and stared at my boots. But try as I might, I couldn't shake the image of the huge amount of blood hanging from the ceiling, running down the wall, and flooding the yellow linoleum of Ruthie's kitchen floor. It was that blood and the smell of it that was worse than the ragged and torn chest bristling with shattered rib bones covered with exploded intestine. And the nearly unrecognizable broken remnants of a face and head half gone. That image tortured me--but the smell was the thing.

It was then that the screams began again on the side lawn.

I got to my feet and walked down the driveway after Smoke.

As I approached the road I saw Smoke returning in his GMC. From the other direction the Ryback ambulance was coming as well.

I stepped back into the pasture to let the ambulance by. Smoke had slowed to let them go first, then he pulled in behind them, but not before the ambulance had stopped beside me.

Pappy, our EMT, rolled down his window.

"Charlie radioed from Huey's to say he doesn't want anyone to leave, Paul," he said. "Come back to the house." And he continued on.

Smoke pulled forward and opened the door for me.

"Climb in, Pardner," he said. "I just happen to have a bottle of scotch in here for us."

"Charlie said we have to go back to Hammersmith's"

"Figured," he said. "But first things first," he added, pulling the bottle out from behind the seat for me to see.

Chapter
Fourteen

We parked at the edge of the gravel below the ridge close to side of the house. Smoke turned off the lights and killed the engine.

"Here," he said, handing the unopened bottle to me. "It'll settle you."

I twisted the cap free and took a shallow sip with my dry lips. It warmed my throat, and I could feel it hit my constricted stomach. Smoke was right. Within moments my insides began to unclench. And the stink left my nose.

Pappy was working over MacAvity's man who was moaning with each breath in low, mournful howls. Pappy lived in a tiny cottage on the far side of Lana's garden, and had earned his nickname because he was the spitting, bulky, white-bearded image of Ernest Hemingway. He was hooking up an IV drip while Shay, who had managed to hop aboard as a volunteer, was applying compression cuffs on the mangled legs.

Charlie arrived ten minutes later and disappeared with MacAvity and Hammersmith into the house. The kitchen window repeatedly burst with the white light of Charlie's flash camera.

Smoke and I passed the bottle back and forth and waited. I looked at my watch. 3:13.

Charlie eventually came back out, put his camera back on the front seat of the Expedition, and opened the rear hatch. He took out several ziploc bags and returned to the house. I noticed he was wearing surgical gloves.

Shay pulled the gurney from the ambulance and carried it over beside the patient. Pappy gently lifted the man's torso onto it by his shoulders while Shay held his knees stationery. Then they each took a knee and a foot and lifted them on as well. The man shrieked in pain and went unconscious again.

Together they lifted the gurney into its rolling position and soon had him slid into the ambulance and strapped securely into place. Pappy, who had once been an Army medic, came over to my window.

Smoke handed the bottle across me to him, and he took it willingly and took a large mouthful, held it with eyes closed, and swallowed slowly.

"Thanks, Smoke," he said. "But my mommy says I can't come over and play with you boys no more."

"That's a shame, Pappy," Smoke said.

"I know. She says you play too rough."

"How are things at Huey's?"

"Charlie says Huey left for his mission," Pappy said, taking another large swallow before handing the bottle back to Smoke. "That true?"

"Yup."

"Well thank God for that!"

Smoke ground out his cigarillo on the flat side of his Zippo, hanging both out his window and dropping the dead butt to the gravel.

He looked at Pappy. "You give that fucker morphine?"

Pappy gave his barrel chested chuckle, "Nope. I figured he was enjoying himself too much. Don't want to spoil the ER doc's job at Magnet, either."

"Then do us a favor, will you?" Smoke asked after a thoughtful moment.

Pappy waited.

"Pull over on the way in and tell him real close and personal that he and his pardner killed the man who owns that house they torched." He paused. "Ya know, Pappy, that was what them and their pals wanted to do, so why disappoint them. Know what I'm saying?"

Pappy nodded, an evil grin spreading beneath his mustache. He headed back to the ambulance. We heard his driver's door slam, and Shay and he pulled out and wobbled down the ranch road and out onto the pavement headed for Magnet Hospital. Soon their flashing lights no longer showed against the tops of the hills, and they were gone.

MacAvity and Hammersmith, followed shortly by Charlie, came out of the house. Charlie carried six or more ziplocs that swung from his fists. It was then I noticed Hammersmith was carrying one as well, and it had the dead man's pistol in it. I could see now it was a Glock.

Smoke and I got out and went over to the back of the Expedition where they were placing the bags in a blue, plastic bin. Charlie stepped back, stripped off his gloves and dropped them into a small hazmat bucket which he snapped a lid over.

The four of us stood silently watching as he did these things. He shut the hatch and turned tiredly towards us, pushing his cowboy hat back on his head. He wiped his hands, sweaty from the latex gloves, down the tops of his jeans.

"I'm tired, men," he began. "I'm bone tired. I was tired before I went to bed. And I can't begin to tell you how much I appreciate you getting me up and bringing me out here to your fire and slaughter houses. You know how far off my ranch is?"

"Now wait a minute here, Charlie," Hammersmith growled.

Charlie reached for the bottle that was still hanging from Smoke's right hand. I thought he was going to confiscate it or something, but he surprised me by taking a pull from it and handing it back.

"I'll tell you exactly what I'm trying to say, Eric," he said, looked around at us and stopping on Hammersmith.

"I'm willing to do anything that's necessary to enforce the law and protect you people. That's what you hired me to do. That's what you pay me for. That's what I said I'd do. And that's what I will do." He voice was beginning to develop thunder clouds. "But Rojas wasn't one of these men. Cano wasn't one of these men. If they were, I would believe they were doing exactly what you led me and those two assholes from the FBI to believe. But that's not the case, is it?"

He rubbed his hands together briefly and leaned back against the side of the expedition, crossing his arms over his chest and cocking one of his cowboy boots up against the rear tire behind him.

Hammersmith and MacAvity waited him out.

"You told us that you arrested Rojas on suspicion of atrocities and he was killed by the VC while attempting to escape. He was listed as MIA, and your story checked out 100%.

"I, on the other hand, provided you with the information that Cano was his son. I also provided you with Cano and his friend's backgrounds, though I withheld the fact the FBI wanted them in connection with arson murders in both Tacoma, Washington and Vancouver, BC.

"Now we have two *new* perps." He looked at the ground and then back at us. "What's that tell you?"

I cast about trying to find something to answer with, and came up with nothing whatsoever except maybe I should offer him another sip.

Hammersmith cleared his throat. "When's the team going to be here?" he asked.

"Probably not for another hour."

Hammersmith turned back to the front of the house, nodding for Charlie to follow him. We all did.

Hammersmith went up the steps and took a seat in one of the half dozen chairs scattered in the porch's cozy interior. I took a seat furthest from the closed front door in case any of the smell from inside leaked out.

Charlie took a seat against the wall, pulled off his hat and placed it on his crossed knee. He wiped dust from the heel of his boot out of habit and waited for Hammersmith to say something.

"Rojas was a fearsome fighter," Hammersmith began. "He was five foot seven or eight, thin and muscular, dark as our chairs here, and mean as a snake. His squad didn't care for him, and he figured, wrongly, it was because he had been a child soldier for Guatemalan rebels. That's what he told me. But it was because he was a loner and he loved to kill things--anything--and it creeped his team out."

"You ever actually *see* him kill an animal or anything?" Charlie asked.

Eric looked at his gnarled hands as he rubbed them together.

"No. His men said that he loved to shoot water buffalo and dogs. And VC. They had gone in on the night I told you about on a STAB, a SEALS Tactical Assault Boat. At their target, they were ambushed. The target was the village they were in at the time, and they had two of the sympathizers' leaders in custody as planned. Then, for no reason, Rojas reputedly started shooting everything and everyone that moved. This alerted a large group of VC that happened to be nearby, who then descended on them from the jungle.

"So Rojas kills their prisoners and gives the village a parting spray, knocking down screaming women and their children. The squad battled their way back to the STAB. There they found their medic killed and the boat burned to the waterline. That's when they radioed for a dust-off."

Eric wasn't finished.

"Teofilo, one of the team, requested to speak with me in private the following day after the debriefing. He informed me of his discomfort over what had happened in the village because of Rojas, and to protect his life I had him immediately flown in Huey's Seawolf to COMNAVFORV to give a full report.

"I sent my second SEAL squad to the village with heavy back-up to assess the situation, and what they found confirmed Teofilo's story. In fact, they found three men in the village willing to testify to the fact."

I noticed that Charlie had taken out his notebook and was writing down points of what Hammersmith was saying.

"After things had cooled down for five days, I talked the doctor of our MEDCAP's team, a group that gave the villagers in our region medical assistance, into bringing these three out. I had them flown to COMNAVFORV as well. Two days later I was told to place Rojas under arrest and ship him along under guard."

Charlie was nodding. MacAvity was looking blankly at his hands folded on his lap. Light from the living room window slanted across him as he sat as silent and still as a post.

"A couple things that will interest you, Charlie," Hammersmith added, "Teofilo Ray was shuffled out of the service with full pay and was found ten months later in the ashes of his suburban Oklahoma home with two .22 shots to his skull like the store owners on the Tucannon."

Charlie considered this. "What about the three villagers that testified?"

"They, their children and wives were given passage to our Naval base at Bremerton, Washington. I'd assume they've been citizens for decades by now."

Charlie got to his feet.

"That's a start, Eric," he said. "And I appreciate it."

He squared his hat on his head and went down the steps to the flagstone path. He stopped, turned back to face us and added, "I want you, MacAvity here and Smoke to talk this over and decide what kind of arrangement we can agree on that will allow you three to tell me the whole story, Eric." He slapped a mosquito on his left forearm. "I'll do what you want to help you protect whoever you're protecting. Understand? I can promise you *that*."

He walked off, saying over his shoulder, "Good night gentlemen. You might want to put coffee on for the team when they get here."

Chapter
Fifteen

Huey Houston's farmhouse had been built in 1903 of the same brick clay as MacAvity's, and like Grandpa Coe, Huey's grandfather wagoned the clay in and kilned it in Ryback. He had then wagoned the warm bricks back out to the Houston's homestead and started laying them. He, his wife and Huey's father, a small boy then, began the farm and lived in their "prairie shack" during the two years the construction took.

Huey was the sole survivor of the clan. A widower and the only child of an only child, the family tree came to a dead end with him. He did claim, however, that he had a pack of kinfolk that had descended from his grandfather's brother. They seemed to have farms of their own scattered over North Dakota.

The town's phone tree called a meeting the next morning. Our phone rang at nine o'clock, and thankfully Lana didn't need to wake me since the meeting was to be held at noon. She didn't get me up until eleven-thirty and had a late breakfast of eggs, toast, sausage and strong tea waiting for me.

I was wobbly on my feet when I came to the table. I took up my cup, took a large, satisfying swallow and began to eat.

Between bites, I filled her in briefly about the night's bloody events and she listened intently, asking questions and nodding.

I was done with my breakfast and two additional cups of tea by the time I had completed the account, and

I asked her about her night. She told me the three of them had killed a fifth of rum and Don had gone out to the abandoned bunk house so he could get some sleep. Lana also told me that Hammersmith and MacAvity had engineered for Ruthie to be out of her house.

Apparently those two old war horses had "a nasty feeling" something might happen that night, and rightly so. Luckily, Huey had not been at home. Shortly, I was to find out that *that* had been arranged as well, which explained Huey's rather abrupt departure. No one had foreseen that the "nasty feeling" involved the total incineration of his farm.

The tables and chairs had already been set up on the town hall's wood planked floor above the firehouse by the time Lana and I arrived. So far about fifty people had arrived and were either in the kitchen setting up or standing in groups discussing the night's bloody history. I stood in a short line for a cup of coffee, and Lana went over to where Don and Jake were sitting to reserve spots for us.

In the next twenty minutes nearly the entire town, probably close to a hundred and forty people, had filled the hall. Lonnie, our mayor and Union Manager, was talking with MacAvity as they came in. They took their usual seats at a table at the end of the room where a microphone had been set up.

Sheila, the town's volunteer recorder, saw them and brought over sandwiches and coffee. She took a seat at MacAvity's elbow where her white legal pad and a ball point rested.

People wrapped up their conversations and took their paper plates and cups to their seats. Slowly the hum of the crowd quieted and Lonnie snapped on the mike with a huge hand and leaned forward on his elbows.

"Thanks for coming, folks," he said somberly. "I know you all had other matters to attend to today, but it has been suggested we need to do something about last night's arson."

The crowd went silent and many people nodded their agreement.

"So I'd like to take suggestions one by one. If you will stand, I will call on you."

In the ensuing hour more than thirty men and women suggested everything from holding a church bazaar and raffle to buy Huey a double wide to buying Huey's land so he could retire in luxury in Palm Springs. But everyone understood deep down they needed to organize and rebuild the beautiful Houston house, though each and every one of them understood it would not be as grand.

"So," Lonnie recapped. "MacAvity tells me Huey had adequate insurance, so we don't need to worry about the actual construction or architectural costs of the house and out buildings, is that right?" he asked, looking to MacAvity.

MacAvity nodded.

"So our job as a town is to salvage the brick and stack it on pallets." He paused, looking everyone over. "All agree?"

"Aye," the townspeople said as a single voice.

Lonnie nodded and checked to see that Sheila was getting it all down.

Jables stood and was recognized.

"I'll bring my thirty foot flatbed over and we can use it as a chipping platform."

"Good," Lonnie said. "What else?"

Two others said they were going to bring their front loaders. Richter, who owned a construction company, said he'd come out with his Hitachi EX200 bucket excavator to pull down the remaining walls and lift the rubble and brick out of the basement hole. Food, beer, and shade tarps were all volunteered.

"How long will it take?" someone asked.

Richter stood again to answered that. "If everyone shows up with a shovel or hammer and chisel--anything you can think of that would help clean brick--well, we could have his place on pallets and the rubble hauled off in a week."

People liked that, and several stood, anxious to get back to farming.

"Anything else?" Lonnie said close to the mike.

Chairs were pushing back in a growing din.

"Then, thanks for coming folks. Coffee and rolls will be waiting for you tomorrow morning at seven. Let's have the machinery in place by tonight."

It didn't seem like anyone was listening, though they were, even as they folded up their individual chairs and crowded over to stack them against the side wall.

Jake and Don remained seated with Lana and me at the end of our table. I knew what they wanted, and so over my half-empty, second cup of coffee I gave them the short version. They remained silent, and by the time I was done, the hall was empty except for our volunteer firemen who were taking the garbage cans of paper plates and cups down the back steps.

I wondered why Smoke hadn't come to the meeting. Just snoozing? But I fully understood how exhausted and unsettled MacAvity and Hammersmith must have been. If I had been them, I would spend the entire week doing nothing more than sleeping and quietly sipping tea and looking out over the fields.

As if reading my mind, Lana asked if I was going to call them today?

"No, I don't want to disturb them," I said. "Let's just go home and hang out today."

I took a three hour nap that afternoon and didn't budge from the house that night.

Lana put me to bed at nine with a tea made from two of her homemade tinctures. I'm not sure if that tea allowed me to sleep or knocked me unconscious, but I slept soundly and didn't wake until nine the next morning. A personal record of some kind.

I had just finished my late breakfast when the phone rang. Lana answered it and handed it to me.

It was Charlie.

"I understand the town's going to help Huey rebuild?" he said.

"Yup. We were just on our way out there," I said. "What's up?"

"Have MacAvity or Hammersmith talked to you or Smoke yet?"

"I haven't heard from either of them."

"OK. I'll give Smoke a call." I heard some papers rustle. He was calling from his desk. "I had Butte in early yesterday afternoon," he said, "and Eric in afterwards. I'm trying to keep this a local matter, but I don't think it's going to stay that way. Pfeffer, in particular, indicated that in so many words this morning."

"I understand," I said, a trickle of anxiety coursing through me.

"So, I want to get your statements down before he starts in. Could you come in at one, Paul? It'll only take a half hour or so."

Lana drove me to the County Courthouse in Magnet, dropped me off at the back where the prisoner transfer garage and main door leading into the Sheriff's Department were located. She gave me a kiss and drove off for the half hour to get groceries.

I didn't know the young dispatcher sitting behind the glass barrier inside the door, but she seemed to know me. She buzzed the inner door open for me. I walked the short hall past the small deputies' room that was mostly cabinets on one side and a wall mounted bench desk on the other with three flat screen computers. Around the corner was a larger room where Charlie and his Chief Deputy, Dale Romsland's desks were.

Charlie was the only one in and looked up. Getting to his feet he motioned for me to have a seat at a small, elliptical oak dining table and four chairs set between the door and the two desks. He carried over a small Sony tape deck and put it in the table's center as I took a seat closest to the door.

"You don't look worse for wear," he said, turning back for a yellow legal pad and ball point.

"Thanks," I said. "Looks can be deceiving."

He flopped the tablet on the table's far end, went past me and shut the door. He took his seat and rocked back, sighing.

"Want to be updated, Paul?"

I nodded, relaxing a bit.

"We're lucky in one important regard," he said. "MacAvity knew enough to stop the second man, not kill him. The shooter lost both his feet, by the way. Nothing left of them.

"And Hammersmith was in the right when he killed the first guy. So that's fine," he continued.

"You know who they were?"

Charlie dropped back on all four chair legs, put his elbows on the table and studied the pen he turned slowly between his two hands.

"Those two guys were Canadian contractors--guys who solve other people's problems for them." He looked to see if I was following him.

"They were hired killers, Paul. So they fall into the FBI's jurisdiction, and frankly, I'm glad to get rid of that aspect of what happened. Special Agent Gibson was kind enough to tell me that the Canadians have been trying to collar those two for nearly ten years. In fact, they were surprised to learn that they had taken a job in the U.S."

Charlie dropped the pen and leaned over on one arm of the chair, relaxing a bit himself.

"Among other things, there were two road flares and two glass liter bottles of gas in the trunk of the car. Primitive but effective. So it's pretty obvious they did Huey's after tossing it. Then they were intending to torch Hammersmith's as soon as they had killed him and Ruthie. No .22s, however. That seemed to be Rojas and Cano's M.O. There was also a five pound slide hammer in the trunk, a pound of C-4 explosive, detonation cord, blasting caps, fuses, and water bottles with hangers to be suspended as tampers."

"Why the slide hammer?" I asked.

"It shows how the Taurus was stolen. There was a threaded cap at the end of the slide hammer. A person puts a sheet metal screw through a hole in the cap, tightens it back on the slide, twists it into an ignition key slot and pops the whole works out. A simple screw driver or knife point inserted into the opening can start the car like a key. The car was stolen from a Ford dealership in Missoula, Montana, and the plates were from a teacher's car in Darby."

I nodded.

"What we don't understand is why Huey and Hammersmith would warrant this kind of attention from someone, nor what Cano and Rojas have to do with it. We don't know for sure if they are connected, but it seems pretty obvious they are. And we also don't have a clue where Cano is--if he's alive."

Charlie looked at me and smiled. "So, you see, we don't know shit. I've had Hammersmith and MacAvity in here and they are still holding out on me. Now what I want from you is to tell me everything that you did before, during, and after what happened at Hammersmith's-- beginning with the decision you three made to protect Eric and Ruthie from harm."

He reached over and turned on the tape recorder, recited the date, time, and my name. He nodded, "Go ahead, Paul. Take your time. I won't interrupt unless I need clarification. OK?"

Chapter
Sixteen

When I was done, Charlie turned off the tape deck, popped the cassette and wrote the date, time, and my name on it with what I assumed was a five digit case number.

Finally he looked over at me. He hadn't said a thing during the entire time I had given my account.

"Those years on the Trib. slowed, Paul. It's rare that I don't have alphabet soup with these interviews. It usually takes me longer to straighten out the information than to get the actual recording."

He put the tape into a card file box on the window sill behind his chair.

"I do have one question for you, though," he said, turning back to face me. "Where's Huey?"

The question understandably threw me. "What do you mean?"

"When was the last time you heard from him?"

"When he phoned the house to say goodbye."

Charlie laced his fingers together with his index fingers pointing upwards and rested his lips on them like he was lost in thought.

"For his mission, right?" he finally said.

"Yeah."

He then placed both hands, palm down on his desk.

"Only problem is, Paul, he didn't buy a plane ticket, and he didn't leave the country."

He studied my reaction like I was a particularly curious plant species.

I was startled by what he said and, at the same time, suddenly worried for Huey's safety.

Finally I found my voice. "Honest to God, Charlie, this is news to me."

He continued to study me. "I can see that."

I hesitated. "You think he's all right?"

"I don't know. I hope so."

"Are you sure he didn't leave?"

Charlie pushed back his chair and stood.

"Yesterday, Special Agents Gibson and Pfeffer took turns at MacAvity and Hammersmith here in this room," he said. "I was present, as I demanded. What was interesting about the whole thing was these two agents were much more congenial than they have been previously. I guess the way MacAvity and Hammersmith handled themselves the other night earned them their respect.

"For one thing, Pfeffer surprised me by telling them that the two shooters were contractors from Canada. But what really seemed odd was they weren't interested in the attack and they weren't interested in the arson. What they were interested in was anything and everything they could learn about Huey."

He motioned to the door. I got to my feet, and he followed me out of the office and down the hall to the inner door. Before we reached it, he put a muscular hand on my shoulder.

"You be careful with the choices you make, Paul."

He stopped and I faced him. Beyond the glass, Smoke, who had been chatting up the new dispatcher while he waiting, was now watching us closely.

"I appreciate you coming in, and I appreciate your candor. You have any questions about the ramifications of anything you are considering doing, call me. It will be off the record and I'll give you my best advice."

He held out his hand and we shook. "OK?"

"I will, Charlie," I said.

He nodded at the dispatcher, and the door buzzed. I went into the tight waiting area, and Smoke grinned at me and then at Charlie.

"You letting this bastard go, Charlie?" he said.

"He's too clever for me, Smoke, but fortunately you're here now. Come on in."

Smoke slapped me on the chest as he squeezed by.

"Meet me at MacAvity's. We'll hatch a plan to steal Charlie's cattle," he said.

"Get in here, you moron," Charlie said, and the door latched shut behind me.

Outside in the lot, Lana was slouched down in the driver's seat of the Tundra reading a new paperback. I looked at my watch. She had been waiting for a bit over an hour and a half.

The message light was flashing on our answering machine when we walked in. It was three thirty. I hit the play button.

"You white folk done killing each other for a day or so?" Micha Wirestone's voice rasped. Micha was a Camas tribal elder whom I respected a great deal. During my years at the Trib. he had helped put out more gossip and rumor fires than anyone I have ever known. When it came to matters on the rez, I relied on Micha to give me guidance, and he never once let me down.

There was nothing more to the message. I took my personal phone book from the kitchen drawer below the phone and called Micha's nephew, Josiah Longbeach, whose doublewide shared the mouth of Lutheran Canyon with Mica's ancient log cabin. Lutheran Canyon was the next canyon upstream from Rattlesnake Gulch. I asked for Micha, received a grunt, and hung up.

On the reservation, only a few people had phones to the outside. But everyone had "walkie-talkies," the Motorola FRS ten mile range ones. A good idea, as far as I was concerned. Beat Ma Bell to the check.

Lana started pulling down pans to begin supper.

I went into the living room, folded myself into my leather cushioned oak chair and leaned my head back with a sigh. I waited for Micha's call. Whatever he wanted to tell me would not be frivolous. It never was. When Micha spoke, much less phoned, it was because he wanted to say something of importance.

I could imagine him shuffling his way up the hundred yard trail through the sugar berry trees between his place and Josiah's. I guessed his age in the nineties, but it was hard to tell. He was only five feet five inches or so, and he had long white hair in two braids hanging down over his chest. Hatless, he always wore insulated flannel checked shirts and old polyester pants that were bought for him at the Goodwill in Confluence. He also liked Nike running shoes. He was a prince dressed as a pauper.

The phone rang. I went back into the kitchen and lifted it to my ear but said nothing. Part of the routine.

"You bring my old friend MacAvity and cousin Hammersmith with you tonight to my house," he said. "And bring a little White Horse, you ask MacAvity, OK?"

"OK," I said, and the line went dead.

I had no idea what Micha had up his sleeve, nor did the others. Eric and Ruthie showed up at our place at six with Butte in tow.

Hammermith explained he didn't want to leave Ruthie alone in the ranch house that smelled of Spic'n Span, steam, and blood, and so he delivered her to the couch beside Lana. The two of them looked eager for us to be on our way, and I wondered if we would return to find Jake with them, discussing the shortcomings of today's husbands. The thought made me smile.

It was pushing seven o'clock by the time we turned off the two lane highway. The sun had just set, leaving the rims of the Clearwater Canyon glowing a deep pink and the canyons filled with blue darkness.

We bumped over a cattle guard onto Lutheran Canyon's narrow dirt road. This turnoff was practically invisible in the dense grove of wild apple and sugar berry trees that choked the canyon's mouth. Two hundred yards ahead, the dim yellow light of Micha's small front window peeked through the limbs, and beyond, sitting on a slight rise on the canyon floor, stood Josiah's double wide, its large view window ablaze with light.

We pulled onto the packed dirt in front of the tiny log cabin. Overhead were two towering ponderosa pines. The cabin had been built between them, and its nearly flat corrugated tin roof was obscured by their needles and fallen pine cones. The air was sweet with them.

Hammersmith's grandfather had been a Camas, which made Eric a cousin to everyone in the tribe, it seemed. So it was not impolite for him to open the cabin door and let himself in. He motioned for us to follow him.

I had been in Micha's place only twice before, and I loved the inside smell of cut firewood, smoke and fry bread. The room was perfectly square and had a metal framed bunk in a back corner under an assortment of clothes hanging from wooden pegs driven into the logs. A small wood burning kitchen range stood in the other corner below an array of plank shelves holding his dry goods and few dishes. A cast iron lidded pot always sat on the stove with meat and vegetables simmering.

The front half of the cabin was normally occupied by a small table, two wooden chairs and a wooden chest. But tonight, as we crowded in, I noticed that the table and chairs were pushed up against the side wall. I was about to learn why.

I halted behind Butte and looked down at the base of the other wall which he and Eric were studying.

Lying naked on a blanket was the dark skinned, black haired figure of a man who was staring up at us from sunken eyes. His ribs showed under the skin drawn tight over his chest. His face, head and arms were laced with ropes of new, pink scar tissue, and one forearm was splinted and wrapped in cloth and duct tape.

But what I stared at was a dog chain nailed hard against a log above him. The lightweight chain lead to a thin, rigid, six inch lace of rawhide that had dried around his testicles. The rawhide had been looped with precision so that when it had dried, it could not be removed yet did not cut off circulation either.

Hammersmith began to chuckle and then laugh.

"Micha," he choked. "You are a caution, you are."

Wirestone smiled slightly at the praise.

"That's our man, fellas," Hammersmith said.

"Who the fuck are you?" the prostrate figure croaked, not moving an inch.

Eric looked down at him. "I'm Lieutenant Commander Hammersmith," he said. "And you, Cano, if you cuss me again, will be left here with Mr. Wirestone for the rest of your short life."

"You're *Hammersmith*?" he moaned. "Oh God!"

Cano looked up at Micha, then at MacAvity, who was grinning back at him, then at me. He rolled his head back and forth on the blanket and squeezed his eyes shut tight.

Then he opened them and addressed Hammersmith again. "You going to kill me?"

"Not now, Cano. I haven't decided exactly how, yet."

MacAvity held up an unopened bottle of White Horse.

With that, Micha ushered us out of the house, nodding at the two chairs pushed up against the opposite wall. Eric and Butte brought them along.

We went out back to a patch of grass lit by the square of light thrown from the cabin's back window. Waiting for us were two men sitting in lawn chairs around the coals of a fire ring. They stood as we approached to be introduced.

Both Hammersmith and MacAvity knew them, and the four of them shook hands.

"Do you know Paul?" MacAvity asked.

They both nodded, though I'd not met one of them before.

"Thanks for taking my call, Josiah," I said, shaking his hand.

"This is Oscar Redtail," he said, and I shook Oscar's hand as well. They resumed their seats. Josiah put two pieces of pine on the coals, and in moments they flamed up giving us light. Under the limbs of a giant lilac sat a wooden rocker and the dilapidated remains of Micha's plaid covered easy chair. He eased gently into the chair's stuffing, leaned back, and waited for MacAvity to hand him a jelly glass of the scotch.

Chapter
Seventeen

In the firelight Micha's face shone like carved mahogany, and the parted mane of white hair marked his movements like a dancing ghost.

MacAvity and I sat in the wooden chairs they had brought out, and Hammersmith took his place of honor in the rocker at Wirestone's right.

Josiah and Oscar were tribal police who also worked security and enforcement at the tribal casino. They both wore tight Wrangler jeans, cowboy boots, white shirts and the casino's string ties. They had police badges clipped to their western belts, and they both carried snug Para Ordnance P12 .45s on their right hips. Josiah wore a braid down his back, and Oscar's thick, black hair was cut full but short.

They had been sipping cans of Bud Light and declined the scotch MacAvity offered them. Instead, Josiah produced plastic cups for us from behind a cooler I hadn't noticed.

We drank in silence. After several minutes, Micha extended his glass, and Butte refreshed it.

He took a sip. "I hear your friend Huey is at your elk camp at Trilby Lakes," he finally said.

I was puzzled. Huey was at the camp?

Hammersmith said, "He settled in all right?"

"Yes." This was Josiah. "Oscar and I spent last night with him. He's doing fine, but he's unhappy about his farm burning."

"I can imagine," MacAvity said, "I hope he stays put, though."

"He said he would."

Trilby Lakes was where Hammersmith and MacAvity had purchased a clapboard miner's cabin and claim as their hunting camp. The lakes were surrounded by the Nez Perce National Forest, considered by the Nez Perce and Camas as their land, and were five miles off to the south of the one-hundred and twelve mile long 4WD track of the Magruder Corridor. This remote crossing stretched from Palace, Idaho, through the Bitterroots and dropped down into Montana from Nez Perce Pass. It was unusual for more than one vehicle to cross it in a day--except during hunting season. Then, after the snows seal it shut, only a rare parties of well outfitted snow mobilers attempt the crossing.

I had been to their camp only once, four years ago, during one of their hunts. I was the designated cook. On that trip Huey and Smoke had also come along, as they sometimes did. But basically, this was Eric and Butte's getaway.

It must have been written on my face that I had no idea what was going on, but MacAvity patted me on the knee, and in the firelight I saw him wink.

It was Josiah that explained. "Oscar Redtail is also working for Special Agent Joy Chu," he said. "She's DEA and is helping the casino and the tribe control a sudden influx of methamphetamine into the tribal area."

He looked to Oscar to see if he should go on. Oscar nodded.

"Seems the stuff is flooding Montana and western Alberta, and has now crossed over to our side of the Bitterroots."

Oscar leaned forward and in a low, gentle voice said, "It's showing up as crystal meth and tiny pills called 'yaa baa,' mad pills, and Joy Chu says they are both manufactured in eastern Mayanmar. She's not positive how they reach Montana, but we're pretty sure they're being brought into Idaho and Washington over the Bitterroots through the Magruder Corridor."

"So Butte and I let Oscar and Josiah use the cabin where Huey's laying low for awhile, Paul," Hammersmith explained to me. "They have a key to the gate and are probably bankrupting Huey at poker."

Josiah laughed. "Not very likely," he said. "And we thought he was a church goer."

MacAvity said, "I been meaning to ask if you saw that Taurus come through the Magruder the other night?"

"You mean the night you bushwhacked those guys?" Josiah asked, grinning.

MacAvity nodded, humorlessly.

Josiah shook his head. "I don't think a Taurus could make that trip. Even if it could get traction, it would be gutted."

I wanted to ask something that had been puzzling me. "I though meth was a homemade problem."

Oscar shook his head. "In its infancy it was, but the precursor drugs, the raw materials, have been pretty much squeezed dry. Plus, demand has gone through the roof worldwide." He looked at Josiah. "Ask Joy Chu if you get the chance. She can answer that better than I can."

MacAvity said, "You know, speaking of controlled substances, it doesn't seem Cano wants to eat very much. How much you poisoning *him*?"

Oscar chuckled quietly and sipped his beer.

"Peyote is not poison," Micha said from his chair, his voice creaking with the scotch. "It is the wings of the mind, and his mind is lost."

Josiah added, "We give him a little onion, apple, peyote, and carrot each morning. After his mind takes flight, sometimes the women come, and the children come to play on the floor around him. Sometimes the children use him as a ridge and place little plastic soldiers on him and have their wars, and he entertains us with his talking."

We heard coyotes up in Lutheran Canyon yipping for a few moments, then go quiet.

Josiah went on. "He says his father was not to be fooled with--was deadly." He stopped and took a sip of Bud. "When his father came home from Cambodia a year ago, he got drunk and high and stayed that way."

"Rojas." Hammersmith said.

"Him." Micha said. "He found Cano a short while back and beat the shit out of him and made him come to work for him." He sat back thoughtfully. "Cano's inside, Cousin, waiting for you." he said, nodding to the cabin. "Josiah, his back-hoe have a deep hole waiting him up the canyon."

"That's our new garbage pit, Uncle," Josiah said.

"It will do," Micha said.

Everyone laughed.

Hammersmith shook his head. "He's better with you for a bit more, Micha. Could you do that?"

Micha nodded.

Josiah looked sideways at Oscar Redtail as he spoke. "How long will that be, Eric?" he asked. He turned back to wait the answer.

Hammersmith considered a moment.

"If we hand him over to the FBI now, we run the risk of not finding Rojas. Or learning who is holding Rojas's reins, Josiah," he said. "They want Cano for a string of killings. Cano and his childhood friend, Salas Valladores, liked to kill Vietnamese living here in the U.S. and then burn their homes down on them." He swirled the scotch in the bottom of his plastic cup. "That seems to be all the FBI wants. I doubt they're as interested in the meth problem.

They want Cano and they want to know more about Rojas and where he is, too. I just think all they'll do is drive Rojas underground even deeper if we give up Cano. Rojas is an ex-Navy SEAL and not one to be caught easily."

"How long have you known Rojas was alive, Hammersmith?" Oscar asked.

"Huey recognized him at the West Bassac River Mission in Cambodia twelve months ago. We always assumed he'd been killed by the VC in 1968, but we weren't positive. It was a shock for Huey, though, to see him in the flesh. Apparently Rojas was instrumental in the mission's operations."

He let that sink in.

"Was that Huey's mission?" This was Josiah. I suspected he knew about all this from talking with Huey at the elk camp.

"No," Eric said. "Huey volunteers at a large and successful Lutheran mission in Phnom Penh. He was helping organize Christian missions for the ongoing post-tsunami relief efforts when he saw Rojas. The West Bassac River Mission is situated between the Chuor Phnom Kravanh mountains and the coastal town of Krong Kaoh Kong on the Gulf of Thailand. There's another one, East Bassac River Mission, on the Bassac River itself at Phumi Prek just south of Phnom Penh."

We thought this over.

"Did Rojas recognize him?" Josiah asked.

"No," Hammersmith said. "He didn't even see him. He was too busy explaining something to an American businessman outside the mission. Huey backed off and caught a flight to the States as quickly as he could and is afraid to return to Cambodia until this blows over."

"I don't blame him," Josiah said. He placed another chunk of pine on the coals. "So why did Rojas come back to the states after all these years?"

"Maybe Huey was wrong," Micha said from under his lilac. "Maybe the businessman saw him. Knows him." He hesitated, "You need to use Cano for barter," he added. "Make the government do your work for you."

MacAvity nodded. "Good idea."

Hammersmith turned to Josiah Longbeach and Oscar Redtail. He was thoughtfully clicking the edge of his plastic glass with a thumb nail.

"How does Special Agent Joy Chu get along with those FBI boys, Gibson and Pfeffer?" he asked.

Josiah chuckled. "She doesn't mind Dwayne Gibson so much, but Pfeffer is another story. I don't think Pfeffer thinks a female, much less someone he calls a 'chink,' should be in law enforcement."

"That's what I thought," Eric said. He paused. "What if you gave Cano over to her?"

Both Josiah and Oscar laughed.

"They'd be pissed," Oscar said. "But why would we do that? Cano is not Chu's concern."

He hesitated and looked hard at Hammersmith, then at MacAvity, "Is he?"

Hammersmith set his drink on the ground and stood up stiffly. He brushed the seat of his pants before answering.

"I think it's time we called Huey on the satellite phone," he finally said. "Tomorrow's Sunday--it's time to feed the lions to the Christian."

He reached out and shook Josiah and Oscar's hands and looked down at Micha with a smile.

"Do you think you two could talk Micha out of Cano?"

"What do you have in mind, Hammer?" MacAvity asked. We were all on our feet now.

"Something I should have done thirty-eight years ago," Hammermith said.

We rode back up the grade from Confluence to the Bench in silence. It wasn't until we were on top and the glow of Ryback's lights could be seen that MacAvity from the back seat repeated his question, "What are you planning, Hammer?"

Hammersmith cleared his throat.

"What Micha said makes sense," he began. "We need to get Cano off our hands, and the DEA people are just the ones to do that for us. Like I said, the FBI is too focused on a narrow aspect of what is really going on to do this right, and if Josiah and Oscar are helping out Special Agent Joy Chu, she's gotta be a stand-up agent. I think we should trust her, but we've got to get Huey's permission. He's got to be the one that decides to do it. He's the one with the most at stake."

"That means some secrets are going to have to be told, Eric," MacAvity said. "You know that."

"I know, Butte. I know," Hammersmith said soberly.

They dropped me off on my corner at ten-thirty. There was only the one living room light on. I looked at the barn. The Tundra was still there.

I went up the sidewalk to the front door and went in quietly, expecting a note on the kitchen floor. It was there and read, "Ruthie is spending the night in the downstairs room. Quiet."

Undressing for bed, I reflected on two interesting side notes we had learned at Micha's, one indirectly. Josiah had said that he and Oscar had been waiting for Cano at the bottom of Rattlesnake even before Kimmy Musselshell had called. They had helped him up from where he collapsed on the highway side of her stock gate and had taken him to Micha Wirestone's for whatever reasons. How'd they learn about the crash so quickly?

Then the obvious became clear to me. Just as Hammersmith had scanned into MacAvity's and our frequency during our stakeout, the Tribe had been listening to the Bench's CB harvest chatter all these years. They had listened to Channel 11 on their CBs and had followed the chase just as I had sitting in Leap's grain truck. In fact, they listened to each other's FRS radio frequencies as well.

In reality, then, no one in the Tribe was isolated. If anyone was in danger or ill or unhappy, everyone knew about it. In that regard, Ryback was no different. But I, at least, hadn't known that the Camas were watching over us, too. In their own way, they had been there like big brothers ready to lend a hand if we got ourselves into trouble.

And they were about to do just that, now.

I slid between the sheets and fell asleep within minutes.

Chapter
Eighteen

The next morning I heard the kitchen phone ring and Lana answer it. I rolled over and saw it was seven o'clock, and I continued to lay on my side, trying to wake up. I could smell coffee from the kitchen.

Then I heard Ruthie talk on the phone. I had forgotten she'd spent the night. I swung out of bed, pulled on my jeans and a clean T-shirt.

I came out through the living room and into the kitchen. It had been fifteen minutes, and Ruthie was still on the phone, apparently with Eric.

Lana handed me my cup of tea and I pulled up to our long country kitchen table. Ruthie moved into the living room and moments later was finished with the call and came back in, placing the phone in its cradle. She and Lana resumed their seats with their coffees. Coffee was something Lana only occasionally treated herself to. It was Ruthie's regular morning brew.

I had never seen Ruthie look frail, but this morning she did. She had white hair these days, with strands of black through it, and she wore it long and twisted into an Asian sort of knot at the back. It looked good, but her face this morning was pale and drawn, and her eyes wet with anxiety. Both her thin agitated hands gripped her cup, her powerful fingers shifting about on its sides as if they were sorting beads.

She looked up with her dark eyes, catching me studying her. Lana was still.

"That was Eric," Ruthie said.

I nodded.

She sighed deeply and shook her head. "I feel sorry you and Lana have become involved in this," she said. "I'm sure last night was very unpleasant for you."

I said nothing. Her lips were unsteady.

"What I'm about to say is not about you or Smoke, and we are very grateful to you all for your concern for us and your willingness to protect us."

"Thank you, Ruthie," I managed. She was speaking like the experienced wife of a Lieutenant Commander. I wondered how many women she had comforted whose husbands had been lost in combat.

She continued. "Eric told me about last night and about today's plans," she paused. "Don't take this personally, Paul," she said, "But Eric feels only he and Oscar Redtail should be at the meeting."

"Why?" I asked, feeling a little crestfallen.

"They aren't including Smoke or Butte, either, Paul," she said, reading my feeling. "They have come to some kind of arrangement, and Ms. Chu knows about Cano being held prisoner and being unconventionally interrogated by the tribe. It's complicated, and Eric says she's trying to do the best for everyone."

She seemed to relax a bit, having said that. She took a sip of coffee, replaced the cup on the dark pine table, glanced at Lana and then back at me.

"Eric was phoning from Josiah's house. He wants me to tell you that Ms. Chu is having Charlie pick Cano up this morning. He's to be held in Magnet's facilities to wait for the FBI and DEA agents to take him. Eric also said she's requesting phone taps. So we're all going to be listened to, and we're not to discuss anything about this over the phone after about noon today."

Both Lana and I nodded, holding back our puzzlement.

"What else?" Ruthie asked herself, looking for a moment at Lana's large collection of cookbooks on the kitchen's back wall.

"Oh. He also said he's calling Smoke and Butte right now, and will meet with all of us tomorrow afternoon at the pub when they return. He said he promises to explain everything then."

Ruthie smiled for the first time that morning. "He asked if I could stay here with you one more night."

Lana scoffed. "No way! Out of the question!" They both laughed.

"Is Huey coming back, too?" I asked.

Ruthie shrugged her slender shoulders. "Eric didn't say."

Lana got to her feet. She pulled a large chef's pan down from the wall, lit a burner under it, and began to make us french toast and chopped melon for breakfast.

Ruthie pushed back her chair, smiled at me kindly, went through to the basement stairs and descended them carefully. Soon we could hear the house's pipes indicate she was showering.

At nine, the three of us went out to Huey's to help in the brick chipping. It was cool out, not cold, the type of day I associated with football and the first semester of university life. Willow leaves along Ryback Creek were falling to the water, the air was still, and the sun shone warmly though the fresh air. I like this time of year.

We rounded the slight bend in the gravel road, and Huey's farm came into view. More correctly, what came into view was an empty void in what had been a familiar landscape. What had been a beautiful, green roofed, round topped, white barn, a long metal machine building, and a two story, steeply roofed brick mansion, was now three small patches of rubble under a blue sky. Only the large hundred year old willows and poplars and the juniper hedges along the road resembled anything I remembered of this fine Norwegian homestead. It was mind boggling.

There were pickups and cars parked in the stubble on the north side of the ruins. Nearly forty people were at work, many standing around Jable's flatbed trailer hammering mortar off the bricks that had been dumped down its middle by the front loaders. Behind them were pallets of cleaned brick, already piled ten courses high and wrapped in clear plastic.

Richter's Hitachi bucket excavator was at the edge of the cellar hole scooping out brick that three men sorted and tossed into the buckets of the two front loaders. Off to the side, saw horses laid with planks held more bricks that had been piled and were being chipped clean.

Under the skirts of the huge willow that grew from the center of the back yard, Jake and several other women had set up a sawhorse and plank table of their own where they had put out coffee pump thermoses, doughnuts, pies, cookies and sausage muffins. Jake waved when she saw us swing in to park and came over to greet us.

"Where have you shirkers been?" she called good naturedly.

We went over to meet her.

"My my," Ruthie exclaimed. "Three days and you're at least half done!"

"Over ten thousand cleaned and stacked," Jake said, sweeping a hand over the operation. "Richter says there is another ten to go--plenty to build a nice one story house for Huey."

From where I stood the scene looked like a minimum security labor camp for elderly felons.

One of Richter's enormous dump trucks came thundering down the road from the north, returning from the county's landfill. It slowed in a cloud of gray dust and made its way over to the side of the excavator to be filled again with charred timbers, pipes, tin, and shattered brick.

I walked over and looked in the hole. Don was down in the bottom with Shay and Leaps. They had a frame set up and were working debris through its half-inch screen. They were located under the place where Huey's office and the dining room had been. Against the rock foundation, leaning sideways and charred, stood his three foot square safe. The safe's door lay on its face a foot away, its hinges destroyed.

I climbed down to join them using the narrow slope where the basement's back door had been.

"Find anything?" I said.

"'Bout time you showed for work," Leaps said, holding out his hand. He pointed to a sheet of plywood. "Go look for yourself."

I negotiated the brick and twisted pipes over to the plywood, noticing, as I did, that one front corner of the rubble was still smoking and smelled like wet, burned wool or garbage.

The plywood was littered with remnants. They had recovered the barrels and parts of more than ten rifles and as many pistols. All of them had grown white hot and had warped. There were also several globs which appeared to be melted silverware, and spread over an area of about two square feet were the oxidized ribbonless medals Huey had earned in the service. And finally, heaped into a gallon jar, were burnt coins and family jewelry they had recovered.

There was pitifully little left of the proud, rich Houston family. It was sad, to say the least.

Don stopped me as I turned back to the ramp.

"That safe was blown before the place was torched," he said. "You know, Paul, I have a feeling Hammersmith and Huey must have something someone is willing to kill for."

"I think you're right," I said, shaking my head. "Does Charlie know about the safe?"

"Yup. Charlie said they had used C-4."

I had brought a hatchet with me and headed over to take a spot at the flat bed, not noticing until I was ten feet away that Smoke, chisel in hand, was standing with his back to the piled brick, waiting for me.

"Well, pardner," he said through the smoke of a cigarillo stub, "it only gets worse."

"What does, Smoke?" I said, taking a spot beside him.

"Did Ruthie talk to you?"

"Yeah, she did."

"Did she tell you Charlie is going to turn Cano over to the FBI?"

"Yeah."

"Well, here's something she didn't tell you. Hammersmith said this morning that our illustrious federal court system will be handing our footless fucker over to the Canadians."

"Isn't that a good thing, Smoke?" I said. "I mean, they probably have enough on him to have a open-and-shut case."

Smoke dropped his stub and ground it out under the heel of his boot.

"Oh, I'm sure they do. But they don't believe in the death penalty up there, and Ryback is way overdue for a good old fashioned hanging," he said. Then added evilly, "Course we'd have to tie some window weights on his legs to make up for the missing feet. Wouldn't want him to be unbalanced in his swinging."

I shrugged my shoulders and picked up my first brick. I began to chop off the mortar, brittle from the heat, and had it clean in less than an a minute. I pulled over another and kept at it.

At ten thirty, twenty some cars and pickups streamed in together and parked. Church was out.

As the vehicles emptied, I could see that everyone had changed into coveralls and work clothes before coming out. They were burdened down with food and the church's folding tables and chairs, and in minutes a regular cafeteria appeared under the trees. These people were not about to let Huey feel they didn't love him.

To me it looked like two thirds of the town was now here, and coming down the road in a billowing cloud of dust were two back hoes and three grain trucks. They pulled in and without hesitation started tearing into the remains of the barn and machine shop. Most of the Lutheran men went over to help them, leaving their wives to finish setting up for lunch.

Smoke nudged me, watching it all happen. "I love this fucking town, pardner, know what I mean?"

I nodded. "Yup, I know what you mean."

Chapter
Nineteen

We returned to Huey's at ten the next morning. There was a ground fog trying to burn off on the Bench, and tails of it painted the farm's trees in bands of slowly moving, white light. The fields smelled of wet straw, and I could feel winter's growing interest in our part of the world.

Less than twenty people, all men, were back at the task. The diesel smoke from the excavator lifted from its stack reluctantly and drifted with the fog.

Lana and Ruthie let me out, turned the Tundra around and headed back to run errands and pick up some groceries in Magnet. They said they'd to be back in time for the afternoon's meeting.

I walked through the dust to the flatbed where Smoke, Shay and Jables were hard at it and joined in for the next five hours.

It was just three o'clock when Ruthie, Lana and I entered MacAvity's kitchen from the back stairs. MacAvity, Hammersmith, Smoke and Sheila were seated along the kitchen table. Waiting for us in the table's center was a plate of small square crackers and three bowls filled with dip and hung with shelled shrimp. Sheila's touch.

Butte stood, went to the oven and removed a warm platter of garlic bread wedges. He put these on the table beside the crackers. He resumed his seat.

Lana and I took places to Smoke's left across from Butte and Sheila. Ruthie sat at the corner at Eric's right. He was at the head of the table and had a pile of paperwork in front of him.

"How do we want to begin, Butte?" he asked, folding his hands atop the papers.

Butte sighed. "With Huey?"

Hammersmith nodded and leaned back in his chair.

"What we're going to tell you isn't to leave the room," he began, addressing Lana, Smoke, Sheila and me. "Ruthie already knows all this and always has, and you, Sheila, a bit.

"You already know about Rojas, his arrest by me on the Bassac, and his attempted escape. And you know the circumstances surrounding his apparent death at the hands of the VC. But until a year ago, we had no idea he lived. So that's where we all stand at the moment.

"What you don't know," he said, clearing his voice with a cough and leaning forward, "is four months before I had Rojas placed under arrest in Vietnam, he pulled a gun on Huey and his crew during a dust off. He had twenty pounds of marijuana with him and demanded it be brought along. Cambodia was then, as it is now, the largest producer of marijuana in the world, and marijuana was common among our forces, I'm sad to say. It was everywhere. But Rojas wanted us to freight it for him that day, and Huey refused, even with a hush puppy pointed at his head.

"The thing about Rojas is he's a sociopath with a fierce temper, and Huey said Rojas's face changed dramatically as hatred swept over it. Huey felt for sure he was about to die. And he might have if the three members of his crew hadn't intervened. They said fuck it. Rojas cooled and they lifted off with the marijuana on board."

Hammersmith leaned back again in his chair.

"We all know Huey," he resumed. "He understood he could be court martialed for what he'd done. But worse, his conscience started to nag at him. And when he saw what Rojas had done to the people of that village, he blamed himself."

"How?" I asked.

"He was convinced that had he and his crew notified me about the marijuana, and Rojas had been arrested *then*, the killings would not have taken place."

I nodded.

"When he returned from the scene of the massacre, he came directly into my ship's office, broke down in sobs and told me about it."

He looked around the table at us before going on.

"I'll never be certain, and I don't want anyone in this room to repeat this to Huey, but I suspect he and his crew landed in that rice paddy because they knew Rojas would attempt an escape, and they knew there were VC at the jungle's edge who would kill him.

"I heard rumors and learned later the crew chief didn't take the wound earlier, and they didn't, as they claimed, land to attend to him or check the craft. The crew chief took the bullet when they were lifting off *after* Rojas was gunned down. And from the ground crew I learned the door gunner hadn't use his weapon that day."

Smoke whistled. "That's our boy!" he said, grinning.

Hammersmith frowned at him and tapped the pile of paperwork with his right index finger.

"So he has done penance. For these past decades, as you know, he has dedicated his life to the people of Cambodia through his missionary work. But this here," he said, placing his hand on the pile, "is what he also did. He has used his influence with his parishioners to collect information and evidence on the extensive drug trafficking from labs in Mayanmar down the Mekong and Bassac rivers.

"When he recognized Rojas at West Bassac River Mission, he was acting on a tip that Father Cabrera, its acting minister, was actually The Black Snake, the man responsible for brokering the drug shipments to Hong Kong and Taiwan. He had serious evidence that the 'ant army' was trafficking heroin, methamphetamine 'yaa baa,' club drugs, and more recently crystal meth, or 'ice.' They were using the old Communist trails through the Chuor Phnom Kravanh Mountains to carry it from where it had been brought ashore at Phum Prek and the East Bassac River Mission.

"So," Hammersmith asked us, "who was Father Cabrera?"

"Rojas," Lana said.

"Right. Rojas was The Black Snake, the cruelest, most murderous bastard of all the dozens of narcotics brokers scattered throughout Cambodia, Laos, and Vietnam. Only the UWSA enforcers of the United Wa State Army of Mayanmar could rank with him.

"And somehow Rojas knows Huey made him. Also, it's obvious he put two and two together and knew that the rumors that Huey's mission was spying on his network were true. He also knew that Huey was behind the spying. He'd figured out something else, too."

Hammersmith took a breath. I had never heard him speak in his "commander's" voice before, and I was looking at him with deep respect.

He went on. "He has figured out my part in it as well. When I had him arrested in 1968, I confiscated everything in his possession to help in his prosecution. There were two things I held back, however. One was his notebook. I read it, and it contained a list of names that were obviously contacts and ants in a growing drug trafficking operation he was developing with the Cambodians. But after Huey came to me, I kept that back to protect Huey, figuring Rojas had more serious charges against him already, and that without him, his narcotics ring would collapse by itself."

MacAvity had been listening very seriously to all this without moving a muscle. Now he said, "Rojas knows you held back and still have his journal and probably all of Huey's evidence, too. Right?"

"That's my guess," Hammersmith said.

"Which means Cano knows all about this as well."

"Yup."

Sheila interrupted, "For God's sake why didn't you guys kill Cano when you had the chance?"

"Only in a perfect world, Sheila," Butte said quietly. Then to Hammersmith, "What was the second thing you held back, Hammer?"

Eric addressed Sheila. "It's not all bad. We've taken out four of his bunch and killed two of them. And one of them I killed the other night with Rojas's old Ingram Mac 10. That answer your question, Butte?"

Smoke busted out with a laugh. "Nice touch, pardner."

Sheila got to her feet using Butte's shoulder, came around the table and brought over a pitcher of ice water from the refrigerator. She motioned we should enjoy the snacks before the shrimp wilted. She then went to the cabinet and mixed Smoke a scotch with a splash which she placed by his ashtray.

"And Agent Chu knows all this?" I asked.

"We told her today," Hammersmith said. "Huey gave us the go-ahead."

"Was that a good idea? I mean, won't that place you both in a world of hurt?"

"What can they do to us old timers, Paul?" he laughed. "And besides, I traded the notebook to her. It's half in code, which should be easy for them to interpret. I'm hoping there is a name in it that will lead us to whoever it is that's at this end of the narcotics trail."

"God almighty," Lana moaned. "We're in deep shit."

Hammersmith reached past Ruthie, who was smiling faintly, and placed his hand atop Lana's.

"No," he said, "Rojas and his bums are in deep shit, and they know it." He reached into the pile and pulled out two sheets of paper and handed them to her.

Lana took them and studied them for a moment.

"These are reservations to San Francisco for tomorrow morning!" she said.

"For you, Sheila and Ruthie," he said. "If you want."

I knew at that moment he was afraid for them.

"Does Ann know about this?" Ruthie said, taking the two pages from Lana and looking them over angrily.

Ann was Ruthie and Eric's only child. She had developed a successful travel and consulting business on Geary Street. Far East Travel Consultants. Her specialty was helping diplomats, missionaries, and corporations do their jobs successfully in Asia, particularly in China and Taiwan. She had never married but had adopted a Chinese baby she named Levi who was now a freshman at Stanford.

Hammersmith answered her. "She's probably setting up the three guest beds as we speak."

"Two!" Sheila blurted.

"What?"

"She only needs to make *two* beds, Eric. I'm not leaving here and miss a good fight."

MacAvity now laughed. "Better listen to her, Hammer."

"For Christ's sake, Sheila," Hammersmith managed, letting the matter drop. He reached for the shrimp and dip and chewed for a moment. He popped a garlic wedge after it.

"I'm staying as well, Eric," Lana said, glancing briefly at me.

We waited for Ruthie's answer.

She handed the pages back to Hammersmith with a forced smile. "I understand your concern, Honey, but we should have discussed this first."

Hammersmith took the reservations from her, tapped them square on the table, and put them back on the stack.

Ruthie put a hand on his wrist.

"But I'm going," she said. "You've never been this concerned for me before, so I'm frightened myself, now."

She faced Lana. "Can you drive me to the airport?"

"Is it that bad, Eric?" Lana asked.

Hammersmith crossed his arms under his chest, leaned against the table edge and looked squarely at her before answering.

"We killed two of his men, crippled another, and put his son back in custody for life or possibly to be put to death. We have evidence of his criminal activities and have given it to the sheriff, the FBI and the DEA.

"I'd say The Black Snake of Cambodia is in a towering rage right now. I'd say he'd love to torture and kill each and every one of us. What do *you* think, Lana?" Hammersmith said evenly.

Lana looked at me and held it a moment. I gave my shoulders a slight shrug.

She turned back to Hammersmith.

"Well, Eric," she said at last, "I think it's been too long since I've visited Ann and Levi with Ruthie and spent a ton of money in San Francisco's restaurants."

Hammersmith nodded.

"Getting back to what Paul asked," he said, wiping his lips on the side of his thumb, "Butte loaded us up with enough stuff to outfit Josiah and Oscar's guys, and Huey is going to direct operations in the Magruder Corridor. If Rojas and his crowd come over that way, as Oscar is convinced they will, they'll be in trouble. Oscar is a DEA MET, Mobile Enforcement Team leader. Has been since 1997. He maintains that the Magruder is the pipeline.

"Also our calls are going to be listened to by the DEA folks at their Seattle Branch Office. Joy is hoping one of us is contacted with threats or perhaps with an offer to bargain or make an exchange of some sort for the evidence. Even if a call comes from a cellphone, they will be all over it.

"She told us that they know crystal methamphetamine, Ketamine, as well as the synthetics MDMA, AMT and GHBs are pouring from Hong Kong and Taiwan into Vancouver, Canada. One leg of it is coming through Alberta and down into Montana...they don't know how... to be distributed and the money laundered by they-don't-know-who."

"Well," Butte said, "Rojas for one."

"But Joy Chu says it takes a large organization and lots of money to do what's needed at this end. That's not Rojas, or at least not Rojas alone."

"Do they know who paid for Cano's defense back when he was seventeen?" I asked. "I mean, that must have taken some serious green, too."

Hammersmith nodded, smiled and took his cell phone out of his shirt pocket. He got up, slapped me on the back as he passed behind me, and went into the living room, dialing as he went.

Smoke lit up for the first time since we had arrived, studying me as he did.

"You know, Paul," he said, "for a dumb fuck, you do have your moments."

"Gosh! Thanks Dad," I said, grinning.

Hammersmith returned to the kitchen.

"I had to leave a message for Joy to call me," he said. "And Paul, I want you to follow our example. I don't want you to be more than two feet from the Glock that Butte loaned you. I want you to carry it and sleep with it constantly. Wear that barn coat of yours and carry the weapon under your belt in back until we get past this mess."

He paused. "OK?"

"OK," I said.

Lana put her hand on my knee under the table and gave it a squeeze. Like she had said, we're in deep shit, now.

Chapter Twenty

It was nearly noon by the time Hammersmith and I returned to my place after dropping Lana and Ruthie off at the tiny airport. Smoke and Charlie were sitting on my front porch drinking coffee and toasted me as we passed by on our way to park at the barn.

"I'd better come in with you," Eric said, getting out.

We went down and around to join them.

"Isn't this "criminal trespass, Charlie?" I asked as Eric and I reached them.

Charlie smiled. "Nope. We have a search warrant."

"But we had to toss your place," Smoke said. "How were we to know you store your coffee in the freezer? As beans, no less. So then we had to find the grinder. Then the Mr. Coffee. Aren't you and Lana Americans?"

Hammersmith sat on one of the porch chairs. I went in, poured cups for us and brought them out. I handed one to him and took a seat by Smoke.

Charlie motioned over the town with his cup.

"Why does every truck in town have a rifle in its back window today, and why does Jables have a DPMS .308 SASS in his? What's going on?"

Smoke laughed. "Jables is afraid of deer. Thinks they might charge if wounded."

Hammersmith took a swallow of coffee and said, "MacAvity told Jables, Leaps and a few others in the pub last night how he was worried about more night attacks by arsonists," he said. "Told them he was expecting reprisals on the pub, my place and possibly Paul's and Smoke's as well."

"Oh my aching ass," Charlie moaned. "So I suppose the whole damn Bench knew within the hour and is now armed and mobilized?"

"Pretty much," Smoke said, lighting up.

"I don't deserve this," Charlie said. He began talking into his cup like there were people in it. "These AARP militants are a threat to national security. Ryback is a terrorist camp. What is a law biding sheriff to do?"

He looked up at us.

"I'm going to assign two cars and four deputies to keep an eye on this," he said, adding, "This is a 'neighborhood watch' thing, right?"

"Right," Smoke said.

"But with assault rifles and WMDs, right?"

"That's Ryback for you." Smoke tapped an ash over the porch rail onto the frost killed flower bed.

Charlie took out a Mead Memo pad and made a note to himself. He hesitated, and frowned.

"When's deer season begin in the Magruder Corridor area?"

"Saturday," Smoke told him.

"This Saturday?"

"Yup."

Charlie looked at Hammersmith thoughtfully.

"Tell me, Eric," he said. "Do you think that Rojas and his people would take advantage of the confusion of opening weekend to make a crossing?"

Hammersmith put down his cup.

"Butte asked me that last night," he said. "It's a good possibility."

"Are you and Butte going up there to help out Huey and Oscar Redtail?"

Hammersmith shook his head.

"Nope. We're both sticking close to our places."

"With lots of help, right?"

"Right."

Charlie removed his Stetson, wiped the band, and put it back on.

He was about to say something when Smoke said, "Butte called me last night expressing an interest in a couple packages of venison. He said he thought Paul, here, might want to join the hunt."

He continue. "He also got a call late yesterday afternoon from Huey on that satellite phone you loaned him. He needs two more propane tanks and a bunch of other stuff."

"Tell him next time he calls he's running up a bill for the county at damn near a dollar a minute using that phone to place grocery orders," Charlie said. Then, "When you going?"

Smoke looked at me. "Wanna go Saturday morning, Paul?"

I'd been so intent on the conversation I had forgotten I was there.

"Uh, sure," I managed.

They laughed. Smoke slapping me hard on the leg.

Charlie stood and handed me his empty cup.

"I normally hunt on our ranch," he said. "But I've always wanted to hunt the Magruder."

Smoke asked me, "The Tundra, Paul?" Smoke asked.

"Sure."

"OK, then. Let's meet here at six AM Saturday," Smoke concluded, getting to his feet. "Work for you, Charlie?"

"I'll make it work. But I'll be following in my ranch's pickup," Charlie said. "I'd hate to see the Expedition mistaken for a game warden's rig and get shot full of holes."

I spent the rest of that day and the next two with Smoke helping finish up Huey's place. We were done with the brick cleaning, more than seventeen thousand salvaged, by late Thursday morning and helped with the cleanup for the rest of that day. Friday the machinery finished and was moved off, and a street party was held in front of MacAvity's Pub to celebrate.

McGregors pulled in a huge barbecue, and the church returned with their tables and chairs. MacAvity set three kegs of beer and a carton of cups on one of the tables, and then retreated to his living quarters to gain solitude. There was a "gone to party" sign on the locked front door.

The whole town turned out, and small ad hoc groups gathered here and there to discuss everything that had happened and what they would do *if*.

I showed up long enough to have a burger and pint of Henry's Draft, but since Smoke, Hammersmith, and Butte weren't there, I was soon surrounded by people wanting me to recount what had happened at Hammersmith's and to ask why I was carrying a pistol in my belt. I bowed out, ducking the questions, and went home to pack, feeling a bit rattled.

By nine that evening, the Tundra was loaded with the supplies Smoke and MacAvity had purchased that afternoon. Much of the produce was loaded into three large, six-day coolers. I also threw in cots and lawn chairs for Smoke and me, our own supply of toilet paper, and also, fortunately as it turned out, Lana's and my large Equinox base camp tent. I assumed, rightly, that in the morning Smoke would bring his arsenal and the surveillance equipment that MacAvity said we should continue to use.

Lana and I had hiked and done mountaineering our entire lives, so my personal stuff included rather specialized, lightweight rain gear, a twenty degree down bag, capilene long johns, down underwear, lightweight wool pants and pullover, a down hooded jacket, a pair of mountaineering boots, and gaiters. I was good to -20 before I would have to retreat to the tent and sleeping bag. I also tossed in a day pack, small MSR pocket-rocket camp stove, full fuel canister, one quart pot, thermos, cup, bowl and spoon. A gallon ziploc of snacks and tea rounded out the load.

I was in bed asleep by ten.

It was still dark at six the next morning when Smoke pulled into my driveway, and my side of town was jarred awake by his tailpipes and his truck horn blaring out reveille.

I scrambled out of the house before he did the ooga, tossed a large thermos of tea into the Tundra's cab and helped Smoke haul over his two large Navy duffles with USS Bonnie Dick stenciled on them. They were heavy with equipment, and as we slid them into the back seat, Smoke's made the telltale clink of bottles.

We were headed back to the house for fresh coffee when Charlie rounded the corner in his blue and white 1995 4WD Ford 150. Loaded in the back was a Honda four-wheeler. He gave a nod as he pulled in behind Smoke's truck and pulled the emergency brake, letting the engine idle.

We went over to his open window.

Like Smoke, he had a large duffle bag with his gear in it. It rode in the bed of his truck with the ATV in a mixture of straw and dirt, half a roll of barbed wire, and a high-lift jack. Racked in the back window of the cab was a scoped bolt action deer rifle, but under that was the Bushmaster A2 carbine I thought he had only been joking about.

Charlie was dressed as he did as sheriff, except for the hat. Instead of his Stetson, he now wore a stained, nicked, drooping cowboy hat he must have had since he was a teen. It was wide brimmed like one his grandfather might have handed down to him. I loved it.

"Shall we, gentlemen?" he said.

"Lock and load," Smoke said, going back to the Tundra.

"You following then?" I asked.

"Lead on," said Charlie. He shifted back into gear, released the emergency brake, and backed out to wait.

The eastern horizon didn't start to color with light until we had reached the edge of the Bench. Then we dropped down the one-thousand, five-hundred foot grade to the Clearwater and reentered the charcoal predawn darkness at the canyon's bottom. The river shone in the hard gloom like the scales of a giant silver snake, and Charlie's headlights danced in my rearview mirror. I was excited to be on the road.

Fifteen minutes upstream we crossed the Clearwater on a long concrete bridge and headed south for Winchester Grade. Soon we were climbing into the timber, winding below giant railroad trestles clinging to the canyon walls. In another half hour we broke out at the top into the expansive Camas Prairie that stretched for fifty miles east to the Nez Perce National Forest and the Gospel Hump Wilderness.

By now the sun was up in a sea of yellow light. Smoke turned his visor to block it from his side window, adjusted his rolled jacket between the back of his seat and window and settled in to sleep.

Charlie killed his lights behind us, and we continued on. I held the speed at seventy. The narrow asphalt and the sweeping bends slid by smoothly.

By eight, we had crossed the Camas and dropped down into the dark shadow of the South Fork of the Clearwater. This too was a deep canyon, but much narrower than the main branch of the Clearwater. There was barely enough bottom to accommodate both the river and the road. In places granite had been blasted to make way, and the curves took concentration to navigate.

There was no traffic, so I pushed as hard as I could, and Smoke continued to sleep soundly even though his head was rocking back and forth as if attached by a failed spring. Charlie's Ford kept pace, but he had once more turned on his lights and hung back to keep them out of my mirrors.

An hour later we found we had climbed enough to reach the sunlight again, and the canyon walls had given way steep hills. We threaded between them and over confused side canyons that dumped small streams into the diminishing South Fork. At the point where it had shrunk to the size of a small stream, the pioneers had felt a name change was in order. So beyond a major confluence meadow, the prestige of the South Fork Clearwater ended abruptly, and it became simply Red River.

Above this meadow, dropped like so many boxes on the grassy hillside, were the dozen or so clapboard buildings of Palace, Idaho.

We rolled slowly through this random settlement on its rough, tilting street, and Smoke stirred from his sleep and sat upright.

He studied the broken trucks, mud-caked four-wheelers, and neglected snowmobiles cluttering the weed choked gaps between the buildings.

"How much snow they get here, you think?" he finally said.

"Three, four feet?" I ventured.

He reached for a cigarillo, rolled down the window and lit it.

"Not enough," he said, taking a drag. "Gotta have at least fifteen feet to bury this shit heap."

I studied the town to see what he meant. It looked fine to me. In fact, I liked it. Smoke apparently didn't wake up well, so I let it go.

From Palace, we dropped back to Red River and left it ten miles later, turning onto a steep, narrow gravel and dirt road that headed east into deep wilderness and the Magruder Corridor.

For two hours we stayed high, winding between peaks, huge timber stands, gray swaths of old lightening strike burns, and through meadows with boggy bottoms. Surprisingly, we only encountered three pickups with hunters in them. They each stopped and nodded amiably as we edged by them. Then we dropped into Bargamin Creek Canyon to crawl back out the other side and up Three Prong Ridge to Dry Saddle. By now the road had deteriorated into a 4WD track that humped over exposed rock and crude water bars.

Dry Saddle was an exposed, dangerous hairpin corner blasted from the granite at the top of the ridge just below a fire lookout tower. At nearly eight thousand feet it was the highest point on the Magruder Corridor and commanded a sweeping three-hundred and sixty degree view of Idaho's wilderness interior.

Also, it was here, off to the right of the corner's apex, that MacAvity and Hammersmith's nearly indestructible steel pole gate was set in poured concrete.

I stopped, and Smoke and I got out, stretching. Shortly, Charlie pulled in behind through our dust and sat waiting for us to open the gate.

It was a bit past noon. The sun was warm on our faces, even in the cold mountain air, and the pine forests were fragrant and hollow sounding.

There was a 5269 American Lock on the gate housed in a section of steel pipe that couldn't be sawed or torched open. But it was difficult to even get to the lock, and Smoke cursed roundly, his head in an upside down position, as he tried to look up into the pipe's cavity. He fumbled with the key MacAvity had provided us and nearly dropped it twice before he had the lock off and was able to swing the pole back.

I hopped back in, and with Charlie on my tail, we pulled through. Smoke hooked the gate back into place and locked it behind us.

Chapter
Twenty-One

Smoke had his hand on the Tundra's door handle and was about to climb back in when a man dressed in camo and a green balaclava stepped from the stunted alpine firs behind him. He pointed a standard issue M-16 assault rifle at Smoke and told him to raise his hands.

I had my hands in plain view on top the steering wheel. I glanced in the mirror and saw Smoke raise his hands slowly and turn to face him.

"Hi," Smoke said, grinning. "How's hunting?"

The guy remained wary, but Smoke held his attention.

"Tell you what," Smoke continued. "Get on your radio and tell Huey that Smoke, Charlie and Paul are here, OK?"

The man lowered his rifle and gave a thin smile. "We've been expecting you."

He motioned for me to proceed and then turned and went back into the trees.

Smoke climbed back in, and I pulled forward.

He shook his head. "Christ! Didn't he see we had a fucking key to the gate?" He fumbled for a his lighter, forgetting he hadn't taken out a cigarillo. "Damn near shit myself," he mumbled. "Coming up behind me like that."

From nerves or what, I started to laugh. Smoke looked sideways at me, and I laughed harder.

We bumped slowly over the overgrown old mining track that ran along the narrow crest of the ridge. The grass was crushed down by the recent traffic, but aside from that, one would not have guessed this was still traveled.

The track went for a quarter mile until it dropped into a shallow col at the base of Dry Saddle's second peak, Spread Creek Point. Here it pushed out onto the mountain's east face and crossed five hundred yards of talus slope on a hair-raising, rock littered dozer track.

I stopped, stared at this hazard a moment, then shifted into compound low and edged out uneasily. I'd forgotten how bad this stretch was because the time I'd been over it before, I had not been driving, and it had been at night.

Looking down from my side window I could see the two lakes about four hundred feet below us. The talus slope I was crossing formed the walls of a cirque which funneled winter snow melt down to an emerald green meadow. The meadow fit into a hollow pressed into the side of the towering ridge like a giant heel print. It rested there securely, one third of the way down to Sabe Creek thirteen hundred feet below. Excellent hunting country. Excellent country to get lost in intentionally or by accident.

A dense ring of timber enclosed this hanging valley on three sides, sheltering it from view below. The open side was formed by the rubble of the talus slope above and was laced with rivulets of water that joined and ran through deep grass and flowers to the lake nearest us. In turn, this lake fed the second smaller one which was only a few yards further on.

From where we were, the small, tin roofed cabin and its chimney could be seen at the south edge of the meadow, half tucked into the timber. Across the hundred foot wide lake, catching the southern sun, was a well aged, white wall tent typical in elk camps all over Idaho. Its tin stack was trickling smoke, and a guy was stretched out on the grass in front of it. He had binoculars trained on us and was laying on one elbow talking into a hand held radio.

I drove along at walking speed. Smoke got out and rolled a rock off the track. MacAvity said that each year, when he and Eric first came in, they would roll or pry bar off more than fifty rollers that had accumulated over the twelve month interim.

Finally we reached the far side, negotiated a hair pin turn, and came back through the timber. Soon the back of the cabin came into view, and we pulled up where four other rigs and four ATV's were parked under the large ponderosa pines. Huey's truck and four-wheeler were among them.

I heaved a sigh, and Smoke and I climbed out. Charlie came up behind, parked off to the side and joined us. At that moment Huey and Josiah Longbeach came around the cabin to greet us, all smiles.

We shook hands, and they ushered us to the cabin. I looked across the small lake, and the guy in front of the tent gave a slight wave, which I returned. Huey clapped a hand on my back.

"Glad you guys could come, Paul," he said, adding, "We can sure use the help."

"Glad to be here. You've got quite the operation going, Huey. Enjoying yourself?"

We reached the door and followed Charlie and Josiah in.

"Not so much," he said. "But I understand I'm ready to begin rebuilding when I get back, right?"

"Looked good to me," I told him.

On the back wall of the cabin there were four bunks that were strewn with sleeping bags and clothes. There was a wood burning cast iron range on the west side of the cabin where the kitchen counter, wash basins and shelves were, and in the room's center was a three-by-six foot kitchen table and seven wooden chairs that were of the old schoolhouse design. The table was littered with playing cards, a USGS map, two Motorola radios, several cups and an empty glass. Two coolers were set below the window in the wall opposite the range. There were also windows on each side of the front door leading to the eight foot wide porch. Everything inside had been given a coat of white paint once, which had held up remarkably well. The outhouse was out back in the trees.

"We saved a bunk for you, Charlie," Huey said. He went over and lifted some coats off the upper right hand bunk and tossed them on the bunk below.

In high school Huey reminded me of what a jolly Dane should look like. He had a round face, twinkling eyes, and ruddy cheeks. He looked like Saint Nicholas with a crew cut--only Huey's build was full, very powerful, and hard.

He was called back from Vietnam in 1967 because his wife and unborn child had been killed by a drunken driver on Highway 95 just south of Magnet. The driver had a record of DWIs and was driving with a suspended license. It had been almost noon, and he was in their lane coming around a corner. They had been trapped against the guardrail and crushed.

After the funeral, Huey, in full uniform, headed to the jail. Naturally, they didn't let him near the cells, and, in fact, obtained a restraining order against him.

After Vietnam, Huey came home a changed man. He never remarried, he never dated, and his happy high school face had run away. He returned to his parents' farm, eventually buried them both as well, and remained in the large house by himself for the decades that followed.

Only in rare instances did happiness wash over him, and usually it was Smoke's antics and displays of love that triggered them. I wondered, now that the farm was gone as well, if even Smoke could achieve that again.

We took seats around the table, and Huey opened one of the ice chests and gave each of us a dripping bottle of Miller. He took a seat opposite me.

Hammersmith had kept Huey, Josiah and Oscar Redtail well up to date on events, but still there were many details that Smoke and I added. For instance, Huey was understandably interested in the town's generosity and labors at his farm. At one point he hung his head as if in prayer, and I thought he might be crying, but when he lifted he eyes to listen further, he was dry eyed and intent.

Smoke suddenly remembered something.

"I've got something here for you Huey," he said, reaching inside his jacket.

He placed a thick five by seven envelope between them. Huey picked it up and withdrew a half inch pile of photographs. They were night photographs of the fire and more of the cleanup and street celebration.

We watched in silence as he went through them one by one, carefully placing each face down on the table in a neat stack.

Smoke smiled kindly and said, "Lonnie had everyone make copies for you."

Huey cleared his throat and tipped his face from view. He stood and went over and acted like the range top needed wiping down.

The shadow of Spread Creek Point that loomed over us had thrown the cabin's interior into a twilit darkness. I opened the large box of kitchen matches that sat beside an ashtray, stood, levered up the chimney of the kerosene lantern hanging from the ceiling over us, and gave us some light.

Josiah Longbeach, as if he had been waiting for Smoke and me to finish our narratives, now focused on Charlie. Josiah had the nervous habit of flipping his long hair out of his face, even if it was braided as it was now. He spoke first.

"Any word from the RCMP about the contractor?" he asked.

Charlie shook his head.

"He's a professional. He won't say a thing. I assume the Canadians will give him a public defender, and he'll just take his lumps. He'll undoubtedly get life in prison, and he knows what will happen to him in there if he says a single word. They are hoping to link him to nearly thirty homicides. Him and his pardner have been dropping the hammer on people for nearly fifteen years."

Josiah and Huey, who had returned to the table, nodded.

Huey asked, "What about the notebook, Charlie? That's got to have something in it."

"Dewayne Gibson, Bob Pfeffer and Joy Chu have a bunch of people working on it. Pfeffer is being very cooperative. Giving Cano to him was a turning point--he respects us now."

"Bully for him," Smoke muttered.

Charlie gave him a glance and continued, "They aren't getting anywhere with Cano. Cano is cop smart after twenty years on the inside. But Gibson and Pfeffer, and particularly the DEA, were astonished at the data you and Hammersmith have collected on drug trafficking in Cambodia. I bet it has all been xeroxed a dozen times.

"Joy says Thailand is most helpful, and a copy was sent to them as part of the DEA's 'Operation Warlord.' The Royal Thai Police, including the Narcotics Suppression Bureau, the Office of Narcotics Control Board, and the Anti-Money Laundering Office are all involved. What you gave them gives a clearer picture of the ATS, amphetamine-type stimulant, trafficking in that neck of the woods."

He paused.

"From what she says, it all goes back to the UWSA, United Wa State Army in Eastern Mayanmar. She said the problem is so big that in 2003, a single raid in Kentucky seized 111,650 methamphetamine tablets, and the trafficking is ten times worse now.

"But Rojas's notebook, Huey, is not only over thirty-five years old, the names are in code." He reflected a moment. "However, one name seemed to carry more importance for Rojas than any of the others. It's the code name 'Spider.'"

Huey nodded. "I know. It's 'the Spider's web,' or 'wait for Spider's stuff,' and several times the name is changed to 'Sea Spider.'"

Charlie leaned back. "Where'd you and Eric keep all that stuff, if you don't mind my asking?"

"In Eric's safe," Huey told him. "He keeps the safe in MacAvity's basement vault."

Charlie shook his head. "Now it's a 'basement vault.'"

He looked us over. "There is nothing about you people that can surprise me any more. You're a bunch of devious bastards. But I truly envy the way you stick together," he added.

Charlie leaned back in his seat. "Paul had a question, too, that Pfeffer has taken on--though he hasn't gotten back to me about it." He looked at me and said, "Paul asked who financed Cano's defense back when he was sentenced for those arsons in Utah."

Both Huey and Josiah smiled.

"Good one," Josiah said. Then, "Oscar will enjoy that. He has a special place in his heart for Cano, a place that Cano is lucky he escaped. I just hope giving him up earned you what you needed from the Feds."

It was the first I had really looked Josiah over since we had arrived. He was still wearing cowboy boots and Wrangler jeans, but his white shirt and casino string tie had been exchanged for a dark green, pearl snap-button western ribbon shirt that showed off his round shoulders and flat stomach. He still carried the Para Ordnance P12 tightly on his hip, and I figured Oscar Redtail would be carrying his too.

The radios on the table suddenly chirped four times.

"That's my shift, men," Josiah said, getting to his feet. I've got to roust my deputy."

He went over to his bunk, pulled a camo balaclava down over his long mane of black hair, slid into a army surplus jacket and grabbed an M-16 from under his sleeping bag.

"I just hope he remembered to make extra grub," he added, heading for the door. "You three kept me from my cooking, what with your white man's tall tales of international intrigue and murder."

He flashed us a grin that was brilliantly white against gloom, and was gone.

"Yeah," Huey said standing up wearily. "If you guys want to carry in the provisions, I'll rustle something up."

Chapter
Twenty-Two

Charlie began hauling the coolers and boxes of food into the cabin and to the tents, and I carried the two large bags holding the tent and poles to a flat spot up in the trees behind the elk tent. I had camped there before, and I knew that the trees provided warmth and shelter from the wind. It was also above the ten foot deep layer of fog that often settled in on the meadow during nights.

Behind Oscar's camp two deer were already tagged, bagged, and hanging from a high pole tied with fence wire at both ends between two trees. I expected we would have ten deer to cart out before long; they were that plentiful on the ridge.

It took me a half hour to set up the yurt-like tent and the cots and to haul the duffle bags and my pack in. I was soon working by headlamp in the dark. By then the two four-wheelers had returned, and smoke drifted up to me from the elk tent.

I zipped my tent shut and headed back to the cabin which was dimly lit from the inside by the lantern. I crossed the porch and pushed the door open. The inside smelled of onions and ham, and I realize with a start how hungry I was.

Smoke had a bottle of scotch on the table and glasses were all around. Oscar Redtail grinned and handed me a half full glass.

"My man didn't shoot you?" he asked.

"No, but he scared me to death," I told him.

"Saves ammo."

Charlie was at the stove dishing up bowls for us. It looked like rice and beans with lumps of ham in it. There was chili oil and a tub of butter set out on the table.

"Where were you?" I asked Oscar.

"In the lookout tower," he said. "I had the forest service unlock it for us and take the plywood off the windows. I also outfitted it with some trick DEA surveillance equipment."

Huey nodded. "Anyone coming from Nez Perce Pass has to cross that big burn on Sabe mountain across from here. They're totally exposed for half a mile before they drop into the canyon and climb up to us."

"Right," Oscar said. "We have nearly twenty minutes from the time our long-range infrared and night vision equipment spots them to the time they reach us. By then we'll all be waiting."

"How will we know whoever's coming isn't just some hunters?" This was me.

Huey answered, "Because we haven't had a single person come through at night. It's too difficult to negotiate the track from here east if you're only wanting to reach a hunting camp."

"And," Oscar added, "we've only had two trucks come through today in daylight. And this is opening day."

I nodded.

Charlie put the steaming bowls in front of us and pulled up a chair himself. He shoveled a forkful in his mouth, chewed thoughtfully, then said, "How are you operating, Oscar?"

"We're doing six-hour watches," he said. "Huey stays here with the satellite phone and radio, and either I or Longbeach go out with one of our deputies. They watch the road from cover, and we take the tower."

"And now?"

Oscar looked to Huey, who replied, "Now we can do four hour watches," he said as he chewed. "You, Longbeach and I will make three teams, and Huey and Paul can rotate here at the base."

"Sounds good," said Charlie, taking another large bite.

Huey got up, went over to the stove and adjusted down a damper that was flickering from the wood fire inside. He then put on a mitt, creaked opened the oven door, and took out a sheet of biscuits. He came over and slid them out onto the middle of the table, took the sheet back to the counter, and resumed his seat.

We dug in.

After we had eaten and washed the dishes in the basins filled with lake water, Oscar radioed that we were coming up for a tour.

We went out into the dark with headlamps and helped Charlie ramp his four-wheeler off his truck. Huey helped him duct tape over his tail lights, one headlight and all but a slit of the second. We climbed aboard all five machines and headed out, our slitted headlights casting thin bands that danced over the ground like skip ropes. The night air had grown cold, and our exhausts fogged behind us.

Oscar lead us back up the mining road and across the talus slope. Josiah was there to meet us at the gate, and after shutting down our engines, we followed him in silence across the saddle and up a boot path. We wound through thinly spaced alpine fir and rock outcroppings as we climbed by starlight. To our right, a quarter moon, orange on the horizon, gave us faint light to go by. Then, two hundred yards above the road, we reached the legs of the lookout tower and ascended narrow wood stairs that climbed in short flights, creaking ominously under our weight. At the top we stepped up onto a narrow plank walkway that surrounded the glass-walled exterior of the lookout.

Oscar Redtail opened a narrow, glass paneled door, and we entered the warmth of the dark room. It was lit dimly by several green and red LED lights on equipment that was strung along a window shelf on the east wall.

Josiah introduced us to Jerry Hobbs-Smith, his lookout, who, like Oscar, was wearing his radio's headset. He also had a night vision goggles pushed back on his forehead.

We shook his hand and he pointed out for us the large night scope. It was basically a very large pair of binoculars powered by a battery pack resting on the floor between its tripod legs. To its left, there was a similarly powered scope, the infrared unit, that fed into a receiver and six inch square LCD screen. And on the window shelf was a larger radio that was identical to the one back in the cabin.

Oscar explained.

"We'll work out the details tomorrow for our larger numbers, but basically, whatever comes along we trap and stop. Up until now it's been one man to stop it on the saddle's turn, two to flank it, and the lookout to drop down onto the road behind it for the block. We cleared a trail from the lookout to the road, and each night we mark it with cat eyes, tiny light sticks. With no moon, they make the descent easier."

"And if there is more than one rig?" Charlie asked from the darkness.

"Hopefully they will be running tight--military style. If not, we have enough of us now to double the stop and double the rear," Oscar said.

We considered this.

He went on. "Do you guys have any idea how much crystal meth is worth?"

No one answered.

"The stuff we're expecting has not been stepped on with MSM yet and is ninety-three to ninety-eight percent pure. An ounce of it will sell for no less than two thousand dollars, so the stakes here are high. If we nail, say, twenty pounds of the stuff, we're talking about six hundred and forty thousand dollars minimum."

He let that sink in.

"My guess is it will be one rig, running dark--low profile," he said, "and there will be just two guys. But they will be serious traffickers. They'll be armed and damned dangerous."

He paused. "But there are now eight of us, and speaking for my men, we're pretty fucking dangerous too."

I half expected Jerry to respond somehow, but he remained grim.

We remained there in the lookout for a quarter hour or so. Charlie, Oscar, Josiah and Huey worked out the schedule. I looked through the powerful night binoculars and wondered what a small light was that slowly edged across the face of the infrared's screen. I pointed it out to Jerry who simply said, "Deer on the road."

We were back at the cabin by nine, and I went up to the tent and turned in. I wanted to relax and read for a bit by headlamp and prepare for the next day. My first shift was at six the next morning and would run till noon. Then I had another from six PM until midnight. Huey was to have the other cabin shifts which were more difficult than mine since they started at midnight and noon. His schedule pretty much messed up both his sleep and his day.

During that time, the three teams would be coming and going around the clock, four on, eight off, their cycles also starting at six AM and six PM. Team one, the one I would be starting with, was Charlie and Smoke's. That was good because I knew Charlie would be up and have tea or coffee and breakfast going by the time Smoke and I staggered in. Also, I would have the opportunity to return the favor each afternoon by cooking a supper for them before their six PM watch started.

Chapter
Twenty-Three

I was nearly asleep when Smoke unzipped the tent door and stepped in.

"I'm awake," I said. "Hit the light."

He fumbled around in the dark, found the lantern hanging overhead, and turned it on.

He sat down heavily on his cot and stared at me.

"What?" I said.

He began pulling off his boots.

"Huey got a call from Joy Chu," he said.

I waited. "So?"

"Looks like the information he and Hammersmith turned over to her got into the wrong hands."

I got up on my elbows. "What are you talking about?"

"Apparently our Thai allies compromised it. Somebody in their organization leaked. Fucking corrupt assholes. Probably made a fortune doing it."

Smoke climbed into his bag fully dressed and leaned back.

"So how does she know?" I asked.

"Because," Smoke hesitated for the right words, "gunmen came into Huey's mission, killed the pastor and eighteen parishioners, and wounded close to thirty others. Then they burned the place to the ground."

"Oh shit," I managed.

"Yeah, shit. And get this," Smoke continued. "Rojas's Bassac River Missions have been abandoned, and Huey's informants are being killed and mutilated all up and down the Bassac River and along the mountain trails going to Rojas's west mission."

He swung his legs off the cot, stood in his bag, and turned the lantern off. The inside of the tent went completely dark save for the pale green glow of the LED lights on the radios we had slung near our heads.

He laid back down and said, "Seems Rojas has compromised the whole operation he was a part of. Looks like they were trying to eliminate him as a liability."

I had nothing to say. I was worrying about how Huey might be taking all this. Talk about guilt! He'd blame himself now for all these deaths just as he had for letting Rojas slip away the first time. Only this time more so.

"How's Huey doing?" I finally asked.

"I don't know. Who knows with Huey? He took the call and talked in a normal voice like he was checking on stock quotes. We had no idea--didn't have a clue what kind of news he was getting. We didn't know until he'd hung-up, mixed himself a whiskey, sat down and told us. He was flat normal. Matter-of-fact. It was creepy."

We were both silent for some time, mulling all this over.

"He did say one thing, though," Smoke added. "He said that we should make Rojas come to us."

"What'd he mean by that?"

Smoke rolled over on his side away from me.

"He say anything else?" I asked.

"Nope. Not when I was there. But he has something in mind, I'll tell you that. And he, Charlie, Oscar and Josiah were huddling up when I left."

He was silent for awhile.

Then, "Remember to sleep in your clothes, Paul," he said. "We need to be ready to move fast." He coughed. "G'night."

How do you act around someone who prefers to suffer in silence? You let them, I guess.

I was awake at five-thirty. I got up in the charcoal darkness and hit the light. Smoke rolled over and gave me a foggy look.

I got dressed, pulled on my down coat and fleece watch cap and left him to make his own way.

I threaded back down through the fringe of timber, past the elk tent, and crossed the meadow's cold ground fog to the cabin's warmth.

Charlie and Huey sat at the table with coffees, eating biscuits and gravy Huey had made and was keeping warm on the stove top. It was the end of his shift and he looked about as haggard as I'd ever seen him.

Charlie motioned to the coffee and food, and I went over and loaded up, trying to be quiet since Oscar was asleep in his bunk. Each bunk had snap ties over them that held rolled blankets that could be dropped for privacy. His was dropped.

I put my plate and steaming cup on the table and took a seat.

"Smoke told me last night," I said to Huey. "I'm sure sorry."

Huey pushed his cup away from him and gave me a weak smile.

"I told her not to let the DEA send the Thais that stuff," he said. "The DEA doesn't know that part of the world the way we do."

I assumed the "we" was referring to MacAvity, Hammersmith, and himself. And possibly Smoke.

"They fucked it up," he said. He took his dishes over to the basins, washed them, and put each back quietly on the shelves as he dried.

He turned and went to his bunk.

"I warned them," he added, pulling off his boots.

He rolled into his sleeping bag, zipped it up, and dropped the privacy blanket just as Smoke came through the door.

Charlie hadn't said a thing. He had watched Huey head off for bed, then glanced at me, shaking his head sadly.

Charlie and Smoke were gone in ten minutes. I heard them talk a moment; then they started their four-wheelers and left through the trees. The sound of their engines was a soft purr, and I couldn't hear them at all after a few moments, thanks to the SES, Stealth Exhaust Systems, considered a necessity by Idaho hunters.

Twenty minutes later, Josiah and his man returned, and Josiah came into the cabin in a rush of cold air. He stripped off his coat and put it, his balaclava, radio, night scope, and M-16 back into his bunk. He joined me for the last of the breakfast.

It was growing light out, and through the window I could see smoke was lifting from the tent's stack and falling back into the fog that lay on the two lakes. A low pressure system was developing. Snow?

I made us a second pot of coffee.

"You ever been snowed in, Josiah?" I asked.

"I've tried," he said, talking as he ate. "But you can't trick an Indian, right?"

"Know anybody that has?"

"Sure. Two guys down by Sun Valley. Got trapped in Muldoon Canyon. Lived in their Ford van eating the deer they had shot. Built their fires right inside."

He didn't go on.

"How long were they trapped?"

"One guy, after two months, walks out. Took him twenty-one days to go less than twenty-five miles. They flew a chopper in to rescue him and the other guy, but when they got to the other guy they found he'd killed himself. He'd gotten his feet wet and they had frozen. Gangrene set in and got too painful, I guess."

He gave me a grin. "They were white guys."

He thought for a moment and looked at me.

"Know who the helicopter pilot was?"

I shook my head.

He nodded at Huey's bunk.

"Really!" I had known that Huey had flown for Fish and Game after the war to pay off some farm debt. But this was one story he'd never told us. Come to think of it, he rarely told any stories about himself.

After Josiah washed up, he put his coat and baseball cap on and went out the door.

I looked back out the window as Jerry met him at the head of the lakes. He handed Josiah a deer rifle, and they walked into the timber.

Oscar got up at nine, and I fried some eggs and ham and started a fresh pot for him while he was casting his vote in the outhouse.

I was glad he had gotten up because sitting around in a cabin watching radio dials does not make the time pass quickly. Fortunately, I had found a dozen or so ancient hardbacks stacked in plain sight under Huey's bunk, and selected out *White Fang*, by Jack London. I had read this book twice while in junior high. Unfortunately, what had thrilled me when I was thirteen no longer had the same punch. But it was something to do.

Oscar sat down to his late breakfast, thanked me, and dug in.

"Want me to cook for your deputy?" I asked him.

He looked out the window at the tent.

"He's up," he said. "Probably cooking eggs and deer liver. Probably back strap tonight." He took his last bite and wiped his plate with one of Huey's left over biscuits. "He's fine."

He had no sooner said that than the radios sounded for the first time.

"Check them." Then, "I'll back you up."

It was Charlie's voice.

"Right," Smoke replied.

Huey's blanket pulled aside, and he held it open as he listened.

After nearly five, long minutes. "They're friendlies." Again, Smoke.

"Roger that."

And that was that. Not what I had expected at all. At least when we were driving harvest there was an attempt to be informative, even funny on our CBs. Oh well.

Huey dropped his blanket and, I assumed, went back to sleep.

Oscar left with his man thirty minutes later, and soon Charlie and Smoke came in and headed for the coffee.

"Damn cold on the ridge, Paul," Charlie told me.

They sat and Smoke pulled a ten ounce flask from a breast pocket in his flight jacket and poured a good two ounces in his cup. He held the flask up to Charlie who shook his head. Smoke grinned and took his cup out onto the porch to light up. This was a polite thing for him to do, particularly since the porch faced north and was practically always in the shade. It was an icy porch for someone to fall on.

The day pretty much went like that. After I had made myself a canned soup lunch, I climbed up and took a walk along the barren ridge from Spread Creek Point above us, south three miles to Ring Creek Point.

I was surprised to find another lake, deep in timber and wind fall, on the far side of the south wing of our cirque. I later learned it was Spread Point Lake. I could also see from Spread Point's summit that there was a small lake directly above our cabin, and just above its shores were the granite tilings of the claim's mine.

I followed the rounded edge of the ridge south and circled around a third cirque and still another lake, Saddle Lake, before reaching the stony summit of Ring Creek Point which was just short of eight thousand feet in elevation. There were five cow elk bathing in this lake to keep the horse flies off, and sleeping in the grass on its north bank, taking the sun, were their three calves.

I leaned back against a smooth rock, took off my watch cap, and enjoyed the sun with them.

After nearly an hour, the cows got out of the lake, shook the water from themselves like dogs, and started off single file across the grass to traverse the north ridge. The calves woke up and began to bleat pitifully as they hurried to catch up. They all disappeared into the trees.

I got to my feet as well and started back to camp, thinking about the time Lana and I had stumbled onto a herd of over four hundred elk. That herd's nursery had held nearly fifty babies. It also had at least ten ruling bulls in charge.

We had found them in a cirque like this one in the Wallowa Mountains of Oregon. They had decided not to share the meadow with us, and ashamed we had disturbed them, we decided that the harm had been done and sat to watch them organize their departure. This task was not an easy one for the herd. They were concerned with the little ones and the steepness of the cirque's walls, and they weren't done with the exodus until three quarters of an hour had passed. The hoots, grunts, barks, mews, and trumpeting they seemed to all be making simultaneously created such a sustained din that Lana and I had laughed ourselves silly.

Chapter
Twenty-Four

That evening, Charlie and I played a few hands of rummy after he and Smoke came in from their six to ten watch. Smoke looked on vacantly, nursing a scotch. Huey and Josiah were sleeping behind their curtains, and the cabin was warm and snug.

At eleven, Charlie put down his cards, went out to pee, came back in and climbed into his bunk as well.

Smoke said, "Yup," and went out the door headed for our camp.

I had found a 1948 SILVER SPUR catalogue on a shelf with some other old magazines, and picked it up to look at its collection of saddles, spurs, hats and the like. I was amazed at what a dollar could buy in those days. A Tex Tan saddle went for eighty dollars, elk hide shotgun chaps for thirty-five dollars, Five-X Lazy Square Stetsons for nine dollars, and for the kids, a metal cast "Kansas Marshal" western cap pistol, complete with full grain saddle leather holster and belt for five dollars.

At a quarter 'til midnight, I put a couple short chunks of pine into the range's firebox, poured fresh water into the coffee pot with a scoop of Folgers coffee, and put it on to heat. Then I went over to Huey's bunk and in a low voice woke him.

Huey pushed back the blanket curtain and got out fully clothed except for his boots. He stretched and went to the side window and studied the stars that gleamed through the tips of the pine trees.

"This is Sunday night, right?" he asked, not turning around.

"Yup."

He walked over to the radio set, checked to see that it was still on channel 11, Ryback's traditional channel, then went and looked out the window of the front door at Jerry's camp.

He tapped the door lightly with the fingers of his right hand, then said, "This is the night, Paul. This is when the shipment will come through. Mark my words."

"You think so?"

"I can feel it."

He went to the range, lifted the lid of the coffee pot, saw it wasn't hot yet, and turned to face me.

"Get some sleep. If we roll, I want you to ride with Charlie up to this side of the gate where we'll have the four-wheelers parked. I want you to make sure no one makes it past you out onto our ridge."

He watched my reaction. I just nodded.

"Now listen, Paul. This is important." He hesitated and lowered his voice for emphasis. "If it happens, do not--I repeat--do not confront them. If they see you, they will kill you. Use one of the four wheelers for cover and use your .45. Aim at their belt buckles."

"I understand, Huey," I said. "I'll do what you say."

"All right then," he said, pulling down a coffee cup. "See you in the morning, if not before."

I pulled on my down jacket and fleece cap and went outside, shutting the door quietly behind me. I stood on the porch a moment, adjusting my eyes to the darkness, and looked out over our wilderness hideout.

The two lakes had already developed a wisp of fog that clung to their surfaces, and the moon's light, whiter now, was throwing the barren summit of Spread Creek Point into a bright relief against the night's stars. There wasn't a breath of air, and the night was absolutely silent.

I crossed over and climbed up to our tent. Looking to my right I noticed one additional deer tagged and bagged hanging from the high pole.

Smoke didn't stir a muscle as I unzipped the door flap and came in. I unlaced and removed my boots and slid into my bag.

I fell asleep slowly, thinking about Huey's prediction.

I had only been asleep perhaps an hour when the alarm sounded. Both Smoke's and my radios gave four loud buzzes, and we frantically grabbed for them, at the same time trying to extricate ourselves from our bags. Everyone in camp was doing the exact same thing, I was sure.

I hurriedly adjusted the headset. Smoke turned on the lantern, pulled his .243 out from under his bunk, and grabbed his boots. He had been fully dressed as well. I was fumbling with my laces.

"This is it!" Oscar's voice came over the headset just then. "We have three four-wheelers coming our way in a tight formation. They're twenty minutes out. There is one dirt bike riding point four-hundred yards ahead of them. So hit it hard! Get here now!"

We grabbed our coats and hats and bolted from the tent. Ahead of us Jerry was running across the dimly lit meadow headed for the four-wheelers parked in the timber. We followed hard on his heels.

Charlie had started his four-wheeler and was waiting for me. I swung up behind him, and we started off.

In moments we had cleared the timber, which he had negotiated with lights off, and were bouncing up the slopes. He had his head and one arm through his coiled lariat and was wearing his black police jacket and SWAT mask.

We were behind Josiah's four wheeler. He had his lights out as well. Jerry was ahead of him, and Smoke was behind us, coming up the rear.

Oscar came back on.

"Charlie, trap the rabbit. Smoke, take the lookout for the block. Jerry and I'll trap the tail. Paul, take the ridge." Then, "We're dropping the log on this one. Do it like we planned," and the radio went silent.

I was bucked a foot in the air as Charlie took us over a water bar. I took a strong hold on the rails of the haul deck and realized I was shaking with adrenaline.

We reached the col and climbed up the short bank and onto the smooth, silent grass of the ridge. In moments, we skidded to a stop where Josiah and Jerry had parked. Twenty yards past them, past the narrow opening the track made through the firs, the silhouettes of our two guys could be seen running and ducking under the gate's pole.

Charlie cut the engine and I jumped clear as he swung a leg off. Smoke pulled in behind us and hit running.

Charlie pointed to the four-wheeler that was the second furthest from the gate. "Get behind that and don't move," he said in a low voice. He took his Bushmaster from its ATV clips and worked his lariat off over his head. "And don't let anyone by, Paul. Shoot them."

And he was gone, running with his assault rifle in one hand and the lariat in the other.

I pulled the Glock from under my belt and squatted down behind the four-wheeler he had indicated. Low like this I had a clearer view of the road and saw that four figures were standing a large log up from where it had apparently been placed on the embankment earlier.

Using ropes that were already tied to it, they balanced it in the ditch so it leaned slightly out over the road. They tied it off with two long ropes attached to the upper end, leaving it suspended. Done, the men vanished into the cover of darkness.

Oscar came on again. "Point's across Sabe. Still running 400 yards in front. ETA eight minutes."

Three minutes passed. Then, "Acoustic booster sounds like they're slowing. They're nervous."

I was shaking with excitement. My heart was thudding in my ears, and sweat was trickling down my spine. My eyes burned from staring down the dark track to the gate and road.

Then I heard the muffled purr of a dirt bike. Moments later it came into my field of vision, rolling slowly along the road, its headlamp pointing dimly at the ground. The rider was dressed in camo, and the butt of an assault rifle stuck from a hard plastic scabbard on the front forks. He wore a black stocking cap and a miked headset. He stopped, stuck out his left leg to brace, and said something. He waited a moment, then continued on around the bend and out of sight.

At that moment, the ground thumped. The log had dropped into place, blocking the road.

A minute later, the first of the four wheelers rounded the corner and halted five feet from the log. Its rider instantly pulled his assault rifle from its handle bar clips and bailed into the ditch at the foot of the bank. Behind him the second four-wheeler stopped, throwing dust into the air.

I heard some angry yelling, and then all hell broke loose.

Bursts of automatic weapons fire sounded from seemingly everywhere on both sides of the saddle. One burst and then a second fractured the air only twenty yards down the slope directly below me.

I braced the Glock in both hands over the seat of the ATV. And waited.

As abruptly as the shooting had started, everything went silent.

Then, again right below me, there was a single shot fired, followed by a terrible scream, and then another burst of automatic weapon fire.

Over my headset someone said, "Fuck!" Then, "Thanks Longbeach. I owe you."

A minute passed. Silence.

Oscar came on. "Charlie, you read?"

"I'm here," Charlie said. "I'm coming up the road with the rabbit. He'll be on his bike, so hold your fire. I'm right behind him."

"Everyone OK?" Oscar asked.

"Peter had his mike shot off his head," Josiah said.

"Plus part of my fucking ear, Longbeach," Peter said.

I hadn't met Peter yet but knew he was in Josiah's watch.

"How about you, Paul?"

"I'm fine," I said.

"Come on out then," he said.

Huey, who had been monitoring us and standing by the satellite phone, came on.

"Do we need a medevac?" he asked.

"No," Oscar said. "We have one live one and three dead. Wait until we have something to report on their cargo and have let the rabbit run."

"I'll wait," Huey said.

I put the Glock back under my belt and went to join the others. I reached the gate just as Smoke came walking up the road from where he'd dropped down from the tower to block any retreat. His headlamp was on and he held his rifle in front of him.

Coming up from the other direction the dirt bike and its rider came into view followed by Charlie, also with his headlamp on. Charlie held his Bushmaster like a pistol in his right hand with its stock trapped under his elbow against his side. In his left hand he held his partially coiled lariat which, I suddenly realized, was looped around his prisoner's neck.

I ducked under the pole gate and fell in beside Smoke who grinned at me.

"Looks like Charlie roped him, pardner. Musta pulled him right out of the saddle like a nineteen-forties western." He laughed. "Caught him by the neck. Bastard won't be able to talk for weeks."

We edged our way around the end of the log to join the others whose headlamps swung random puddles of light over the area. They were already unloading the four-wheelers onto the road.

I looked over to where I had seen the lead driver hide and saw he was dead, face down in the ditch with his arms under his chest and his legs sticking straight back. The second driver was laying face up in the road a couple yards from his machine, his legs and arms stretched out like spokes. His weapon was another three feet off towards the bank. There was no sign of the third driver.

Charlie edged his captive past us and stopped on the downhill side. He told the driver to shut his bike down but didn't handcuff him. I found that odd.

Oscar and Jerry came walking up the road out of the dark. Oscar had a digital camera in his hand. As soon as he reached us he began walking around the scene photographing everything repeatedly.

He was taking pictures of Charlie's prisoner, a white man in his late twenties. A Celtic tattoo banded his neck above the collar of his leather jacket, and below the tattoo was a purple rope burn. I almost laughed.

Josiah answered Charlie's question by pointing back towards where I had been. He said, "Both the driver and Peter's headset are in there about twenty yards."

"And some of my fucking ear, too," Peter said. He had a blood soaked bandana tied around his head, and blood was running down his long black hair and staining the front of his jacket. He was lifting red plastic gas cans off the leading four-wheeler.

"Was that you who screamed?" Oscar asked Peter.

"Ummm, yeah."

"Christ, we heard you clear down the road."

Peter suddenly stopped what he was doing and shook one of the cans.

"Hey, Hammersmith," he said to Charlie, "we have something here."

Hammersmith?

Charlie, who still wore his SWAT mask, walked over.

Peter had the lid off the gas can and sniffed. "Vanilla?" he said. He poured out a handful of small green pills.

"Holy shit!" Charley said. "If there's more of that, we're rich!" and added, "Radio Huey. He's got to come up here from the cabin to see this."

I stepped closer to look, as did the others, including Smoke. I looked over my shoulder to see who was guarding the prisoner and was astonished to see he was alone on the road and was toeing down his kick starter preparing to flee.

"Hold it!" I yelled, reaching behind for my weapon. Smoke grabbed my wrist. The motorcycle jumped to life with a howl and the prisoner screamed into the dark, laying flat on his handlebars. Charlie opened fire with his Bushmaster, shooting into the sky. Practically every one else did the same thing. The din was deafening.

Smoke let go of my hand.

"Run rabbit, run," he said, grinning. "You almost fucked up the plan, Pardner." He slapped me on the back.

This is the plan? I asked myself.

There were three red plastic five-gallon gas cans on each of the three ATVs. Of each set of three, one held gas and another held about twenty-five pounds of the green pills which were marked with the letter "R" and actually did smell like vanilla.

The third cans had had their bottoms cut off one inch up the sides. The bottoms had then been pushed back into the cans and fixed into place with sheet metal screws; but not before they had been filled with small, factory sealed vacuum packets of what looked like nearly transparent crystals.

"I'm going down and bring Huey up here," Smoke said. "He's gotta see this. It's fucking unbelievable."

He walked behind me to head for his four-wheeler. I grabbed him by the arm.

"Why'd we let him go?" I whispered.

"He's our rabbit, Paul. "We want him to run back and tell Rojas that Huey and Hammersmith are here and *stole* his merchandise."

He continued on. "Rojas will go out of his mind. He'll be here tomorrow night in the killing mood, and we'll be waiting for him."

He shouldered by me to get to Huey.

"Oh," I said aloud to myself.

Oscar and Josiah were explaining something. I moved into the group to listen.

"Seventy-five pounds of yaba and thirty-five pounds of 'ice' methamphetamine," Oscar was saying. "These are absolutely the best half-gram street packets of ice I have ever seen. They are worth fifty dollars or more each, so there are one million, seven-hundred and nine-two thousand dollars here on the ground."

"You did well at math in school, Redtail?" Josiah asked.

"Shut up. And these tablets are 'yabas' which are part methamphetamine and part caffeine. They add ethyl vanillin--synthetic vanilla--to mask the terrible taste and smell of the chemicals. These babies are the number one most popular form of meth in the Asian community worldwide."

"And they're showing up in our casinos lately," Josiah added. "They sell for about six bucks each. So there's about, uh..."

Oscar helped him out. "About seven-hundred and seventy thousand dollars of 'yaba' here," he said.

I was stunned by the value of what we had seized. It was worth two and a half million dollars! Of course, that was peanuts compared to what some CEOs, athletes and movie people earned every month. But still.

By four in the morning, everything had been cleaned off the road and moved a hundred yards down the track and into the firs out of sight. The bodies were zipped into the body bags Oscar had anticipated we'd need and had brought along. Then the drugs, along with the bodies, were loaded into the back of Oscar's red Dodge Ram 2500. Charlie collected our blood stained latex gloves in a hazmat bag, sealed it, and tossed it in as well.

The whole load was covered with a blue tarp and lashed down.

Peter got into the Dodge for a trip to the clinic and left, promising to be back by nine that night.

Charlie followed in his Ford that he had reloaded with his four-wheeler. "Happy hunting, fellas," he yelled out his window, waving.

They rolled out in a flurry of dust and tail lights.

Back in the cabin, we found that Smoke, who had slid out of the work an hour earlier, had prepared a huge breakfast of eggs, biscuits, sausage, coffee and even hot water for my tea.

The entire crew filed in over a period of twenty minutes, cold, tired, and hungry. Soon we were standing around the cabin eating off paper plates, chewing without conversation.

When Huey was finished, he placed a call to Hammersmith and was still talking to him when the last of us staggered off to bed.

Chapter
Twenty-Five

I wasn't awake until ten. Smoke was still asleep on his back with his mouth open and didn't stir until I worked the zipper. He was groaning himself awake as I walked down towards the cabin.

It was a beautiful fall morning. The low pressure zone we were in had brought warmth with it. It must have been in the seventies, and there wasn't a breath of air.

Apparently Smoke and I were the last ones to wake up. Jerry was sitting in the grass in front of his tent with Longbeach. They had cups and tin plates on the grass beside them, and they stopped talking as I approached.

"How was she?" Jerry asked. He had his shirt off and was laying on it like it was a beach towel.

"Who?" I asked.

"The girl you were dreaming about," he said.

I sat down on the cool grass. "Oh, you mean your sister. Great!" I said.

Josiah laughed, "Your sister's something, ain't she, Jerry?"

"The best," Jerry said, not quite happy. He pointed to the tent directly behind them. "There's coffee on the stove, Paul."

"I'll get my cup."

I stood and circled the lake to the cabin.

Huey was putting the satellite phone back on the window bench when I came in.

"Everyone out there?" he asked.

"Smoke isn't," I said, "but he's awake." I got my cup. "Where's Oscar?"

"He's scouting around," he said. "Peter won't get to Confluence with the dope for another hour, I'd guess, so we've been on the phone with Charlie's people, and with MacAvity and Hammersmith. Hammer is worried that when Charlie tells Joy Chu about this large bust, she'll tell the press and screw us up. I mean, a two to three million dollar bust in her jurisdiction can't harm her career much, I'd say."

He came over and got his own cup. "Let's catch some sun," he said, heading for the door.

When we reached the others, Jerry got to his feet, took our cups and went inside his tent to fill them. At that moment Oscar stepped from the timber with Smoke in tow, and they flopped down in the grass beside us. Jerry came out with our coffees, nodded to Oscar and Smoke, ducked back inside, and returned with two tin cans which he'd filled with coffee. He held them gingerly by their rims to avoid burning his fingers.

Smoke accepted his. "Elegant chinaware, Jer," he said.

"Fuck you, Smoke."

Huey blew on his coffee several times before taking a cautious sip. He looked around at us and said, "MacAvity agrees we'll be hit tonight."

"He would know," Smoke said.

"How would *he* know?" Jerry said.

Smoke nodded the question over to Huey.

"He trained Special Forces in the 60s and SEALs in the 60s, and Rojas, our man, was a SEAL," Huey explained.

Jerry nodded.

"And MacAvity wants us to set up a perimeter and lure Rojas and whoever he brings with him deep into its center. I won't repeat what he felt we should do to them then. I'll let you use your imaginations." He paused. "But he and Micha Wirestone are old friends, if that helps."

Smoke was sitting with his knees drawn up, his elbows hitched around them, both hands holding the hot cup carefully. "Any suggestions?"

Longbeach spoke up from off to the side. "Keep smoke coming from the tent stack and leave the cabin's lamp on like always," he said.

"Not enough," Smoke said.

"Why's that?"

"Because, like we just said, he's a fucking SEAL. If anyone can smell a trap, it's one of those guys."

"So what do you suggest?"

Smoke looked evenly at Huey. "I suggest we stake Huey out like a goat in plain sight," Smoke said. "Sit him at the table right under the light."

"Are you crazy?" I blurted out.

Huey put up his hand to stop me. "I agree," he said.

I felt like moaning.

Huey went on, turning to Oscar. "How does the area look to you?"

"Could be worse, but not by much," Oscar said. "If he were to snipe you, he'd have the front windows, door window, and east window. If he were to breach you, he could come from the timber behind and alongside the cabin. There will be six of us out here, and we all have night vision, but it's still pretty damn thin, particularly if he brings three or more men with him."

We waited for him to finish.

"In our favor, on the other hand, he thinks we stole the shipment and have it stashed somewhere here on the grounds while we get ready to move it. Which means he's not going to blow us all up."

Blow us up?

"So, I say we lay it all out this afternoon, dig in, cover our holes with limbs and brush, established a mike-click signal code, and put Paul on the point above us with Oscar's tricked-out night vision binoculars."

He looked at me. I nodded.

Huey said, "I want to see if I can't move that table so my east flank isn't vulnerable."

Jerry, who had been silent, said, "Cover that window with a blanket. He'll think it's always like that. Leave the front windows bare as a whore's ass. He won't be able to resist."

"That's good," Huey said. "But I'm still going to push the table back towards the bunks. I'm not comfortable with it being right under the lantern."

"Plus," Smoke said, "If you're pushed back away from the front he'll have the porch roof in the way if he tries a long-distance sniper shot with a .50."

"Beautiful," Huey said. "He could do it too. You can see the cabin clearly from the north side ridge here above the timber."

"Yeah, but not without Paul spotting him," Josiah said.

"That's a point."

So it went until lunch. The details remained basically the same, and after we had eaten, everyone went about preparing their positions. I climbed to the summit and made a nest with a low wall of rock piled to look as natural as possible yet still high enough to conceal me. I had brought up my thermarest mattress, and once everything was in place, I hiked over and retrieved the night vision binoculars, their tripod, and the heavy battery pack. Once I had those things in place, I scrambled back down to the road and returned to the meadow.

At the tent I stuffed my day pack with my down coat, thermos, hat, pee bottle and headlamp. As an after thought I added my down pants and a green nylon six by eight foot tarp. Then I went to the cabin where I found Huey and Smoke tacking the blanket over the window with nails that looked like they had been pulled from the roof's shingles.

I glanced at my watch. It was three-thirty, about three hours until sunset. I stood in the center of the cabin in the spot the table had been.

Smoke noticed my hesitancy and asked, "What is it, Paul?"

"I'd like to borrow your deer rifle," I said flatly.

He grinned at me. "Well, I did ask you to check with me before you ever touched it, Paul. Glad you kept your word." He went over to where it leaned against the front wall and handed it to me. It had a brand new Austrian Swarovski 3-12x50 scope mounted on it.

"You know how to shoot this thing?" he asked.

Huey stepped to my defense, "Just because he's given up hunting, Smoke," he said, "doesn't mean he's not still a damn fine shot. Isn't that right, Paul?"

"Nope," I said. But I did know how to shoot practically straight down a hill, which I might have to soon do. I also knew that I would be able to kill anyone, anyone at all, who was trying to kill one of us. Last night had taught me that.

"Well," Smoke said dubiously, "just don't scratch it, OK?"

I looked at him. "What if I drove your truck over it?" I asked. "That OK?"

He just looked at me.

I filled my water bottle on the kitchen counter with water carried from a spring behind the cabin and sorted through our boxes of supplies for something I could eat up top for supper. I noticed, too, that the coffee pot was full and hot, so I filled my thermos, capped it, and put that in my pack as well. I swung my pack on, adjusted it, and picked up Smoke's beautiful .243.

I stopped at the door and said, "I'll be careful with it Smoke. I was kidding."

"I know you will, Paul, he said. "Be careful with yourself up there, too." And then, "Your radio batteries charged?"

"I put in charged ones."

"Good."

"Good luck, Huey," I said awkwardly.

"Don't worry," he said, turning to face me. "We have it covered. Stay warm."

I nodded and left for my position.

Chapter
Twenty-Six

A little after five the meadow and cabin were deep in shadow. A breeze began to blow over my position, and in moments the temperature dropped at least fifteen degrees.

"Smoke, you feel that up there?" I asked over the radio.

"Yup," he said from the tower. "There is a black wall coming our way from the northwest," he said.

"How far out, Smoke?" Huey asked.

"Long ways. Through these 30x glasses it looks like it's at the Lochsa River. Maybe on the other side of the Crags and Fenn Mountain. Fifty miles?"

"So we have five to ten hours?" Huey speculated.

"That's my guess."

"Hang on. I'm going to tune into NOAA for a minute."

We waited. I looked over at the far ridge. Smoke and I and Sabe Mountain were still bathed in light. Beyond, the Bitterroots were layered in progressively lighter shades of deep blue haze.

Huey came back on. "We have a large weather front coming, men. It's going to have snow in it, and it's moving right along. Temperatures down to thirty, which isn't too bad, but if you're not prepared to hold your positions in that kind of weather, come in now and load up. And while we're at it, Jerry, you need to empty your tent of stuff and stash it in the timber."

He paused. "We're all going to have a radio link with MacAvity at 6:30. He wants to talk to us. Peter phoned a bit ago too. He will be arriving at seven, Smoke, so don't shoot him. He's going to park the truck up on top past the gate."

"If I do shoot, I'll try to miss," Smoke said.

Below, Longbeach and Jerry came in from the timber at different angles, crossed over to the tents and began carrying things back up to near where Smoke and I were camped. They didn't reappear after that.

Snow. I guessed the temperature, which was continuing to drop, was down at forty-five. I did a quick inventory and knew that I'd be fine if I stayed dry. My hooded down jacket and down pants were good to minus twenty. With the tarp pitched over me, it would be like a living room in my rock shelter. Or more like a bunker. I could lay on my stomach with only a two foot high, three foot wide opening for my rifle and binoculars. Perfect. And if the wind continued from the northwest, I'd have it off my left flank and it would sweep over the top of me. I felt almost smug.

So the satellite phone could plug into Oscar's large radio set. I wondered what MacAvity wanted to tell us. I looked at my watch. Six ten. Time was crawling.

It was a few minutes later when I realized that an intense pinpoint of white light was shining on the horizon just below the south slope of Sabe Peak's summit. I swiveled the powerful binoculars on their tripod and directed on them at the spot, adjusting the focus. The image pulled into view was crystal clear, and I realized that what I was seeing was the setting sun reflecting from the passenger's side window of a partially exposed black Humvee.

An electric shock ran through me as the implications became obvious.

"Huey!" I said into the mike. "We have a Hummer parked on the road below Sabe Peak."

Huey answered immediately. "You see it, Smoke?"

"Let me check," Smoke came back. Then, "No. Can't see it."

"Is it alone, Paul?" This was Huey.

"I can only see its front half. There might be another behind it, but I don't know."

Smoke said, "That explains why I can't see it. It's around the bend too far."

There was a pause as everyone digested this. The reflection was fading rapidly as the sun sank lower behind me. Had I not glanced when I did, I wouldn't have seen it.

Huey came back on. "What do you think, Oscar, Josiah?"

"This is our first break," Josiah said. "I think they're hoofing it down that little drainage below them to Sabe Creek and will come upstream to our drainage and follow it up until they reach us."

"How long will that take?" Huey wanted to know.

"It looks close from here, but it'll take a good tough five miles of bush whacking to reach us. Say, three hours?"

"I agree," Oscar said. "Let's run this by MacAvity, Huey. He's trained these SEALs. He'll know how to handle it. Can you ring him up now? It's nearly six-thirty anyway."

"Yup."

We waited. The sun slid behind the horizon, bathing everything in a momentary pale yellow-red glow, and then the cold descended on us in earnest.

Over the headset, I heard a phone ringing. A receiver was lifted. I could hear ice tinkling in a glass and then MacAvity's gruff voice said, "Hello."

"It's me," Huey said.

"I was to phone you. What's up?"

"You're patched in to all of us, Butte, and we have a development here. Paul spotted a black Hummer parked nearly out of sight around the bend below Sabe Peak."

"How long ago, Paul?" he asked.

I was amazed how clearly he came in. It was like a direct phone link. "I saw it about ten minutes ago," I told him.

"How long do you think it was parked there?"

"I don't know, Butte. I only noticed it because the sun was reflected back from a side window."

MacAvity thought about this a moment. Then, "A black Humvee is just Roja's style, gentlemen. We can assume it's his. So what do you men think he's doing now?"

Huey spoke, "Josiah thinks they're coming to us by following the drainages."

"I think he's right," MacAvity said. "It's what I'd do."

"Should we snipe them?" Josiah asked.

"Don't even think about it. You'd be moving the fight into his arena. We need to keep to the plan. To catch a fox you have to use a snare."

No one said anything.

MacAvity went on. "When Peter gets there, Smoke, tell him what's going on. He needs to keep on going and take that Humvee out. Rojas will have a man left behind in it to do the pick-up when they're done with us--if we don't do them first."

"What if Rojas has two rigs?" Smoke asked.

"He won't. That many guys can't make it through tough country in the dark without being detected. It's the driver, Rojas, and two of his best men." He let that sink in. "There will only be three of them, maybe four, but they will be a handful, believe me. If any of them get away, they'll realize a pick-up isn't going to happen, and they'll return to where the Humvee had been parked. When they find it's gone, they'll know they're fucked."

"How so?" This was me.

"Because they will be stuck out in the wilderness with a pack of Redskins tracking them down."

"Nothing is more frightening than Redskins," Jerry chimed in.

MacAvity ignored the remark. "Be ready for a diversion once they reach you," he continued. "It will be all you can do to remain under cover. It will be designed to draw you out into the field of their night visions. Lay low and wait. It will only take moments."

Huey said, "We have a blizzard coming in, Butte."

MacAvity laughed. "Our second break of the night. They are at a huge disadvantage if it snows. Especially if they're retreating. They won't last the night. I can guarantee they won't be prepared for freezing temperatures, much less a foot or two of snow."

Time was passing. I looked at my watch, and I was growing very nervous.

As if he had read my mind, Butte said, "Smoke, come in from the tower as soon as Peter takes off. Leave the lookout and join Paul. I can imagine one of them coming in from the north or south ridges. You'll be able to pick them off easily from where you're stationed. It might be the shot that starts the whole thing rolling, and it will take them by surprise. They obviously don't think you'll be up there, or they would have parked the Humvee further back out of sight."

He waited a moment, then, "Anything else?"

"That's about it, Butte," Huey said. "We'll let you know how it goes."

"Good luck gentlemen," MacAvity said. We could hear his receiver rattle as he hung up.

It was five to seven when Smoke came back on. "Peter has arrived. He's on his way to Sabe," he said. "I'm coming over to you, Paul. Don't kill me."

"I'll think about it."

I switched on the night vision and swung the binoculars over to where the road climbed up from Sabe creek and crossed the burn. I was curious how Peter would traverse it without Rojas and his men detecting him and radioing a warning to their driver. I waited.

Five minutes passed, and I heard Smoke climbing the shale slope that led to my position. When he arrived he was out of breath and flopped down on his back beside me, letting out a sharp moan.

"What the fuck you laying on, broken dishes?" he said, sitting up. He held up one of the walnut sized rocks I had leveled the floor with.

"I'm on my mattress," I told him. I looked through the binoculars to see if Peter was climbing yet. He wasn't.

"Didn't you bring up my cot?"

I handed him back his .243. He traded me back the M-16 he must have borrowed from Oscar's stores.

Suddenly Peter's Dodge came into view. He had the lights off and was apparently feeling his way along using his night vision goggles.

I moved out of the way so Smoke could have a look.

"Won't Rojas hear him?" I asked.

"I doubt it," Smoke said. "He'll be following the drainages because they will provide game paths for him to walk, and the streams will mask any noise he and his men make. The water will also drown out any noise Peter's truck makes. Peter'll stop and go on foot before the guy sitting in the Hummer can hear him."

I considered this. "Seems like Rojas has chosen a bad plan," I said.

"I don't know," Smoke said. "If you hadn't spotted the Humvee it might have been a damn good one. Didn't sound to me like MacAvity was that thrilled."

I turned the Thermarest sideways so both Smoke and I could keep our stomachs and elbows off the sharp gravel, and at that moment the temperature took another plunge as the breeze strengthened. We got to our feet and stretched the tarp over the walls and held it in place with rocks. Roofed over, the interior was much warmer.

We checked on Peter's progress and watched him slowly approach the timber where the burn had halted. He was about four hundred yards from the bend, and it was another fifty yards around it to the Humvee.

Rather than enter the timber, he parked, left the road, and started up the mountain on foot. He followed the edge of the trees and took advantage of the clearing created by the fire. About two hundred yards above the truck, he turned into the timber in the direction of the Humvee and was out of sight.

That left us with nothing to do but wait. We took turns at the binoculars watching both ridges that bracketed our meadow, and to help the time pass, we chinked the gaps in the windward wall with smaller stones that were scattered around inside. I opened the thermos and poured us a cup which we passed back and forth. I poured a second, enjoying the warmth spreading through me.

Peter came back on. "No one here. I'm going to pull its wires and come back." About five minutes passed, then, "Whoa. There's a duffle in here with at least five pounds of C-4 with all the goodies. There's a bunch of other shit too, including a nifty Colt 1911. Want me to bring it along?"

"Affirmative," Huey said.

Chapter
Twenty-Seven

At a little past eight-thirty, we saw Peter step out of the woods on the road and climb back into the truck. He begin backing down the grade, and at a wide point he turned it around and continued on.

"I hope that's Peter," I whispered.

"It is, pardner, never fear," Smoke said, patting me on the back.

He got on the mike and clicked twice. He got two clicks back and whispered, "Peter's coming back." He got a click.

By nine we spotted Peter sneaking quickly down the north ridge. He radioed with two clicks, got two, then said quietly, "I'm setting up above Paul and Smoke's tent. I'm in the open and will take to the rocks in a moment. I'll stay put."

He got a click.

"That takes care of one ridge," Smoke whispered. "We'll give him cover from a flanking maneuver and watch the south ridge at the same time."

"Right."

According to Josiah's estimates, Rojas would reach us anytime within the next sixty minutes. We were alert and tense.

"Man," Smoke mused, "I would have loved to take out that Hummer with my A-4 Skyhawk." He thought about that for a moment. "My cannons would have turned it into metal filings. I think Oscar should provide us with one next time."

It was at that moment that a thundering explosion shattered the night, and Jerry and Peter's tent lifted into the air riding atop a ball of rolling flame. The concussion drove grit through the mouth of our shelter into our faces and lifted our tarp in a snapping billow.

"Holy shit!" Smoke said.

We studied the lakes and meadow in the flames' diminishing yellow light. Nothing moved. I swung the binoculars to the front of the cabin. From our position I couldn't see in the windows, but I had a clear view of the area in front. Nothing. I began scanning the edge of the woods and along the back side of the meadow. Still nothing. The brush at the back of the tent was on fire.

Suddenly there was the rapping of automatic weapon fire followed by two quick rifle shots. Then a figure appeared on the porch of the cabin and darted inside. There was a pop and simultaneously a flash of blue light accompanied by a shotgun blast. Seconds later, just below Peter, a gun battle began in a mix of rattles and booms among the trees and continued in starts and spurts. I looked at Peter's hiding place and could see the muzzle of his M-16 waiting.

The gunfire stopped, and I saw a stooped figure running, hugging the edge of the timber along the bottom of the bare ridge. Peter's rifle flash-boomed, and the man turned to dive into the timber when Peter hit him with a quick roaring burst. The man was thrown to the ground and rolled limply up against a rock and stopped.

At that moment Smoke's .243 thundered in my ear, knocking me senseless. I stared out the opening to see a man running towards the cabin from where he had been hiding in the talus directly below us. Smoke squeezed off another round and the runner fell to his knees. He began crawling frantically to where his rifle had been thrown.

He was dragging a leg. Smoke squeezed off a third round and the man's head hammered down on his left shoulder as he was flattened to the ground by the bullet's impact.

On the far side of the meadow there was a sudden flurry of fire from several automatic weapons. Their muzzle flashes strobed the bottoms of the pine limbs over them. The firing continued for several seconds. Then they went silent as well.

A minute passed. Smoke asked to use the binoculars, and was slowly scanning up and down the meadow and over to the cabin and woods with them. The flames at the camp were sputtering along slowly.

Two minutes. Three.

A mike clicked twice. There was no response.

We all waited, not moving.

A mike clicked twice again.

No response.

Then Oscar came on. "I'm going for the cabin. Something's wrong. Cover me."

I strained to see anything. For the moment, Smoke's muzzle flashes had partially blinded my one good eye. He watched through the binoculars.

"I see Oscar," he said. "He's coming from the far side slow and easy, keeping out of view." Then, "He's out of sight now. He's probably setting up to see past the blanket in the side window."

Then Oscar said, "Huey's down. I'm going in."

I could see him run into the light that flooded the porch from the front windows. He bolted through the door and was inside.

We waited anxiously.

Finally he came back with, "He's alive. But he's bad."

We waited.

"Secure the area," Oscar said. "Someone bring the med. chest." Then, "Smoke, get down here and treat him. Hurry."

Smoke turned on his headlamp, plunged from our shelter and practically skied down the shale onto the road. I watched him run the road to the edge of the talus, then continue straight down through the bear grass until he reached the meadow. In moments he was met by Josiah who was lugging the medical chest from where the trucks were parked. They went in together.

Peter turned on his head lamp and climbed down to the man he'd shot.

Longbeach came on. "Make sure the dead are concealed, men."

Peter dragged his kill by his feet into the timber and went out of sight.

Josiah and Jerry came over, got Smoke's victim and dragged him behind some firs just below me, dropping his legs like lumps of wood. Without looking down at him, they went back to put out the fire. They got two canvas camp buckets and hauled lake water over. Soon they had it under control.

I got to my feet, slinging Smoke's rifle over my head to carry along with the M-16, and descended along his skid marks. My headlamp lit up a large area in front of me so that I reached the meadow easily. I swung its beam over to where his victim had been stashed and wished I hadn't. Half of his head had been blown away--the closest half. It looked like someone had taken a helmet filled with a mixture of blood and pudding and propped it on its side so the contents could spill out.

I reached the cabin porch just as Jerry and Peter came out dragging a body by its arms. For a horrifying moment I thought it was Huey and stopped in my tracks. But it was a dark skinned, wiry man in his late fifties. His hair was salt and pepper, and he had a pencil thin beard that looked like it had been drawn on his jaw line with charcoal. He was dressed in black jeans and combat boots. The front of his navy blue down jacket was a sodden pile of blood soaked feathers. He had taken a round of buckshot at close range.

I followed Jerry back into the cabin and edged my way towards the stove to see past the others. On the floor by the bunks Smoke was laboring over Huey with Oscar working from the other side. They had moved the table Huey had been sitting behind out of the way. On its surface lay a pistol-gripped twelve gauge pump. It was covered with blood.

Smoke reached for another compress Oscar had unwrapped and handed to him, and I was able to see past him. He had clamped two hemostats in through Huey's open mouth, and was now fitting compresses over his shattered jaw and the gaping exit wound. Huey's chest and pants were soaked with blood. Oscar finished setting up an IV, stood and taped it to the side of the bunk.

Longbeach and Peter came in just then. Josiah took one look at the scene and went over to the satellite phone. He pulled a small book from his back pocket and punched in numbers. He then pulled a GPS unit from a cargo pocket on his thigh and placed it face up on the window sill where he could read off it. He turned his back to us, faced the window and talked quickly, his voice low with authority. When he was done, he turned back and said, "Two of you get six flares out of my truck. A Geotze Air Service chopper will be here from Schumacher Meadows in about forty minutes. When you hear it coming, mark off a landing zone. Huey's being lifted to St. Luke's in Boise."

He looked us over. "Everyone remember this." He waited until even Smoke looked up. "Huey shot himself by accident while showing us his new Ruger Mark III, got it?"

Chapter
Twenty-Eight

We heard the whump of rotors thirty-five minutes later. It was a quarter till eleven, and Jerry and I struck the flares and placed them upright in a flat spot near the base of the talus slope where Smoke's victim had fallen.

Shortly a black Bell 429 Light Twin helicopter lifted up into view from the canyon over the trees, lights strobing the blackness. Its landing lights suddenly came on, flooding us in their glare, and the helicopter dropped its wheels and landed. It cut back its engines, which whined down as the four blades slowed.

The pilot and a crewman jumped from the wide starboard door, dragging a wire mesh stoke after them. They each took a side and jogged over to the cabin with us right behind them.

We stood outside to keep out of everyone's way and waited. When they finally reappeared they were both at the head of the stoke and Josiah and Oscar were at the foot. They came off the porch carefully, then hurried past us back to the chopper in silence. Huey's head was in some kind of brace, and Smoke was alongside holding the IV bag over his head.

For some inexplicable reason, I suddenly filled with tears which began streaming down my cheeks.

Jerry put his hand on my shoulder. "It's been a big night, cousin," he said.

I could only nod, not trusting my voice. We walked towards the landing zone, and with effort I got myself under control.

The pilot and crewman jumped into the helicopter, turned and pulled the stokes after them. Smoke got in with them, still holding the IV bag. Josiah and Oscar helped lift Huey onto the cargo deck and climbed in as well. In the white glare of the ceiling lights I could see them lift the stoke onto a set of brackets. Smoke hung the IV bag from a stainless hook, and Josiah and Oscar jumped back out into the grass. The crewman was strapping the stoke in place as the pilot climbed forward into his seat and pulled on his flight helmet.

Smoke buckled onto a fold down seat against the far wall, and the crewman slid the door shut. The engines gained rpms quickly, and with a howl, the twin jet turbos lifted them into the air. The helicopter then tipped forward and left in a gentle turn to the south, streaking back down the canyon headed for Boise.

A silence fell over all of us. The flares hissed in the grass, a wind was working in the tree tops, but there was nothing to say.

Finally Oscar started back to the cabin, then stopped. "I'm going to get some rags out of the truck," he said. "Peter, Jerry, let's clean the blood up in the cabin and bag the bodies."

Longbeach came over to me and walked with me back through the grass.

"We're going to hide the bodies tonight," he said. He looked at the ceiling of cloud that was closing in over us. "I'm not going to ask you to help. It's a pretty ugly business. But could you take Smoke and Huey's stuff back to them?"

"No problem," I said. "I'll go down to Boise to pick up Smoke in the morning. What about Huey's truck?"

"We'll handle that." Then Josiah added, "You know that was Rojas Huey killed, don't you?"

"I figured as much."

"I'm going to give you his weapon to give to Huey. Smoke will tell him the self-inflicted wound story. But also Huey can have something to remind him that his nightmares can end now any time he wants them to."

He paused. "Old habits don't die easily, I guess. Rojas was a head shooter. He popped Huey with a .22 LR hollow point from that spanking new Ruger Mark III. Damn thing looks just like his old hush puppy Charlie showed me."

"Don't forget Smoke's .243 when you leave," Josiah said. Then, "Speaking of which, where'd he hide my M-16?"

"I'll bring it over to your truck," I told him. "Was that your shotgun Huey had used?"

"Nope. Oscar made him take it. A .22 against a scatter gun. Not much of a contest in tight quarters, is it?"

It was just beginning to snow when we arrived back at the cabin. Inside, it smelled of blood, soap and water. All the windows had been pushed open, and we left the front door ajar.

Josiah went to one of the coolers and pulled out a half case of Miller High Life. I reached up to the shelf where Smoke had stored two bottles of White Horse and took one down along with a cup.

We pulled our chairs up around the warmth of the stove that was roaring full-bore and relaxed.

It was the first time I had had a chance to take a good look at Jerry and Peter. They looked to be brothers. They each wore their hair in a long braid like Josiah's, they both wore lined flannel shirts over hooded sweat shirts, and they both wore tan Carhartt carpenter's pants. They were also kind looking men. They did things without complaint and knew how to laugh. The only difference between them that I could see was that one of them was wearing Converse sneakers, and the other was wearing calf high moccasins similar to MacAvity's.

Oscar caught me studying them. "You didn't know our deputies are brothers, did you Paul? Jerry and Peter Hobbs-Smith."

"No I didn't," I said, standing to shake their hands a second time. They leaned forward and shook lightly as the Camas do.

"They live inside their minds just like you," Oscar said. "Jerry is a historian and story teller, and Peter teaches grade schoolers."

I nodded. Jerry, I noticed, was working away on a sheet of paper towel with a ball point.

"What are you doing there, Jerry?" Oscar asked.

Jerry looked carefully at his writing and said, "Counting coup."

They laughed.

"Here's how it stands," he said consulting his notes. "We have killed four deer and seven white men on this hunting trip. The Indians are ahead with five kills and zero prisoners to the white men's two kills and zero prisoners." He looked at me. "But roping has powerful coup and sets a new standard."

We toasted Charlie in abstentia.

I offered, "As long as you're counting, you forgot we had a kill on Rattlesnake and another at Hammersmith's," I said. "We also took a prisoner at Hammersmith's." I paused. "Of course, you took a prisoner out of Rattlesnake."

He put his notes on his knee and filled that in. "You want the monthly total? OK. Indians: five and one, Whites three and one and one roping." He looked up. "But we still have one white man left, isolated and surrounded in a remote mountain cabin." He grinned evilly at me.

"Tell me something, Jerry," I said. "When was the last time someone put a brown recluse in your bedroll?"

"Oh shit. Don't ever say that," Jerry moaned. "I'm afraid of those fuckers."

We laughed and drank to Jerry.

"Paul's been hanging around Wirestone," Oscar said. "Better watch your ass."

"Have you ever seen anyone that's been bitten by a recluse?" Jerry asked.

I shook my head. The others were nodding.

"Charlotte Riba was bitten three years ago on her calf. She was out getting an armload of wood one night and it crawled up her pant leg. Before it was over, her whole calf rotted away." He sipped his beer. "Wirestone saved her life. Those doctors at Confluence didn't know what to do except cut and cut. If we hadn't stolen her out of the hospital and taken her to Micha, there'd a been nothing left of her but a pile of shavings."

They were quiet for some time remembering that.

Snow was beginning to blow in the windows. Peter and Josiah got up and closed them but left the front door open.

"You know," Jerry said, opening a second can of Miller, "I can see the fat cats who are behind all this sitting in their mansion somewhere. They're saying, 'What the fuck. Send those two cons over to get that evidence shit back and pop those two lame-ass medicare recipients. Simple.'

"So after one con is burned alive and the other is tortured for weeks by an old Injun, they say, 'Screw it. Hire a couple professionals from Canada. Problem solved.'

"So they do and one of the contractors gets his feet blown off and the other is shot to shit. Now they say, 'Forget those old fucks. What are they to us?'

"So then the old fucks take two and a half million dollars worth of drugs from them, kill three more of their guys, and take another prisoner by roping his head nearly off his body."

We're howling with laughter.

"Now they say, 'Tell that sorry-assed ex-SEAL muthafucka Rojas, to get in here,' and they read him the riot act and tell him to solve the problem or they'll bury him in a hay field somewhere.

"So Rojas says, 'I'll take care of those assholes, don't you worry.' He spends all night crawling up and down mountains, getting the shit scratched out of him by the brush, only to find that a bunch of stinking Indians have teamed up with the lame-ass geriatrics who then proceed to kill every fucking one of them.

"So, right now those fat fucks are sitting around their huge log mansion fireplace smoking Cuban cigars and drinking gins saying, 'So, whose fucking idea was it to mess with those old shits anyway?'"

We're mopping our eyes and coughing.

Peter was scratching at the white bandage that covered practically half the side of his head. He looked like he was falling asleep on us. Then he remembered something. "Can we see Rojas's .22?"

Josiah got up, went to his bunk and returned with the pistol wrapped in a paper bag he expected me to carry it in. He handed it to me.

I took the Ruger Mark III out and showed it to them. Its handle was swept back, it had a stainless finish, a round trigger guard, and a long, fluted barrel. It looked as deadly as it did elegant. It got passed around. They understood it was the weapon used on Huey. They also understood it was the weapon of choice for a professional drug trafficker and murderer responsible for an untold number of atrocities. They each studied it carefully, looking for meaning, I suppose.

Then Oscar spoke, getting to his feet. "Let's drag those bodies up to the mine shaft." he said. "And Peter, bring along a pound of that C-4, a blasting cap, crimpers, and ten feet of fuse."

I stood, put the bottle and cup back on the shelf and headed for the door. Peter handed me back the gun he'd rewrapped in its paper bag, and I went out, leaving them to their macabre tasks.

There was a half inch of snow on the meadow, and I could see my breath in the cabin's receding light. The air was still, and I fell asleep to the slight hiss of flakes striking the tent's sides and roof.

Sometime in the middle of the night an enormous, rumbling boom startled me awake. It took a few moments before I realized what it had been. "Nighty night, boys," I said to myself, falling back to sleep.

Three inches of snow accumulated during the night. It had built up in a silent layer on the tent's roof. Outside it was still falling quietly, slowly rocking its way through the gray dawn into the meadow, blanketing the cabin's roof and the boughs of the pines. The air was very cold.

Smoke was drifting up from the cabin's chimney. I crossed the meadow hoping for tea and a substantial breakfast, stamped the snow off my boots on the porch boards, and went into the cabin's warm interior.

Oscar was the only one there. He was seated at the table with a cup of coffee and was writing in what looked like a police binder. I realized he was making out his DEA report covering what had happened, but only with the drug bust. The rest would be lost to the winds of time.

He looked up, "Morning."

"Where is everybody," I asked.

"Hunting," he said, turning back to his work. The dirty plates stacked by the dish basins indicated they had all eaten.

I went over and set about frying up three eggs and some sausage links. I brewed a cup of tea and sat opposite him and ate. Afterwards, I did the dishes and stepped back outside to spent the next hour breaking camp and loading it all into the Tundra. Someone, probably Peter and Jerry, had loaded all of Huey's things into the back seat.

I started the Tundra and left it to warm up while I went in to say goodbye.

I pushed open the cabin door and stuck my head in. "See ya, Oscar. It's been lively."

He pushed his chair back and came over to shake my hand. "Have a good trip, Paul. Give our best to Huey and tell him he can live with us while we help him rebuild his home."

"I will," I told him. Then, "What about the Hummer and those guys' four-wheelers?"

"Josiah will come back with a trailer for the ATV's," he said. "The Hummer is going to get wiped and parked at the Boise airport. Whoever they're working for will think they took the drugs for themselves, stashed them somewhere, then left the country for awhile."

Clever.

I went back out to my truck, swept the snow off the windows, climbed in, shifted into low-range, and pulled out onto the wide tracks left by the Hummer. I carefully made my way up the drifted-in mine road and out onto the relative safety of the ridge. The pole gate had been left open, and I locked it behind me. I swung onto the Magruder Corridor and let out a sigh of relief.

Boise, here I come. And Lana, I'm about to call you.

Chapter
Twenty-Nine

The snow gave way to thin rain as I descended Three Prong Ridge to Bargaman Creek, which was flowing blackly through the fog. Climbing up the far side to the next ridge and Granite Spring, I was back into the light snowfall, though it was wet and stuck to the Tundra's windshield, cut by the wiper sweeps. From Mountain Meadows on it was steady rain, and the road's softness pulled me side to side.

I pulled up to the general store, the only store, in Palace and stepped into the shelter of its porch where a pay phone was bolted to the wall. I was about to call Lana when a well dressed couple got out of a Subaru Outback and approached me.

The woman was wearing Eddie Bauer style outdoor clothes and had short, blond hair and heavy makeup.

"We saw that you came in from the Magruder Corridor," she said. "Can we ask you some questions?"

"We're reporters from The Country News in Brunsfeld," the man added.

I placed my hand on top of the phone to give them the message that I was busy.

She moved closer, smelling of soap. "Can you tell us about the Native Americans' drug seizure up in the Bitterroots? Are they still in there?"

I got out my wallet and removed my phone card before answering.

"You planning on driving in there with your little Subaru?"

"Oh yes. It's four-wheel drive and is great on country roads," she said happily.

I nodded. "Well, the passes are snowed shut," I said.

"We can make it," the man said. "Don't you worry about that."

I could imagine him trying to push the car out of the snow, slush thrown onto his designer jeans.

"You're determined to talk to the Indians?"

"Absolutely," he said. She nodded vigorously.

I reached back, and put my hand on the receiver ready to lift it.

"In that case," I told them, "It's only fair to warn you that they were driven out by the snow like I was. They left last night for a big Indian gathering at Clark Fork, Idaho. You know, on east shore of Lake Pend Oreille."

I thought that lie would settle the matter and picked the receiver up. I had underestimated them.

"Do you know where they're staying up there?" the woman asked.

I considered this. "They usually stay at the River Bend Motel, Restaurant and Lounge," I said.

The man's eyes closed down to cynical slits. "You're lying," he snarled. "I know Clark Fork. There's no such place."

"I haven't seen any Native Americans in the Bitterroots, either," I said. "So quit bothering me."

All their sweetness evaporated, and they went back to their car, but not before the man could mumble loud enough for me to hear, "Fucking hillbillies."

I typed in my calling card number and took out the slip of paper with Ann's phone number on it and dialed.

Apparently, everyone in Palace had given the reporters the same run around because they angrily ripped out of town and headed back to the South Fork road. I felt guilty about the way I'd treated them. I knew how hard it was to be a reporter and how well meaning many of them were. I blamed my own bias against the way they were dressed and the way they smelled. Now if they had come up in an older truck.... Ann's answering machine picked up.

As usual when an answering machine waited, I couldn't find anything to say, but managed, "It's Paul. Tell Lana I'll call again tonight."

I went to hang up but stopped short, "Oh, and tell her I'm fine. We're all fine. And I love her."

What a fucking moron.

It had stopped raining by the time I reached the Salmon River Gorge, which was also locked in fog. I turned left and followed it on upstream due south on highway 95. Within the hour I had climbed back out onto the thirty mile long expanse of Schumacher Meadows. There the fog had lifted, leaving a leaden ceiling of cloud and a black strip of wet asphalt. I drove through Brunsfeld and past the Brunsfeld Airport. I looked over and saw the Bell helicopter that had lifted out Huey and Smoke parked by the Goetz Air Service hanger. Its blades drooped sadly in the wet air.

It took me a half hour to drive the length of Schumacher Meadows. At their south end the mountains squeezed in from both sides, leaving only an extremely narrow notch carved by the North Fork of the Payette River. I took a deep breath, since I disliked this part of the drive, and slowed to thirty-five as I entered the slot. It would be an hour before I broke free into the flats below Boise Ridge and entered the turmoil of run-amock suburban mania.

I was told at St. Luke's reception desk that Huey was in surgery. A young volunteer, a clean cut teenage girl dressed in pale pink hospital cottons, was assigned to show me where the surgery's waiting area was. I found Smoke there, reading a well-worn copy of People magazine. He looked up.

"How'd it go?"

I took a seat at his left. The waiting area was a long, ten foot wide room with an "authorized personnel only" door at the far end. The wall opposite our padded chairs was all windows, twenty feet high, looking out at Boise Ridge. The city was pushed up against its slopes like a bath tub ring.

"OK," I said. "You been able to talk to Huey?"

"Nope. I've sat with him, but he's pretty messed-up. Lost heaps of blood and went shocky in the air."

He groped for a cigarillo out of habit, then dropped his hand. He looked pretty spry aside from that.

"What are they doing?"

Smoke flipped the magazine onto the end table at his right and leaned back.

"They have a plastic surgeon working on him today. I talked to the guy, and he's about forty something and looks like he knows the ropes. Said he volunteered for awhile in the Gulf War. I guess that'd iron out some beginners' wrinkles.

"Anyway, he said he was going to take some bone out of Huey's pelvic area to rebuild the missing parts of his jaw and screw plates on the rest. He showed me one of the plates he uses. It was a quarter inch wide sliver of stainless, about an inch long. It had tapered holes in it so the screw heads would be flush."

I nodded. "Grim."

"Shit, Paul, it's not that bad. He'll be up and around in a matter of weeks."

He paused, looking squarely at me. "Don't worry, I'm not going to bore you with a 'casualties I have seen' account."

"I wasn't thinking that, Smoke," I said.

We remained silent for a moment.

"Did you tell him about the alibi?" I asked.

"Nope. He was too bonked out on morphine, but I'm not leaving his side until I can. It's only a matter of time before the fucking FBI is in here. The local cops have already interviewed me concerning the gun shot wound. I told them, but when Gibson and Pfeffer get the chance, they'll be breaking down my motel door."

A sense of hopelessness descended on me. I had this feeling that everything in my life was about to turn to shit. No home, no Lana, no Ryback, no pension, no Social Security, and possibly no balls...they'd take those too.

Smoke studied me.

"You know, Paul, these things go away faster than you can imagine. I give the fan two to three weeks to spin free of shit. It takes damn good lawyers to keep a fire sizzling along month after month...that's how they earn their bread. A pair of divorce lawyers in cahoots can keep an unhappy couple in turmoil for as long as it takes to empty their meager treasuries."

"I know what you mean," I said. "That's the stressful part of reporting. Bread goes stale in three days. I've got to remember that, I guess. Thanks."

"You get my stuff?" Smoke asked.

"All but your .243, Smoke. In the confusion I think it was left in the mine shaft when we blew it."

He didn't buy that for a moment.

"Nice hiding spot," he said, grinning. "Those guys are sharp."

"Where are you staying?"

"A clean little courtyard motel of 50s vintage," he said. "I hate modern motels."

"You have a name and maybe a phone number for your shit hole in paradise?"

Smoke leaned forward and pulled a brick sized billfold out from his back pocket and handed me a Motel Gardens card with address and phone number.
"You staying on?" he asked.
"For tonight."
"Good."
"How you getting around?"
"Budget rental. They gave me a Camry." He shook his head woefully. If he wasn't in his beloved pickup with his beloved .243 he wasn't content.

I sat with Smoke for another hour and filled him in on every detail since he was flown out. His favorite part was the story of my abusing the yuppies.
In the hospital's lobby I made two calls, one to reserve a room next to Smoke's, and the second to Billy O'Connor of The Idaho Banner, Boise major newspaper. Billy had worked with me at the Confluence Tribune for a few years before moving up in the world. He was a genius at research and investigation, and I liked him.
It was already two o'clock when I left the hospital and headed over to the Banner. I was starved and snagged a burger from a mom'n pop's on the way. It was gone by the time I pulled up in front of the old established brick front of the Banner building. Giant sycamores shaded the paper's parking lot off the side. The place smelled of tradition and old money. I had a pang of jealousy at Billy's success. Had I been as fortunate, I'd still be working. Maybe.
The interior of the building was what one would expect: rich oak doors and trim, marble floors, offices with frosted glass windows with names painted in black and gold, and wooden desks heavy with authority and history.
Billy's office was pointed out to me, and I walked a long hall to his door, which was on the right, second from the end.

I went on in.

His desk was pushed up against a tall, deeply framed window that looked into the limbs of the sycamores. He was working in front of a twenty inch flat monitor. He swiveled around in his wheeled oak desk chair to greet me.

"Un-slumming, Paul?" he asked, taking my hand in both of his. "Great to see you."

"Likewise, I said. "But I need you to run a name for me Billy."

He motioned for me to take a seat in a leather captain's chair against the wainscoting beside his desk, and sat back down.

"So much for the chitchat, huh?" he asked. "Do I get an exclusive on that drug bust you participated in, then? Is that what you're offering?"

I was amazed.

"How does everyone know about that?" I said. "On the way here some yuppie reporters were trying to get in there to interview our pesky redskin brothers."

"I know, Paul. If you'll recall, I am Billy, the one and only Billy the Wonder Boy."

"At age, what? Sixty three? You're still the boy?"

"Sixty one. But is that what you're offering?"

I blew through my lips, shaking my head. Then, "OK, Billy, better you than anyone else I know."

"I won't release a thing until you say to," he offered. "Though it violates my moral well being to do so."

"OK, then," I said with misgivings.

He leaned back, reached out his left hand and hit a key that cleared the screen, leaving it a blank window of blue.

"What is it you want?" He didn't need a notepad; he had a nearly perfect photographic memory.

I began. "In 1982 Cano Franzani and Salas Valladores were arrested in Dillon, Montana, on two counts of arson-homicide, one in Provo and one in Ogden, Utah. They were tried and convicted in Ogden."

I spelled out the names for him. He was nodding, hands clasped across his small beer belly.

"I want to know who paid for their defense and what firm their lawyer was working for."

Billy sat up straight in his chair. "That *it*? That's all you want, Paul? You could have done that yourself." He shook his head. "Man, you don't owe me an exclusive to do that for you."

He spun around and unleashed his pale, manicured fingers to begin their lightening fast dance on the keyboard. He tapped into archival and newspaper research sites I had only *heard* of in my long career. They flashed momentarily onto his screen only to be passed by quickly as he went in deeper and deeper.

After about five minutes, he let out a "Bingo!" hit a key, and the HP Laser printer on a stand against the opposite wall spit out two sheets of paper. He spun around, grabbed them, and handed them to me with a self-satisfied smile.

I took the two pages.

The first sheet was a synopsis of the case as defended by Rice Litteneker of Litteneker and Gentry. He was representing a certain Bahamondes Valladores, father of one of the defendants, Salas Valladores.

Salas's father? I felt let down. It was so reasonable.

The second sheet, however, was what nearly stopped my heart. I leaned my head back against the plaster wall.

"Oh my fucking ass," I moaned. "Oh shit."

Billy sat bolt upright.

"What?"

He looked down at the page I was holding, then spun back to his computer and went to work.

Chapter
Thirty

Billy and I left the Banner two hours later. He took me to an Irish Pub near the center of town. On the inside, the pub didn't look too much different than his newspaper's building or MacAvity's Pub.

The owner knew Billy well and led us up a flight of stairs, past an ornate bar, and around a corner to a glowing fireplace. Arranged around a coffee table directly in front of the fireplace were two deep leather chairs and a leather couch. The bartender brought a round tray carrying two Guinnesses, a bottle of Green Spot Irish Whiskey, and two glasses.

He put these on the table in front of us and placed next to them a narrow menu he pulled from under his apron towel. He went back to the bar. The owner, who looked in his fifties and was ruddy from a life of booze, opened the whiskey and filled the shot glasses. He gave Billy a pat on the shoulder as he left, saying, "Drink up lads."

I took up the beer and began to tell Billy every single detail of the drug bust, and he listened without interrupting. I told him nothing about the attack on the camp, and when I was done, I refilled my shot glass for the third time and sat back.

But Billy would have none of it.

He studied me carefully, swirling his Guinness in its glass.

"You know, Paul, you're holding out on me. What you've told me does not justify your reaction to the research

I've so generously and probably unethically provided for you."

I squirmed.

"I have kept my part of the bargain we struck this afternoon, but you have not been forthcoming." He watched my every move. "However, you have given me the exclusive on the drug bust, and that's what I bargained for, so I'm willing to let it go."

He leaned sideways and signaled for the bartender. When he arrived, Billy said we'd like two corned beef and potato soups with rolls, and then turned back to me.

"You know, ol' chum, if I want to do even a little more digging, say into this guy Bahamondes, I'll eventually discover whatever it is you're afraid to tell me, right?" he asked.

And that was exactly the terrible mistake I had made. I had come to one of the best investigative reporters in the western United States without thinking it through. Thank God he was honest, and he was my friend.

I sighed. "Right."

"So what do you want me to do?" He smiled almost sympathetically.

"I don't know, Billy," I admitted. "Let me sort some of this out. I'm not going to stiff you, OK? I promise that you will come to understand and eventually be content with everything I can give you. It won't go stale, and I will keep you informed. That's the best I can do."

He nodded. "OK."

I still couldn't get Lana on the phone. I used the motel's phone and left another message around eight o'clock, leaving my room's phone number on Ann's machine. I wasn't too surprised they were out because San Francisco is one of the premier dining cities of the world, and no one eats before nine.

I heard Smoke unlock his room door just before ten. I struggled to my feet and went out and knocked.

"Come in, Paul. It's open," he said from inside.

He was sitting on the edge of the bed, tiredly pulling his boots off. He had a smoke in his mouth and squinted up at me as I took a seat at the small round table by the window curtains.

"How is he?" I asked.

"Swollen shut, I'd say. His face is drum tight from the swelling, black as a berry, and eyes just slits. Man, he looks terrible," he said pushing he boots to the side. "He's conscious, now, but loopy as all get out."

"Were you able to talk to him?"

"Yup. I said, 'You shot yourself by accident showing us your new Ruger Mark III.' I told him the same thing three times. He started making writing motions, so I slid my pen between his fingers and he wrote on the bed sheets, 'I get it. Shut up.'"

I busted out laughing.

Smoke started laughing as well. He got up, opened the room's tiny refrigerator and took two Millers out, handing one to me.

"To Huey," he said, twisting his open.

We sat, drank the cold beer, and Smoke sat back on the bed. We relaxed for a moment in silence.

"I have an old newspaper friend who did some research for us today, Smoke," I began, setting my beer on the table, "and I have some bad news for you."

He said nothing, leaned his head back on his piled pillows and grew still.

"That wasn't Rojas Huey killed," I said. "It was Salas Valladores' father. I saw a printout of his picture."

Just like that.

Smoke surprised me by grinning his evil grin.

"Well ain't Rojas the clever shit," he said. "I'll be fucking go to hell." He was shaking his head. "Damn, this is some really bad-ass news, Paul."

"I know."

I took my beer back up and drank deeply. "Turns out we might be wrong about Rojas. Bahamondes is known as 'Baha.' He was a realtor for Spreiter Realty in Missoula and financed Salas and Cano's defense."

"Which means he has to know Rojas," he said, looking back at me.

"Yup. And the attorney, a Rice Litteneker, is still in the picture. He never did represent Baha directly; he was the attorney for Spreiter Realty. And still is, only it's not called that anymore. It's a multi-state company called Western Summits Investment Group. It's still headquartered in Missoula but has branches in North Dakota, Wyoming, Nevada, and Colorado. It's worth millions, and Baha is one of its five vice presidents."

Smoke mulled this over.

"Well, Paul, I guess you know now who paid for the defense. You kinda popped our cherry, though, didn't you?" he said.

"But Billy printed out promo pictures of this guy Spreiter, Clifford Spreiter, and the five VPs. I asked for them because I want to show them to Charlie, Joy Chu, Hammersmith, MacAvity, Huey and you. Wanna see them?" I asked. I put my drink down and got ready to stand.

"Damn straight," Smoke said, finishing his beer and getting up for another.

I went to my room, pulled the promo from the top of the pile of printouts Billy had stuffed into a folder for me, and came back.

I handed the seven pages to Smoke. The top sheet had a large photo of Clifford Spreiter with a list of his accomplishments. The next sheet was the company's mission statement followed by a detailed report touting the fortune to be made by investing in Western Summits Investment Group. Next, there were five more pages, each with a photograph, short biography, and individual mission statement for each of the five VPs. Bahamondes Valladores' sheet was the first of these.

"That's him, all right," Smoke said, tapping Baha's face with an index finger. "Right down to that skinny pimp beard of his."

"Recognize anyone else?" I asked, resuming my seat at the table.

"Nope. Should I?"

"Well, I was hoping Rojas was one of these guys," I said.

"Might be, I don't know," Smoke said. "That was a long time ago, and people change. Plus, I'm not sure I've ever met the guy anyway." He lit another cigarillo. "Hammer would know."

The phone rang in my room.

"Later," I said, heading out the door.

"Make it morning," Smoke called after me.

I grabbed the phone before Lana hung up.

"So, you guys are famous," she said as soon as I put the phone to my ear.

"Hi, Sweetie, glad you called, I've missed you, sure can't wait until you come home, and what are you talking about?" I said.

She laughed. "I deserved that," she said. "Would you like me to read a few of the various headlines I copied down? I got them all from a news stand on Mission Street."

"Sure."

"OK then, and I quote, *Three Killed in Wilderness Shoot-Out. Vigilantes Attack Drug Shipment. Locals Go On*

Rampage, Kill Three. Locals Help Camas Tribe in Drug Bust. Ryback Takes Revenge on Drug Traffickers. Elderly Citizens Take Law into Own Hands. Vietnam Vets in Shootout With Traffickers. Truckload of Dead Carried From Bitterroots. Locals Give Meth Traffickers Warning. Charges Against Vigilantes Considered."

"Wow!" I said, glancing at my reflection in the wall mirror. "Sounds pretty grim. I wouldn't want to mess with those local elderly citizen vigilante vets, that's for sure."

She gave a light laugh. Then asked in a soft voice, "You OK?"

"I'm fine," I said. "A bit tipsy from spending the evening with Billy O'Connor, though."

"The Wonder Boy?"

"The same. We drank some very rare Irish whisky at a pub he frequents. The place is almost identical to Butte's only it has a fireplace."

"Damn, I miss all the fun," she said, a note of sarcasm thrown in.

"You guys having fun?" I asked.

Lana hesitated. "I picked up a surprise for us yesterday," she said.

"What is it?" I was watching my own expressions in the mirror.

"It's a surprise, get it? We signed up for a wine tour and joined six other people to van around in the Santa Cruz Mountains hitting a whole bunch of these tiny, farm-type wine operations. Some of them had only one cask and one wine to offer. It was a blast!"

"So you bought us a farm?" I asked, joking of course.

"Nope. You'll see when we get back." She paused. "When should that be?"

"I don't know. Soon I hope. Has Ruthie asked Hammersmith?"

"He's not answering his phone. She phoned the pub and they keep missing each other. Tonight she asked Sheila to make sure he calls her. He's only called once, and that was only to say he missed her, was bored, and hated to cook."

I had brought my beer with me from Smoke's room and took a pull.

"Well, both he and MacAvity have been kept abreast of what's been happening," I said, "but they're doing it over encrypted satellite phones. Tell Ruthie he can't tell her, nor can I tell you anything over our home phones since they're tapped."

"He still could from a pay phone in Magnet," she said.

"Where'd he call from before?"

"His home. But he didn't tell us a thing."

I considered this.

"Well, he can tell you if you can return or not."

"I understand that, Paul. And I hope he does tomorrow. I want to come home."

"I agree. I want you to too. I have heaps to tell you. But I'm going to assume our house is bugged, so I'll tell you out on a hill or something."

She giggled. "I know what you have in mind."

"No, no," I said. "Well, maybe." Then, "Actually, that's kind of a fun idea, sweetie. Remember..."

"That's enough," she interrupted. "I'll phone you tomorrow night. Where are you going to be?"

"Home sweet home," I said.

I got to my feet and we said our goodbyes.

I had just hung up and was headed to the bathroom when the phone rang again. I came back and lifted the receiver.

"Give me one lead I can follow, Paul, so I can get the fuck to sleep," Billy slurred, before I could speak.

I considered this for some time and listening to random cars pass outside in the darkness.

Then, tentatively, "OK, Billy, I'll give you something to follow if you promise not to call me again tonight."

"Yes?"

"See if you can figure out if Bahamondes and a guy named Rojas Franzani know each other. Then see if the connection is in trafficking narcotics."

Billy let out a terrific belly laugh.

"I love you, you fucking shit," he said. "Why couldn't you have told me this earlier?"

"Because you're too easy, hot shot," I said. "Besides, I'm jealous of your office furniture."

He thought this over. Decided I was joking.

"OK, Paul."

I hung up and headed for the bathroom.

Time to turn in.

Chapter Thirty-One

After Smoke and I had excellent omelet breakfasts at a small brick cafe filled with college students, I followed him to Saint Luke's.

Smoke led me to Huey's room, but the room was empty. A floor nurse told us he was having a drain installed, but we could visit him in a couple hours when he came back.

I looked at my watch. It was already pushing nine o'clock and Ryback was six hours north.

I turned to Smoke, "You going to stay on?"

"Yup," he said. "The doc says he should be ready to be moved to Confluence General in three days. I think I might ride along."

"They're going to take him up that windy-ass road?"

Smoke shook his head. "His buddies at Geotz Air Service are going to give him a free ride as soon as he can handle it. Saint Luke's has a helipad on the roof right over our heads."

"That's very cool," I said.

"Yup. Geotz and Huey were in flight school together."

I nodded. "Small world, isn't it?"

"Especially if you are a helicopter vet and live in Idaho," Smoke said. "So you staying?"

I shook my head. "I think I should get Billy's photos and research up home. With Rojas still out there, who knows what will happen?"

Smoke thought this over.

"Well, I can see that MacAvity and Hammer need to know all this, but what are you going to tell Charlie?"

I'd been thinking about that all morning.

"I'm going to tell him about Huey's 'accident.'" I marked the air with quotes. "And that Billy has found out who financed Salas and Cano's defenses."

Smoke nodded.

"And then I'm going to point out that there must be some kind of link between Baha and Rojas since their sons ran together. He doesn't need to know we killed Baha." I paused.

"You've been thinking again, Paul. Does it hurt?"

I ignored him.

Smoke said, "Don't contact Charlie, Paul. So a realtor's son becomes a criminal and runs around with the son of a drug trafficker. That doesn't make him involved in anything. I think you're making a leap here."

He paused. "We've given them the biggest drug busts in Idaho's history. It's time for us to drop under the radar. Keep Charlie, the FBI, and the DEA out of this. Keep them out of Ryback."

I said, "You're speaking from Charlie's point of view, right? I mean, you and I know that Rojas is involved. He tried to murder us for taking out a drug shipment."

"Right. But if Charlie is going to come to that conclusion, it will be without our help. We already know all this, and how we came about that information can't be revealed to anyone, much less the authorities. Even Charlie."

I saw his point.

I sat on the foot of Huey's bed. "That's why it's important for Rojas to be one of the V.P.s," I said.

"He won't be," Smoke said, flatly. "He's been in Cambodia for the past thirty some years. They don't make you a Vice President of a real estate investment group the instant you're smuggled back into the country, Paul. Rojas has to remain underground for the rest of his life."

"Unless he can wipe the slate clean," I said.

"Too late for that, pardner," Smoke pointed out. "He already tried that, and we thanked him for his efforts by turning the goods over to the authorities."

I nodded. "So, the fact that Baha is with Western Summits doesn't mean the investment group is involved with him?

"That's what I'm thinking," Smoke said. "But it still stands to reason there's a good chance they are. And we're also pretty certain Bahamondes and Rojas are in it together." He looked at me. "What else?"

"I want to ask Hammersmith if he recognizes Rojas among the Western Summits Investment Group photos. If he doesn't, I don't know what to think. If he does, well, I guess we'll know Western Summits is laundering international drug money and trafficking with Rojas's help."

Smoke shook his head. "Never happen, Paul. Rojas isn't in those photos. Like I said. We know Baha was dirty. We know from Huey that Rojas is dirty. We can imply that they are in cahoots. That Western Summits is involved is only conjecture."

"I'm worried about Billy, though," I said.

"Why?"

"I asked him to see what the connection between Bahamondes and Rojas is. And, thanks to Micha's torturing Cano, we know Rojas is back in the States. But I'm afraid he'll find out that Baha is missing."

We left the room and walked back to the elevator for the lobby. Smoke pushed the button, then faced me.

"Do you think for a moment, Paul, that a bunch of drug runners are going to go to the police and report that four of their hit men have gone missing?"

He waited for my answer.

"Oh," I managed.

We rode down to the lobby and stepped out. Smoke walked me to the large glass doors and stopped and shook my hand.

"I'll see you in a few days," he said. And then, "I assume you're going to tell everything to Lana, right?"

I nodded.

"It's your choice, Paul." He opened the door for me. "But I'm not going to tell anyone, and I'm hoping you won't bring anyone else in on this."

"Look, Smoke," I said, facing him, "I understand, OK? Billy has provided us with information the FBI hasn't given up to us, even if they had it. And no one but Billy can help us. I'm not going to tell him about the attack on the cabin. There's no need to."

He waited.

"But I'm not going to carry around secrets in my own house. Lana is my wife, and if I didn't trust her one-hundred percent, I wouldn't have married her," I said.

"Are we having an argument here?" Smoke said.

"I'm not arguing."

"But you aren't listening, Paul. I didn't imply that Lana is untrustworthy or that you shouldn't tell her. I asked, number one, *if* you were going to tell her because I wanted to know, and two, I wanted to be assured you weren't planning on bringing anyone else in. You're the one that said you were concerned about Billy, not me."

I was suddenly feeling extremely defensive.

Finally I said, "I was listening. But let me tell you something, Smoke. You don't need to remind me of something so blatantly obvious. I'm not an idiot. You don't need to lecture me. In fact, I think it's about time you gave me a bit more credit."

"So we are having an argument."

"No," I said. "We're reaching an understanding that's long overdue."

Smoke looked at me like I had just farted in church.

"That's a nice 'fuck you, Smoke.'"

He grinned. Then, "But I guess we're all under stress, and we don't need this conversation."

He put an arm around my shoulders.

"Come on. I'll walk you to your truck."

We pushed open the the heavy sheet glass doors and went out and down a grass parking island to where I'd left the Tundra.

I climbed in and rolled the side window down.

"You have Oscar's satellite phone number?"

He took out his wallet and pulled free a corner torn from a sheet of paper.

"Right here," he said. "What d'ya have in mind?"

I took a ball-point down from the visor and a tablet from the glove box and wrote the number down.

"I've got to call Billie and warn him not to call my house and leave a message over our tapped lines. I'll use a land line for that."

"Whew! Good call," Smoke said.

"Then I want to use the satellite phone to give MacAvity my ETA so Hammersmith can be there when I arrive. I'll bring them up to date before I do anything else."

I put the pen back, tore the page with the number on it from the notebook, shoved it in my shirt pocket, and put the note book back.

I remembered something. "Where do you want me to drop off your stuff?"

"You'll be returning MacAvity's equipment, right?" Smoke asked, lighting up a cigarillo, something he couldn't do in the hospital.

I nodded.

"Leave my gear with him, too, OK?"

I started the engine and reached over to shake Smoke's hand.

"Have a good flight, Smoke."

He took my hand in his powerful grip and grinned.

"See you in three days, pardner," he said. "I'll call you so you can pick me up at the Confluence Hospital."

I backed out and was on my way.

Chapter
Thirty-Two

I broke free of the clouds north of Brunsfeld just before dropping down to the Salmon River. The sun streamed in through my back window, and tamaracks, dogwoods and alders flared in brilliant reds and yellows on the sides of the surrounding mountains. The ridges overhead were capped with a dusting of snow, and here, on the river's edge, the air had warmed and smelled sweet with rain. I drove the rest of the way home with the side windows down and enjoyed the cool air buffeting me, anxious to reach the sweep of the Bench and its rolling fields.

I pulled into Ryback at three-fifteen and drove directly to MacAvity's. Hammersmith's GMC was parked out front, so I knew that Butte had reached him.

I parked at the back near the basement door, killed the engine, and walked around to the front with my handful of Billy's research.

Butte and Hammersmith were in a rear booth with drinks. Butte stood as I entered, and Eric looked around at me from the corner of the booth.

"Welcome home, Deer Slayer," Butte said, motioning me to sit where he had been. He was dressed in his Wyatt Erp finery, and the sight of him made me feel good.

Hammersmith reached across the table and shook my hand.

"Damn good job you guys did," he said. "You'd make a fine scout in the SEALs, Paul. Sharp as a tack."

"Thanks, Eric. It was interesting."

Eric brought me a Wiser's ditch, put it in front me, pulled up a chair, and sat with his elbows on the table.

"Well," he began, "Longbeach and Oscar Redtail have us up to speed with everything on the Magruder, and we got off the phone with Smoke about a half hour ago."

He hesitated to watch for my reaction and got none.

"Smoke is a bit nervous about you contacting your reporter friend at the Boise Banner. I guess you know that."

I nodded. "You might say that I couldn't convince him it was OK," I said.

MacAvity said, "So explain it to us. We're not bone headed fighter pilots like Smoke."

I took a deep swallow of the smooth Canadian blend and reflected how glad I was to be back home in the safety and company of these two friends.

"Billy O'Connor worked with me at the Trib. for several years," I said. "He's the best investigative reporter there is, he's as honest as they get, and he can unravel things the DEA, FBI, CIA, INS, Interpol, and God Himself can only hope to."

They listened closely.

"To make a long story short," I began, "within only two hours he provided us with a link between Rice Litteneker, who defended Cano and Salas, and Salas's father, Bahamondes "Baha" Valladores. He also made the connection between Baha and Western Summits Investment Group in Missoula, which had financed the defense. Then, he produced a photo of Baha which revealed we hadn't killed Rojas as we had thought."

I took another swallow.

"You see what I'm driving at?" I asked. "He did that in a matter of hours, not days or weeks. And he shared the info, unlike law enforcement."

I reached down and took up the pile of paper and put it on the table on my left. I took up the top six sheets with the photos and bios and spread them out so they could see them.

Butte and Hammersmith handed them back and forth one by one. They studied the pictures carefully, then returned them to the table top.

I waited.

Hammersmith took a sip of his White Horse and looked up at me.

"So?"

For a moment, I thought he and Butte were dismissing the importance of all this. Then I realized they wanted me to go on.

"So you don't recognize any of these men?" I asked, knowing the answer from their lack of reactions.

"Nope," they said in unison.

I let out my breath.

"Well," I said. "As we've been told, it takes a heap of money to fund international drug trafficking, and Baha was working for a multimillion dollar outfit. Western Summits Investment group sits right in line between Alberta and the Magruder Corridor. And they have branches in North Dakota, Wyoming, Nevada and Colorado. It's a sweet setup for laundering money and trafficking narcotics."

They nodded their understanding.

Hammersmith tapped the table top with an index finger like he always did when he wanted to state a point.

"*If* they are laundering money and trafficking narcotics," he said. "Smoke mentioned that what's missing is proof that the men killed along with Baha were all financed and linked to Western Summits, right?"

I nodded.

MacAvity asked, "So what do you think this friend of yours, Billy, can do to help? That's why you brought him in, isn't it?"

For the second time that day, I felt myself grow defensive.

"Billy doesn't know that Baha and his buddies are dead, Butte. The only thing he knows is that Baha is Salas's father and works for Western Summits. But he's no fool, so I told him to see if there was a connection between Baha and a man named Rojas Franzani, and if that connection had anything to do with the drug shipment we busted."

"I like it, Hammer," MacAvity said.

"So do I."

Hammersmith took another sip and put his glass carefully back on the table before he spoke.

"If he links those two, how can we show Western Summits is involved?"

I shook my head. "I don't know."

Then, "But if Western Summits is involved, no matter what, Billy will find it out. I guarantee it."

Hammersmith picked up the picture of the realty's founder and president, Clifford Spreiter. He studied it a moment, then turned it so that it faced us.

"This is the link right here," he said. "This is our man."

"Smoke and I think so too," I said. "We want to show it to Huey when he gets his sight back."

"What for?"

"Well, if Spreiter is the same man Huey saw talking to Rojas at his West Bassac River Mission in Cambodia, we have our link."

He put the picture back on the pile. "I wouldn't be surprised."

Butte asked, "How's Billy contacting us?"

"He's going to phone my house and leave a message. I have to contact him."

They nodded.

"Let's call him now," Butte said suddenly.

He pushed back his chair, grabbed his drink, and headed for the stairs.

Hammersmith gave me a questioning look, took up his drink, slid out and followed Butte. I joined him.

"Aren't our phones still tapped?" I asked him as we climbed the stairs.

"Charlie picked up his satellite phone this morning. Said they stopped the taps the day after the drugs were seized. Seems that's all the FBI and DEA wanted." We stepped into Butte's living room. "Seems their show of concern for our safety was only to obtain our permissions for the taps."

Sitting on MacAvity's coffee table was a speaker phone. Apparently he had been using it enough to bring it in from the kitchen. He handed the phone to me.

I checked my watch. It was a quarter past four--five o'clock Boise time. Billy might just barely still be at his desk at the Banner. I took his card from my wallet and dialed his number, then laid the phone back down on its cradle. We listened to the phone ring on the other end. Almost immediately, Billy answered it.

"It's Paul."

"Glad you got my message," he said.

"I haven't been home yet," I told him. "I'm with two of my friends who helped set up the drug bust, Billy. They're sitting right here. You're on a speaker."

"Got it," he said. "Can I have you gentlemen's names?"

They gave them, and Hammersmith said, "We really appreciate the information you've gotten for us, Mr. O'Connor," he said. "It's been very helpful."

"Glad to hear it. Are you working with the authorities on this?" Billy wanted to know.

"No," Eric said. "We're just trying to determine the source of the shipment. Kinda on our own. Gives us something to do."

Billy laughed. "Yeah, right. OK. I'll tell you why I called, and you can do what you want with it."

We could hear some papers shuffling in the background. We waited and sipped our drinks. After nearly a minute, Billy came back on.

"This is extremely interesting shit you guys are into," he began.

Hammersmith and MacAvity gave each other worried glances.

"First of all, I looked into Western Summit's vice presidents' and the president's backgrounds. I hit a wall with Clifford Spreiter, the president, right?"

We heard more paper being moved around.

"The guy was a "Greenie," an Army Special Forces dude. A Green Beret in the mid 60s. His records were sealed by the D.O.D. and are inaccessible."

Billy chuckled.

"So I called a source, who will remain anonymous, who also was a Greenie in the 60s, and who also had his records sealed. In fact, he once tried to prove his military service to receive benefits and failed.

"Anyway, in 1954 he was involved in the CIA's Operation PBSUCCESS."

Hammersmith said, "I'm familiar with it," he said.

"Right." Billy went on, "Their job was to help overthrow the democratically elected, left-wing president of Guatemala, Jacobo Arbenz Guzman, and replace him with a military junta headed by a murderous Colonel Carlos Castillo Armas," he said. "Guzman had wanted to buy Guatemala's uncultivated land, eighty-two percent of which was owned by a U.S. company, United Fruit, and let it be homesteaded by the country's impoverished peasants. United Fruit went ape-shit, of course, and in that Joe McCarthy, cold-war mentality, the whole idea sounded too communist."

We waited. This was classic Billy O'Connor. He should have been a history professor.

"Anyway, my source said he knew Spreiter."

We all sat up with that.

Billy continued. "Spreiter was a greedy prick. A 'king rat.' He made bucks-deluxe keeping a small following of fellow pot heads provided with marijuana. This was well before the 60s, mind you. He was known as 'Spider,' get it? Spreiter--spider? Or," he said, "'Sea Spider,' as in C. Spreiter."

"Oh man!" Butte said aloud, shaking his head.

"That rings a bell with you cats, right?" Billy asked.

"You have no idea," Hammersmith put in.

"Yeah, I do have an idea," Billy said. "But let me tell you something else."

MacAvity had his forehead in his right palm and was massaging his temples.

Billy resumed, "I looked into Rojas, Paul," he said. "And while I was at it, Bahamondes Valladores."

He paused. "You'll love this. And by the way, you guys owe me some big time pay-back," he added. "So both Rojas and Baha grew up together in Monterrico, Guatemala, until they were sponsored at age eighteen for immigration to the U.S. by none other than the 'Spider' himself."

He laughed, "Don't you love it? So I run that by my Special Forces buddy, and he says that Rojas and Baha were the same two little twelve year old shits that were Spreiter's runners. And when they weren't doing that, they stole the platoon's equipment every chance they got. He said those kids were little fuckers, and would have been shot if it weren't for Spreiter."

We were silent, and Billy waited us out.

Finally, I said, "What can we do for you, Billy? This is terrific information you have given us."

He chuckled.

"I'm glad you came in yesterday, Paul. Been a long time, and I wish you lived closer so we could hang out and drink Irish whiskey more often."

We could hear his chair squeak as he leaned back.

"You men made a front page drug bust. Period. But I know, and you now know, who was behind it. What I don't know is what happened to Rojas after he dropped off the radar screen in 1968. Is he still alive, where is he, and how does he fit in with all this? You guys know, and I want to be told."

He waited a moment while that registered.

"Second, I want to know what you are planning to do with the information I've given you. And third, why you are working covertly and with the help of the Camas Tribe."

He paused. "Can you do that for me?"

Hammersmith looked questioningly at Butte, who nodded.

"On our timer?" Eric asked.

"On your timer." Billy said. "This is how I make my living, gentlemen. I'll take care of you if you'll take care of me."

"OK, then," Hammersmith said. "We'll see about number two, but you're going to have to come up here to MacAvity's Pub. It isn't a phone thing. We'll discuss it then."

"Right. I'll be up late tomorrow evening," Billy said.

MacAvity said, "Come to the back door. We'll be upstairs in my private quarters. You can stay in my guest room."

"Done."

The phone went dead. MacAvity got to his feet and disconnected it from the speaker. He turned back to us and grinned.

"Bingo," he said. "Time to lock and load."

Hammersmith switched off the speaker and got back on the phone and called Oscar at the cabin. He gave Oscar a summary of what we had learned. It didn't take long. He disconnected with, "And when you get in, Charlie wants the satellite phone back."

He turned to face us without lifting his hand from the receiver. "You know, MacAvity, you need one of these satellite phones."

"Glad you see it my way," Butte agreed.

Eric said, "What do you think about Ruthie and Lana coming back?" he asked.

Butte thought this over. "I don't know," he said. "Do you think Spreiter would risk another encounter to accommodate Rojas?"

"What would he gain by it?" Eric asked.

Eric nodded, and went on, thinking out loud, "Seems to me Rojas has become a serious liability to the whole operation. His Cambodian supply lines are down. He failed trying to get your evidence on him back, which resulted in the entire package getting turned over to the DEA. His son is in the hands of the FBI, who are undoubtedly still interrogating him, hoping he'll plea bargain. They're out two and a half million for a drug shipment which they now know, from the press, is in Charlie's hands. And they lost a vice president, the vice president's son, and six other men. I'm not even counting the Canadian contractors."

He paused, stood and went to the liquor cabinet. He continued, his back to us as he got out the White Horse.

"He's bungled the whole thing from the very beginning. Ever since he realized Huey recognized him at his West Bassac River Mission he's been making bad choices. I'm surprised Spreiter hasn't killed him."

"What should he have done, you think?" I asked.

Hammersmith answered this, the phone still in his hand, "He should have shut down his two missions, dropped out of sight until things blew over, and then started up again at new locations with a new cover," he said.

Butte came over, put a drink in his hand, then joined me back at the table.

"I think," Butte began, "that Ruthie and Lana will be fine coming home. I don't think Spreiter will let Rojas do anything but keep his cars washed and waxed. He'll be too busy mending his fences and explaining Baha's disappearance to his investors."

"OK, then," Hammersmith said.

Chapter
Thirty-Three

Hammersmith placed the call to Ann's home. He was brief and explained to Ruthie that the coast was clear, and they could come home anytime they wanted.

There was a long pause which I assumed was Ruthie discussing it with Lana, and then Hammersmith said, "Yeah, he's here. I'll tell him."

Then, "When? Good. Love you," and he hung up.

He turned back to us. "Lana gives her love, Paul, and they are going to try to get on tomorrow's eleven-thirty flight. They'll call back."

"They just can't stay away from you hunks, can they?" Butte said. He reached for the phone, called Sheila to come in early, then went down the stairs to the bar.

"How are you doing, Paul?" Hammersmith asked, turning to look at me.

"I'm OK. It was certainly a learning experience, Eric," I said.

He studied me.

"I hope you didn't mind our asking about Billy."

"I understand," I said. I drank the water melted out in the bottom of my glass. Hammersmith got up and returned with the bottle of Wisers and refreshed both our glasses with it.

"You called it right, getting Billy involved. He's a gold mine."

I nodded, just as Butte returned.

"Come into the kitchen," he told us. "I'm going to rustle up your last bachelor dinners."

He went to the refrigerator. We came in behind him and sat at the long table.

"How's tenderloins, mashed potatoes and tossed green salad sound?" He didn't wait for the answer and added, "You're doing the mashed potatoes, Paul." He lifted four russets from a zinc lined drawer and placed them on a cutting board with a peeler and sharp knife.

I got to my feet and went over with my glass.

The phone rang and Hammersmith went back into the living room and answered it.

Butte turned on the grill to heat and began rubbing garlic and pepper into three one pound tenderloins.

"Leaps and Jables were at the bar," he said. "They told me to congratulate you on the drug bust. You and Smoke are regular Clint Eastwoods around town, aren't you?" he grinned.

We often helped ourselves in the pub if Butte stepped out for a minute. Leaps and Jables, like the rest of us, would leave money on the bar when they left. No problem.

Hammersmith came back in.

"It's a go for tomorrow morning...." The phone rang before he finished. "What is this, Ma Bell?"

He went back out again.

"You heard from Joy Chu or the FBI twins?" I asked Butte.

He shook his head. "The feebs have vanished, but Joy called to say that she and Charlie had a long talk. She also talked with Oscar and Josiah on the satellite phone."

He brought out a head of cabbage and iceberg lettuce and began cutting. He continued. "Anyway, you and Smoke have been classified as volunteer observers. She's grateful that you pistol packing vigilantes never dropped the hammer on any of those guys yourselves. Saved the Agency a ton of paperwork."

They obviously hadn't and wouldn't hear what happened at the cabin.

Eric returned again.

"Your phone next time, Paul," he said, dropping into his seat. "That was Smoke. St. Luke's is releasing Huey tomorrow at noon to be transported to Confluence Hospital, but he says Huey wants to be brought back to Ryback."

He took a large swallow of his Wisers.

"This is pretty good, Paul," he said, raising his glass to me. "A good break from White Horse."

I put the peeled and cubed potatoes in a pot of water Butte had set out for me, and he moved it over to a lit burner.

"So I told Smoke to have the chopper land in the pasture between the house and the road at my place. Huey's going to stay in that huge childhood room of Ann's. Give me an excuse to dust it and let some air in."

He grinned, adding, "I hope he doesn't mind sleeping with all her dolls along the window sill and a lamp shaped like Little Bo Peep."

"When will they be landing?" Butte asked.

"Two thirty, three. They want the helicopter back to Schumacher Meadows before dark."

Butte speared one of the potato chucks with a knife point. Satisfied, he slapped the steaks on the grill and switched on the hood fan. The fan was on the roof of the building and could hardly be heard, unlike mine at home, which sounded like a 747 warming up.

After we ate, we went down the back stairs with Hammersmith to see him off and to load Huey's stuff from the Tundra into the back of Eric's GMC. Once he was on his way, we carried Butte's and Smoke's stuff down into the basement vault room. Then I headed for home as well.

Driving the four blocks home, I wondered why we hadn't discussed what to do about Rojas. It seemed odd to not have mentioned him at all. But then, we didn't know where he was, and until Smoke got back, there was no point in discussing it anyway. For dishing out a life of misery to Huey, and recently being responsible for the destruction of Huey's farm and for him getting shot in the face, I was certain that Eric and Butte were going to make Rojas pay with his life. I guessed Spreiter's days were numbered too, though I doubted they would kill him. But one could never tell with these two old war horses.

The last thing Butte had said to me before I left the pub was that my place had been staked out by a dozen reporters. There were still two of them left, determined to talk to me. As I rounded the corner I saw he was right.

Parked across the street under the security lights at the elevators was a white Inland News van with a satellite dish on the roof. As soon as I parked, they opened their doors and came across the street to intercept me. I headed through the dark from the barn to my back gate, and they reached me just as I was about to push through into the back yard.

They were a two man team, one with the video camera, and another with a mike. They both wore jeans and simple jackets.

"Mr. O'Shea?" the interviewer asked.

I stopped. "That's me."

"Would you be willing to answer some questions about the Magruder drug seizure?" he asked, moving the mike within inches of my face. The camera's light came on at that moment, blinding me temporarily in its intensely white light.

"Inland News is a Spokane TV station, right?" I asked. Lana and I didn't use our TV for anything other than watching movies.

"Yes," he said. "You were one of the men who made the bust, isn't that right?"

"Do you know who Billy O'Connor is?" I asked.

He hesitated, then signaled his cameraman to stop filming for a moment.

"You've already talked to O'Connor?" he asked.

I nodded.

"And he has an exclusive?"

"Yes."

He let out his breath. "And you are a retired newspaper man yourself, right?"

"Right."

He shook his head woefully. "Well, thanks anyway," he said. "And sorry for interrupting your return home."

The light switched off, and they started to leave.

"Wait a minute," I said. "Give me your card. If I think of anything I can toss your way, I'll be in touch."

He took a card from inside his jacket and handed it to me.

"Much obliged."

And they were gone.

I went through the gate with my first armload of stuff, and unlocked the back door. As I stepped inside I was greeted by a reek of eau de garbawge. I had forgotten to take out the compost before leaving with Charlie and Smoke, and the smell was intense. I left the back door open, went to do the same with the front door, and opened the kitchen windows to get some cross ventilation. I decided I would take out the compost with my next trip to the truck.

There were eighteen messages on my answering machine, and I scrolled through them. There was one from Charlie asking if I would call him as soon as I got in, but the rest were from reporters. The only reporter I planned on answering was Shapiro at the Confluence Tribune.

It took me fifteen minutes to empty the truck and scatter my gear over the living room floor, and then I phoned Charlie.

I got his dispatcher, as I expected I would, and she transferred me to his voice mail. I told him I was home, that I was picking up Lana tomorrow morning at 11:30, and that we would be at Hammersmith's by two o'clock to welcome Huey back. I told him Huey was flying in by helicopter and would be staying with Eric and Ruthie.

I hung up and took a long shower before flopping down on my pillows. I lay there, too tired to do anything more, and studied the familiar patterns the elevators' security lights made through my blinds on the bedroom ceiling and far wall.

I fell asleep wondering what Lana had gotten for us that she had kept secret. In a matter of hours I would know.

Chapter
Thirty-Four

I was having my morning oats and tea when Hammersmith called.

"Can you bring Ruthie home, Paul?" he asked. "The Lutheran church is mobilizing the town for a homecoming here at the ranch to honor you drug-busters."

"No problem. Charlie and the Camas Tribe been told about this?" I asked.

"I don't know. I'll notify them myself just to make certain. Charlie said he was coming down this morning anyway to pick up the satellite phone and to arrest you, so I'll just tell him to show up at two this afternoon."

Until five years ago the Confluence airport consisted of a hanger and a large Quonset hut that had glass walls at each end and served as the terminal. It was located south of town on the level top of a ridge above the Snake River. Our new terminal wasn't much larger than three classrooms pushed together, but it was nice. There were thirty seats in the waiting area, ten in the secured passenger area, restrooms, and a two station check-in counter to handle the four Alaskan Air flights each day. There was also an espresso cart by the water fountain.

The airstrip ran the length of the ridge, and the bush pilot types that flew the small turbo prop under-wing planes that served us tackled it in all kinds of weather, no matter what.

Ruthie and Lana were the second pair to descend from their plane. They came down steps that folded out with the door from the plane's side. But before they walked over to the terminal doors, Lana went to the hand-pulled baggage cart and opened the door of a pet carrier. She withdrew what looked like a black and white fox, half ears, half body, with short little legs. It was squirming with excitement, and she had to clutch it to her chest to keep it from breaking free and falling. She saw me in the window and managed a quick wave as they came over.

"I couldn't help it," Lana explained later as we were heading up the grade.

Ruthie nodded. "Isn't she darling, Paul?"

I had to agree. It had climbed up onto Lana's shoulders and had fallen asleep behind her neck against the head rest.

"We were at the Voss Ranch above Los Gatos on Skyline tasting their brilliant burgundy," Lana said, "and there was a wire enclosure by the barn filled with straw, and on the straw was a beautiful corgi with five pups all suckling away. The foreman, a guy named Lopez, said I could step over the fence and pet them if I wanted too. I was still there twenty minutes later when Ruthie and the others returned from sampling the wine. The foreman came over and said he'd give me one if I wanted."

"Is it some kind of mutt?" I asked.

"Not at all," Lana said as if I had insulted her treasure. "She's an eight week old border corgi. At least that's what I call her. Mr. Lopez's neighbor has a border collie that paid his lady corgi a visit one afternoon."

Making sure I understood this little dog's true value, she added, "Ollie's a descendent of ancient Celt herding dogs. Legend has it they were ridden by the wee fairies of Wales. They run like the wind and are considered one of the most attentive dogs there is."

"Ollie?"

Lana nodded. She was smitten by the bright-eyed little pooch.

We reached the Hammersmith's at one o'clock, and already there were over fifty people in the front yard and out in the pasture. Cars filled the barnyard and lined the long lane. Yellow tape had been strung on metal posts in a circle where the helicopter was to land, and the Lutherans, true to form, had set up their long tables and folding chairs on the grass under the three large locust trees in front of the house. One table was being arranged as a buffet, and two men at the house were taping helium balloons to the porch posts.

I saw that someone, probably Jake, had driven Smoke's truck to the farm and had it parked at the side of the house. There was an empty spot beside it, and seeing me, Don and Jake came off the porch and signaled for us to park there.

They opened both our doors and ushered us to the porch. Ollie rode on Lana's bent arm, a bit overwhelmed by the crowd. Suddenly people noticed we had arrived, stopped what they were doing, and clapped and hooted.

Eric came out on the porch with Charlie and gave Ruthie a long, tender hug.

"So now we're heroes," Charlie said, shaking my hand.

"Looks like it," I agreed.

We followed Eric into the cool, dark living room. I could see four women back in the kitchen preparing food. Ruthie and Jake went happily back to join them.

Lana and I sat down on the couch, and Charlie and Hammersmith settled back in overstuffed chairs. Ollie nestled in Lana's lap watching us closely.

Charlie took off his hat and placed it on his knee.

"Your Boise Banner buddy Billy is quite the soothe, isn't he?" he asked, proud of his alliteration.

"He's the best, Charlie."

He nodded. "So it all hinges on if we can show there is a direct connect between Rojas and Spreiter, am I right?"

"I guess so," I said. "Right now no one seems to know where Rojas is, and the only thing we do know, and that's word of mouth, is that Rojas and Bahamondes Valladores were childhood pals. Apparently they had been delivery boys for Spreiter's pot deals in Guatemala in the 50s."

"I understand that," Charlie said. "Eric has filled me in. But what do you think will provide a usable bit of evidence that they are all connected?"

Hammersmith answered, "What if Huey IDs Spreiter as the man he saw talking to Rojas in Cambodia?"

Charlie turned his hat around on his knee. "That would help, Eric, that's for sure," he said. "I'd also like to talk to Spreiter and this Bahamondes guy, but they're not in my jurisdiction, and I'm not comfortable bringing Joy Chu in on this just yet. Maybe Oscar could pull it off, though."

We thought this over.

Jake came from the kitchen with coffees for all of us and set the tray on the table. She scooted onto the couch with us and snuggled up with Lana and Ollie.

Lana reached for a cup, dodging Ollie's curious nose, and took a sip.

"You know," I said, "I'd like for Lana and me to take a road trip in the camper and train Ollie to be a good traveler and hiker." I added, "Plus, I could fill Lana in on what we're all talking about. We could drive to Montana, and while we're at it, we could drop in at Western Summits Investment Group and meet these guys."

Charlie whistled. "I don't like the sound of that," he said, shaking his head. "It's a good idea--but man!"

Lana said. "People must drop in all the time, Charlie. They don't need to know who we are or where we're from--we'll just meet them, get some information, maybe be given a tour, who knows?" She paused. "We'll pretend we're rich, mildly interested investors from California who saw his building and just dropped in."

Before Charlie could answer, a great din of car horns sounded from out on the road. We went onto the porch to see what all the commotion was about.

Coming up the road from Rattlesnake Grade was a long line of cars and pickups. Their lights were on, they were blasting their horns, and the backs of the trucks were filled with children and people in lawn chairs holding brightly colored streamers that fluttered behind them. It looked like the entire Camas Tribe was arriving as if they had won the state basketball championship. It was exhilarating to see.

They parked in the grass along the shoulder of the road and scrambled out. They formed a line that stretch nearly a hundred yards back and began walking single file up the lane to the house. As they got closer our people began to clap and cheer and lined both sides of the lane so they could walk between them.

At the head of the line was Micha Wirestone. He was walking briskly, followed by Oscar, Josiah, Jerry and Peter. Some of the children, further back in the line, were skipping and clapping in rhythm. Every woman was carrying something in the way of food to be placed on the tables, and three of the men behind Peter were carrying packages of wrapped meat. Jerry, I noticed, had the bandage off his ear, probably Micha's doing, and the stitches looked like a column of black ants crossing where the top of his ear had been.

I looked at my watch. It was nearly two o'clock. Perfect timing.

We hurried down the porch steps and took places in line with the others. As the tribe entered the gamut, everything broke apart and we milled together, shaking hands, hugging, and laughing. The children dodged between us, many of whom had found Lana and Ollie and were swarming them. Lana went to the lawn and they followed. She sat on the grass with them and put Ollie down to run from one to the other for petting all around.

Soon the tables were heaped with food, and people were chatting in groups. The packages were deer meat from our hunt. Oscar told me to distribute them among the six of us, which included Hammersmith and MacAvity. We accepted the frozen paper bundles and carried them to the back door and down the stairs to the basement where Eric's freezers were kept.

Charlie and I went back up to take seats on the porch and wait for Huey and Smoke's arrival. The festivities filled the yard in front of us and extended around to the back and to the barn, and more people kept coming up the lane all the time.

I glanced at Charlie and could tell he was feeling just as happy as I was.

We heard the thup thup thup of the Bell helicopter before we saw its gleaming, black shape skimming over the fields towards us from the south. It did a fly by to show off for us, then slid easily inside the circle of yellow tape and cut the turbines. The blades slowly came to a stop, the side door opened, and there was Smoke crouching beside Huey's wheelchair, grinning.

The crowd went nuts with whistles, cheers and clapping. We all surged forwards to the edge of the tape. Oscar and I ducked under and went to help Smoke lift Huey and his chair down onto the grass. Smoke turned and shook the two pilots' hands before dropping down to join us. The turbines began winding up again as we reached Josiah, Jerry and Peter, who were holding the tape up for us to roll Huey under. The crowd parted and made way for us. At the steps Jerry and Peter grabbed hold and carried the chair, with Huey still in it, up onto the porch.

We turned around and everyone waved as the helicopter beat the grass flat and lifted back into the air. It tilted forward and did a high speed loop of the ranch that ended with a steep climb and a swooping dive, skimming across the pasture's surface. It wiggled its tail at us as it sped away, and everyone cheered wildly for the aerobatic display.

Smoke was grinning from ear to ear. "I love those guys," he said. "They've got class." Then, looking down at Huey he asked, "Know any of these assholes, Huey?"

Huey's eyes peeked out at us from purple slits and he gently shook his head. We laughed.

"You're lucky," Smoke said, pushing him inside and back to Ann's old room. As they passed Ruthie in the living room, she broke into tears at the sight of his swollen, discolored face half buried in bandages. Eric took her in his arms, and as Huey rolled past, he reached out and touched her on the back of her right hand. She cried all the harder for it.

We waited in the living room while Smoke helped Huey out of his clothing and into bed. When that was done, Smoke poked his head out the door and signaled we could come in. Ruthie went first, followed by Lana and Ollie, Jake and Hammersmith. At that moment, MacAvity and Sheila, who had just arrived, came into the house. Eric motioned for Butte to come along too. Smoke came out to make room and produced a pint of Black Velvet, which he put on the coffee table for us to share as we waited our turns to visit the wounded soldier.

Outside, the feasting had begun, and a fiddle and banjo began playing under one of the locust trees off to the side. Things settled into a burble of conversation punctuated by the sporadic squeals of the children at play. I leaned against the back wall of the living room and watched through the front window as a hero's table was set up on the porch. Jerry and Peter were helping.

It was nearly a half hour before Charlie, Smoke, Oscar, Josiah and I were able to go into the spacious bedroom. MacAvity and Hammersmith were seated by the window, and Huey was propped up against a mountain of pillows. He sagged with exhaustion.

Smoke whispered to me. "We need to make it quick, pardner," he said. "Our boy here looks like he's had enough for one day."

No one stirred. I unbuttoned my shirt enough to draw out Spreiter's photograph. It was folded in thirds, and I spread it out and held it for Huey to study.

"Is this the man you saw talking to Rojas?" I asked quietly.

He nodded carefully and hissed between his wired teeth, "Yesss, datss 'em."

He closed his eyes and leaned his head back.

Ruthie and Micha Wirestone suddenly appeared at the door.

"Everyone out, gentlemen," she said. "Enough is enough. We're in charge here now. Out."

And out we went.

As we reached the living room I heard Charlie say behind me, "Bingo!"

Chapter
Thirty-Five

Stretching almost the entire length of the porch were two of the eight foot tables that had been pushed together for the Magruder Marauder Bunch, a moniker people were now applying to us. Venison roast, sweet potatoes, pickled beets, fry bread and ice tea were served to us at our place of honor. Shortly Micha came out to join us and took the central seat. Hammersmith spotted Lonnie, our mayor, in the buffet line and yelled for him to come join us, too. He came over, all grins, and took the seat to Micha's right.

"Looks like a dangerous group up here," he said.

"It is now," Micha said, patting Lonnie's arm good naturedly.

I looked out over the growing crowd. Nearly two hundred had arrived, and from time to time others came strolling down the lane with lawn chairs, coolers, and dishes of food.

Sheila was sitting beside MacAvity on the other side of Lana. She suddenly remembered something and asked Butte, "What about that guy from the newspaper? Does he know we're out here? The pub's locked up."

"No," he said. "I'd completely forgotten about him." Then, "I'll give you fifty bucks if you go pick him up around eight and bring him here without sexually molesting him," he said.

"Keep your fifty," she said. "I need the sex."

We laughed.

One by one people finished eating, and MacAvity's wood pile was raided. A large fire was started in the middle of the pasture, and people dropped their paper plates on it. Mike, Eric's man, was alarmed by the fire and trotted back to the barn. Ten minutes later he returned with the tractor carrying an old, six foot diameter galvanized watering tank with a rusted out bottom. It had two foot high walls, and he dropped it by the fire. Men lifted it over the flames and set it in place as a fire ring. They congratulated Mike on his ingenuity, and he took the tractor back.

As it began to grow dark, people left to return later with more firewood, bales of straw to sit on, tents, musical instruments, bedrolls, and warmer clothing. By the time Sheila returned with Billy in tow, elk tents, dome tents, pup tents and bedrolls were set up randomly all over the pasture.

Off to the east side of the roaring bonfire an impromptu band was playing. There were three guitars, an accordion, base, two fiddles, a banjo, a mandolin, and nearly five skin drums. They sounded pretty good, particularly since the banjo and fiddle players, who had triggered the whole thing to begin with, just kept on playing tune after tune, and the rest of the musicians just tried to play along. The drummers kept up a hypnotic beat, and people were delighted. Old people were waltzing, youngsters were galloping around polka style, teens were imitating everyone, and the rest were doing their own thing.

Sheila finally arrived and delivered Billy over to where Smoke, Lana and I were standing.

"What the hell's this all about, Paul?" he asked.

"Billy O'Connor, Smoke Atkins," I said.

"We're being celebrated as the Magruder Marauders," Smoke said, shaking his hand, adding, "And you're an honorary member if Sheila hasn't stolen your member on the way over here."

Suddenly a tall, skinny guy was twirling around near the fire, punching his fists at the air, bellowing he'd take on anyone not too chicken shit to fight him. Everyone was laughing at him, which just made him rage the more. The music kept playing right over the ruckus he was creating.

Then Josiah walked up behind him, reached down, and pulled both his feet out from under him. He landed hard on his chest, and Josiah place a knee firmly on his neck and cuffed his hands behind him. He then invited the children to drag the guy around the pasture by his cowboy boots, and nearly fifteen kids came running to oblige. They sat one little girl on the man's back and pulled her around like he was a sleigh.

People howled with laughter as kids and their victim went zipping around, and the musicians switched into a rendition of "Rawhide." Josiah finally had to stop the children since they were preparing to drag the man into the fire.

Once uncuffed, the now sober drunk pumped Josiah's hand sobbing, "The little devils woulda killed me, Josiah! They woulda killed me!"

People applauded and laughed.

Josiah sat him on a bale, and walked back to the porch.

Billy turned to Smoke. "Ever read *Lord of the Flies*?" he asked.

"No need to," Smoke said. "We just watch these little shits at work. Same thing." Then, "Let's go find MacAvity and Hammersmith," he said. "They might let you drop in on one of our hunting accidents while you're here."

We went back up onto the porch. The tables had been cleared away, leaving the folding chairs where everyone except Micha and Lonnie were still seated. I looked around for Micha and saw him in a Kennedy rocker on the far side of the fire at the mouth of an elk tent. He had a flock of tiny children sitting around his feet, and by the way he was using his hands, I knew he was telling them a scary story.

I introduced Billy to everyone, and MacAvity and Hammersmith stood and invited him into the house. After they went from sight, I looked at Smoke questioningly. He just shrugged his shoulders, and pulled out a cigarillo to light.

They were behind Eric's closed study door for close to an hour. When the door finally opened, only Butte came out.

"You Magruder boys wanna come in a moment?" he asked, adding, "And you too, Lana. This concerns you as well."

Charlie came with us, and we filed in and stood along the book and picture lined walls.

Hammersmith was seated behind his large desk and Billy and MacAvity had the two leather seats.

Hammersmith motioned with his hand at Billy, "Well, we have two things here that will interest you," he said. "You want to repeat what you found out for us, Mr. O'Connor?"

Billy cleared his throat. "Well, I have a thirty year old picture of Rojas for you men to make copies of," he said. "He probably hasn't changed too much since then--hard to tell." He passed a black and white picture of Rojas that a war correspondent had taken. He was standing beside a tall, blond SEAL on a river bank, and they appeared to have just returned from a mission.

Rojas was a dirty, angry looking man who looked to be no more than five and a half feet tall. He had leather colored skin and a hawk nose that swept out from a tipped-back forehead. Unlike his son, Cano, or his pal Baha, who both looked Spanish, Rojas appeared to be a full-blooded Mayan Indian. But besides those striking features, his eyes were what held my attention. He truly looked like he wanted to cut the camera man's throat. The picture was very unsettling in that regard, and from everyone else's reactions, I saw that I was not alone in that feeling.

"And something else I found out for you guys," Billy said. "Spreiter looks to be about as squeaky clean as a politician up for election," he said. "He not only is an active player in the Missoula community and a wildly successful businessman, he is a huge contributor to four Christian missions. And that's not counting the two you say were abandoned in Cambodia."

Billy handed around another three sheets of paper.

"As you can see from these IRS figures I had a pal put together for me, he donates and gets large deductions for monies sent to missions in Hong Kong, Taipei, Antigua, and those two in Cambodia. Plus a place in the Cascades above Vancouver which is called Gospel Haven, whatever that is."

Charlie said, almost under his breath, "Seems like he has missions at major points along international trafficking corridors."

Oscar and Josiah both nodded in agreement. Then Oscar asked, "Just what part of this information do we share with Joy Chu and her people, Hammer?"

"That's what we need to discuss," Eric said. Then to Billy, he said, "I'd like to express our deepest appreciation for all the help you've been giving us, Mr. O'Connor. And we've told you everything we know about this. Now, can you share with us what you intend to do with this information?"

Billy nodded. "Sure thing." He racked together the pages and the photo we had returned to him and handed them across the desk to Hammersmith.

"First of all," he said. "I'm not going to write about the Magruder drug bust. That's ancient history now." He paused. "But I have a veteran reporter's nose for when something big is about to happen, and I suspect you guys are the ones that are going to cause it. In fact, I know you are. That's what I want to be in on."

He got to his feet. "I know you people want to discuss this in private, so I'll ask Sheila if she will drive me back to your place, MacAvity."

Butte nodded.

"But before I leave, there are two things I would like to say. Number one, there is a piece missing from your accounts of what happened up there on the Magruder." He looked at Charlie. "And if Sheriff Rand here is OK with that, then I am too."

He paused.

"And second, you folks are probably going to trigger one of the largest drug busts in the history of the Western United States. And *that*, and only that is what I want to write about."

MacAvity and Hammersmith both got to their feet. They shook Billy's hand and Hammersmith said, "You'll have everything you want, Mr. O'Connor. You can count on it."

As we began to file out behind Billy, Eric said, "Paul, can we have a word with you and Lana?"

We stopped and let Jerry and Peter past. Then came back into the room.

Eric looked at Lana and then me.

"We have discussed what you and Lana said about dropping in on Western Summits."

He paused to choose his words.

"Are you two serious about taking that kind of risk?" he asked.

Lana looked briefly and me and nodded. "I don't think there will be any risk," she said.

"Well, it isn't a bad idea." he said. "We'd like for you to go ahead and do it, if you still want to."

"Fine with me," Lana said.

I nodded.

Butte said, "Do you think you could leave tomorrow?"

Lana's eyebrows went up. "I think we can get ready by noon."

Then to me, "Don't you?"

I shrugged. "I suppose."

Chapter
Thirty-Six

It was six-thirty in the morning, and Lana was on the phone. I wondered who would be up that early and willing to take a call? Someone in New York?

Then I heard her at the computer, and soon the printer began to grind away.

I got up and went into her room to see what was going on. She was still in her PJs and had just finished cutting a business card from a sheet of tan card stock. She handed it to me, grinning.

I turned the card around and read, Burdock Ventures, with an e-mail address beneath it. Nothing more.

"What is this?" I asked.

"Our business card," she said. "We're a venture capital firm in San Francisco, and we're interested in going into something with greater potential now that property values have tanked. It's a vulture's market."

"Is this a real e-mail address?"

"It's Ann's," she said.

"You woke her up for this?"

Lana looked hard at me for a moment. "Ann's up and into her second cup of coffee by six, Paul. Give me some credit here."

Oops.

We had our clothing and food loaded into the camper and the camper loaded onto the Tundra by eight o'clock. I locked up the house, started the truck, and Lana settled in beside me with Ollie on her lap.

The summer months are the only time the four hour stretch between Confluence and Missoula sees traffic. But this was late fall, and as we got nearer to Lolo Pass we met less than twenty rigs, mostly semis, each hour. It's a beautiful drive, and even though the road is narrow and winding, it was enjoyable. Particularly with it this deserted.

We stopped under a stand of old growth cedars on the water's edge about half way up the Lochsa to have lunch. It was cold in the shade, so we took our folding chairs and plates of ham sandwiches and apple slices down to the small beach and ate in the sun.

Relaxing, I took the opportunity to tell the entire story of the past week while Ollie explored. I left out no details, and Lana listened in silence watching my face for tells, and only occasionally asked for clarification on points.

When I finally finished the last of it, Lana sat up straight, stretched and said, "So basically, what you're saying is that unlike Ann, Ruthie and I, who had a blast ripping around San Francisco and eating in elegant restaurants, you guys sat around in the cold woods doing nothing--except for the occasional gunfight. Right?"

"Pretty much," I said.

The afternoon slipped away and we decided, finally, to build a fire, open a bottle a shiraz and spend the night right where we were. Missoula could wait.

It was that evening that I saw my first cougar. Practically everyone I knew, including Lana, had seen these beautiful cats and had stories of how cougars had followed them or how they had followed cougars on the stock trails lacing Idaho's interior. But for me, this was a first.

The sun had just dropped behind the mountains across from us, and we were sitting by the beach fire eating rice and beans when Ollie started whining nervously at the far bank. We looked across the river to see a muscular cougar step from the undergrowth and glide gracefully down to the water's edge using the tops of smooth river stones as steps. It appeared larger than I expected a cougar to be-- possibly because of its long thick tail that trailed behind like a sweep oar.

He stopped briefly, looked us over, then lowered his head between his shoulders and lapped the water with a long pink tongue.

Lana reached down and stroked Ollie's head trying to soothe her. Ollie looked quickly up at her but resumed whining, staring hard at the huge cat.

When the cougar had his fill, he sat back with straightened front legs and watched us in the same way we were watching him. The end of his tail tapped the gravel off to one side thoughtfully, and he studied Ollie and us with beautiful golden eyes. Finally he turned, did a mighty leap ten or more feet up the bank, and vanished back into the timber.

With that, Ollie went nuts with tiny yips, and Lana swept her up onto her lap and stroked her.

"Wow!" I managed. "That was something!"

Lana lifted Ollie up to hold her against her shoulder and looked over at me. "Daddy, can I have a mountain lion? Pleeeze?"

I grinned, "Only if you feed it puppies, Sweetie."

We reached Missoula by ten the next morning and drove directly to the airport. We parked the truck, climbed into the camper, and changed into different clothes. Lana pulled on a pair of slacks, a salmon colored silk western shirt and scarf, and the cowboy boots Jake had once given her. I slid into clean, pressed Levi 501s, snap button tan shirt, and my own cowboy boots.

Inside the terminal we rented a Budget Toyota Camry with Montana license plates and picked up a map of Missoula from the desk clerk. We were set.

Western Summits Investment Group was a stone and log building on the banks of the Clark Fork River on the northwest side of town off Interstate 90. It sat on three acres of landscaped humps of mowed lawn strewn with boulders and planted aspens. A man-made alpine stream ran twenty feet down a slope of rock and heather to a small pool. On top of a knoll built in the center of a circular drive were three flag poles. A huge American flag hung from the center one, bracketed by a Montana state flag on one side and a white flag with a Christian fish done in green on the other.

We parked in a slot just short of the covered apron in front.

"Well, this should be interesting," Lana said, getting out. She turned back and settled Ollie into the front seat. We locked the car and crossed over to the front and through the large, heavy plate glass doors. They opened assisted by hidden pneumatics that hissed.

The lobby's ceiling was steeply pitched, and a three tiered chandelier made from deer antlers hung from its log ridge pole. The entire interior was done in western motif. Even the receptionist's glass topped table was made of polished logs.

Lana went up to the middle aged blond receptionist who, thankfully, was dressed like a business woman and not Sacajawea.

She had been watching us with faint interest.

"Can I help you?"

"The Burdocks of San Francisco to see Mr. Valladores?" Lana said in a happy voice, handing the woman the Burdock Ventures card. "He's expecting us," she added.

The receptionist delicately placed the card on the table in front of her, assessed that Lana was the boss of our outfit and said directly to her, "I'm sorry, but Mr. Valladores' sister is very ill. He flew to the family estate in Guatemala a few days ago to be with her."

"I'm sorry to learn that," Lana said. "Do you expect him back soon? We're only visiting the area for a few days."

"It's hard to say. It's a large family business his sister has been managing. He might be gone for some time."

She tapped the business card thoughtfully with a long red nail.

"Would you like to talk with Mr. Spreiter? He's our firm's president."

"That would be wonderful," Lana said.

She picked up the phone.

I whispered to Lana, "They learned the Hummer was at the airport."

She nodded.

We were led past the receptionist's desk. Off to both sides down the wings of the elegant log structure were individual offices and conference rooms. Two men dressed in dark brown slacks, white shirts and colorful ties were talking leisurely in one of the halls. They paid us no mind as we went to the back of the central building into the largest office I had ever seen in my life. It was more like a lavish living room with towering peaked windows comprising the entire west wall. The view of the Bitterroot Mountains and the Clark Fork River was fabulous.

Spreiter stood up and came around his thick pine desk to greet us. The receptionist handed him our card and excused herself. He ushered us over to two leather couches that faced each other in front of a stone fireplace.

Billy had told me that Spreiter was in his late sixties, but he looked only about forty-five years old. He had thick blond hair buzzed military style, and he was a muscular six feet tall. He looked like he had worked out every day of his life and participated in triathlons on a weekly basis. He also looked like he used a sun bed, had capped teeth, and possibly took steroids, but that might have been my envy at work.

He studied our card. "Ventures. Capital ventures?"

Lana was all charm and grace. "It's not what it was five years ago, is it?

He beamed a blinding smile at her. "No it isn't."

"But Western Summits is buying now, is that correct?" she asked. "I'm talking about property."

He swept an index finger from her to me and back. "Are you two...?"

"Yes," Lana said.

He nodded.

I leaned across the glass topped coffee table between us.

"Frank Burdock," I said.

He shook my hand, and turning to Lana, "And you're..."

"Elaine," Lana said, extending her hand loosely.

He sat back sideways and crossed his knees. He had on expensive cowboy boots and jeans creased like slacks. He also wore a plain black cotton shirt, only his was a pearl snap western shirt and was unbuttoned so that a wisp of chest hair showed.

"Yes," he finally said. "We're buying. The selling balloon is deflating, so we're buying land."

"Like you did in the eighties?" Lana asked.

Apparently Lana had done her internet homework.

He nodded. "And in the nineties we built neighborhoods, particularly south of Denver. And I mean neighborhoods with diverse living styles, parks, shopping centers, markets and coffee houses. The whole ball of wax."

Lana smiled knowingly, encouraging him. I marveled and couldn't keep my eyes off her.

"We began selling in the mid nineties to about 0-four," he concluded. "The prices ranged from two-fifty to one mil. We were clean before the bottom fell out."

He paused, watching her reaction.

"Would you like coffee or something stronger?" he asked.

Lana stood. Spreiter and I took her cue and got to our feet as well.

Lana looked at him sweetly. "We really can't stay. But we wanted to drop in, meet you and..." she hesitated, "we would be very interested in having a copy of Western Summits' folio," she said.

A little over an hour later we were back at the airport where we returned the car and changed into our normal clothing. We grabbed burgers at a Burger King on highway 93 going south and ate them as we drove, glad to be rolling.

"God, that was fun," Lana said, tousling Ollie's neck fur. "I think I'm going to make crime my new occupation."

I nodded. "You'd make the perfect scammer," I agreed. Then, after a bit, "See what all that stuff is he gave us. At least we learned how they're covering up Baha's disappearance."

Lana pulled up an inch thick shiny blue folder of printouts, photos, brochures, and spreadsheets Spreiter's secretary had brought from a side door of his office and given us.

She opened the folder on Ollie's back as if she were a lap table and started reading through the contents. Among them, slid in as if by accident, was a pamphlet describing Three Crosses Ministry Haven and Seminary.

We were on the south side of Missoula when Lana pulled it out. She read it carefully, then looked out the side window a long time.

"What is it?" I asked, glancing nervously at her.

Finally she turned and quietly said, "I think we know something else, Paul. I think I know where Rojas is."

Chapter
Thirty-Seven

From Missoula the Bitterroot River Valley runs a hundred miles south between the Sapphire Mountains to the east, and the looming, snow capped peaks of the Bitterroot Mountains to the west. We could still see the expansive lands where buffalo and elk had once grazed, and where later the now famous Montana cowboys worked giant herds of cattle. But now these lush grazing lands and meadows were filling with McMansions that stood out like fat drunks at a grade school picnic.

We drove on through Lolo rather than turning for home and continued south through Stevensville, Hamilton and on to Darby. Darby was once a true cattle town. But it had changed with the times and reinvented itself as a stage set of the Old West. It attracted tourists who came each summer in droves.

Fifteen miles further south, we turned on a narrow paved road that followed the West Fork of the Bitterroot River and reentered the mountains.

Twenty minutes later we turned right again and began edging our way up a one lane road that was deep in cold shadow. Soon the asphalt turned to thin gravel, and we tunneled through dense timber shouldered by cliffs. The road was cut into the north bank of the Nez Perce Fork and ran along the water's edge climbing west towards the Continental Divide.

We had entered the beginnings of the eastern end of the Magruder Corridor.

We drove slowly, looking for even a hint of a place we could pull off and camp by the stream. Finally the canyon opened briefly, and we turned on a short dirt track that led to a single fire ring twenty yards off the road in a stand of cedars. Ground fog was beginning to form, and the air smelled of damp wood and granite.

We parked, popped the camper top up and scrambled in with Ollie. We switched on the lights and furnace, and soon were snug, happy, and sipping Chilean merlot at the table. Ollie worked industriously on a rib bone she had been given at Hammersmith's party. The only sounds were the clucking of the small stream ten feet from our door and the gentle hiss of the pressure cooker Lana had started.

I took a Benchmark Montana Atlas out from the storage tray under the mattress and opened it. I placed the Three Crosses Ministry Haven and Seminary pamphlet on it and tried to determine how far away it was from where we were camped. Lana watched me, enjoying her wine.

The Haven and Seminary's location was easy to spot. According to the photo on the cover of the pamphlet, it was set in a meadow at the mouth of a canyon, and there was only one such place anywhere along this stretch of the Magruder. It was where Watchtower Creek came from the north and flowed into Nez Perce Fork, about ten miles further on.

Lana saw the recognition on my face.

"So?" she asked.

I spun the atlas around and showed her what I had determined.

She studied it closely, then said, "Looks good to me. So what's the plan?"

I settled back against the dinette cushions.

"Don't have a clue," I confessed. "And you?"

She shook her head. Then, after a moment, "We want to find out if Rojas is there, right?" she asked.

"Right."

"So we need to spot him, right?"

"Right."

"So how do we do that?" she asked.

I thought about it.

"Beats the shit out of me."

She poured us the rest of the bottle and dropped the empty into a plastic grocery bag we had hanging for trash.

"Why don't we do a drive-by," she suggested, "and see if we get any brainstorms after seeing the place in person. How's that sound?"

I shrugged.

"Did you bring your digital camera along?"

She shook her head. "And too bad too, huh? Wouldn't it have been nice to have had it when the cougar was having a cultural exchange with us last night?"

The pressure cooker, filled with venison roast, garden carrots, potatoes, and Micha's "secret seasoning" suddenly gave a loud burst of steam, making us both jump.

The fog was burning off under a white sun by the time we got on the road the next morning. It dripped from the cedar bows and the air was absolutely still, cold and sweet smelling. It looked like the beginnings of a near perfect fall day. We had gotten a late leisurely start, and it was now nearly ten o'clock.

Eight miles from camp we rounded a bend. The mountains receded here leaving a broad meadow created by an alluvial fan from Watchtower Creek.

Lana got out a Montana road map, and I slowed to a stop on the narrow gravel road. She unfolded it completely so that it blanketed the dash.

She said, "Let's do the drive-by slowly with the map in plain sight as we planned, but come back like we're lost and ask for instructions. Unless we see Rojas on the first pass."

"If only we could be that lucky," I said.

"If we see he's there, we'll just turn around further on and drive back on by quickly like we figured something out."

Two hundred yards further we broke out into the clearing. The road continued along the river bank and a narrow strip of young aspens for a quarter mile before reentering the timber. To our right on the north side was a lush, mowed meadow that ran another quarter mile back up to the base of the mountains.

In front of a cluster of log buildings were three twenty foot tall pole crosses and at their base a carved sign advertising Three Crosses Ministry Haven and Seminary.

The log buildings sat on river stone foundations and appeared to have been a CCC camp in the thirties. There were two small cabins at the east edge of the timber near us. Only one seemed to be in use, and a Toyota 4-Runner was parked in front of it. A long bunkhouse stretched across the back of the compound where a dirt bike and an older Ford pickup were parked. A small chapel stood in the meadow's center next to a dining hall.

Between the cabins and the chapel there was a long garden. Two young women in sweaters and bib overalls were working in it, loading potatoes into two red wheelbarrows. They looked up as we rolled past, and Lana waved to them. They waved back and stood watching us.

Behind the hall were two log houses set back into the edge of the pines. The one nearest the road was an old CCC or Forest Service headquarters with a new dark green Suburban parked in front. It appeared the building was still being used as a headquarters office, though not for the NFS any longer.

The second house was what caught my attention. It was a tidy, two room cottage that sat directly behind the headquarters. It had a small porch out front, and parked parallel to the porch so that it faced the road sat a black Humvee. I tried not to stare at it as we passed.

Back into the timber I tried to count how many days it had been since the Humvee we had confiscated had been left at the Boise Airport. If it had been reported stolen, there might have been just enough time to get it back up here. But I doubted it. Maybe Rojas and Baha both had one. Trophy rigs between childhood friends or something.

"Nice place," Lana remarked. "I wouldn't mind being a drug trafficker if I could live *here*."

I nodded. "I wonder how Spreiter got it away from the government?"

"Who knows?" Lana checked the map, then looked up at me. "What's eating you?"

"You see that black Hummer?" I said.

"Garish, wasn't it?" Then she stopped herself. "You're thinking it's the same one you guys stole?"

"You have a way with words. No, I can't figure out how it *could* be," I said. "Might be a second one, though."

"Rojas's,"

"Right," I said. "Makes better sense, too. I don't think Spreiter would report a stolen Hummer one of his men had used on a killing mission."

"So, when should we turn around and go back to ask questions?"

I shrugged my shoulders. "Where do we think we're trying to go? We need to asked them questions to *somewhere*."

"Well we don't want it to be up here because then we'd have to drive the whole Magruder to get back home."

"Right."

She studied the map. "If we hadn't turned right off West Fork Road onto this cow path, we would have hit Painted Rocks Lake and State Park." She put the map down on her lap. "In fact, we should have stayed there last night. They have showers."

"How far away is it?" I asked.

"About the same as to here."

I said, "Let's do it then."

Ten minutes up the road I found a spot just wide enough to do a five point turn around, and we headed back. Approximately twenty minutes had passed by the time we made it back to the meadow. I slowed, and we swung in up to the front of the crosses and parked in a gravel lot marked off with washtub sized rocks painted white. Two young guys had come out and were sitting in the morning sun in front of the bunkhouse. Both of them were smoking. Not very ministerial of them, I thought.

One of the women came through the garden's low gate and over to Lana's window. She was in her early thirties and had very pale blond hair and eyelashes. A Finn?

"Hi," she said. "Lost?"

Lana nodded, trying to calm Ollie, who had just woken up and was trying to jump out the window into the woman's arms.

"Cute dog!" she said. She reached in to give Ollie a couple pets. Ollie licked her hand, and the woman smiled happily.

Lana wrestled the map around to show show her.

"We're trying to find Painted Rocks Lake."

Just then I noticed a man come out on the porch behind the Hummer. He was dressed in gray sweat pants, black muscle shirt, and had his long gray hair tied in a knot at the back of his head. He was staring at us.

I turned back to act a part of the conversation. At first I had thought the man was a Blackfoot Indian, but then I had a glimpse of his Mayan profile. I knew now it was Rojas. No doubt.

"Thanks a lot," Lana said. I had missed the rest. "I thought as much, but some husbands--"

The woman gave Ollie a parting rub and turned back to the garden. I turned around in the parking lot and went back onto the road. Glancing in my rear view mirror, I saw Rojas turn and walk leisurely back inside the cottage. I gave a sigh of relief.

"You OK?" Lana asked.

"Did you see that guy on the porch?" I said.

"Briefly."

"It was him," I said.

"Really!" Lana said excitedly. "Rojas? That's excellent." She gave me a high-five. "We're the best. We rule the universe. We are The People From the Land of Border Corgis!"

Chapter
Thirty-Eight

We were back to Darby by noon and pulled into the Kensington Pub and Eatery because it looked like a place that would serve micro brews and healthy food. We were right. Plus, its clientele dressed like they enjoyed snow boarding, mountain biking, rock climbing, and pot. And they were one-third our ages and didn't look as if they had killed anyone in the past thirty days. It was refreshing to sit among them.

We shared a large salad, a feta, walnut, pesto pizza, a pitcher of the local IPA, and afterwards relaxed with Americanos.

Lana was watching people pass outside on the sidewalk but then turned to me and asked, "Why did Oscar and Josiah feel they needed to hide the bodies?"

The question took me by surprise. I for one was thinking how nice it would be to build a cabin above Darby.

"Well," I attempted, "I think Oscar said something about how a person needs to deal with criminals in a way they understand. I'm not sure."

She thought this over a minute.

"But it was a clear case of self defense. You guys could have loaded the bodies in a pickup, just like the first time, and taken them to the local Sheriff like Charlie did, and after a hearing, you'd just go home."

I admitted to myself that this had been nagging on me as well. I didn't know the answer and said as much.

"Well," she offered, "is tribal justice that much different than the court systems?"

I shook my head. "I doubt it, but I really don't know," I admitted. I thought about it, and Lana waited, sipping her coffee patiently.

"Remember those sensationalized newspaper headlines you read to me over the phone?" I tried.

"Yes."

"Well I'm thinking that maybe a lot of all this is a matter of perception. I don't know. But with the drug bust we did, the only excuse we had for being up there in the first place was that our hunting camp was there. Charlie was out of his jurisdiction, just as Oscar and Josiah were. That means all of us were. We were out of the scope of their respective agencies. A law enforcement agency should have had a SWAT team or raid team set up to take down the shipment, not us. And I'm sure Charlie, at least, will be facing some kind of disciplinary action because of what we did."

I thought of some of the possibilities.

"I mean, we could all theoretically be the objects of a homicide investigation, even though being cleared would be a given. We could even be charged with the felonious taking of personal property for having confiscated the drugs, even though the drugs were illegal. Then, we could be charged with the possession of controlled substances because we had those in our possession afterwards. You see what I'm driving at?"

"Yeah. But aren't you exaggerating?"

I grinned. "These things would all be sorted out in our favor, and it would be in a federal court since it took place in a National Forest, and it would take time, possibly years, and money to go through the motions. And what a drag."

Lana nodded.

"Now think about the nightmare the gun fight at the cabin would have started."

She did. Then said, "That sounds a lot easier to me."

I shrugged. "You're probably right," I admitted. "But it also sounds like we purposely lured them into an ambush and slaughtered them."

She nodded. "I see what you're driving at."

I wasn't so sure I did, though. I was more talking to think than thinking to talk.

"I'll be honest," I said. "This whole month has been way over my head. I suspect that everyone knows exactly what we're doing except for me."

"There you go again."

"No, really," I said. "I've been thinking about this, and I think they stashed the bodies because they knew that the outcome, if it had gone through the judicial system, would have been the same, only the results would not have exposed the men behind the drug trafficking. It would have only driven them underground as the police actions in Thailand and Cambodia did."

I hesitated to add, "I think Micha is the mentor on many of Josiah and Oscar's decisions, and I believe, perhaps reluctantly, that his advice is based on a more universal and just system than our own."

I thought about what I had just said a moment.

Then, "I mean, we killed and buried a bunch of men who were poisoning our citizens, and one of their leaders is a homicidal maniac guilty of nearly forty years of atrocities. Do his gunmen's corpses deserve more than being sealed in a mine? That's the only crime we're talking about here."

Lana, who had always been the first to see things clearly, nodded.

"So when are you going to phone MacAvity and Hammersmith?" she asked.

"If you'll take care of the bill, I'll do it on the outside pay phone right now," I said. Apparently we had talked our way to some understanding of things. Time would tell.

I was getting up to go to the phone when Lana said, "And by the way, Paul, while I was on the computer yesterday morning just before we left home, I tapped into the Idaho statutes as well. I learned that 19-201 says you guys had the right to defend yourselves at the hunting camp, and 19-205 says that it was OK to be helping peace officers."

She smiled at me. "So aren't you men angels?"

I shook my head and went out into the lobby, smiling. Lana. Always ahead of the game.

I phoned MacAvity on my calling card. He picked up on the fourth ring.

"MacAvity's Pub," he grumbled.

"It's me. Got a minute?"

It was like he put on another voice and suit of clothes. "Paul! What'd you find?"

"We found Rojas. I saw him with my own eyes," I said.

"Oh shit!" Butte said excitedly. "The little bastard is in our sights. Where is he, Paul?"

"Fifteen, twenty miles up the Nez Perce Fork at some sort of ministry retreat."

Butte laughed. "At the mouth of the Magruder," he said. "Wouldn't you know it? What's the layout?"

"It looks like an old CCC camp that was taken over by the Forest Service before Spreiter got his hands on it. Just a bunch of log buildings in a meadow."

MacAvity thought this over. "Where are you calling from?"

"Darby," I said. "I'm at a pay phone."

"You have a phone book there?" he asked.

I stepped back to check the phone book shelf. Amazingly, there was one there--the only one in America that hadn't been stolen off its chain. I pulled it up. "Yeah. Right here."

"Look at the motel accommodations for me, will you?" he said.

I thumbed through the narrow phone book's yellow pages. There were more than ten motels, hotels, lodges and B&Bs listed for the little town. I read them aloud.

"Tell me more about Chaffin Creek Cabins," he said.

"I read to him, 'Ten cabins. Two with queen beds, two with twin beds, six larger cabins with bunk beds and twin beds. Views of Trapper Peak. Open May 15 to September 15. Call for seasonal prices."

MacAvity grunted approvingly.

"So they're closed right now," I said.

"Can you call them anyway?" he said. "See if they would open for a group?"

"What are you talking about, Butte?"

"Just do it will you? Then call me back."

I did as he asked. Lana had come out and had taken a seat on a bench. She was leaning back against the restaurant's front wall, waiting.

It took nearly ten minutes for me to negotiate with the woman who answered. Then I phoned Butte back.

"They said they are remodeling the interiors of all but the six bunk cabins. If we don't mind the construction during the day, they'd open three for us, but we'd have to take all three if they're going to the effort of dewinterizing them. They said the minimum is three nights, and it will cost us six-hundred dollars a night," I told him.

"Give me their phone number, will you?" he asked. I did.

Butte then asked if there was an air strip in Darby.

I flipped through the phone book. There was a paved air strip in Hamilton, and one of the lodges beneath

Trapper Peak southwest of Darby advertised they had a short dirt strip. I told him this.

"Good," he said, adding in a hurried voice, "Smoke will have charts that show that dirt strip which will probably be either grass or gravel. I'll bet it's grass. You need to find out exactly where it is too."

"Why?" I asked, growing frustrated.

He sensed my impatience. "I'm just putting this together in my head, Paul. Sorry. I'm going to see if Smoke will rent a plane for us so he can fly Hammer and me in early tomorrow morning."

"But why do you want that many cabins? Lana and I have the camper to stay in."

As soon as I asked I knew the answer.

"Because I'm going to phone Oscar and Josiah," he snapped. "We're going to get this fucking job done once and for all."

"OK, Butte. No need to get upset," I said. "What do you want us to do? And what about Charlie?"

"Go park at the cabins. I'll have them reserved by the time you get there. I'll ask them if you can camp until we arrive. Call me at six tonight so you'll know when to pick up Smoke, Hammer and me. We're going to rent and load the plane this afternoon." He paused. "As for Charlie, he has his hands full right now explaining to the Idaho Attorney General his role in the drug seizure."

"Is he in trouble?"

"I asked him that, and he said it was a matter of setting the record straight. Paperwork."

After we had hung up, I phoned Billy in Boise. Lana was window shopping. She had worked her way a block and a half down the street.

Billy picked up on the first ring.

I briefly told him where we were, and that we had developed some leads concerning major drug trafficking.

Leads, which as far as I could tell, might possibly turn up something we could hand over to him. That he should get up here immediately.

"Can you get them to open one of the cabins for just me tonight?"

"I doubt it," I told him. "I don't know yet if even Lana and I can camp there. I haven't been out there yet."

"Forget it," Billy said. "I've stayed in Darby's Best Western before. It's good. I'm going to have our contracted pilot fly me into Hamilton this afternoon. I'll rent a jeep there."

The Boise Banner. Always first class.

He thought a moment. "Come to the motel around six," he said. I'll buy you guys the best supper Hamilton has to offer, and let me tell you, they serve some excellent tenderloins and t-bones in that burg."

I asked, "Before you come up here, could you check to see if a black Humvee has been towed from the Boise Airport?"

Billy laughed. "Always the mystery man, ain't you? Yeah, I'll find out. See you."

And he hung up.

Chapter
Thirty-Nine

Eighteen miles south of Darby, we turned west on Chaffin Creek Road and a mile later reached the base of Sugarloaf Peak and a large stand of aspens that were bright yellow in the autumn grayness. The cabins were scattered among the trees and were low ceilinged and modern. Each had log walls, stone foundations and fireplaces, and a picture window that looked east between the gray-green aspen trunks to the Bitterroot River Valley.

The cabins looked as if they had been built within the last fifteen years, and their construction was done in such a way that the natural landscape and foliage of the setting had not been damaged or altered. In fact, to reach the cabins we had to park in a single, small parking lot away from the trees and walk in on a narrow, barked trail.

Lana, Ollie and I got out and headed towards the sound of a table saw coming from one of the cabins. A slender red haired woman in her thirties dressed in tan Carhartt bibs saw us and came out onto the porch and down the steps to greet us. The sound of the saw stopped, and a man her age appeared at the window for a moment, waved, then went back to what he was doing.

She greeted us, holding out her hand. "You must be the couple that's with the group coming in?"

Lana shook her hand and Ollie wiggled around excitedly at her feet. "Yes. Glad to meet you."

She led us between two of the cabins and out to the back of the aspen stand where three larger cabins stood with their doors open, airing in preparation for our arrival.

She was quick to explain that we could stay parked that night in the parking lot, but that we could drop no waste water, gray or black. She said we could move into the cabins and use their bathrooms in the morning. She added that our group was on its own because she and her husband would not be there after five each night. During the winters they lived at their house in town because it was easier for their children to attend school that way when the snows came.

Back at the camper, Lana said, "Well, pretty upscale, I'd say."

I agreed. "They seem nice and real sensitive to the environment, don't they? I guess we'll be living in luxury for a day or two."

"So what do you want to do now?" Lana asked, lifting Ollie back into the truck and getting in after her.

"Make arrangements for tomorrow's landing on the private air strip and then check out the town," I said.

Back in Darby we got directions to the town park that shouldered the Bitterroot River. There we popped the camper and spent the next four hours just hanging out, reading, drinking tea, and taking strolls along the miles of river bank trails that went both north and south from the park.

At six o'clock, we pulled up stakes and headed to the Best Western to meet Billy.

Billy climbed into the Tundra with us, sat in the extended cab's back seat with Ollie, and guided us to a steak house in Hamilton, twenty miles north. He claimed this place had the best steaks he had ever eaten and at the best prices except for a comparable restaurant in Sydney, Australia. He was not wrong.

We were seated in a deep rich booth towards the back and were soon sipping Glenfiddich single malts and ignoring the menus. Billy was in great form, excited, I supposed, to be in the field as a reporter, which was his true love. He said if it wasn't for the hurtful aspects of bullets and beheadings, he would love to be covering the Middle East right now. Action. Excitement. Danger.

He was dressed in a dark blue Ex-Officio large pocket shirt, jeans and hiking boots. A tablet and ball point, his signature, were in the shirt's left pocket, and he was nearly vibrating with energy. It was contagious. Lana and I were grinning.

"Anyway," he said, "guess what I found out about that black Hummer." His eyebrows were lifted clear up to his hairline as he waited for our answer.

"Don't tell me," Lana squealed, "it's Hoffa's!"

"Oh, drop dead," he groaned.

"So what'd you learn, Wonder Boy?"

Billy took a sip of his scotch and sat back with both hands wrapped around the glass.

"Called a buddy who is the head of airport security. The Hummer, which is worth nearly seventy grand, was over-parked in a two hour zone directly in front of the terminal, not a hundred feet from the front door. It made him nervous.

"So he had the police run the license plate, which he can do being security, and it came back as registered to a Clifford Spreiter."

He was grinning and waiting for us to be shocked and dismayed. When we practically shrugged, he said. "You knew that already?"

"Not really," I offered. "But it points out it was associated with the drug bust, doesn't it?"

"Well yeah," he said, a bit crestfallen. "That's the point, isn't it?"

Lana reached across the table and patted the top of his left hand. "Go on, Billy. Ignore Paul. He's an ass."

He snapped back remembering something better.

"So he said that a man was flown in by private plane, picked up the Hummer, paid the three-hundred dollar ticket for creating a security risk, and drove off. When I asked what the guy looked like, he said like an Indian."

He took another sip while we waited.

"I asked him if I could send him a fax of a guy's photo to see if he recognized him, and he said sure and gave me the fax number. I sent him Rojas Franzani's photo, and he phoned me immediately and said it was the guy."

Lana and I both nodded, happily.

"That answers a major question for us, Billy," I said. "That Hummer is right now parked up the canyon in front of a cottage at some kind of ministry retreat. We saw it there. We also saw Rojas come out onto the porch."

"Wow," he said quietly, studying us carefully. "That's getting pretty damn lucky. But why was the Hummer important?"

"We wanted to learn who it was registered to and if it was stolen. You answered that for us."

"But you knew it was at the airport. How's that?"

"We can't tell you Billy."

"But you knew it was there."

"Yes," I said.

He thought this over. "But you aren't going to tell me how you knew?'

"No."

He spun his scotch around in his glass and then asked, "So who'd you think it belonged to? Can I ask that?"

"Spreiter, Rojas, or Baha originally," I said. "Then it was narrowed down to Spreiter or Rojas."

"Why not Valladores?" he asked.

Lana glanced at me then said to Billy, "We talked to Spreiter this morning. He said Vice President Valladores was called back to Guatemala to manage a family business because his sister had fallen ill."

Billy gave a short laugh. "Not very likely," he said. "He was probably the one who left the Hummer at the airport, but I had airport security check, after I learned it was Spreiter's rig, to see if anyone from Western Summits had taken a flight. I faxed him Spreiter's name and the V.P.s' names, and tossed in Rojas's as well. He came back with negatives on all of them."

The waiter came up, and Billy ordered tenderloins for all three of us, medium rare, and more single malt.

Lana watched this.

"Say Billy," she said, "what if I had become a vegetarian since the last time you did that?"

"You haven't," he said flatly. "You would have said something. Or done something violent under the table," he added.

He handed the menus to the waiter who left.

"So, in my opinion, one of three things is going on here," he continued. "Either Baha wants Rojas and Western Summits to think he's left the country because he's afraid of them for some reason, or he wants the cops to think that. Either way, he had to do it with some high quality document forgeries because he would need an assumed name, passport, etcetera. But as I'm learning more about these guys, I realize those things would be a cinch for him to get."

I found it very difficult to keep the truth from him and to keep that inner struggle from showing on my face. Lana, on the other hand, acted keenly interested in his theories and was leaning forward hanging on his every word with bright eyes and vigorous nods. I couldn't help but marvel at her guile. Fortunately, this drew his interest totally away from my transparency.

"So," Lana asked, "What's your third theory, hot shot?"

"Well," he concluded, grinning, "and this is my pet theory."

He paused for dramatic effect.

"That the citizens of Ryback have slaughtered the whole pack of these smugglers, and aren't telling."

He grinned wickedly at us.

"No, no," Lana chirped, "That's tomorrow, Billy. And we're going to pin it on you. That's why we invited you along."

"Ohhhhh," he said. "It all makes sense now."

But with that, he gave me a quick, searching glance just before he turned to accept the second round of scotches the waiter was placing in front of us.

Then he relaxed and asked, "So what's on for tomorrow?"

Lana suddenly said, "Oh my gosh, we forgot. We've got to call MacAvity right now!"

I jumped out of the booth so she wouldn't trample over me, and she headed for the courtesy phone off the waiting area.

"Smoke's flying Butte and Eric in tomorrow morning," I answered. "They're landing on a grass air strip south of Darby. Oscar and his bunch are driving in later, and we're going to make some plans at the cabins."

"Am I included?" he asked.

"I'm pretty sure you are, Billy. At least they'll expect you to stay with us. I think you'll be in a cabin with the Ryback bunch so that the Camas warriors don't kill you in your sleep."

"A regular reunion of the Magruder Marauders, right?"

"Right," I said.

Chapter

Forty

Few things, in my estimation, beat sleeping in late and waking up in a mountain meadow on a frosty morning. It's magic. Particularly when bacon and eggs are put on to cook to mingle their aromas with the smell of freshly perked coffee. Within the hour we had eaten our breakfast with home canned peaches and coffee for dessert and had gone up to the cabin and taken long, hot showers. It was nine AM when we left to join Billy at the airstrip. Smoke was due in thirty minutes, and he was rarely late.

The airstrip was nothing more than a mowed runway in a level hay field that ran along the banks of the Bitterroot River. There were two small, galvanized plane sheds, several tie-downs poured in concrete, and a yellow turbo propped crop duster sitting beside the nearest shed. The owner of the strip lived in a small nearby ranch house in a stand of cottonwoods beside a hay barn. He wanted twenty dollars a day for tie-downs, and I had given him twenty and told him if my friends stayed longer, they'd square things with him before they left.

We pulled up alongside Billy's yellow rented Jeep, and he got out to greet us in the cold morning light. The smell of wood smoke from the chimneys of scattered ranches filled the golden air, and the grass was wet with melting frost. Like us, he was bundled in a down mountaineering jacket.

"When the frost is on the pumpkin, that's the time for peter dunkin'," he greeted.

"Then that must be a real disappointment for you, Billy," Lana said.

"And good morning to you, too."

She gave him a hug.

"Well," I said, coming around the front of the Tundra, "do we want to wager lunch on when they get here?"

But before Billy could answer, we heard a single engine plane coming through the mountains behind us.

"I'll bet damn soon," Billy said. "What about you, Paul?"

"I'll bet you're right."

A small blue and white plane showed against the trees at the mouth of the West Fork of the Bitterroot River Canyon and came north towards us. It had bush tires mounted, and as it got closer I recognized it as the Maule 235 Smoke liked to bush pilot with. I knew from flying with him that these little tail draggers could practically land and take off on a football field. Nothing beat them in that regard.

Out of habit, Smoke did a fly over to check for game or livestock on the strip, then banked, came back around, and slid in sideways for a pinpoint landing. He taxied up to us, selected tie-downs beside the crop duster, and killed the engine. We went over to help with the gear.

MacAvity, who had been riding up front, practically fell out of the plane. He came walking stiffly from under the wing leaving Hammersmith to struggle out from the back on his own.

Free of the plane, Butte leaned back his head and yelled at the sky, "I'm alive! Once again Smoke failed to kill me!"

We cracked up.

"That asshole flew every fucking stream from Magnet Airport to here, and he never got more than three inches off the water, I swear," he bellowed.

Smoke was securing the plane and yelled over, "At least we got some good digitals, ya cry baby."

Hammersmith came up and said, "We flew past that compound, Paul. It was right where you said it was. Butte took a couple pictures of it."

He grinned at Billy, "You made it, too. Good for you." They shook hands.

"But my plane was a twin turbo with a wine bar," Billy told him.

"And you're an asshole just like Smoke," said Butte.

They had with them only their winter clothes, which they were wearing, and two extremely heavy duffle bags. Hammersmith asked Billy and me to load them into the jeep and to leave them there until our landlords had left for the night. I assumed they contained the weapons and other gear we would be using. What startled me, however, was that as we were loading the duffles, Eric said we were going to move on the target this very night.

"Hit fast, hit hard," Butte said. "That fly over, even though Smoke did it off to the side and at a thousand feet, might still have made them a bit wary. The pictures really didn't show much anyway. The damn plane was bobbing around in the updrafts like a cork going through a hydroelectric turbine. I was lucky I wasn't thrown out the window."

Smoke scoffed.

Ever since high school, when Lana and I had worked together on the school paper, she has been an artist. She had developed an at-home profession for herself as a book illustrator as far back as the early seventies. A SE Washington University art professor we met at an English Department party had taken an interest in her work and had eventually introduced her to a Manhattan agent named James Macias. Jimmy kept her as busy as she wanted to be.

We had gathered in the second cabin waiting for Oscar and his bunch to arrive. Butte and Eric were on their beds, leading back against the headboards on pillows, and Billy and Smoke sat at the table with Lana and me. Lana had brought an eighteen by twenty-four inch tablet of lightweight drawing paper in from the camper, and was at work with a soft, 4B Derwent pencil, sketching the layout of the Ministry Haven. Smoke and I watched her idly and drank coffee.

Like many artists I have seen work, usually on contract with the Trib., she had near perfect visual memory and worked quickly, the pencil making swift sure lines like magic. It only took her twenty minutes to complete a striking drawing of the entire place, crosses and lettered sign included. Even the trees and vehicles seemed to be in the correct spots.

When she was satisfied, she said, "There you go, boys. That's the best I can do."

MacAvity and Hammersmith got slowly to their feet, and Billy and I gave up our seats to them. They pulled the chairs up to the table to study the drawing closely.

Hammersmith pointed to the SUV in front of the headquarters building. "That there when you guys were?"

"Yup," I said.

"We saw the Hummer," he said, "but not that Suburban. How many people did you see?"

Lana said, "Two women, who probably stay in one of the cabins together, and two young guys at the bunkhouse."

"Rojas came out onto the porch of this cottage," I said, pointing it out.

Butte nodded. "We saw the pickup and the dirt bike," he said, tapping the drawing, "but what's that thing?"

He was referring to what looked like a concrete box half buried in the hill behind the compound."

Hammersmith said, "Haven't you ever seen a root cellar, Butte?"

"Oh yeah. I see it now," MacAvity said, adding, "With the guy gone from the headquarters building, they're pretty damn light in staff. Where is everyone?"

Smoke scoffed. "We killed them all, Butte. Whaddayathink?"

"Not so fast," Hammersmith said. "Oscar told me last night they probably have had their narcotics resupplied, since we confiscated the last shipment. I'll wager they're waiting for new recruits to arrive to mule them over."

He looked around at us. "Just one more reason to make the move in the next twelve hours."

He was just about to explain something else when we heard two trucks pull into the parking lot. Billy and I went out and down through the alders to greet the them. The sun was at its autumn highest now, and the yellow leaves of the alders flickered like gold coins.

Our warriors didn't come unprepared, I'll give them that. Jerry got out with six boxed pizzas, and Peter had a case of Miller High Life under each arm.

"Ayyye," Jerry greeted us. "You still have your scalps."

Billy shook his hand. "Anything I can carry?" he asked.

"Grab that duffle of bows and stone hatchets, will you?"

"Can't do." Billy explained how we didn't want to call attention to ourselves. He nodded to the nearby cabin where the the owners were at work.

I made it to Oscar and Josiah's truck just in time to explain they shouldn't unload their gear either, but they did pull a wooden grub box from the back of the truck and carry it between them up to the third cabin.

With Billy and me on their heels, Jerry and Peter took the pizzas and beer into the second cabin where Lana was still explaining the layout. In moments Oscar and Josiah joined us, bringing along their cabin's chairs.

Smoke, MacAvity and Hammersmith greeted them as if it had been years, not days, since they'd last seen them. Everyone but Billy and me pulled up in a tight circle around Lana's drawing and studied it.

Lana started to explain it again, when Billy interrupted her.

"Ah, folks," he said, "As a neutral observer, and though I appreciate your apparent trust, I'm not completely sure, with the way this meeting is developing, that I should be a participant."

Peter whistled. "Now that is one pile of words, Billy. Does everyone talk like that in Boise?"

"You saying something, or are you asking something?" Oscar added, looking up from the drawing.

Billy flushed with embarrassment. I'd never seen him do that before, and I had to suppress a laugh.

"Well," Billy said, thinking it over, "I guess I'm asking what my part in all this is going to be."

Jerry and Oscar were about to take another turn at him, but Hammersmith intervened.

"That's a good question, and you deserve for it to be answered, Billy."

Everyone became still. I could see how Hammersmith had become a commander. It was obvious he knew how to control men. More, he knew how to control a pack of men ready to go into combat.

"What we're going to do is make you the most famous investigative reporter in the history of Idaho," Eric said. "First off, tonight we're going to correct a wrong that for thirty-eight years has affected me, Huey, and, not least of all, Cambodia.

"Next, if we find the cache of drugs the DEA thinks is being readied to replace those we confiscated at the pass, we're going to destroy them.

"And finally, we hope to find documentation in this building," he tapped Lana's drawing of the headquarters building, "which we will turn over to you."

Billy had become very serious and restrained. "What kind of documentation?"

"The kind that will allow you to write an article that will be the front page news of every major newspaper in North America. The kind that will bring down the second largest drug trafficking cartel at work in the United States."

Hammersmith hesitated, looking kindly at Billy.

"That's what we're doing, thanks to the information you have provided us, Billy. That's what we're doing now, and that's how we're going to repay you."

Everyone waited for Billy to reply.

He cleared his throat at last, and said, "Well, that's sweet of you, but don't you think we should eat those pizzas first, before they get cold?"

Hammersmith laughed and slapped him on the back.

Smoke began popping open beer cans like he was shucking razor clams and handed them around.

"Good to have you on board, Billy," he said.

So began a long afternoon and even longer night.

Chapter
Forty-One

After we ate, Billy opted out of the tactical planning and, with Lana's permission, moved his stuff into our cabin next door. Jerry and Oscar carried the grub box over for him to cook from, and Billy then left in the Jeep for Darby to get the ingredients he needed to make what he called "a Texan Branding Iron Chili."

Lana, Ollie and I saw him off, then turned to go back to the cabins just in time to see the sun slide behind the towering peaks of the Bitterroots directly overhead. It was hard to imagine that the face of these mighty mountains extended two hundred miles north and south with only three roads crossing them.

The owners pulled up in their truck while we waited for Ollie to finish checking out a mole hill.

"Everything to your satisfaction?" the woman asked cheerfully from the driver's window.

"Lovely," Lana said. "Thank you."

The woman glanced in the direction of our cabins. "You having a business meeting?"

Lana grinned. "More of a reunion of old farming friends," she said. "But don't worry, they're harmless. They do this every year."

"Well have fun," she said.

They pulled out and headed back to town just as Oscar, Jerry, and Smoke came down the trail. We helped them unload the gear and carry it back up to the cabins. The few duffles Jerry and Oscar carried into their cabin seemed much lighter than ours. I suspected they only contained their M-16s, ammunition, and warm clothing, which seemed adequate to me. Who could guess what Butte had loaded into his, though. A Sherman tank?

Soon, the three empty bunks in Smoke's cabin were strewn with gear. MacAvity was showing off his new satellite phone, and on the bunk he had our radios and three M16 A1s with night scopes. Then he reached deeply into the end of the duffle bag and pulled out three grenades, which he placed beside the M-16s.

Hammersmith shook his head, turned away, and went over to sit at the table.

"And, of course," Butte continued, "one must have their M-67 baseballs and an old thermite, just in case."

"Oh yeah!" Smoke said enthusiastically. He picked up the thermite grenade that was shaped like a beer can. "You've been hanging on to this all these years?"

MacAvity grinned. "I just hope it still works,"

Smoke put the grenade back on the mattress carefully, and went over to open his own bags. I suspected Oscar's bunch were in their own cabin doing the same thing we were.

Lana, from the stove where she had started tea water, rolled her eyes at me. She had always been dismayed by what she thought was MacAvity's obsession with weapons, and the grenades capped it.

Hammersmith just sat at the table looking at them thoughtfully.

Butte then shook out a box of latex gloves, ten pairs of "E-Z Cuff" nylon disposable restraints bound in strips of blue paper, and reached back into the duffle and bought out five black lycra ski masks. He then held up what looked like a pocket sized, rubber coated camcorder.

"And this," he said proudly, "is my second new toy. An IR/X-100 Compact Thermal Viewer." He put it back on the bunk.

"Well," he said. "That's the lot."

"I'm surprised at your austerity, Butte," Lana said.

"I'm sorely disappointed in you as well, Butte," Hammersmith said. He accepted a cup of tea Lana handed him. "Did you plan for the two of us to get close enough to toss those baseballs? Why didn't you bring the blooper?"

"What's a 'blooper'?" This was me.

"A grenade launcher," MacAvity told me. "It's like a single-shot shot gun, but 40mm. But for this operation," this was to Eric, "it's just too damn cumbersome. And besides, it's not needed."

"Whatever you say, Butte," Hammersmith said, respectfully.

Smoke came over and put his .243 into my hands.

I said, "I know, I know. Don't scratch it."

"I just don't want you to feel left out, pardner," he said. "Butte also fitted a night scope to it for you, so you're ready to roll."

Josiah came through the door at that moment, followed closely by the others. They pulled chairs back up around the table to resume discussing options for that night.

We joined them and the planning began in earnest.

Lana's drawing became more and more worn from being poked and drawn on.

Hammersmith had out his small farming notebook and was keeping notes, adding suggestions and scratching them out as they were dismissed.

We didn't stop until eight that night when Billy announced that his killer chili was being served in the first cabin. We scrambled to our feet.

After dinner Lana and I stayed in our cabin with Billy to help do the dishes and clean up. We knew by then what the general plan was. I was basically to do the same thing as twice before--be a lookout--and Hammersmith wanted Lana on hand to talk to the two women.

Hammersmith lingered behind as the others went back to continue working out details and packing up the gear. He stopped at the door, shut it after the others, and turned to face us.

"Can I talk to you three a minute?" he asked.

He leaned back against the log wall to the side of the door.

"There's a good chance the two women and the two young guys are only working there, or worse, actually *are* doing seminary studies." He looked down, rubbed his left hand over the top of his right, studying the bumps and gnarls life had left on them, and continued, "There's also a remote chance that a real minister actually does occupy the old headquarters house."

We waited. I heard Billy take a deep breath beside me and let it out slowly.

"There may not be any drugs at all, either," Eric continued. "But, we know that Rojas is in the cottage. And Butte's and my conviction is that wherever Rojas is, that's where the drugs are.

And," he added, "if Rojas is living in the smaller of the two houses, then something or someone more important than him is in the large house...and it isn't the drugs. They wouldn't keep drugs in the house. And that's what we'll find out soon.

"Anyway," he said to Billy, "I want you to come along in your rented Jeep with one of Butte's radios. I want you to park where the rest of us will be leaving the trucks."

Billy nodded. He was a bit flushed in the face from either cooking or sipping Irish whiskey--I couldn't tell which--but he looked fully alert and eager.

Hammersmith pushed off the wall and stood, hand on the doorknob.

"When I contact you to come on in, I want you to drive to the headquarters house and park in front. If we find what I think we will find, you'll be a happy boy."

He smiled for the first time. "And right now I want you, Billy, to come over to the cabin with me and call your pilot on Butte's satellite phone. Can you get hold of him in the evenings?"

"Yup," Billy said. "He's on call 24/7. What do you want me to tell him?"

"I want you to have him waiting for you at three AM, six hours from now. Do you think he can make it?"

Billy saw what Eric was driving at. A huge smile spread over his face. "Damn straight!" he said. Then, "Thanks, Hammersmith."

"OK," Eric said and went out.

"Oh, this is going to be sweet," Billy said. He grabbed his down jacket off one of the wooden pegs driven in a wall log and followed.

"My oh my," we heard him say.

I looked at Lana questioningly.

She shrugged her shoulders and started to clear off the dirty dishes.

Chapter
Forty-Two

Jerry and Peter left the cabins at eleven o'clock. They were dressed in black jeans and camo jackets and had with them, besides their M-16s and night goggles, a canvas bag with a pound of C-4 and the makings. They wanted to find a spot we could pull off the road out of sight and still be near the meadow. Lana and I talked this over, and the only possible spot we could suggest would be practically in the meadow itself.

After they pulled out, Lana and I got into our capilene long johns, down coats and fleece caps. Billy had nearly the same clothing as us--a common occurrence among people who liked to hike in the high country.

We were about to go out the door and over to the other cabins when Lana put her hand on my forearm and stopped me.

"Are you all right?" she asked.

"Yeah, I guess so," I said. "I have a bucket load of adrenaline in me right now, though."

"You'll be fine when we start doing something, Paul," Billy said. "It's always like this. Pre-game jitters." He grinned. "Maybe we need MacAvity to give you a pep-talk."

"God, not that," Lana said.

I picked up my black lycra ski mask and put it in my jacket pocket along with a pair of the latex gloves Hammersmith said we were all to wear. In my other pocket I put the radio and headset. That done, I took a deep breath and picked up Smoke's .243 and night scope.

"Well," I said, "I guess I'm ready."

The night was iron cold, clear, and full of stars. Hammersmith and MacAvity rode with us in the Tundra, and Smoke and Billy followed in the Jeep, with Josiah and Oscar bringing up the rear.

When we entered the blackness of the narrow Nez Perce Fork canyon, Hammersmith had us stop. I looked in my rear view mirror. Oscar had gotten out of their Dodge and was slit-taping the head lights. I climbed out, went back and borrowed enough tape to do ours as well. Smoke joined me, and soon we were rolling again.

Twenty minutes passed. I began to wonder if we had missed Jerry and Peter and might be headed directly into the meadow. I strained to see into the blackness of the trees past the thin strip of headlight dancing over the graveled road surface.

Another three or four anxious minutes had passed when I spotted both of them standing like tar covered posts in the middle of the road. One of them flashed his headlamp at us, and I came to a stop and rolled down my window.

Jerry came up to me. "Shift into four wheel drive and cross the stream. We had to drop a few small trees, but we're parked on the far bank in a hole we've cut into a stand of aspens."

Butte made room, and Jerry climbed in beside him. I could see in the mirrors that Peter was back telling the others the plan. He then climbed in the Jeep and waited for me to lead the way.

I could just barely see the tire tracks in the grass and brush marking where Jerry and Peter had left the road. I shifted into four wheel drive compound low first, and eased over the side and down through the brush over a four foot bank. Fifteen feet further I squeezed between two cottonwoods and dropped off a foot high step onto the gravel of the narrow stream which was no more than sixteen inches deep. Almost immediately my front wheels humped up on the far bank and onto a swatch of grass.

Jerry jumped out and led the way into a stand of aspens where two sawed stumps, maybe four inches in diameter, marked the entrance to the hide. Deep in the trees, I made out the tailgate and bumper of their truck.

We parked and got out. Billy had pulled off to the side on the grass, and Josiah and Oscar came into the grove next and parked directly behind us. Then Billy did a turn around and backed in.

We gathered around MacAvity and Jerry.

"We're a good three quarters of a mile from the compound," Jerry began. "Peter trotted up there to check it out while I was sawing out the trees."

"The place is dark except for one yard light," Peter said. "So we're lucky. Means they probably don't have motion sensors. And none of the windows showed light, so everyone must either be asleep or preoccupied."

MacAvity said, "Three quarters of a mile. That's fifteen minutes of road walking. We'll allow another fifteen minutes to get into position."

"We need to know which buildings are hot," Oscar said. "Who has the thermal viewer?"

MacAvity said, "I do. When we get close, let's cross back to this side of the stream and get opposite the place. From there we'll hopefully be able to get a clear enough view of the buildings to tell who's where. Also, by then our quarter moon should be high enough to help our approach."

He paused. "Now that we're here and we have a feeling for this, I have a suggestion for you, Lana," he said. "See if this works. Rather than having you go in with Oscar and Smoke to get the two women, I'd like for you to come in with Billy. When he stops at the main house, you can go over to interview them then. Find out who they are and what they're doing there."

"Sure," Lana said.

"Oscar? Smoke?"

They both agreed.

"Well, let's go, then," he said. "Keep your lamps off. We'll have our night eyes open and focused by the time we get there."

Lana gave me a quick kiss and whispered she loved me. I slung the .243 over my shoulder and gave her a hug, then hurried to catch up with the others who were leading off.

We followed MacAvity back to the road at a brisk pace, flooding our boots with ice cold water as we crossed the stream. Hammersmith was directly ahead of me and was walking along smoothly, though I did notice he was breathing harder than I was. Still, he and Butte were both seventy-eight years old. Amazing. Or maybe it was amazing that more people didn't remain that active.

Walking and listening to my footsteps and thinking in the dark.

And Billy had been right. Now that I was moving through the night along with these men, these friends of mine, I had become completely relaxed and filled with a kind of strange joy. It was like how I had felt when I was returning home from Hammersmiths that bloody night. Was this the emotion I had missed by not playing sports or going to war with Huey and Smoke? I wondered about that and listened to the hypnotic rhythm of our boots striking the gravel.

Suddenly we turned left back into the brush, crossed the river again and entered the tall, thick-trunked aspens that I knew grew across the river from the meadow. We slowed and moved very quietly through the trees. Here the far wall of the canyon came down to meet us, but there was also an open strip of low brush and grass that ran like a hallway between the trees and the slope.

The dim yard light of the compound began to flicker between the trees on our right as we moved forward. When we reached a point directly opposite the center of the property, everyone but MacAvity stopped and sat on their heels. I followed suit.

MacAvity began to climb the slope behind us and was soon out of view. Minutes passed. Then he was suddenly behind me and eased past to squat down among us.

"Gear up," he whispered.

I put on my mask, gloves and headset, adjusting the mike so it was close to the side of my mouth. I hadn't noticed it before, but everyone else had either a shoulder bag or day pack, which they were opening and taking gear from. Jerry handed Josiah the canvas bag with the C-4 in it.

They set about adjusting their night vision goggles, headsets and weapons, and MacAvity whispered, "The main house is cold, and the cottage, bunkhouse and middle cabin are hot. Based on what Paul and Lana saw yesterday, let's assume that the two guys are in the bunkhouse and the women are in the cabin."

He handed Hammersmith one of the baseball grenades and Oscar the thermite grenade. My heart was thudding with excitement.

"Let's go," he said.

As planned, Jerry, Peter, Smoke and Oscar peeled off to the right to cross the stream and circle around behind the cabin and bunkhouse. Hammersmith and Josiah followed MacAvity to the left to get behind the two houses, and suddenly I was by myself.

Well, here goes, Paul, ol' boy. No problem.

I eased back into the trees, noticing that MacAvity had been right--a quarter moon was now peaking over the west rim filling the meadow with a pale white light. Thirty feet ahead, it illuminated a four foot wide band of deep grass edging the stream. At its bank, I sat down, swung my legs over and eased onto a thin strip of sand. The stream was a ten foot wide, three inch deep pool at this point. Across it I entered a narrow band of small aspens that bordered the road directly across from the three crosses.

I belly crawled though these trees and was shortly able to poke my head out the other side. Rising to my knees I could see over the top of the grass that bordered the road.

I was surprised how close the compound was. It felt like I was at its very center. The road was only two feet in front of me, and the parking lot and the berm with the crosses on it was just beyond that.

Then I realized I could only see the main house which Josiah was going to enter. My view of Rojas's cottage was partly blocked by the berm. I also couldn't see any of the bunkhouse or the cabins.

This was something none of us had foreseen, even though it should have been obvious. I knew I had to cross the road in plain sight and gain the mound.

I eased up into a stooped position and wondered how I should move across the gravel road and parking lot. Slow or fast? The sound of my boots pressing down on the small stones would sound like I was shoveling it into a wooden box. But hopefully they were asleep. Best not to wake them, I concluded.

I was hot under my down coat by the time I had crept across the road and parking lot to the painted rocks edging the mowed grass. I crawled past the sign and up the side of berm. Then, very slowly, I eased up to the base of the main cross and looked out.

Now I really was in the compound.

I carefully pulled Smoke's .243 up into position, turned on the night scope, gave my radio a click to indicate I was in place, and lay there waiting.

That wasn't so bad, now was it?

The black Humvee had been moved from where it had been two days ago. I could just see the back of it sticking out from the far side of the cottage.

A few minutes passed before I heard two more clicks. That's three of us in position. Those were followed shortly by three more. Six.

I suspected only Jerry and Peter weren't in position. I estimated they had at least one-hundred and fifty yards further to traverse to the back of the bunkhouse.

Minutes dragged by. I could feel the cold begin to seep up from the ground through the compressed down of my jacket, and I could see my breath in the dim yard light. It had to be down in the twenties.

Two more clicks.

I released the rifle's safety and sighted on the cottage's front door. It showed clearly in the scope's pale green light. The red cross-hairs of the scope did not meet at the center. Instead there was red dot. I placed that dot where a man's chest would be if he were coming out the cabin's door.

And waited.

My radio gave a loud beep, and I could hear running. Suddenly, a tremendous explosion and flash of white light came from the back of the cabin, followed by another roar from inside the cabin's front room. The windows sprayed out in silver showers of glass, and the front door shattered in a flurry of splinters, leaving a smoking hole.

My scope was temporarily blinded by the flash. I looked up.

I could see MacAvity crossing the porch, stooped to be under the window sill. He reached the door and peeked past the frame into the cabin's interior. He suddenly ducked back and rolled off the front of the porch into the grass. He lay quietly on his back with his pistol resting on his chest in both hands, waiting.

I put my eye back to the scope.

At that moment, in the scope's green light, a man, naked and black with blood from head to toe, staggered to the cabin's doorway. He held an Ingram Mac10 at his side and swung it towards where Butte was hiding.

I squeezed the trigger, and the .243 roared against my shoulder. I worked the bolt, looking past the scope at the cottage. Only the man's bare and bloody feet were visible.

MacAvity rolled upright and went back to where he had been on the porch.

"I'm entering," he said over the radio.

"Go," Hammersmith came back.

He bolted in over the downed man.

Then MacAvity came back on. "Clear here. Everyone check in."

"House empty," Josiah said.

"Two guys in custody." This was Peter.

"We have the two ladies," Oscar radioed.

Hammersmith came on. "Billy, you copy?"

"We're here."

"Come on in. Make it snappy."

"Got it."

Then, Butte said, "Paul, check in!"

"I'm here."

"Where'd you aim?" he asked.

"Chest."

"Well, you can tell Huey you shot Rojas through the mouth and took off the back of his head. Smoke, you loading hollow points?"

"Yup."

I put on the safety, turned off the scope, and got to my feet. I picked up the empty casing, put it in my pocket and started over to the cabin where Smoke and Oscar had turned on the lights.

Josiah said, "I'm going to shoot a quarter pound of C-4 in the house to blow a safe. Give me five minutes unless you want to eat its door."

"When you're done with that," Hammersmith said, "go check out the root cellar."

"Will do."

"Where you going, Paul?" Eric asked.

I stopped. "Where do you want me?" I asked.

"Wait until Josiah has the safe open. I want you to help Billy in the house. Let Lana do her thing."

"I understand." I turned and stood in the middle of the compound waiting. The lights were now on in the house as were those at the end of the bunk house where the two guys were being interrogated by Jerry and Peter.

Hammersmith and Eric were dragging Rojas's corpse by its feet off the porch. I went over to help. Hammersmith caught sight of me. "No need to come over here, Paul. Stand by. Billy and Lana will be here in a second."

I stopped and waited.

At that moment an extremely sharp explosion and flash came from the house.

"OK. I'm taking house guests now," Josiah said. "It's safe in here again," chuckling. "Get it?"

"Good," MacAvity said. "Come help us get this guy up to the root cellar and bring the makings."

Josiah came out the front door of the house and around. He slung his bag over his shoulder when he reached Butte and Hammersmith. He took Eric's place, who came over to join me.

"Nice shooting, Paul," he said. "You OK?"

"I'm fine," I admitted. I looked over at Rojas's body. They had dragged it nearly to the root cellar.

The Jeep came into view, drove past the flags, turned in and parked in front of the headquarters. Billy killed the lights, and Lana and he climbed out.

Hammersmith and I went over, and Lana came jogging past on her way to the cabin. "We having fun yet?" she asked as she went past. She reached out, and we slapped hands.

"Looking good in the mask and gloves," I called after her.

She flipped me off over her shoulder.

Josiah came back on. "Fire in the hole."

A small explosion cracked the air. We looked over quickly. He had blown a lock off the root cellar's metal door.

"Amazing how useful four ounces of C-4 and three feet of fuse can be," Eric said.

Chapter
Forty-Three

Billy came out of the house with an entire filing cabinet drawer filled with folders. We stopped and let him go past.

"Could you help with the other three, Paul?" he asked, hurrying to the jeep.

Hammersmith and I went into the large front room that took up half of the building. The log walls shined with years of varnish and wear, and the river stone fireplace was blackened by decades of fires. There was no kitchen. In the back there were two rooms separated by a bathroom. One was set up as a bedroom and the other an office. It was the office that held the safe. Its door lay on its face on the floor, and a heavy desk, which Josiah had apparently used as a C-4 tamper, lay shattered everywhere. Off to one side was a filing cabinet that had been thrown on its side by the blast. I lifted it upright and took out a second drawer. Billy was coming in as I carried it out to the Jeep.

"What do you have, Lana?" Hammersmith radioed. He was standing by the fireplace.

"They're high class call girls, Eric," she told him. "They're working off attorney fees here for a man named Rice Litteneker. Name ring a bell?"

"Oh yeah," Hammersmith said. "He's Spreiter's legal council and probably a hell of a lot more as well."

He paused. "Smoke and you stand ready. We're about to move the Jeep. Take them in their 4-Runner five miles up the road before releasing them. One of them might be a jogger. Make sure they're dressed warmly. And find their cell phones and get rid of them."

"We'll stand by," Smoke said.

I came back in, again passing Billy on his way out with the third drawer. I got the last one and had a look in the safe as I did. It was stuffed with five accordion files and seven ledgers. But what looked even more promising was a Dell laptop that was slid in beside the ledgers.

"Oscar," Hammersmith continued.

"Yeah."

"Get your crew ready. You'll roll in three minutes."

"Got it."

Oscar said, "You have those boys secured?"

"Cuffed and crying," Jerry said.

Lana came on. "These women say those two men are working off their debts with Litteneker too. They say they're OK guys."

"Well, remind those two ladies to remember to cut them free when they've hoofed it back here."

"Right."

Billy and I were able to carry the safe's contents out in one load. He was very excited about the Dell.

"This is the jackpot," he said happily.

"Any loot?" Eric asked when we came back in.

"Not a dime," Billy said. Big time crime doesn't work in cash. It's all wire transfers."

"Oscar," Hammersmith said. "Time to roll."

Billy went out and got behind the wheel of the Jeep and started it. Eric and I followed him as far as the porch just as Jerry, Peter, Oscar, and Josiah came trotting up and crowded in with him. It looked like a scene from the phone booth stuffing craze of the 50s.

Billy swung the jeep around the circular drive and headed back down the road.

Hammersmith watched them go, then, "OK Smoke, you and Lana's turn."

MacAvity came up onto the porch at that moment.

"So far so good," he said. "But this fucking lycra mask is driving me ape shit. Why didn't I get us cotton ones?"

"Because you want to torture us?" I offered.

Across the grounds we watched Smoke and Lana escort the two women out of the cabin and over to their own Four Runner. They were bundled up in heavy coats and had their hands cuffed in front of them. They were giggling and climbed into the Toyota's back seat happily. I suspected we had done them a huge favor by killing Rojas and freeing them from Litteneker.

Smoke, in his usual style, started the Four Runner and threw gravel everywhere as he spun it around and headed out of the compound. By the time he went past us he must have been going forty miles an hour. All four of them were laughing.

"You see that?" Butte said. "They're all nut cases."

It had made me apprehensive. Apparently Hammersmith was feeling the same way.

"The only thing that could go wrong now," he muttered, "is if Smoke puts them in a ditch."

"Or hits an elk," I offered.

Jerry's pickup, then my Tunda with Peter at the wheel, came out of the canyon, pulled in and stopped in front of us. We stepped off the porch and went over to them. Josiah had climbed into the Dodge with Oscar and they headed back home. And Billy was alone with his booty, headed for his private plane and a quick flight to Boise. All we had to do was wait for Lana and Smoke to return, and we'd all be able to leave.

I checked my watch. We had been here only twenty-five minutes, though it felt like half the night. I was relieved.

It took Smoke nearly twenty minutes to drop the prisoners off, cut their restraints and get back. We were waiting in the relative warmth of the main room. Jerry had gone around and turned off the cabin and bunk house lights, closed their doors, and shot out the yard light. There was nothing he could do for the shattered cottage. Fortunately, it sat back a bit and might not be noticed for some time, perhaps weeks. The Humvee's driver's side window had been blown out, but neither it nor the grenade's tiny frag holes in the driver's door could be seen from the road.

"In five hours it will be light, and Oscar and Josiah will be back home," Hammersmith said, "and Joy Chu is going to get the best phone call of her life."

This was something no one had told me about.

"Joy Chu?" I asked.

Butte said, "Oscar's going to pass on a hot tip about the new drug shipment she told him was coming. There is at least three times as much of that shit in the root cellar as we confiscated on Saddle Pass. Plus, leaking all over it is her number one most wanted, Rojas."

Eric added, "Oscar's going to tell her that he has reliable information as to the whereabouts of the drugs and the potential for a Canadian revenge hit on its location... namely here."

"That's it?" I asked.

"Not quite," Hammersmith said. "In fact, why don't you do it now, Butte?"

MacAvity grinned. "I been waiting thirty some years to try this thing."

He pulled the two pound thermite grenade out of his shoulder bag, went around the end of the porch and into the dark.

We went to the side to watch him. He was barely visible.

"Thanks for shooting out the yard light, Jerry, you ass," Peter said.

"At least I have two ears," Jerry growled.

There was a muffled thump that vibrated the ground, and the root cellars door, which Butte had apparently slammed shut after tossing in the grenade, flew back in a bloom of fireworks that lasted more than half a minute. It was spectacularly hot and sizzled crazily. We could only imagine what was taking place inside the walls in the white heat. I had never imagined anything could be so hot.

MacAvity's silhouette walked back to us, framed by the inferno he had created.

When he reached us he said, "It worked."

We busted up.

"Christ, man!" Jerry murmured. "You whites are dangerous fuckers."

The 4-Runner pulled up behind us and stopped.

"Time to go, folks," Hammersmith said.

Smoke and Lana got out and stood transfixed staring at the flames that were roaring from the root cellar.

"What caused that?" Lana said.

"Nothing like a little thermite," Smoke said. "But my favorite will always be napalm. Right Butte?"

"Can we take these fucking masks and gloves off now, Hammer?" Butte whined.

"Do it while we're rolling!" Eric said. "For God's sake, people, we've got to get the hell out of here."

Chapter
Forty-Four

Jerry and Peter pulled into the parking lot behind us. They wanted to load in their grub box and personal gear and keep going. We went up to the cabins with them to help, using our headlamps to light the way. It only took one trip, and they pulled out. Jerry stuck an arm out the window and waved as they made the turnaround and started back down the valley's road.

It was two-thirty and very cold. Hammersmith said to leave everything in the camper, lock it, and get some sleep. He and Smoke planned to leave as soon as they managed to wake up and have something to eat.

I said, "We'll probably take off too, Eric, but what do we tell the owners of this place?"

"I told her we usually stay only one night, but she said we'd still have to pay for three."

"God, I'm sorry, Eric," I said. "I should have gotten us rooms at the Best Western."

"It's no big deal, Paul," he assured me. "We needed the privacy. It's covered."

I nodded.

Lana and I entered our own cabin, and Ollie climbed sleepily from her collapsible crate, stretched, yawned, grinned a hello, and promptly turned around and went back to sleep. Lana laughed happily.

"I love that dog," she said, giving my arm a hug.

Smoke knocked on the log wall of our cabin the next morning. I looked at my watch and saw it was already nine forty-five. He passed by the front window carrying a duffle down to the parking lot. Lana got wearily to her feet and went into the bathroom.

It only took us fifteen minutes to bush our teeth, dress, and carry our things down to the truck. The camper was stuffed with all the gear the five of us had brought, but we were ready to roll.

Lana squeezed into the Tundra's back seat between Butte and Smoke on our drive in to Darby, and Hammersmith sat up front with me. Lana only had to slap Smoke's hand off her leg once, so I knew he was exhausted.

"We're going to have to present Huey with the trophies," Hammersmith was saying. "Anyone not going to be free tonight?"

"Holy shit, Hammer," MacAvity moaned. "A man's gotta have his rest, you know."

"Think about *us*, Butte," Lana said. "We've got that long drive still ahead of us. There's no way we'll be back before five o'clock."

"Plenty of time, then," Eric said. "My place at six? We'll serve you all a nice supper."

Smoke chuckled. "Now you have an idea how he used to run everyone ragged. If the Bassac River got too calm, he'd order the STABs and PBRs to go out and make some wakes. Maybe call in some air strikes on elephants or something."

That comment didn't go over too well with either Hammersmith or MacAvity. Everyone was silent until we reached the outskirts of town. Without asking, I pulled into a cafe that had trucks and two semis loaded with cattle parked around it. A sure sign of a place that served hearty breakfasts all day long.

Smoke got out of the back and scanned the sky. A bank of clouds was peeking over the Bitterroots.

He lit up, blew smoke into the cold morning air and studied it. "Let's make this snappy," he said. "One thing about a Maule, it knows how to buck. Those big wings ride the bumps like a cork, and I think we're in for a real dose of it."

Hammersmith ignored him, but Butte looked nervously at the clouds. "You going over that or under?" he asked as we walked over to the front door.

"I don't know yet," Smoke said.

We were at the hayfield and airstrip by eleven fifteen. I parked the Tundra in the grass alongside the Maule, and Smoke made quick work of removing the tie downs from the plane's wings. He was very concerned about balancing the load, and as we took the gear over to him from the truck, he put the duffles in first, and then the clothing bags on top of them. Finally, he hooked a bungy net over the load, shook the pile until it settled in place, then tightened the net further.

Hammersmith had walked over to the ranch house and returned in the cab of the owner's old International Harvester one ton truck, which had a two-hundred gallon fuel tank behind the cab strapped to the flatbed with steel bands. The owner, a weathered old cowboy dressed in jeans, flannel shirt, and ancient felt Stetson, handed the nozzle to Smoke and began cranking the fuel in.

Done, Smoke paid and climbed aboard. He signaled Butte and then Hammersmith to do the same, and the Harvester pulled away and returned to the ranch grounds. Smoke turned over the engine which jumped to life in less than one revolution.

It was now a quarter past noon.

Smoke gave us a brief wave as he gave the Maule the throttle and bumped through the grass over to the mowed strip. Without hesitation, he swung it into line and was airborne in less than a hundred and fifty yards. He wagged the wings radically at us, and they pulled away and up into the sky headed in the direction of Lolo Pass. It appeared he had decided to fly Highway 12 back to Magnet.

Lana and I stood in the silence that descended on us as the plane vanished from sight.

After a moment she said, "Well, I'm going to let Ollie run a bit and do her business."

She went over to the truck, adding over her shoulder, "You boys do take interesting vacations, don't you?"

It was after one o'clock when we hit the snow, or more correctly, when the snow hit us. We had not even begun the steep climb to Lolo Pass when we entered it. It was like driving through Alice's looking glass. One minute we were in the cold sunlight; the next, we were in a heavy blizzard of large snowflakes. They stuck to the windshield and had accumulated on the road an inch deep.

I slowed to thirty miles an hour, and we crept along. Fortunately, we had the road to ourselves going west, and only occasional semis came the other way, snow caked to their grills and mud flaps. We were in for a long afternoon of driving.

Nothing to do but relax, turn up the heat for the defroster, and settle in.

"Looks like we'll be missing dinner," I said.

Lana nodded.

Ollie was asleep on her lap. Lana had gotten her excited at the airport and running circles around her. Apparently the little corgi girl was plain tuckered-out now. I was amazed at how much sleep puppies needed. I decided to not look at her too often, though, because she reminded me how I would love to do the same thing. Besides being tired from the long night's activities, the wipers and snowflakes were hypnotizing me. But I knew Lana would drive anytime I asked, and she was an excellent driver by anyone's standards.

I slowed and shifted into four-wheel drive, then resumed thirty miles an hour and held it there.

At the summit, three inches of wet snow had accumulated, and a huge Rio snow plow came roaring at us up from the west side. The driver, buttoned down in a fur-lined Mad Bomber hat, gave us a wave from inside the towering yellow cab and thundered past. He must have been doing close to forty miles an hour. Impressive.

Now the long, winding hundred miles down began.

Lana had been silent for more than half an hour, but now she said, "You think Smoke can handle this weather?"

I shook my head. "I don't think he'd go though this. Maybe over it."

I thought it over. "Yeah, I'm pretty sure he'll go over it. None of these peaks are much over ten thousand feet, but the clear skies can't be much higher, I would think."

"Let's hope," she said.

She fell silent again. Then, about ten minutes later she leaned against the door and looked at me.

"How do you feel about having killed a man, Paul?" she asked.

I glanced at her, then turned back and focused on the truck tracks I had begun following in our lane .

"Is that what you've been thinking about?"

"Not totally. I was also thinking about a painting I want to do, but somehow that got me to thinking about last night."

Finally I admitted, "Well, I've been thinking about nothing else, to tell you the truth. That mess at

Hammersmith's, what with the shooting off of feet and the total goring of the guy in the kitchen, really put me off my feed. I'll admit that. But this was different."

Lana nodded. "Because he had it coming."

"Yeah, that's a lot of it, I guess. I'm not much on psychology, you know. But I'm glad, I guess, that I didn't have any choice in the matter unless I was willing to watch him kill Butte."

I thought over what I had said, adding, "Plus, Hammersmith wasn't about to let me get close enough to see the results of my handiwork. Apparently it wasn't a very pretty sight. And those two M-67 grenades sprayed little quarter inch chunks of steel spring all over the place. I don't know how Rojas was still alive."

Lana said, "Smoke told me he thought the one they tossed into the back room rolled under his bed. The mattress took most of the damage."

I nodded. "That makes sense. Then the second one got him through the doorway between the bedroom and the front room. But not enough to stop him completely."

I started to feel a little woozy just imagining it. Anyway, it was over. I was also beginning to think that a lot of the justice that's metered out in the world is done just the way we had. And injustices, too. And injustices.

The snow covering the road was quickly thinning, and within ten minutes we were in rain that was falling heavily.

"We need to stop somewhere and call Hammersmith," Lana said. I doubt we'll be home before seven."

I agreed.

I pushed our speed up to forty, then forty five.

Chapter
Forty-Five

Despite the rain we reached Hammersmith's at a quarter till seven. I pulled in behind the house and parked beside Smoke's truck. Lana carried Ollie, and just as we ducked onto the back porch Ruthie opened the door for us, and we went inside to the warm kitchen and through to the dining room.

Smoke, Butte, Hammersmith greeted us from the dining room table where they were working their way through three baked chickens.

Huey was looking on from the living room, sitting in an easy chair with a canned liquid dinner at his elbow on an end table. A long flexible straw stuck from it. He looked pretty good--much better, in fact, than I had expected. Though his face was a sickly yellow and still partially bandaged, there were no purple bruises, and his eyes were wide open.

He got to his feet. Lana put down Ollie and gave Huey a hug, while Ollie squirmed around their ankles.

"You're looking good," I said, shaking his hand.

"That's Micha's doing," Hammersmith said from the table. "He smeared some white salve all over Huey's face and neck the same day you guys took off. Said it was made from leech spit."

Huey hissed, "Iss not nagic. His doctor fhren gae it to hin."

He sat back down.

Ruthie helped him out, "It was an anticoagulant leech topical called Hirudin. Worked like magic."

Beside Huey's strawberry dinner shake was the Ruger Mark III. Apparently Eric and Smoke had already done the presentation. I reached into my pocket and took out the brass .243 casing and gave it to him.

"Hut's dis?" he asked.

Smoke answered over the top of a drumstick he was gnawing on, "Paul here pocketed it after he squeezed off the shot."

Huey nodded and put it on the table beside the Ruger. He then picked up the milkshake and saluted Lana and me with it. He looked down at Ollie who was now lying on her back hoping to have her tummy petted, saluted her as well. He carefully inserted the straw down the side of his wired teeth and drank deeply.

Ruthie took two plates and a bowl of mashed potatoes from her range's warming drawer and placed them on the table. We sat down and helped ourselves to the trimmings, and Ruthie poured us both glasses of chardonay. I could tell from the way Lana dug in she was just as starved as I was. Breakfast had been our last bite of food that day.

"I phoned Billy this afternoon," Hammersmith said. "Told him to go ahead and notify Joy Chu. He said he had his staff digitally scanning every single page of the stuff he'd collected, and they fire-wired the entire contents of that laptop over to his computer. They are also copying everything to an external hard drive and will put it in the Banner's safe. Joy will take all the stuff, but she's not going to know of the copies, even if she asks."

He swallowed the last bit of wine in his glass and reached for the bottle to refill it.

"He also wants to call one of his FBI pals at their Boise office. I told him to do whatever he wanted. Either way, tomorrow morning Joy Chu and that FBI guy will be sitting down with Billy going over the materials his "anonymous source" has given to him. By this time tomorrow night Mr. Clifford Spreiter and Mr. Rice Litteneker will be wondering what they did that brought their little multi-state international empire crashing down on them."

"Plus," Smoke added, "a lot of people will be wondering who would have enough gall to fry a corpse on a funeral pyre made up of seven and a half million dollars worth of methamphetamine."

I had to laugh. "There's a certain poetic irony in that, isn't there?"

MacAvity, who had been busy enjoying Ruthie's cooking, nodded. "Rojas certainly fell on the sword he lived by, I'd say. But we still don't know who was on this end receiving the drug shipments."

"I'll bet we'll know as soon as Billy's staff looks this stuff over tonight," Eric said. "He's got them on twelve hour shifts."

"Personally," Lana said, "I think it's got to be someone either in Confluence or in the Tri-Cities area."

"Well," Hammersmith said, raising his wine glass, and getting to his feet, "Here's to us."

Huey stood and Ruthie went over and put a full glass of wine in his hand with a clean straw sticking up from it. Tears began to roll down his cheeks. We lifted our glasses over our heads, then drank. Ruthie put her arms around Huey and held him as his tears flowed.

Smoke came around the table and took Huey's right hand in both of his. "It's over now, pardner," he said, grinning. "It's now time to rebuild, and I don't mean just your house. Know what I'm saying?"

Huey looked around at all of us. "OK," he managed.

Chapter
Forty-Six

We sat along the bar, Jake, Don, me, Lana, Smoke, Hammersmith, Ruthie, and Huey--straw in hand. MacAvity and Sheila were behind the bar, pouring drinks as fast as they could.

The place was packed. Shay, Jables, Mike and Leaps were standing off to our right listening to Smoke read from the Confluence Tribune, and nearly everyone had a copy and was following along. It had come to our houses around seven that morning. It was only nine o'clock now. MacAvity had been forced to open it at eight, two hours early.

Inch tall headlines read AUTHORITIES MAKE MAJOR DRUG BUST by Billy O'Connor of The Boise Banner and The Associated Press.

Everyone had read the seven full columns at home, but somehow we couldn't help but read them aloud to each other again here at the pub.

"Get this," Smoke was saying through a cloud of cigarillo smoke. "FBI, DEA, Camas Police, and law enforcement agencies in seven states, Canada, and Guatemala arrest 28 ring leaders on charges of international methamphetamine trafficking.

"The 28 have been accused of the trafficking more than 120 million dollars worth of crystal methamphetamine from August 1998 to the present.

"Joy Chu of the Drug Enforcement Agency and Dewayne Gibson of the Federal Bureau of Investigation said the case was triggered by an anonymous source who handed thousands of pages of evidence over to the Boise Banner.

"The case centers on methamphetamine brought in by a multi-state drug trafficking and money laundering organization called Western Summits Investment Group, headquartered in Missoula, Montana.

"Clifford Spreiter, 68, founder and president of Western Summits, Attorney Rice Litteneker, 59, and seven vice presidents are charged with trafficking the methamphetamine in boxes labeled "Mission Relief."

"The methamphetamine was imported through a chain of missions Western Summits had established in Cambodia, Hong Kong, Taiwan, Guatemala, and Canada. The final destination was Three Crosses Ministry Haven and Seminary in the Bitterroot Mountains south of Missoula.

"Ministry Haven was recently the object of what is reported to have been a drug related retaliation. Motivated by an apparent internal conflict, the pastor's cottage was destroyed and the burnt remains of an unidentified man were found in a root cellar. Sources say that nearly six million dollars in methamphetamine expected to be found at the ministry by law enforcement had been stolen by those responsible for the attack.

"Earlier this month, Sheriff Charlie Rand of Magnet County and Oscar Redtail, Josiah Longbeach, Jerry Hobbs-Smith and Peter Hobbs-Smith of the Camas Tribal Police were first to intercept a Western Summit's shipment worth in excess of two million dollars."

Smoke looked over the remainder of the article, then found what he was looking for near the end.

"Here it is," he said. "Joy Chu and Charlie Rand reported that several citizens of Ryback had evidence of Spreiter's Cambodian activities and were targeted by Spreiter and his group earlier this month. Cano Franzani, 40, the son of Rojas Franzani,60, one of Spreiter's Lieutenants, was taken into custody by Sheriff Rand and is cooperating with the FBI."

"Read the last paragraph, Smoke," someone said directly behind us.

We turned around. Charlie stood there, the Trib. folded under one arm. He had his gray Stetson tipped back on his head and his hands in his pockets.

"Ho, ho," MacAvity said, reaching for Charlie's brand of beer. "How are you, Sheriff?"

Charlie put a hand on Smoke's shoulder and read the last paragraph for him.

"Still at large are Rojas Franzani ,60, Bahamondes Valladores, 60,...."

He read the entire list of five. When he was done, he straightened up, and Butte handed him a long neck Budweiser.

The bar had gone absolutely silent.

Charlie took two long swallows, lowered the bottle, wiped his mouth on his cuff, and put his beer down on the counter with a loud crack.

He grimly looked us over. Shook his head.

"I have a feeling," he finally said, "there are people in this room who know exactly where Rojas and Valladores are."

Lana pressed her knee against mine telling me not to open my mouth.

"And I hope you all understand, folks, that this isn't over."

No one said anything. Some of us were watching Charlie warily, others were studying their drinks or the floor.

He picked his bottle back up, drained it, and placed it quietly back on the bar.

Struggling not to smile, he reached into his back pocket and withdrew his well worn, tooled western wallet, opened it, took out a hundred dollar bill and put it on the counter beside his beer.

"Know what I'm saying?"

No one moved.

"Well, never mind."

He put his wallet back into his pocket and pulled his hat back down over his forehead.

"Drink up, folks," he said.

And left.

The relief in the pub was palpable. Charlie hadn't carted any of us off to life in prison but had stood a round of beer instead. Justice served.

When the sound of his Ford Expedition could no longer be heard, some of us laughed nervously, some took cautious sips from their drinks, and others talked quietly among themselves.

Smoke was grinning and studying his cigarillo.

"Does this mean more fun?" he said.

Chapter
Forty-Seven

It was two years later, in the dead of winter, before Charlie's warning proved true. And it wasn't as if we didn't know it would. It was the waiting that had tormented us. It seemed that the threat, over time, paled in comparison to the anxiety we all felt to have the past events, triggered by the break-in at Hammersmith's, all come to an end.

Smoke was holding court from his usual stool in the Pub. He was half tanked, and a guy named Freddy Stripe, who had just strutted out of MacAvity's Pub, had rubbed him wrong.

Butte MacAvity's polished old world bar top and hanging cabinets ran twenty feet along the left side of the pub's long room. At the far end it turned towards the wall for six feet and accommodated three additional stools. Smoke's was one of them. Huey Houston, Eric Hammersmith and I were his audience.

Stripe had sat closest to the door and addressed us from a distance of five empty bar stools in a churlish tone for the length of time it took him to drink three Granddad doubles. He had raged on about "...those rag heads. We need to build a fence around the whole Middle East and let them fight to the last man. Then we'll shoot that bastard. Do the same thing with environ meddle ists. 'cept them faggots don't fight. We'll just kill 'em."

Butte served Stripe his drinks in heavy glasses neat, one after the other.

Smoke had stared at Stripe the entire time. Saying nothing.

None of us said much, but Butte had at least been polite and stood behind the bar halfway between him and us, nodding at the appropriate times like a philosophical penguin.

Finally, Stripe shook his head in hopeless disgust with our company and left.

He had been doing this every afternoon for nearly two weeks.

Smoke, who had actually attempted to make him feel at home the first time, had not said another word in his presence after the first ten minutes of that first visit. Stripe must have assumed Smoke had gone deaf-mute on us.

But he wasn't mute now. Enough was enough. Twelve afternoons, now, Smoke had been holding his temper. We were relieved he has chosen to get it off his chest before he killed the guy. I was a bit disappointed he hadn't, to be honest.

"How many of us," Smoke was asking, "have ever seen a guy that had *ever* seen combat wearing around a ridiculous gold braided Vietnam Veteran's hat?"

None of us were expected to answer, and we didn't.

"None!" he said. "Never. They are all a bunch of guys doing what Halliburton is now contracted to do. They served food and typed letters and now they're strutting around acting like they won the war single handedly. I'll give that wing nut his own fricking war he keeps it up," he said.

"We won the war?" I asked.

He paused and took a sip of his White Horse scotch, knocked a cigarillo out of its pack, lit it, and continued.

"And what about that pearl handled Colt 11 he has strapped to his leg?"

"Hey, hold on there, Smoke," Butte said. He had moved down to stand in the corner so he was in the middle of us.

Butte liked Colt 11 semi automatics, though at the moment he had a Browning 9mm under his leather vest down the back of his pants.

"Well, hell! You know what I mean, Butte. But you don't walk into strange bars wearing a heavy-assed firearm strapped to your leg. He even carries it into the grocery."

Butte grinned. "Actually, I do too, Smoke. But I know what you're saying." Then said the obvious, "So you're saying the guy's a phony, right?"

Smoke slapped the bar.

"That's exactly what I'm saying."

He took a huge swallow to finish his drink, and Butte topped it back up from the bottle that he kept directly under the bar where Smoke always sat.

Huey was swirling his drink in its glass.

"I hear what you're saying, Smoke. But I know that some of the guys that flew with me wear Vet hats like his."

Smoke stared at him in amazed disgust.

"Shut the fuck up, will you? We're having a conversation here."

Butte reached out to take Smoke's drink back. Smoke grabbed his wrist.

Butte's face turned to stone. He stared hard at Smoke.

Smoke looked quickly down at his own hand as if amazed how it was misbehaving.

Eric, the old Navy commander, gently removed Smoke's hand from Butte's.

"OK. OK. I take it back," Smoke growled. "Shit."

He tapped the ash off his cigarillo into a small tin ashtray in front of him, shaking his head.

Butte pushed Smoke's White Horse back to him and gave one of his it's-OK-*this*-time looks.

We all made busy studying the insides of our glasses like geriatric monks seeking meaning, and remained silent. The five of us were comfortable with silence. We'd now known each other for sixty-eight years. Eighty years for Eric and Butte.

In fact, the entire town of Ryback is comfortable with silence.

It's not a bad thing.

That's what was so odd about Freddy Stripe. Very few people ever turn off the highway and come in to visit Ryback. But Stripe did that and more.

Two weeks earlier, during our latest blizzard, he came into town in the middle of the night driving a huge Magna 63 Country Coach RV and towing a '05 Jeep Wrangler. He drove directly to our football/baseball/skeet shooting field like he knew exactly where he was going and parked in the small parking lot that was nearly indistinguishable under the seven inches of new snow. It was like he knew the field hadn't been used in twenty years and was now open for homesteading.

But we assumed that Stripe was just an old Vet that knew enough to find a safe harbor during a storm. That he'd pull out again in the light of day.

But he didn't.

Instead, he ran out hydraulic levelers, ran up a huge American flag on a mast lifted on the side of the RV cab, and shut down the 525 horsepower caterpillar diesel engine. He put on his Vietnam Vet hat, strapped on his Colt 11, and walked the hundred yards to MacAvity's and settled in.

For the winter?

"Is he going to be here in town for the entire winter?" Smoke groused.

Butte shrugged.

No one said anything.

Smoke scanned our faces. "Did you see the plates on his rig?"

We looked up.

"He has British Columbia plates," Smoke told us.

"You sure they aren't Washington plates?" I asked. "They're both white."

"They're BC plates. I got close enough to see through all that road muck covering the lower half of that rolling whore house of his," Smoke said. "BC plates in brackets that advertise 'Pony Express RV, Minot, North Dakota.'"

"So, there you go, Smoke," Butte said. "Lives in BC, Canada, and buys American. Runs up old glory wherever he parks. Carries a damn fine weapon. Is proud to have served in Nam." He recharged my Wisers. "So what's not to like?"

We watched Smoke, waiting for an answer.

Smoke was looking at his hands wrapped round his glass. He shook his head.

"He's a phony," he said quietly.

Butte grinned.

"If his weapon is empty he's a phony. If it's loaded and has one under the hammer, what do you call him?"

"A dangerous phony."

Smoke had had enough of us for one afternoon. He turned on his stool, dropped his boots to the floor, said "A.M.F.," and left.

"A.M.F.?" MacAvity said.

"Adios Mother Fuckers," I explained.

He shook his head in disgust.

"Well," Hammersmith said, "things are looking up around here. Maybe we'll have some fun this winter yet."

Sheila came through the door before it had a chance to close behind Smoke. She hung her coat on the bent hickory coat rack to the right, unhooked her apron from a peg in the wall, and came over as she tied it behind her back.

"What's with Grumpy?" she asked, referring to Smoke.

Butte shrugged. He took Smoke's tin ashtray, shook it over the rubbish bin under the bar, then pulled his glass off and placed it into the sink.

Sheila continued around the corner of the bar and went into the kitchen to prepare supper for Butte and anyone else that might drop by later. Usually between five and fifteen folk came in to have some of MacAvity's and her fine cooking. A change from staying home looking out windows over snow covered fields and thinking about spring.

There were never more than two items a person could select for dinner. There was always tenderloin steak, but the other choice was whatever Butte or Sheila felt like cooking up. It might be elk stew or shredded pork mole wrapped in soft tortillas fresh from the grill, or sweet and sour chicken, or whatever they felt like. One never knew.

"Well I'll be damned," Butte said from the far end of the bar. "Stripe walked off with his glass."

We looked. Butte was staring in disbelief at the wet ring on the varnished wood surface. Apparently Butte wasn't used to people taking off with his glasses. Apparently people were virtuous around a man who had a high caliber weapon stuck down his pants.

Huey, always one to make sure things were perceived truthfully, cleared his throat.

"Um, I think it was there after he left," he said.

Butte slumped visibly and leaned against the counter.

"Christ almighty!" he moaned. "That Smoke. What the hell would he want with Stripe's whiskey glass?"

We considered that.

"Wants to shove it up Stripe's ass?" I offered.

No one spoke.

After a moment Butte pushed off the bar and came back slowly to the sink. He drew some hot water and began washing dishes.

"So," I ventured, changing the direction the afternoon had taken, "what's so special about a Colt 1911?"

MacAvity looked up without stopping what he was doing.

"Actually, Stripe is packing a Colt Browning 1911 A1. Military. Came out in 1926. Improved the 1911."

"It's rare?"

He bent back to his washing.

"Hardly. There were over sixty thousand Colt 1911s on hand before World War One broke out, and another sixty thousand were manufactured by the Springfield Armory before our involvement. After the war started they were made at a rate of one thousand a day. By mid 1918 it was two thousand a day. Do the math. Say half a million by 1920? And of those, one hundred thousand disappeared. Even a thief knows a good thing when he sees it."

Hammersmith whistled between his teeth.

"As for Stripe's," Butte continued, "the A1 was used clear up to very recently when NATO dictated standardized ammunition and selected the 9 mm Beretta. Big mistake. Put a .45 slug in a guy, he doesn't get up."

Don and Jake came in. Apparently they had cleared their road enough to escape the ranch.

They had Lana with them and slid into one of the booths. I took my drink and pile of bills off the bar and went over. Lana made room, gave me a kiss, and MacAvity came around to take their orders.

"It's nearly dark out there, Paul," Lana informed me. You planning on coming home tonight?"

"It's a thought."

Don ordered a pitcher of Guinness assuming I'd help drink it. Jake and Lana, like girlfriends do, both ordered the same thing--martinis with two olives each.

Butte nodded and said, "You want some of my bite du jour? I'll throw in a bottle of Merlot."

"Is it that bad?" Lana asked.

"Of course it is."

"What is it, exactly, then?" This was Jake.

"I'm not sure," Butte said. "It's intended to look like Russian meatballs and noodles."

We considered this.

"Shall we take a chance?" she asked.

"We can always drink the free wine," Lana pointed out.

Butte went back to get our drinks and tell Sheila the bad news.

"So where's that big RV?" Lana asked me.

Eric and Huey turned on their stools with that.

"Whaddaya mean?" I said.

"I'll say it slower."

"It's gone?" Huey asked.

"That would be my immediate conclusion," Lana said, "since it's not there."

MacAvity picked up the bar phone and dialed. And waited. Then he hung up.

"He's home."

"Who's home?" Lana asked.

"Smoke."

"How do you know that?"

"He answered his phone."

Everyone stared at Butte.

"You mean you just hung up on him?" Jake squeaked.

Butte nodded. "What would you have me say? 'You home?' and have him say, 'What the fuck do you think? You're talking to me, aren't you?'"

"But he'll spend the entire night wondering who hung up on him," Jake persisted.

"Be good for him. What else does he have to do? Thumb through his photo albums?"

We thought this over. I wondered what else there was to do in Ryback in the dead of winter. Nothing wrong with photo albums.

"Well," Hammersmith said. "At least he hasn't shot that Stripe fellow yet." He stood and struggled to drag his heavy barn coat on. "I'll see if his RV tracks aren't in the snow going out my way," he said.

Huey reached out and helped Eric pull his coat up over his shoulders and then took up his own.

No one paid them any mind as they went out into the blue black cold.

We watched the door close after them.

"Am I missing something here?" Don asked.

"Smoke thinks the owner of that RV is a phony," I said.

"A phony what?"

Butte came back with a tray and placed the two martinis and our pitcher and two glasses on the table.

"Thinks ol' Freddy Stripe is no more a Nam Vet than that hound you have out on your ranch," he told Don.

"Oh."

"Yeah. Oh."

Lana shook her head and took a tiny satisfied sip of her martini.

"What?" I said.

She sighed. "I hope he is a phony. The last thing we need in this town is another Vietnam Vet."

"What?" Butte and I said simultaneously.

We could hear Sheila bust out in her whiskey voiced guffaw clear from the kitchen.

Jake was hiding her laugh behind both hands.

Butte yelled at the kitchen, "Shut up in there."

Sheila appeared in the doorway holding a huge steel spoon.

"You say something?"

"Yeah. I want some rat poison put in these ladies' meat balls."

She turned back into the kitchen. "*Somebody's* balls are going to get what for. I can promise you *that*."

Chapter
Forty-Eight

The wind had shifted from the west to the north during the night. From the window above our sink, I could see the early light turn salmon against a perfectly clear sky. After weeks, the lid had finally blown off, and we'd be feeling the sun and plummeting temperatures today. A gift from Canada.

The ancient dial thermometer hinged to the outside kitchen window frame read minus two. It would be the sort of day when the house popped as it adjusted to the cold, and coffee, sipped in front of the gas log Jotul, smelled particularly delicious. A good day to sneak a cap of brandy into the mug.

Lana came from her bedroom on Ollie's heels. Our two year old corgi slept with her. Ollie's crate, luxuriantly furnished with a folded down sleeping bag, simply didn't measure up to the thick blankets on Lana's bed. Plus, when the room turned arctic on winter nights, Ollie was allowed under the blankets where she could curl up against Lana's side for additional warmth.

To be a corgi.

Lana poured a cup of coffee and heaved a sigh.

"God! Why aren't I hung over?" she said.

We went in to sit by the fire.

"You are. You just don't know it yet," I said.

"It was Jake's fault."

"Always is."

"I didn't even bring money."

"No."

She sipped carefully. Ollie sat at her feet staring at her without moving. Without blinking.

Finally Lana noticed her.

"What?"

Ollie stared.

"Oh, for Christ's sake."

Lana heaved to her feet and went back into the kitchen. Always the herd dog, Ollie was jumping happily up against the back of her legs the whole way making certain her gratitude had been delivered.

Lana pulled an iron skillet down from its hook on the wall and banged it onto the gas range. She lit the burner, and when the pan was hot, cracked two eggs and tipped the whites into it.

Ollie watched carefully. The raw yokes were glopped into a bowl, and in moments the cooked whites were added. Lana pulverized the egg shells under a spoon and sprinkled them over the top of the mess and put the bowl on the floor.

Finished, she came back in and resumed her seat. Ollie was done and curling up beside her nearly before Lana had taken her second sip of coffee.

"I'm glad you're not hung over," I said.

She said nothing.

The grain elevators out our front window were taking on the sun's yellow light, and the air was filled with tiny glitters of drifting ice dust. Definitely cold out there. Sometimes these ice crystals formed sun dogs and ice bows around the sun. But it had to be sub zero to happen.

Someone pulled in at the barn. We heard a door thump shut and snow squeak under approaching footsteps. There was a knock.

Lana looked at me with raised her eyebrows and upturned hand. It wouldn't be Smoke. He never knocked, nor was expected to.

I hollered "Come in!" without getting up, and the back door opened on cold hinges.

Charlie stamped his cowboy boots on the back porch and stepped in. He took off his thick green hooded sheriff's parka, hung it with our coats, and hooked his felt cowboy hat over it.

"Morning, Charlie," Lana said.

He nodded and headed straight for the kitchen and came in with one of our huge white pannikin mugs. He stirred his usual three spoons of sugar into the coffee and took a seat on the couch.

"So why the police coat?" I said. "What happened to your sheepskin?"

Charlie shook his head. Took a careful sip of his coffee, and leaned back tiredly.

"All night being a sheriff," he said.

We waited.

Charlie always wore his ranch clothes. He only wore the sheriff's coat if he was working with other law enforcement agencies. He didn't trust they wouldn't shoot him by mistake.

"I was on the Rez." He blew on his coffee and took a larger swallow. "Someone took a shot at Micha Wirestone last night. I went down to help figure out who it was."

"You learn anything?" I said.

"Only that he parked near Kimmy Musselshell's at the mouth of Rattlesnake Canyon and came along the base of the ridge and into Micha and Josiah Longbeach's stand of timber."

He rolled his neck, working out the fatigue.

"Micha was saved by the fact he lights with kerosene. If he'd been lit up by electric lights the shooter would have seen that it was Micha's dog sitting at the table eating, not Micha. Shot out the kitchen window and removed the top third of the dog's ear."

Lana looked horrified.

"Shot off the dog's ear?"

Charlie smiled tiredly.

"So Micha sticks that giant double barreled ten gauge out the window and lets go with first one then another thundering load of buckshot."

He shook his head.

"He brought down so many limbs and pine needles onto the snow it looked like a bomb had been dropped."

"Any blood?" This was me.

"No blood. And no shit," he said.

"Maybe he had his cuffs tucked into the top of his boots?" I offered.

"Longbeach said his tracks were strange. Said he didn't roll his feet."

"You know those redskins."

"What do you mean, didn't roll his feet?" Lana asked, ignoring me.

"You know, heel-toe. Like a rocker. The tracks show he didn't walk that way."

We considered this. Lana got up and went in to replenish her coffee. She was moving like she actually wasn't hung over after all. A damn miracle.

"You know anything about a guy named Freddy Stripe?" I said.

Charlie turned sideways on the couch to face me and the fire and to get more comfortable. He draped his left arm over the leather cushions.

"The guy in that luxury yacht parked by the ball diamond?

I nodded.

"No. Should I?"

I shrugged. "It's just that he pulled out last night," I said.

"Last night?"
I nodded.
"What time?"
"Don't know."
Charlie drummed his fingers on the couch's oak frame. Lana had resumed her seat.
"I should have run his plates," Charlie finally said.
"Smoke says they're British Columbia plates."
Charlie's brows shot up. "Really."
"And, Smoke hates him for some reason."
"That doesn't mean too much. Probably the guy's hat."
I nodded.
Charlie pushed to his feet and took his cup into the kitchen, washed it, and replaced it on the shelf.
Lana was on her feet.
"Where do you think you're going?" she said.
"Back to the ranch for some shut eye."
"Wait a second."
She pushed past him and went over to the stove. The egg basket was still out on the counter and she broke eight of them into the skillet and added some salsa before he was able to work up a viable protest.
He watched her for a moment, looked back in at me, shrugged, and went over and started slicing bread for the toaster.
Always helpful, I focused my attention on the way the sky was now taking on the blue of a perfect morning and how the elevators gleamed in the clean light.
Another skillet clanked down on the stove, and the smell of bacon ends frying filled the warmth of the house.

Chapter
Forty-Nine

I walked the four blocks to MacAvity's as I always did. Huey pulled up beside me, parked, and we went in.

Hammersmith and Butte were discussing Stripe's leaving in the dark. I jumped in and told them what Charlie had been doing all night.

"He think Stripe shot at Wirestone?" Hammersmith said.

"He just said he should have run his plates."

"But didn't."

"Right."

"Is he going to have anyone look for him?" Butte said.

"He didn't say."

Huey frowned and cleared his throat.

"Could be coincidence," he offered.

"You mean him leaving the same night Micha's dog is wounded?" I said.

They looked at me.

"Lana's sorry for the dog," I said.

Butte shook his head and turned to get Huey's Black Velvet and soda, and my Wisers with a splash. Tonight he was wearing his blowzy shirt and arm garters, jeans, and packing a Para Covert Black 9mm.

"Where's Smoke, by the way?" he asked.

We looked at Smoke's stool, which stood empty. A good indication he wasn't with us.

Butte put our drinks down in front of us.

"Ya think he might be out wounding dogs, Paul?" he said.

"Be my guess." I took a small sip.

"I think I heard his hopped-up Jimmy rumble by my place about 5:30 this morning," Hammersmith said. "Didn't pay it much mind. Pitch black out there. He might have been going the back way to Magnet."

"Could be."

Most of us use this empty dirt road to go to town. Sharing any road, particularly 95, seems just a wee bit too dangerous for us. Particularly in deep snow.

It was nearing five o'clock when Smoke finally came through the door and took his seat. He had snow on his shoulders. Apparently the sunny day had come to a snowy end.

He shook off his flight jacket and came over.

Butte turned to get his drink. We stared down at our glasses and acted like we didn't know Smoke had finally arrived.

Butte gently put an ugly yellow plastic cup with a cartoon duck painted on the side down in front of him.

"What the fuck is that?" Smoke said.

"White Horse and water, right?" Butte asked.

Smoke stared at him.

"What's with the cup?"

"That's a picture of Fup."

Smoke twirled his lighter between his index finger and thumb. Then stopped and lit his cigarillo and looked at Butte through the smoke.

"I get it," he said. "Like...Fup Duck. Right?"

No one said anything.

"Maybe I took this Fupping glass?" he said.

He took the glass from his jacket pocket and placed it on the bar.

We said nothing.

Smoke leaned back and blew a gentle stream of smoke towards the high ceiling. Drank from Fup Duck. Smacked his lips. Gave a satisfied sigh.

"It's not him," he said after a time.

We waited.

"I had breakfast with Joy Chu."

Joy Chu was still working with the Camas on the meth problem on the Rez and at the casino. She got a promotion for the Magruder bust, but the problem was persisting.

"You drove to Spokane?" Hammersmith finally said.

"Yup."

"Old 95 the whole way?"

"Yup." He grinned. He had one of the evilest grins in the world, and outside of Hammersmith, he was, by far, still one of the most dangerous of men.

"What is it, Smoke?" Huey asked.

Smoke rolled the stolen glass on its edge around and around.

"Freddy Dickweed Stripe is a phony," he said.

We all moaned in unison.

"You've mentioned that a time or two before," Butte said.

Smoke took a deep drink.

"Joy ran Stripe's license. That RV of his is registered to a Freddy Stripe of Kelowna, Canada."

"Wow!" I said. "Registered in his own name!"

"So what?" Hammersmith said.

Smoke continued rolling the glass.

"So, Joy ran his fingerprints from this glass I *stole*."

Now he had our attention.

"And they belong to someone named Casper Leib."

I had the sudden notion that Freddy Stripe might be a phony.

Smoke drained his cup, dropped it on the floor, and handed his glass to Butte.

Butte took it with a nod and reached down for Smoke's White Horse.

"So Joy..."

"Joy was having breakfast?" Huey interrupted.

Smoke said, "Yes, Huey. She had breakfast."

"But we thought she didn't eat breakfasts. She never did before," I said.

"Look," Smoke said. "She had breakfast with me. A bagel. And an orange juice, OK?"

"Go on, Smoke," Hammersmith said.

"So Joy Chu ran the name Casper Leib though the computers, and guess what?"

No one said anything.

"That name is locked by the CSIS! Can't get in. Zero. Nada. Classified."

"What's the CSIS?" I asked.

"Canadian Security Intelligence Service."

He accepted his refreshed and richly colored White Horse in a plain glass from Butte. Butte must have made him a bury-the-hatchet-knock-your-socks-off drink.

Smoke went, "It's Canada's CIA. Only from what I understand they use the CSIS for *intelligence* gathering, not law enforcement, not misinformation. They don't have secret prison camps offshore. They don't torture. They don't assassinate foreign democratically elected presidents with socialistic leanings. They don't..."

"That's enough, Smoke," Hammersmith said. "We get the picture. So why would he live by one name, and have his real name be locked up by the CSIS?"

"I don't have a clue."

We thought about this.

Sheila came in for her shift just then, went directly over to Smoke, took his half empty glass, and went into the kitchen.

Butte shrugged. He went into the kitchen after her and came back out with it. He put the empty glass back in front of Smoke.

Smoke stared into it like an empty well.

"You wanna say something to her?" Butte asked.

Smoke shook his head. He pushed his money out and Butte refilled his glass with ice and poured White Horse to the brim. He pushed the money back.

Sheila returned. I expected her to have her killing spoon with her, but she held out a cordless phone handed it to Butte and gave Smoke a sharp glance before returning to the kitchen.

Butte was a man of few words on the phone. He hated the things.

"What." he answered. "Yeah. They're here," he said, surveying us. "Where?"

He listened for a full minute.

"OK."

He turned and went after Sheila and came back out without the phone.

"Charlie has invited us to Ghost Tree up along the Clearwater," he said. "Wants us to confirm his identification of a body.

Chapter
Fifty

The pub had ten customers by the time Lana walked down to relieve MacAvity. Jables Weinman and Leaps had come in together from a combine repair they were joining forces on. They watched us leave. Curious. Hammersmith didn't join us.

We climbed into Huey's Dodge 2500 pickup. Smoke and I took the crew cab seats and Butte rode shotgun. Snow was whirling dryly in the wake of the building, but on the gravel road out of town it blew straight from the south.

We rode in silence. The small flakes in the headlights formed a funnel that we seemed to be driving down.

Huey slowed as we reached the lip of Coyote Grade where our narrow track twisted its way one-thousand, five hundred feet to the floor of the Clearwater. He drove carefully. We let him.

There was less than two inches of snow accumulated in the canyon. We turned west on a paved road which would eventually reach Lolo Pass and drop down to Missoula, Montana. This road followed the banks of the Clearwater. High in the mountains, the Clearwater forked and forfeited its name. The left fork was called the Lochsa and the right the Selway.

But that was two hours distance. We had only five miles to drive. Butte said Charlie wanted us to meet him at Ghost Tree Park, a picnic/camping/RV park just upstream from the Camas Riverside Casino and Hotel.

The casino's lights in the falling snow could be seen well before it came into view. Then the three story A-frame of the huge Casino's entrance loomed out of the night like a lost city.

A five acre parking lot sat half full of pickups and dull colored sedans favored by elderly couples. The towering mercury lamps that arched over them seemed to be sprinkling snow like shower heads.

Along the back side of the lot were pull-throughs and hookups for RVs. There were eight. We glanced at them in passing, and at the same instant we all saw Freddy Stripe's Country Coach.

"Well fuck a duck," Smoke said. "The bastard hasn't gone back to Canada after all."

Butte nodded. "His jeep has been out and about, though," he said.

We could see what he meant. Stripe's Wrangler had been unhitched and was parked nose to nose with the coach.

Then we were past the casino and entering a pinch in the canyon which soon opened into another clearing. Ghost Tree Park sat along a wide sandy beach in a stand of huge willows on our left.

Among these trees, protected by a four foot cedar fence, was an ancient birch tree that had somehow found its way far from its natural habitat in the Bitterroots. Having put down roots into the rich soil of this river bank, it had achieved a spiritual significance for the Camas for more than a hundred years. It was on its last legs these days, but, as we were soon to learn, had not neglected its responsibilities.

We pulled in. There were enough cruisers parked around Ghost Tree to start a Fourth of July parade. Their light bars had the entire park strobed out like a Grateful Dead concert.

Two large fifth wheels and a pusher not unlike Stripe's were hoisting anchor. They were leaving the chaos that had descended on them. Someone's 1988 Ford 150 pickup with a ratty old camper bolted to it remained. Free parks like this one were often havens for Snow Birds that were loathe to pay Scottsdale, Arizona winter prices. Many of them used reservation casinos as the nucleus of their refuge. And most of them distrusted the police and government in general.

Butte pulled in behind Charlie's Expedition, and we stepped out into the light snowfall. Charlie was standing among a group of ten uniforms. Just he, Josiah Longbeach and Oscar Redtail were in jeans, ranch coats and cowboy hats.

Charley saw us approach and motioned us over.

"'Bout time," Charlie said.

Josiah and Oscar nodded to us, and several of the staters and Dale Romsland, Charlie's chief deputy, glanced over at us.

Charlie walked to the Camas emergency response ambulance and swung open the back doors and climbed in. We went over and Butte went in after him.

Charlie partially zipped open a body bag that was strapped to a fold-down gurney. A terribly bloated and blackened face stared up at the ambulance's ceiling.

Butte said, "Willam Garber, all right."

Charlie zipped the bag shut again and they stepped back out.

Butte looked at Josiah.

"What happened?"

"Had a twenty pound river stone tied to each wrist with rawhide," he said. "Was put twenty, thirty feet up the tree. Head slipped in a fork. Left there kicking till he choked to death."

Smoke laughed.

"Old Camas tradition, Longbeach?

"Use teach paleface not call Camas 'Native Americans,'" Oscar said.

"You redskins sure have funny accents," Smoke said.

"How the hell they get him clear up the tree?" I asked.

"Magic," Josiah said. "Only tracks were the old fart's from the big RV. Out walking his rodent that he claimed was a dog, heard a farting noise in the tree, shined up his flashlight, and there was ol' Garber, dead as stone, belching and dripping away."

"Who's Garber?" Huey asked.

"You Native Europeans can't remember shit, can you?" Oscar asked.

"The contractor Butte shot the feet off at Hammersmith's," Charlie told him.

Huey's mouth fell open. "That's *him*?"

"Had prosthetics on," Josiah said.

Garber had been extradited to Canada, but he successfully rolled over on some people in exchange for a lifetime sentence in a more upscale prison.

"He escaped," Charlie said, reading my mind. "That camper isn't his. Ran the plates. The rig was stolen from a ratty used car/truck dealer in Priest River."

"He's the guy that took a shot at Micha?" I asked.

"You don't miss a tick, do you, Paul?" Smoke said.

"The obvious is never lost on me."

"Come over and sign a few things, Butte," Charlie said.

They went over to the Expedition, and Charlie reached in and brought out a clip board and Maglite. He held the light and Butte took a Bic ball point from under the clip and signed off on two forms and handed them back to Charlie.

He motioned for us to go, and we climbed back into Huey's Dodge.

Huey heaved a tired sigh.

"I can't believe this is starting up again," he grumbled. We said nothing.

The diesel engine kicked over. Huey twisted on the lights, found reverse, turned us, and pulled onto the asphalt headed home.

"Am I going to have to sell out and move to the North Pole to get away from these guys?" he said.

"Nope," Smoke said. "The pole is melting. By the time you sell your weed patch all you'll need up there is a boat."

Huey smiled weakly. But at least it was a smile.

"You think the Camas killed Garber?" I asked.

Butte turned in his seat so he could look back at me.

"Oh yeah. You heard what Longbeach said. No tracks. High up in a tree. Rawhide and river stones. My dad told me that once when he was a kid Gramps took him down to see the tree. There were six cattle rustlers notched up in its limbs. All had stones tied to their feet."

He gave a dry laugh and pushed his flat brimmed Stetson back on his forehead.

"But, of course, I had to shoot his feet off two years ago. He had to have the stones tied to his wrists."

"Damned inconsiderate of you, Butte," Smoke said.

"I know. Shameful's what it is."

The casino came into sight.

"Turn in, Huey," Smoke said. "I wanna check out Stripe's rig"

"What's the point?" I said. "He's either in it or in the casino. You trying to provoke a fight?"

"Smoke's got a good point," Butte said. "No harm looking it over."

Huey swung into the plowed lot and drove slowly back to the RV slots and crept past Stripe's Jeep and Coach.

"You want to get out, Smoke?"

"Just for a second."

Huey came to a rolling stop fifteen feet past Stripe's slot and parked so the Dodge was half out of sight behind the neighboring RV.

Smoke opened his door quietly and left it open as he worked his way past the RV in a crouch and over to the Jeep. He was back in less than sixty seconds, slid in and closed the door carefully.

"No winch on the front. Tires cleaned by snow. Some kind of trick radio or CB built under the dash. Lock box behind the seat."

Huey pulled away and drove back through the brightly lit lot towards the highway.

I looked out the back window. There was a dome about the size of a large punchbowl on the roof of Stripe's RV. It sat centered about eight feet from the front and was the same dark brown as the rest of his rig. There were also three whip antennas just behind it.

I didn't say anything.

Chapter
Fifty-One

Lana and I were crossing over Cup Hand and dropping down towards Magnet. Lana was at the wheel of our Toyota pickup working the snow blown drifts across the road. Sun cut through the timber and across the road in brilliant panes of light.

Once a week we drove to Magnet to stock up on groceries at Safeway and the Food Co-op in the center of town.

The next portion of our ritual is to buy rich Co-op coffee and fresh-from-the-oven sweet rolls, sit at one of the small round tables at the front windows, and spend a half hour feeling metropolitan.

Also, two days had passed since Garber had been lowered from his Ghost Tree, and I wanted to talk to Charlie about it.

"You want to help with the shopping first?" Lana said.

"Whatever you want."

She considered.

"I'll drop you off and when you're done, walk over and meet me for coffee."

"Sure."

"That way I can actually see what's in the store."

"Because I want to get what we need and leave?"

She nodded.

"Because I usually speed the cart around the aisles throwing stuff in one-handed, tipping around the corners, and shooting towards checkout with my wallet open?"

"Exactly."

"So what is it about Safeway that rivets your attention? Makes you linger as if it were a museum of fine art?"

"I cook."

"That's true."

"What do you cook?" she said. "When I'm, say, visiting family on the coast?"

I gave my best defensive shrug.

She answered for me.

"You calculate how long I'll be away and make a stew that will get you by the entire time. You have two pots of tea and oatmeal for breakfast, grilled cheese for lunch, Wisers at 3:30 until dinner, and then hit the stew."

"You can depend on me."

"So what I'm saying is that I get new ideas as I *thoughtfully* peruse the aisle

"Wow!"

We passed Magnet's graveyard and Lana threaded the residential streets.

She dropped me off in back of the elegant county courthouse where the sheriff's department was hunkered out back in an ugly cinder block one story extension.

Very few people know about the high-tech security and labyrinth of rooms and cells that lie beneath Charlie's offices. And the ones that do are pretty sure they don't want to have it shown to them again.

Charlie came down the hall and signaled the dispatcher to buzz me in.

"I figured I'd see you sometime soon," he said.

He lead me back to his office.

"It's in my blood," I said. "Too many years reporting for the Trib."

Besides Charlie's desk backed up near the window and his chief deputy's small steel desk off to the side, the room had a six foot long, heavy oak table down the center with five chairs pushed up to it. He motioned for me to sit at the end closest to the door, dragged a chair out for himself and leaned back against the wall.

He studied me a minute.

"You wanna know if your Freddy Stripe killed Garber. Right?"

I nodded.

"Did he?"

"Don't know."

He dropped the chair and went over behind his desk and picked up two sheets of paper stapled together.

"Vics' report," he said.

Sherman Vics was our coroner, forensics guy, undertaker, shrink and a dozen other things. A multi-tasker.

"Ol' Garber, it seems, had a liver full of hemlock. Must have been paralyzed maybe for three hours before he nested in that tree."

He turned to the second page, glanced at it, then dropped the report back on his desk. He came back around and sat on the desk's edge and looked at me.

"Interesting, huh?"

"Wirestone?"

"Hemlock grows damn near everywhere on the Rez," he said. "The plants grow six feet tall. Dangerous to even touch that shit."

He shook his head.

"Leaves look a little like pot leaves. Amazing at least one kid hasn't tried it out and killed themselves."

"I think they're discriminating smokers these days, Charlie." I said. "They smoke bud, not leaves, and by their eighteenth birthdays have doctorates in pharmacology."

"And D's in math and English."

"Right."

We thought about that.

"Find out how he got up that tree?"
Charlie shrugged.
"The staters swept the snow back and found a set of tire tracks. Heavy pickup. Helped confirm Garber was in the tree about the same time."

He shook his head. "Might have used a truck winch to get him up there."

"Not a Jeep, then?"

Charlie looked at me curiously.

"Explain."

"We saw his Coach at the Casino. The jeep had been unhitched."

He nodded.

"Yeah. Longbeach told me he'd come in. Seems he went straight there from MacAvity's. Came in, ate, went out, unhooked and drove off. Spent the following afternoon in the Casino working the slots and talking about how the 'wetbacks,' his words, were ruining the country."

Wetbacks?

"Jerry Hobbs-Smith was called over and he told Stripe if there were any wetbacks around it was the white man come clear across the wet Atlantic kill Camas."

I grinned.

"Stripe had the good sense to keep his mouth shut after that. Ate supper, and drove off again in his Jeep. Wasn't back until about eight PM."

"How do they know all this?"

Charlie got to his feet.

"The casino has more surveillance cameras inside *and* out than all the airports in Idaho combined."

He walked towards the door to suggest he had work to do and it'd be nice if I left.

I stood.

"You know," I said, "the tracks might not match a Jeep, but that doesn't mean Garber wasn't given up."

"Exactly," Charlie said. "We don't have a clue how this thing went down."

"So Stipe is still in the game?"

"Absolutely."

I thought this over.

"On our way back we pulled in and Smoke looked the Jeep over and it didn't have a winch."

"OK."

"But it had a tricked out CB or something in it and a locked trunk behind the seat."

Charlie nodded.

"Anything else?"

"Well," I said, "there was a dome on the roof of Stripe's RV and three whip antennas."

"Ain't that quaint?" Charlie said. "Our boy Stripe must have a police scanner, some bitchin' communication equipment, and something under the dome to boot."

He went back behind his desk and picked up his phone.

"Could you get Dewayne Gibson to phone me?"

He hung up.

"You remember Dewayne."

"He and Bob Pfeffer were the FBI assholes that pissed MacAvity off so badly."

"Right. I want to know if that dome had some kind of government-issue satellite communications or phased array antenna gear in it."

He sat back down in his desk chair.

"I'm thinking this Freddy Stripe isn't what he appears to be," he said.

Chapter
Fifty-Two

The wind came up that night and rattled the windows in their wooden frames. I got up and latched the front porch screen door to keep it from beating itself to death.

Like nearly every house in Ryback, ours was built in the 30s by union men grateful to have jobs and proud of their journeyman skills. Every wall was plumb and met at right angles and was framed with rough-cut old growth clear fir and covered inside and out with rough cut one by twelves. Fiber board covered the interior walls and ceilings, clear lap cedar the outside. The floors were red fir. Craftsman homes. Tight. Warm. Solid as bomb shelters.

By morning the wind howled with snow. It wrapped the town, scoured the fields bare to the west and piled the snow in ten foot, corniced drifts on the lee side of the rolling hills. Ryback's streets caught the snow, and drifts formed and grew in long rows between the buildings, houses and barns. The tombstones in the Lutheran church yard vanished under them. Doors remained shut. The lower third of windows were crosscut by the accumulations.

By noon Ryback was sealed off, and by nightfall, the power and phones went. Lanterns were lit and placed on tables, wood stoves were fired up, and guide ropes were strung between the houses and the barns.

The people of the Bench were no strangers to Idaho winters. Truth be known, we enjoyed them.

We felt secure and snug. Our homes had cellars bulging with canning jars filled with fruits, meats, and vegetables. We had bins of flour and rolled oats. Salt, sugar, and spices lined shelves in kitchen pantries. Root cellars held wooded boxes filled with potatoes, apples and carrots packed in wood chips. And under the snow lying dormant we had kale, chard, leeks and parsnips.

We made no effort to clear our streets. Instead, those who had snowmobiles came to pick up those who didn't. An adhoc volunteer taxi service.

MacAvity's, which had a large military surplus generator for backup, became increasingly crowded as night settled in, and Lana and I pulled on our winter clothes, strapped on our snowshoes, and went down to join the fun.

Sheila and Butte never cooked individual meals during the Bench's great storms. Instead, they brought out the crock pots so that by evening there were chilies, stews, roasts, soups, pastas and rice dishes simmering away. They would bake loaves of bread, toss salads in two-gallon stainless bowls, and bake apple and berry crisps. They put an empty coffee can by a stack of plates, bowls and a tray of flatware, and folks dropped whatever amount of money they thought was fair into the can for helping themselves to the food.

Card tables and folding chairs were brought up from the basement, unopened cots leaned against the back of the long room for overnighters, and three plastic milk crates of playing cards and table games were placed on the floor by the stereo cabinet.

Those with visiting grandchildren in tow had MacAvity's living room floor upstairs to make pallets on, but the little ones were welcome downstairs in the pub, and the attention lavished on them soon had them too tired to stand.

We loved a storm. And we liked to remember the great ones of the past. 1948-49. 1953-54. 1968-69. Storms that brought things to a standstill for weeks. Months.

Where temperatures reached -50. Where the cuts made by Highway 95 through the hills filled in smoothly with snow so that the remaining highway between them looked like dams.

There were nine snowmobiles parked haphazardly in the middle of the drifted street when we got there. They were bathed in light from MacAvity's three large front windows. We threaded between them, unstrapped our snowshoes, and jammed their tails into the snow along the pub's outside wall, kicked the snow off our boots on the steps and went in.

The warmth and the aroma of hot food and damp wool greeted us. As did Smoke who had commandeered one of the booths and had Huey and Eric Hammersmith sitting across from him.

I snagged a folding chair and Lana slid in beside Smoke. He went to squeeze her thigh and she deftly slapped his hand away.

Smoke laughed and craned his neck to catch Jake's attention. Whenever Jake and Don came in from their farm, Jake liked to help at the bar. Butte and Sheila let her.

Smoke signaled for drinks all around and Huey swept up their pinochle cards and score pad and pushed them out of the way.

"Did Charlie call you guys today?" Hammersmith asked.

"We don't have a cell phone, Eric," Lana reminded him.

He nodded. "I forgot."

"Why?"

"Why did I forget?"

"Why did you ask?"

"Oh. He said he was going to."

We waited.

"And he didn't, Eric," Lana said.

Smoked took out a cigarillo, lit it with his Navy Pilot Zippo.

"Because you don't have a cell phone," Smoke said.

"Yes," Lana said very quietly, "We don't have a cell phone, Smoke, so we didn't get a call from Charlie, so will you guys stop fucking with me a second and tell me why he was trying, though unsuccessfully because the phones are out and we don't have a cell phone to call us?"

He grinned.

Huey said, "Charlie and Joy Chu have been working all day with Dewayne Gibson and Bob Pfeffer."

"Our favorite Feebs," Hammersmith said.

"And Joy, bless her Asian heart, has friends in L.A. who, along with 3,000 other Japanese Americans, were relocated near Death Valley into the internment camp, Manzanar, during the bad ol' WWII days..."

Jake had managed to work her way through the crowd with a round cork lined tray with our drinks. She placed them down in a bunch between us, kissed Lana on the cheek, and hurried off.

"Free drinks?" Smoke said.

"No, Smoke. She trusts most of us," Lana said.

Hammersmith selected out his Beam and tonic from the group of glasses and took a sip.

"...from their fishing and cannery village on Reservation Point back in the bad old days by Executive Order 9066," he continued. "The place, called Terminal Island, is now a federal minimum security prison. Gordon Liddy's ol' hangout."

"And where our favorite murderer and drug trafficker Clifford Spreiter managed to cush his life sentence," Smoke said.

"And from where, Joy's people tell her, Spreiter has managed over the past two years to reestablish his drug trafficking operation from behind the fence."

Lana moaned.

"How?" I asked.

"It's a gift," Smoke said. "You take 3,000 hard working successful California fishermen that are American citizens and slap them in a concentration camp in the middle of the fucking desert, destroy their homes, steal their boats, canneries and livelihoods, and you've made enemies." He tapped off an ash. "That's what we do best. Vietnam. Afghanistan. Iraq. You name it."

When Smoke got it going, we were quiet.

Except for MacAvity.

None of us had noticed, but Butte had come up behind Hammersmith and had been listening.

"Charlie says some of the children that were at Manzanar were pissed enough to form a gang called the Furusato, the 'Home Sweet Home Gang.' Apparently Spreiter connected with some of their least savory types, now in their 80's, among the various twelve hundred prisoners serving inside Terminal Island. These people had flourished as criminals, thanks to having been relocated."

"For revenge?" I said.

"Probably more out of necessity, too."

"And Spreiter says to hell with his Canadian connections?" I said.

"But not yabas. Just the crystal meth," Butte said. "And here's Spreiter and all his connections working out of a minimum security prison right at the very mouth of Los Angeles Harbor between Long Beach and San Pedro?"

He shook his head and walked off, back to the kitchen. I watched him go.

Jake had made me a Dugan's Dew, instead of a Wisers. I took a sip and felt it slide hotly down my throat. It was good, so I took another sip.

"How'd Cano Franzani get out?" I asked.

Hammersmith shook his head. "Charlie says he didn't and he won't. Says he choked his cellmate to death after lock down in the medium security prison at Herlong, California. It was caught on surveillance camera, and he stabbed the first guard barging into the cell in the neck with a wire, nearly killing him. He's now in the worst of the worst, Florence ADMAX in Colorado. Solitary for life. Is let out only two hours a day to shower and exercise by himself in a small room."

"What about the guy in the tree?" Lana asked.

"Garber? Prefer says he walked away from Ferndale Institution up near the Fraser Valley in British Columbia," Eric said.

"I thought he went to prison?"

"That's what Canadians call them. Institutions. Like the one at Herlong, California. Federal Correction Institution, Herlong. More sanitized."

Lana shook her head and got to her feet.

"I'm hungry. God almighty."

She walked over and joined Ruthie Hammersmith and two of Ruthie's friends who were dishing up. The two friends were, like Ruthie, in their eighties, and like Ruthie, looked fifteen years younger than they were, though slower moving.

We watched them. Hammersmith doted on Ruthie. It showed on his weathered face.

"Gentlemen," Smoke said. "Here's to a good blizzard."

"Cheers," I said, and we toasted the wind and snow.

"Did Charlie say anything about why Garber came back here?" I said.

Smoke and Eric shook their heads. Huey was swirling the ice in his glass and remained silent.

"Anything about Freddy Stripe?"

"Nope," Smoke said.

I got up and went over to join Lana, Ruthie, and the two ol' gals with them. I wanted a full stomach for an evening of catching up. A storm is a good time to get back in tune with your neighbors. And wives, for that matter.

Chapter
Fifty-Three

Power was restored to Ryback two days later, and a little after noon the state opened our road from the highway clear into town and down Main to the pub. But the town itself and all the other roads leading out of it remained deep in the drifts, and the farms and ranches in the Bitterroots were still sealed.

No one minded. The winds had died.

Charlie came in to visit and have supper at MacAvity's late that afternoon before the evening rush. Smoke, Hammersmith, Huey and I looked up from our booth when he came in. He nodded to us and hung his heavy parka on the rack and zipped off a pair of lined Carhartt ranch pants. He clumped over to the long table and loaded a bowl with chili, grabbed a spoon and took a seat at the bar. He put the overfilled bowl down carefully and hooked the heels of his cowboy boots over the stool's rungs.

Butte brought him a Bud to wash the chili down, and they talked together quietly.

We turned back to our card game and waited. We'd know soon enough what was up.

When Charlie had finished his chili he nodded at Butte, turned around on his stool and walked to the back of the room. He disappeared through a door on the side wall that opened to a narrow staircase and went up to MacAvity's living quarters.

Butte went into the kitchen, said something to Sheila, and came back out over to our booth. He stood and pulled up one of his sleeve garters thoughtfully.

We put down our cards.

"You gentlemen have a moment?"

"At my age, that's all I got," Hammersmith said.

We slid out of the booth and followed Butte up to his richly furnished old Ireland living room.

Charlie was seated in a wooden chair at the eight foot long farm table in the center of the kitchen. He was studying several sheets of paper he had unfolded in front of him.

He didn't smile.

We took seats along the table's sides and Butte sat at the end facing Charlie.

We said nothing.

We waited.

Charlie smoothed the pages with a palm, bent over to scan them for a moment, then looked up at us.

"The feds took finger prints off the truck Garber had stolen. They've come back with the results," he said.

"There were lots of them. Garber stole the heap from a lot, but Garber's prints were clear and predominantly on the passenger side."

He let us consider that.

"He had prosthetics, but we're sure he could drive. Seems he preferred to let someone else. Which gave us another set of prints. A Canadian shooter named Alex Byrd. A skinny little guy with the face of a dull ax and as friendly as a heart attack."

Charlie turned to the second page and passed around a laser print of the guy's mug shot, front and side.

Smoke handed me the page after looking briefly at it.

Alex Byrd did, in fact, have a face like a dull ax. Under a pitch black military crew cut, his dark eyes, unnaturally close together, looked as if they had been pushed up against a narrow nose that was too small for his long, clean shaven face. Lean and ugly. I handed the picture on to Butte and sat back.

"Pfeffer and Gibson, our FBI friends, think he's still in the area," Charlie said.

I heard Huey let his breath out slowly.

"Now," he turned to the last sheet. "Here's the fun part."

He read for a moment, then looked up again.

"Apparently this guy Byrd earned his stripes in L.A. before going independent first in Chicago and then up in British Columbia. Seems he's now working out of Kelowna, Penticton, Salmon Arm, Kamloops and Vancouver. But there has never been enough evidence to prove that or to convict him of anything."

He glanced at Butte's pressed tin ceiling.

"He's been seen with an old colleague of Clifford Spreiter's, that friendly real estate developer you guys put out of business. The buddy's name is Trent Mazollan. Lives in Kelowna. Has a land development office in a glass five-story that sits on the lake's edge."

Charlie sat back and laced his hands behind his head.

We said nothing.

Smoke got to his feet, looked at Butte. Butte nodded and Smoke went to an old, beautiful glass-doored cabinet in the living room and took out a fifth of White Horse.

"Anyone?"

He brought out four small, heavy glasses, poured, and brought them in. Huey and Charlie abstained. Smoke lit a cigarillo, then sat back down.

"That dickwad Freddy Stripe's from Kelowna too, right?" he said.

Charlie nodded.

"And this guy Mazollan is from there, and Spreiter and he used to work together."

"Right."
Smoke sipped his drink thinking this over.
"And this shooter, Alex Byrd, works for Mazollan."
Charlie smiled slightly.
We were all watching Smoke.
"And our ol' footless friend William Garber tried to kill Wirestone and came here to do that and came with Byrd."
"Right."
"But missed and got poisoned and hung in Ghost Tree by someone. Probably the Camas. Who don't care to have their elder and best witch doctor fucked with."
We listened.
Smoke shook his head in disgust.
He finally said. "Stripe's in on it."
"We don't know that for sure, Smoke," Charlie said. "We don't have a clue about Stripe. All we know is that his prints are classified by the CSIS. That's all."
"And that all these assholes live in his home town," Smoke said.
Butte cleared his throat.
"You said Joy Chu and the Feebs are pretty sure Spreiter is back in business? From behind the fence at Terminal Island?"
Charlie nodded and placed his palms back on top of the sheets of paper and patted them absentmindedly.
"They're sure of it," he said. "Can't prove it, though."
"Using the Furusato gang?"
"They're sure of it."
Butte nodded.
"They know who the L.A. boss is?"
Charlie leaned forward.
"You're going to hate this, guys," he said. "It's not an L.A. guy. The Furusato gang takes care of L.A. We think the boss is a fat slob named Nelson Yost."

He looked at each one of us in turn.

"And he's right here. Three hours away. He's located in the Tri Cities. In Pasco."

Smoke moaned. I think we all did. He stubbed out his cigarillo and leaned back, folding his hands briefly over his face in total disgust.

"The other end of the Magruder Corridor."

Charlie nodded.

"That's what it looks like, guys," he said.

"What's happening, Charlie?" Butte said quietly.

Charlie took a deep breath and let it out slowly through his lips.

He cleared his throat.

"We think they're about ready to get it going again. Up from L.A.. Through the west coast interior and into Canada. Same deal, opposite direction. By-passing the Magruder and Montana all together. The RCMP is very concerned."

He sighed. "I could sure use a beer right now."

Butte nodded, went to the refrigerator and brought one back. He opened it and placed it and a chilled pint glass at Charlie's elbow.

I watched Charlie pore the can of Bud carefully into the frosted glass so it formed a half inch head and didn't overflow.

He took a sip, then a sizable swallow.

He put the glass and empty can down softly on the table's bare wood.

"But," he looked down at the table, "Joy Chu has a lot of friends--sources--that say Spreiter wants to clean house before they start the narcotics rolling again."

He looked back up at us.

"Looks like he wants to settle an old score."

He spoke directly to Butte and Hammersmith.

"Looks like he wants to have the Magruder Bunch, that's you guys and the Camas--everyone that was involved in busting his chops and killing his men two years ago..."

"Killed," Hammersmith offered.

Charlie nodded.

I didn't trust myself to speak.

"Ain't that just dandy?" MacAvity finally said, making me jump.

"Not so much," Huey said without looking up. "Seems pretty serious to me. Seems like Spreiter isn't in Terminal Island to protect us from him. Seems like his being there lets him do any dang thing he wants and we can't do a thing about it."

"This is one fucked up situation," Smoke said.

Hammersmith chuckled.

We looked at him.

"Nope," he said. "You got it backwards, gentlemen. You're giving him too much credit."

Charlie nodded and grinned.

Eric drained his glass and put it down.

"We know where he is. He can't get away. He can't hide. We know what he's doing. We know who's helping him."

"You have him trapped," Charlie said.

Smoke shook his head.

"But we can't get at him, Charlie."

"Maybe. What we need to do right now is find Byrd before he gets to us. Before the road is clear of this infernal snow. And we need to find out what we can about Stripe."

"He still at the Casino, Charlie?" I managed.

"Yup."

He turned and faced Smoke.

"I'm going down there right now."

He finished his beer in four large swallows, clapped the pint glass back down on the table and stood.

"And I want you to go with me, Smoke," he said. "I'd like to watch you ask him your questions. I might even have a few myself."

Smoke grinned evilly and got to his feet.

"I'm with you, pardner."

Clarlie swept up the sheets of paper, folded them twice, and put them in his shirt pocket.

We all got to our feet and followed them down and saw them out the door.

Hammersmith turned back towards our booth.

"Well, what the heck. Nothing we can do for now."

Huey and I nodded and slid in across from him.

Eric shuffled three times, then stopped and looked at us.

"You know L.A. and San Diego are Navy towns, don't you?" he said. "Maybe there's something an old commander like me could do after all. Maybe call in a few favors."

We nodded.

Chapter
Fifty-Four

Huey, Hammersmith and I played pinochle until 5:30 without mentioning what Charlie had told us.

After the game, they got up to leave, and I went to the front window to see them off. Hammersmith got on the back of Huey's Arctic Cat. Its lights came on with the engine, and they turned onto the now well-established snowmobile track that headed east out of town and past their farms.

I stayed at the bar for a bit longer in hopes of getting a chance to talk with Butte, but he and Sheila remained busy setting up the table for the evening. Folks were already beginning to arrive.

I shrugged into my coat, stepped out into the cold darkness and walked home through the snow and past the boarded up two story school house on my right. It sat eerily dark behind the leafless elms that as school kids we had played under.

Lana had a rolled venison loaf cooling on the stove top. She was at the kitchen table working on a grocery list and smiled when I came in. I hung my coat, poured a drink and sat down across from her.

"How was the game?" she said.

"Fine. Charlie was there. Took us upstairs for a powwow," I told her.

"He learned something, huh?"

"More than I liked to hear. But less than I needed to know, I guess."

I sipped my scotch and put the glass down. I turned it in my hand.

"Seems Spreiter has put something together through a second or third generation Japanese gang in L.A. called the Home Sweet Home Gang. The Furusatos. Same thing as he had before but soon to be trafficking up from California to Canada with a stopover in Pasco. Bypassing the Magruder and Montana altogether."

Lana leaned back.

"Our Pasco?"

"Yeah. The west end of the Magruder run that we apparently missed. Got a boss in Pasco named Nelson Yost and another at the end in Kelowna named Trent Mazollan."

Lana was listening without moving. Looking at me.

"Paul, that seems like a lot of information. A lot more than anyone had the last time we had to deal with these people."

I nodded.

She looked back at me.

"So what is it?"

"Seems Garber had a shooter with him named Alex Byrd, and he's still out here. Or at least they think so."

"Here? Ryback?"

I nodded. "And a snitch inside Terminal Island says Spreiter wants us all killed before his operation is put back into gear. Guess he doesn't like us."

Lana's eyes went wide. Then shut. She put her forehead down on her hands resting on the table. Then she looked up tiredly.

"What's Butte say?"

"I didn't get to talk to him. But Smoke went with Charlie to talk to Freddy Stripe. No one seems to know how Stripe fits in, but it seems to be an accepted fact that he somehow does."

I took a swallow. "Maybe he's connected to this Alex Byrd guy. No one knows."

We both thought about that.

Lana pushed back her seat, stood and started to set the table.

"Paul," she said, "it doesn't matter if Byrd, Stripe or whoever else there is is caught, Spreiter will just keep sending more."

"I know."

"So what are we going to do?"

"I don't know."

She stood over the table holding the meat roll.

"It's like a snake, Paul. You've got to cut the head off a snake."

I nodded.

"Seems like it, doesn't it?"

Then, "I'm sorry I got us into this, Honey."

She put the platter down between us and took her seat.

"No. It's all been there from 1967 to today. Eric and Huey did what they had to do in Vietnam. Smoke, Butte and you had to do what you did to keep them from getting killed, Paul. The only two things you could have done are let them and Ruthie get killed or do what you did."

I nodded.

We ate supper. Discussed the predicament we were in.

We were getting undressed for bed when we heard Smoke's snowmobile whine to a stop at the barn. In moments he knocked at the back door and opened it.

"Any food in this dump?" he bellowed.

I pulled my pants back on and met Lana in the hall.

We went to the kitchen.

Smoke was looking in the refrigerator. He found the platter and took it out.

"Help yourself," Lana said. "Unless you'd like it heated with gravy, some potatoes on the side and some slaw. But of course you wouldn't."

"As long as you insist."

Smoke dropped into my chair. I took one at the end.

Lana dished him up a plate, put it in the microwave and put the coffee on to heat.

"So?" I said.

Smoke shook his head.

"Oscar Redtail met Charlie and me outside Stripe's RV. Stripe didn't invite us in. Charlie told him he was part of a murder investigation. Stripe said we still couldn't come in. Charlie told him he didn't have a choice. That he could talk to us there or in Oscar's office. He said he'd talk to us in the casino. So we went to the casino's restaurant and sat at a round cafe table."

Lana put his heated plate down in front of him on a round cork underlay, and took her seat.

Smoke dug in.

"But," he said between mouthfuls, "he claims he drove the Jeep to Orofino the night Micha's dog got shot. Was back by two. Claims he went to Kooskia when Garber was getting killed. Back by three."

"Did the casino cameras show that?"

Smoke nodded.

"Unfortunately."

I thought about that.

"So what was he doing in Orofino and Kooskia?"

"Said he was drinking and trying to shag some pussy."

"Shag some pussy?" Lana said.

"Yup."

"Isn't that a 50s expression?"

"Still a valid concept."

Lana shook her head hopelessly.

"So did he say if he shagged any pussy, Smoke?" she said.

"Yup."

"Let me guess. Kooskia, right?" I said.

Smoke nodded. "The town bike."

Lana looked at me and laughed.

"Town bike?"

Smoke chewed thoughtfully.

"You know. Everybody rides her. Charlie's going to call around and see if he actually did. Things kinda hinge on if he did or not."

"Call around?" Lana said. "Why not beat the bushes?"

"There's something peculiar, though," Smoke said.

We waited while he finished his last bite. He put down his fork and leaned back.

"That Freddy Stripe ain't what he claims to be."

"Smoke!" I said.

"I know, I know. But a couple times there, when Charlie was really leaning on him, he quit sounding like some kind of Midwestern redneck. Just for a moment. Like he'd fallen out of character or something."

He pushed back his empty plate.

"So, what did he sound like?" I asked.

"Like one of your fucking college grads."

"*My* fucking college grads?" I said. "You went to fucking Annapolis, Smoke."

"You know what I mean. For instance, when Charlie asked him who Casper Leib is--you know, his real name--instead of saying, 'I don't know the fucker,' he said, 'I don't recall anyone by that name.'"

He got to his feet.

"Anyway, I'm beat. Thanks for the grub Lana."

He went to the back door and pulled his coat back on.

"No coffee?" Lana said.

"Too tired."

He pulled open the back door.

"Charlie's checking things out," he said. "Otherwise we got zip."

And he was gone.

Lana looked at me, shrugged, and started back to her bedroom.

"Wanna shag some pussy?" she said.

I gave my best lecherous grin. Apparently not well.

"Or should we drink his coffee?"

"Let's have the coffee and see what develops," I said.

"And cut the head off the snake?"

"And figure out what Stripe's got in that RV."

We returned to the kitchen.

Lana poured our coffees.

"Maybe stolen bicycles?" she said under her breath.

Chapter
Fifty-Five

Lana was on the couch with her morning coffee. I was in my chair. I had a strong pot of Mount Everest tea on the end table at my elbow and a steaming cup resting on the oak arm. Our normal early morning routine, until the light turned gray outside and a band of Homer's rosy fingered dawn edged up over the drifted southeast horizon.

It was a quarter to seven and the phone rang in the kitchen. I went in and answered it.

"Where is everybody?"

It was Hammersmith.

"Don't have a clue," I said. "I suspect I'm in my kitchen."

"Longbeach just called me," he said. "Says Smoke and Charlie scared Freddy Stripe off last night. He took off."

"They know where he went?"

"Left about an hour ago, lock, stock and barrel. Was headed towards Confluence. Charlie isn't answering his phone."

I thought about this.

"Want me to call his dispatcher? He might be coming in from the ranch, Eric. Timing's right."

The line was quite for a moment.

"Yeah, OK.," he said. "I'm going to call Joy Chu."

He hung up.

I called Charlie's dispatcher and left a message for him to call me. Then went back in to the living room.

Lana looked up from her book questioningly.

"Longbeach just called Eric. Stripe has pulled out. Eric wants me to get hold of Charlie."

"Why doesn't Longbeach do it himself?"

"Hammersmith is like an elder to the Camas. He and Micha go way back. They were practically frontiersmen together. I guess Longbeach didn't think it was a big deal but wanted Hammersmith to know."

"And Eric decided Charlie needed to know."

"Right."

I was about to take a sip of my cooling tea when the phone rang again.

I went back in. It was Charlie. I told him about Hammersmith's call. I could hear the Expedition's engine in the background.

"Okay," he said after a moment. "Guess he figured out the only way Smoke, Longbeach and I could know about his movements was with surveillance cameras at the Casino. Guess we played our hand wrong."

I heard him shift down. There was a thump and then he resumed his speed.

"Damn!" he said. "It's still in the twenties out here. Just plowed through a drift must have been three feet deep. Wide, too."

"Least this snow will keep Byrd holed up until we know what's what," I said.

"I'll have my men and the staters keep an eye out for that Country Coach and Wrangler. Hard to miss."

He hung up.

I called Eric back and filled him in.

"I'm still trying to get hold of Joy. She's no better than Charlie."

"Well, Eric, maybe they have more on their plates than we do."

"Crossed my mind."

"So what's with Ms. Chu?"

"I want her to accompany Ruthie and me down to L.A."

That surprised me. Eric hadn't even gotten down to San Francisco to visit his daughter Ann and her adopted son Levi since Ruthie and Lana hid out in her apartment two years ago. And he wanted to go to L.A.?

Eric read my mind.

"We'll stop in and visit Ann and Levi on the way home," he said.

Then, "Let me speak to Lana a minute."

I carried the phone in and handed it to her. She put her book down, took a quick sip from her coffee, and put it to her ear.

"Eric?"

She sat listening. She listened for a long time, giving appropriate uh-huhs.

I took my seat and tried to distinguish words from the burble of Eric's voice.

"Well let me speak to Ruthie," she finally said.

She drank more of her coffee, watching me over the cup's rim. I raised my eyebrows and she gave me the "hold on a minute" look.

"Morning, Ruthie," she said.

Again Lana listened.

Again I tried unsuccessfully to eavesdrop. Drank the rest of the tea in my cup and poured more from the pot.

"Let me talk to Paul, Ruthie," she finally said. "I'll call you back."

She hung up, put the phone down on the large square coffee table, and leaned back.

"What goes round comes round," she said.

"Meaning?"

"Same-'ol same-'ol. Eric wants me to go to LA with them, hang out at Hotel Saint Maarten in Laguna Beach and spend money while he and Joy do business in Los Angeles."

I let out my breath.

"Then what?"

"Make a guess."

I shook my head. "He wants you and Ruthie to stay with Ann until this blows over."

"Right."

I could feel the undertow of despondence pull on me.

"So, did either of them say what the *business* they're doing is?"

"No."

She patted the couch. I got to my feet and went and sat beside her. Close.

She put a hand on my thigh.

"He told me one thing, though," she said. "The old Navy commander was on the phone last night to Washington DC. Seems he use to know a Harley G. Lapping."

She smiled at me.

"Who's he?"

"Seems this guy, good ol' Harley, has been the Director, Federal Bureau of Prisons, since 2003. Eric said he met him at Kent State in the early 80s when Eric was on loan from the Navy as a guest commencement speaker."

I digested this for some time.

"So," I said, "what do you think?"

"It's Eric's nickel..."

"And?"

"Ruthie and I could have a lot of fun..."

She looked into her nearly empty cup.

"I'd love to see Ann and Levi..."

"But you're not scared."

She nodded.

"But you don't want to be running away."

She thought that over.

"No. It's more than that. I want *this* shit to go away. This time for good."

She put her cup back on the table.

"And I want to be with Ruthie. You can imagine how hard this is. This is the second time for them. You know that. And they're in their 80's."

Lana shook her head.

"It's like the fucking Vietnam war just has never left them alone. Ever."

She got to her feet suddenly and went into the kitchen with the phone and her cup. She made like she was interested as she began brewing another cup of coffee. She sneaked a finger up to her cheek as she stood and watched the kettle come to a boil.

"When do you leave?" I asked so she could hear.

"Depends on Joy Chu," she said. "Eric is positive she'll want to go after he talks to her. We'll meet her in Seattle. My guess is she'll have to even if she doesn't want to. Seems Eric has some clout still in DC."

"This morning?"

"If not the 11:30, the 4:30," she said.

She spooned some Taster's Choice into her cup, poured in boiling water and stirred in cream. She then turned to boil up some oats for us, keeping her back to me.

An Alaskan Air Grumman landed four times in Confluence on its way twice a day between Seattle and Salt Lake. I knew that Lana would be packing quickly as soon as we ate.

She dialed a number, put the phone to her ear and held it there as she stirred. I knew she was calling Hammersmith. I got to my feet and went into my room to dress once again for the drive to the airport.

It was all starting up.

Again.

Chapter
Fifty-Six

That morning found us under a black lid of cloud that nearly touched the eastern horizon. The sun slid through this narrow strip of clear blue sky quickly like a lantern passing a door left ajar.

I went out to the barn in the warm gray gloom, rolled open the heavy door and backed out our new Tundra. Back in the living room I resumed drinking tea and waiting with Lana.

Huey and Jables Weinman brought Eric and Ruthie into town on their snowmobiles within the hour. Jables, Hammersmiths' closest neighbor, was bundled in Carhartt Arctic insulated coveralls and had four suitcases strapped on his powerful Polaris 340 Transport.

We heard their engines moaning across the prairie well before they arrived. The engines sang a capella, slowly growing in volume the closer they got, and changed pitch dramatically as they passed between the brick buildings down Main on their way to our place.

Lana and I reached the barn just as they pulled in. They left their engines running, and Lana and I helped Ruthie and Hammersmith climb off stiffly.

Ruthie was overdressed like a toddler in a silver snow suit. She could barely walk in it. Lana took her arm and helped her to the house. Eric followed in old galoshes. He had plain hooded coveralls over his traveling clothes.

Jables unstrapped the luggage and Huey loaded them into the back of the Tundra. I thanked them and they remounted and headed back to their farms.

I climbed into the Tundra to warm it up.

In a bit I heard the back door open. Ruthie and Lana came out wearing long wool coats that reached high topped leather dress boots. Lana had a messenger bag slung over one shoulder and carried a mid sized canvas garment bag. Eric was dressed like a New York godfather on his way to a back room meeting. They were ready to go.

I wasn't back from the airport until two that afternoon. Their flight was late, and I drove home in the gloom of fog and thin rain that had settled down on the Bench like a wet hen. Visibility was down to five car lengths and I kept the speed under thirty, straining to keep on the pavement the entire way.

The phone was ringing when I finally came in the back door. I tracked my way through into the kitchen and answered on the fifth ring.

It was Smoke.

"You ready to go, pardner?" he said.

I shook the rain off my hat over the sink.

"What are you talking about?"

"You and I are going to Pasco," he said. "MacAvity wants us to check out this Nelson Yost guy."

"Right now?"

"You have other plans?

I desperately cast for an excuse. Came up empty.

"I'm going to get my fucking Jimmy out to the road if I have to tow it behind my Caterpillar," he said. "Be packed. I'll be back in an hour."

I went back to the hall, hung my Stetson and shrugged off my wet Goretex mountaineering coat.

Came back to the living room.

The house was empty. Hollow sounding. Ollie watched me from Lana's spot on the couch. Corgi ears towering.

"I suppose you wanna visit Pasco with me?" I said.

She jumped off the couch and began to jump against my leg and bark. I shouldn't have said a thing. No way I could take her.

The phone rang again.

Lordy.

It was Charlie.

"Where is everybody?" he said.

"You found *me*."

I could hear him tapping his desk top.

"Joy Chu said she's meeting Eric in Seattle," he said. "You happen to know why?"

"They're going to L.A., Charlie. Lana and Ruthie are going too. I don't know what Joy and Eric are up to, but Eric wants to stash Ruthie with Ann again. Lana's coming home."

" Isn't Ann's place in San Francisco?"

"He wants to drop her off on the way back," I said.

He thought about this.

"You know where they're staying in L.A.?"

"San Maarten Hotel in Laguna Beach."

"Got the number?"

"No."

"Okay. I'll find it."

He paused.

"You find Stripe?" I said.

"He pulled into the Twin River Marina and RV Park in Confluence. My deputies talked to the live-in managers. The wife says he was followed in by two Indian looking guys in a white Ford Explorer. Stripe came in, arranged for a slot, parked the RV without bothering to hook up and drove off in the Explorer."

"The guys Camas?"

"Don't think so," he said. "Canadian plates. And she said there were two short antennas on the rig's roof."

I thought about that. More Canadians.

"Have any ideas?"

"None. I'm leaving a deputy there, parked discretely. I want to get the plate numbers off that Explorer."

Then, "You guys up to something?"

"You have a suspicious mind, Charlie," I said.

"A gift you old farts have given me. So what are you doing?"

I leaned back against the counter and looked out the front window. I could barely see the elevators across the street.

"Smoke and I are about to leave for Pasco," I finally said.

"Jesus!" he moaned. "That fucking Smoke. This his idea?"

"MacAvity's. Just to take a peek."

"Oh. I see. Lovely. Butte thinks I can't do my own police work?" he said. "He thinks I can't make a phone call and have a SWAT team tear Nelson Yost's place apart in the next ten minutes?"

"You asked."

He hung up.

I put on the tea kettle and poured dog food and water into her gravity feeders.

Ollie followed me into my bedroom, hopped up on the bed and watched me pack a small duffle. I put in one change of clothes and my toiletry kit. I had no idea how long Smoke intended for us to be gone.

From the night stand I took out a compact Walther PPK .380. Lana had given me the automatic because it was what 007 had carried, and she thought the Glock MacAvity loaned me once was ugly and Sean Connery was gorgeous. Couldn't ignore the logic there.

The PPK was held in a cordura clip holster I could comfortably slip under my belt down the back of my pants. I popped the clip, made sure it fully loaded with one in the chamber, and dropped it on top in the duffle.

I went back into the kitchen, poured hot water through the tea pot's infuser and took it and a cup back into the living room. I took a seat by Ollie, picked up the book, *Wolf Man of Alaska*, and settled in.

Chapter
Fifty-Seven

After sitting out the winter in the soul rotting rains at the mouth of the Columbia River, Lewis and Clark and their sodden band left their tiny split cedar fort and headed for home. They followed the Columbia River upstream to where it turned north and the Snake River poured into it. Here they decided to avoid the narrows along the Snake below Confluence by heading inland. They decided to turn up a small river marked by a three story plug of rock that looked like a top hat, and worked their way up the west side of the Blue Mountains to Confluence and their friends, the Camas.

Their route from Hat Rock up the Blues, the Snake, the Clearwater, the Lochsa and over the Bitterroot Mountains to Montana is now Highway 12. It is one of the few east-west roads across Idaho and is more like a winding narrow two-lane strip of asphalt than a highway. It should have been called a road or game trail.

Smoke followed 12 from Confluence for about ten minutes. Here the Snake entered a deep gorge and the road turned left up a side canyon and over Alpowa Ridge to a summit and down to the Pataha River.

We drove speaking little, as always. Smoke drove quickly, even when the wipers were barely keeping up with the fine spray of late afternoon rain, and he didn't take out a cigarillo unless his wing window was open. His tricked-out GMC was too precious for that. Instead, we allowed ourselves be lulled out of time and place by the hypnotic sweep of the road's continuous windings.

We slowed through the listless farming towns of Pomeroy and Dodge, switched from the Pataha River to the Touchet by crossing the Tucannon and entering the foothills. Soon we dropped rapidly down to Dayton, crouched at the mouth of a canyon where the Touchet came out from the Blues and turned west.

When we reached Waitsburg, Smoke navigated between its two-story brick buildings and up a side street that carried us away from 12 and up onto the sweep of Touchet Flats.

We had been on the road for two hours. The fog had lifted to form a featureless ceiling, and whips of mist streaked the river valley. Bare limbs of locust trees rose like fork tines into the heavy still air, and night settled in on us.

Smoked pulled on his lights. He reached under his seat and withdrew a pint of Lauders Scotch and handed it to me to open. I cracked the plastic seal, took a swig, and handed it back. Smoke took a long pull and wedged the open bottle between our seats.

He glanced quickly at me. "How we doing, pardner?"

"Been wondering if Butte or you happened to have a plan," I said.

The road veered away from the river and we began to climb out of the valley.

He dropped into third.

"Nope."

"Any ideas to make me soar with hope we'll live through this?"

"Nope."

"Gee, that's swell."

At the top of the grade the road straightened and began the stretch across Eureka Flats.

Smoke opened it up. In seconds we were riding the truck springs at ninety across the prairie's ocean swells.

Pasco's loom sat dimly on the western horizon where the sun had been.

Smoke took a second swallow and handed the pint back to me. I took a sip and wedged it back into place.

"I know where we're going tonight, though," he said.

"That's encouraging."

"Nelson Yost wholesales hops from an industrial park on the Columbia River in West Pasco," he said. "Highest quality. Sells to micro breweries."

"Canada?" I said.

Smoke nodded. "That's what MacAvity says. Vancouver, Kamloops and, get this, Kelowna. Also, in the states, Bellingham, Seattle, Portland, Eugene and Bend."

"Joy Chu tell him all this?"

"Nope. She told Oscar Redtail."

"And Oscar told Butte?"

"Nope, Oscar told Hammersmith."

"OK. So Eric *didn't* tell you."

"Nope, he did."

I swallowed.

"You're a fountain of info, Smoke."

We suddenly howled into a slot through black walls of an enormous pulp tree plantation. One moment we were in the sage brush steppes and the next in a forest of tightly packed tree trunks that threw the thunder of Smoke's tailpipes back at us. He backed off and the speedometer dropped from one hundred to eighty five where he held it. We were pounded by our own din. The dash lights illuminated his grin. The old fighter pilot catching a deck cable.

It took five minutes to break free of the trees and out under a ceiling of cloud now bright from the glow of the Tri Cities. The Columbia was directly before us and we turned north on a genuine highway and followed the grandeur of the river around its bend to the west.

Smoke dropped back to legal speed, took us into Pasco by the old bypassed highway and pulled into a fifties style courtyard motel. He parked in the neon light of the office and turned the truck's monstrous engine off for the first time in three hours. The silence was palpable.

"Alice and I use to stay here," he said.

Alice, his war time bride and our high school classmate, had died rapidly of pancreatic cancer seven years ago. I said nothing.

He ducked into the motel's tiny office. A heavy elderly woman barely taller than a door knob came through an arch from her living quarters in the back. When she saw Smoke she threw her arms into the air and came around the end of the counter, wrapped them around Smoke's waist, and gave him a long motherly hug.

They talked in the dim light of the office.

I waited.

When Smoke climbed back into the cab, the best he could do was clear his throat and fumble with the ignition key. He drove us to a corner room set back from the street, got out, and opened the door with a brass key that swung from a numbered square of red plastic.

I got out with our two small duffles and carried them in. He was already through a round arch and a door into the tiled bathroom when I entered. There were twin beds covered with white cotton bedspreads, and behind the beds a scene taken of old Honolulu from Clark Gable days papered the entire wall. Tiny lamps with salmon colored silk shades sat on night stands, and in an alcove to the left of the bathroom was a tiny kitchenette done in red and cream colored tile. A two person formica and chrome table and bent legged chrome chairs with red seats sat along the wall. A TV occupied what had once been a writer's desk and chair at the front window. It was cozy.

Smoke came from the bathroom with wet hair combed back.

"Ready for the best fucking burger you've every had, pardner?" he said.

I nodded. "Then seeing the sights of West Pasco, I presume?"

"That's what I'm thinking," he said.

"Armed?"

"Safety first."

We went out.

"Or burgers first."

"Not burgers, Paul," he said. "Best Fucking Burgers."

"Of course," I said, striking my forehead with a palm.

Chapter
Fifty-Eight

It was a little after eight when we located Yost Hops. It was a one story, prefab, concrete slab building that sat in the middle of what had once been a forty acre orchard. A railroad track ran between it and the river. All the buildings in the industrial park were identical and were scattered under mercury vapor lights clear back into a stand of huge cottonwoods growing on the edge. The whole complex must have been erected in a matter of weeks.

Smoke drove slowly into the center of the labyrinth following the winding curbs towards Yost's building. He pulled into a parking space a hundred yards short, killed the engine and lights and rolled his window down.

He looked pissed. He broke his own rule and lit up a cigarillo and blew the smoke out into the artificial light.

"Should be a fucking law," he said. "Zone a farm industrial and let the taxes kill him. Buy the place for pennies and plow under the apples and peaches and cherries and slap down a bunch of fucking concrete cubes. And on a beautiful river bank! Shit."

"This place is like a morgue," I said.

"And these buildings are the tombstones."

I studied Yost's. It had a loading dock at the back along the tracks and a single truck dock on the west side. There were empty parking spots in front, and three new upscale cars were parked by a side entrance next to the truck dock.

Oddly, they were the only cars in the entire park. In fact, the place was deserted except a few company vans and two Swift semi trailers.

Smoke was lost in his outrage.

"Fuckers," he finally said. He opened the door and stepped out. He ground his half finished cigarillo under a boot heel and looked into the cab at me.

"Well?"

"Clearly," I said. "Brilliant plan."

I took my Walther .380 out of the glove compartment, got out and clipped it in back under my belt. I knew Smoke probably had his Kimber .45 in a shoulder holster under the leather flight jacket. I joined him at the tailgate.

He studied Yost's, hands on hips, feet spread.

"Any ideas?" he said.

"We look around?"

"I coulda thought of that."

We walked over and stood in the end parking spot at the corner of the building.

Smoke started to laugh quietly.

"Sneaky bastards, aren't we? Walk right up, folks."

I kept looking between the front of the building and the parked white Lexus, black Acura and imposing black Cadillac CTS-V nearest me around the corner.

"You know what's strange about this?" I said.

"Us?"

I pointed at the cars.

"These are the only cars in the whole park, right?"

Smoke scanned the place, turning slowly.

"I see what you mean. That *is* weird."

"There are five parking spots on this side, and three of them are taken."

Smoke nodded.

"And they are obviously the bosses'."

"Right. And no lights on in the building," I said.

Smoke stepped onto a strip of white gravel that pretended to be landscaping, edged to the side of the building, and cupped his eyes against the window.

"Can't see a thing," he said, standing back.

He eased along the front of the building and I followed on the walkway.

We reached the front door. It was green enameled steel and had a pane of security glass in the top half.

Smoke and tried to look in again. Then he tried the door.

At that moment, three things happened.

One, the door pushed open.

Two, a whoop-whoop siren went off in the building.

And three, we were engulfed in the smell of blood and gunpowder.

"Oh oh," Smoke said, releasing the door. It shut pneumatically. He reached in his back pocket, took out his bandana, and wiped down the doorknob.

"Shall we venture forth, Skywalker?"

"May we run?" I asked.

"Let us stroll rapidly."

And we almost made it.

Smoke had just reached for the door handle of the Jimmy when the first white police cruiser, light bar aflame, siren off, slid to a halt with its headlights pinning us. Two deputies were out instantly with pistols trained on us over the tops of their opened doors.

Smoke and I trained our hands as high as we could at the mercury lamps overhead.

Then, almost immediately, two other police cars came careening into the park.

In a matter of moments we were relieved of our weapons and wallets, cuffed, and put into the back of two separate cruisers.

Two deputies went over to the building's front door and opened it, guns drawn, flashlights out. One of them, then the other, slid in. Almost immediately the second one hurried back out, yelled something to the four other deputies, and all hell broke loose.

A full hour had passed before anyone paid any attention at all to Smoke or me. Both our cruisers were pulled out of the way far off to one side where we were left to sit. Watching the action was like happening upon a major rescue effort at a multi-car/truck interstate accident. There were at least eight police cars, two unmarked cop cars bristling antennas, an SUV, ambulances, a fire truck, cops stringing yellow plastic police tape, a communications truck, the works.

And I had to pee.

And I couldn't lean back comfortably without jamming my cuffs sideways against the flesh on the inside of my wrists.

Plus, I couldn't believe my luck. Charlie had it right. We old farts in fact *should* have the decency and good sense to stay inside our homes and listen to our arteries harden. Much better than being caught in the middle of the night at a slaughter while carrying a Walther PPK .380 down the back of your pants. And having arrived three hours from home in a truck designed to do one hundred and fifty miles an hour in the middle of the night? Lovely.

I leaned my head against the side window and waited. It was going on ten o'clock.

And the irony of it.

Two years earlier I had killed a man and taken part in the killing of another seven or so, and no one said a word to me. In fact, the town had thrown us a party because we'd killed a bunch of bad guys.

Now, here I was, slammed in the back of a cop car for just getting near some more of the bad guys, and they were *already* dead.

The door jerked open and I fell out onto the gravel.

An enormous black cop grabbed me by my upper arm and hauled me to my feet. He walked me over to a brown Chevy Tahoe and put me in the back behind the passenger's seat. The interior lights remained on after he had shut the door.

The driver was an extremely thin, pale man. He had black hair in a buzz cut and was dressed in a wool western dress jacket. He didn't look up but continued reading under a bright mirror light from a note pad he had flipped open. I waited silently.

Finally he turned sideways in his seat, leaned his bony shoulders up against the driver's door, and looked at me from large watery eyes set in dark circles of flesh. He looked like an Egyptian taxi driver.

He studied me passively.

Finally he cleared his throat and said without a trace of Egyptian accent, "Paul. Right?"

"Yes," I managed.

He glanced at his tablet.

"And the PPK is yours?"

"Yes."

"Not much of a weapon, Paul."

"My wife gave it to me," I said.

He looked at me from under his thick eyebrows.

"Sweet of her."

I nodded.

"You or Colonel Harrington enter that building?"

"Smoke?"

"I don't smoke. Ask one of the deputies later."

"No. His name is Smoke."

"OK. Did you?"

"I use to. But I quit a long time ago."

He rapped the notebook on the screen that separated us.

"Did you and *Smoke* enter the building?"

"No," I said quickly.

"Did you know there were three dead guys in there?"

I shook my head. "No. But we smelled them."

"So you opened the door."

"Yeah."

"To go in."

"Yeah," I said quietly.

He wrote that down.

"Why? And I'm not asking why you quit smoking."

Crunch time. I wondered if I should lie my guts out. Decided against it. Hoped Smoke would decide the same way when his turn came with this Egyptian detective.

"The door opened by itself when Smoke tried to peek in," I said.

He shook his head sadly.

"You drive down here from Ryback. You're both armed. You happen to come to Nelson Yost's. You try to peek in. The door pushes open. The entire office complex was shot to shit by automatic weapons and you smell three dead guys."

"We didn't see any dead guys."

He watched me closely.

"Is that right?"

"Yes sir," I said, even more quietly. Seems I had felt this way a time or two before in the old Ryback School principal's office.

He wrote for a minute or two. The silence was heavy.

Finally he turned his attention back to me. He didn't look happy. In fact, he seemed to be getting pissed.

"Tell me. What the fuck are you two doing here, Paul?"

I looked out the side window, then back at him.

"I don't know."

He waited. His large wet eyes looked as large as grenades.

I swallowed.

"Could you call Sheriff Charlie Rand for me?" I asked.

He cocked his head. "I know Charlie. Why?"

"Maybe he can tell you."

He put his tablet down and pushed a button on a radio slung under the Tahoe's dash.

"Yes Sheriff?" the speaker phone chirped.

"Connect me to Charlie Rand, Nita, and put him through to me."

"At his ranch?"

"Ask his dispatcher."

He picked up a Motorola radio the size of a twelve inch length of two by four and got out. He slammed the door, and went over to the crime scene. He went in and brought out a guy wearing a tan lab coat. He pointed to the glass in the door and the guy went to work taking prints off it.

The detective came back over and climbed in. He put the radio on the seat and started copying from another notebook someone had given him. When he was done, he got out again, disappeared into the building, and was back almost immediately.

He closed the door, leaned back against it in exactly the same way he had before.

"Think of an answer yet?"

"No. But I had a good time trying."

"How old are you guys?" he said.

"We're both sixty-eight."

He nodded.

"You know Commander Hammersmith up there?"

"Yes."

He nodded.

"How's he doing?"

"Good."

He thought about that some.

"Were you involved with that Magruder bunch a couple years ago?"

"Yes," I said.

He nodded.

"And Smoke?"

My turn to nod.

He was about to say something when the radio chirped.

"Yes?" he said to the speaker.

"Evening Detective. What can I do for you?"

It was Charlie.

"Sorry to ruin your day, Sheriff, but we have a couple of your..."

"You have Smoke and Paul with you, Asif. Am I right?"

Asif?

"Yup. How'd you guess?"

"Lock those two old shits up and don't let them back up here and I'll send you a fifth of your favorite."

"Done."

"What'd they do now?"

"They barely managed to avoid contaminating a crime scene. I've got three corpses here butchered by machine gun fire."

"Let me guess. Nelson Yost and his henchmen."

Asif (that really his name?) groaned.

"Paul's sitting right here behind the screen, Charlie."

"You hear me, Paul?"

"Hi, Charlie."

"Shut up."

Then, "Cut those two loose and call me back here at home. I'll tell you what I know. It's a can of worms," he said.

"Is Hammersmith involved again?"

"Call me at home. And commit those two to a rest home for the insane."

After taking one of the longest pees in my adult life against Smoke's rear right hubcap, I climbed in to await his release.

While he made steadfast friends with the Pharaoh of Pasco, I sipped from his pint until there was less than a half inch in the bottom. I knew he'd appreciate the gesture.

That night, back on the streets as free men, we celebrated in the bar of a restaurant called Harbor Side over plates of deep fried shrimp. We analyzed our luck, stupidity, bravery, foolhardiness, and other character flaws that had haunted us since high school. I only vaguely remember opening the door to our motel room at one AM and helping Smoke in.

I woke up at dawn on top of the white bed spread fully dressed.

Chapter
Fifty-Nine

Lurking somewhere in the brain is a switch that is thrown when a man turns sixty. It arms a buzzer that wakes us up at five-thirty AM no matter what horrible hour we fall asleep the night before or how miserable our hangovers are.

Smoke seemed to know where we were going. The streets of Pasco were practically deserted and shined with rain.

"The only chance we have to live," he said, "is to eat with the Mexicans. They are practical people and understand these things."

He pulled off the old highway onto a side street, and off the side street into an alley. The alley opened into a paved parking lot in the middle of the block that was nearly full of old pickups, ratty compacts, and a couple dented Econolines.

Along one side of the lot was a long narrow windowless diner with a red door in the center. A half sheet of plywood was nailed to the side with white paint letters that read, *Restaurante y Cafetería   Desayunos y Almuerzos   Comida Casera.*

Smoke parked, and we stepped out and went over. The air was saturated with the smell of eggs and sausage cooking and dark coffee in the pot.

"Here we go, pardner," he said.

The interior was hot, dark and filled with men standing eating off paper plates with plastic forks. There was a long wooden bench along the front wall where perhaps a dozen old men sat holding Navy surplus coffee cups and leaning into one another deep in conversation.

No one paid the slightest attention to us but stepped aside politely to let us pass through to a chest high stainless counter. Behind it fry cooks and young girls busily prepared plates and filled cups that they slid out to the men.

A heavy middle aged woman dressed in tight jeans and a plain blue sweatshirt greeted us happily.

"¿Que les puedo traer?" she said.

Smoke gave her what he felt was his lady-killer smile.

"Demasiado whiskey anoche."

"¿Menudo?"

"Sí. Y huevos rancheros para el gringo."

Apparently everyone had been waiting to hear what we would order because the help went right at it and the volume of talk among the men surged forward cheerfully.

"Well ain't you The Shit?" I said.

"That's what I'm thinking."

"So what'd you order us?

Smoke was watching a truly beautiful little girl of about the age of ten expertly pour us two paper cups of strong coffee. If it hadn't been for his career in fighter jets, I suspect he and Alice would have had a litter of their own.

"Well, pardner, the traditional cure for hangovers is a chili soup with chunks of tripe."

"You got that for me? Shit."

"No. I already know you're a pussy. I got you a tortilla topped with eggs and salsa. Some refrieds on the side. Be prepared for some heat."

"That's better," I said.

"And do you think we should head right for Magnet?"

"To get our asses chewed?" I said.

"With hot sauce. The worst Charlie can do is kill us. Right?"

I nodded.

"But let's call him first."

We ate in the truck cab and tossed our garbage into a dumpster at the back of the lot.

It was just seven o'clock when we pulled into a gas station at the entrance to the highway. Smoke pumped gas into the beast, and I went over and dropped in enough quarters to reach Magnet. I was surprised when the dispatcher put me right through to Charlie's office. An early riser. And ten years short of sixty. Amazing.

After the call, I came back to where Smoke had parked with the engine running.

"So?" he said.

"I don't know."

I shut the door. "He said we were to get home. Said he would talk to us tonight. Said he was coming in to MacAvity's at seven and Huey and Butte would be waiting for him upstairs and we had better damn well be there too."

"He's pissed, then."

"I considered that."

I paused. "No...but something's odd. I think something happened last night while we were down here trying to get thrown into the penitentiary."

We pulled onto the freeway and Smoked surprised me by not reaching the speed limit full-bore. A humbler man for all the whiskey.

"Or the three of them have lead pipes and are going to show us just how sorry they are we weren't," he said.

The road back across Eureka Flat began to dry in sheets of steam as soon as the sun had climbed into a cloudless miracle of a sky. And by the time we reached Ryback, the roads were bare and dry, and the sweeping expanse of snow that covered the rolling hills of the Bench were painfully brilliant. Even an overnight trip to Pasco made me excited to be back home, albeit a slaughter had transpired in the interim. And, at home, Ollie reflected my happiness with great leaps and barks and contortions.

Smoke, still subdued, rumbled off slowly, leaving me to chores, lunch, and some recovery time.

I left two messages on Ruthie's cell phone to ask how things were going and for Lana to call, but it wasn't until I was making a culinary supper of toast and a can of Dinty Moore that she got back to me. I told her about the trip.

"And they let you go?"

"Barely."

"Worst mistake of the year," she said.

"Us going down there?"

"No. Them letting you go."

"So in an hour Charlie wants to talk to all of us."

"'Bout time."

"Eric there?" I said.

"No. He left for L.A. about seven this morning and isn't back."

"Joy Chu staying at the Saint Maarten with you guys?"

"She stayed in L.A. I doubt the DEA has the Maarten in its budget projections. It's really beautiful. Two story. Spanish. Encloses a garden courtyard and fountain. We have to come here on our honeymoon, Paul. Lay in the sun. Watch the gorgeous tan boys surf."

"Just let me throw some things in a bag. I'll fly out tonight and help watch the tan girls in their thongs."

Lana laughed.

"Get a note from your doctor first, Paul."

I walked to the pub at five to seven. Smoke and Huey's trucks were already parked in front and Charlie's Expedition was in back, so I was late. I hurried up the back stairs, gave a perfunctory knock on the door and went though the kitchen to join them.

Charlie was just taking off his ranch coat and hanging it in the entry.

Eric was at the liquor cabinet, nodded at me, and took another glass out as he continued to mix drinks.

Huey and Smoke were seated opposite each other on the heavy couches. Apparently Charlie and Butte intended to sit in the leather cushioned chairs.

No one said anything.

I shrugged off my jacket and went over to join Charlie when the stairwell door opened. Josiah Longbeach and Oscar Redtail came in.

"Evening, folks," Longbeach said. "We late?"

Charlie was taking his seat. Huey got up and joined Smoke, making room.

"There goes the neighborhood," Smoke said. He stood and he, Huey and I shook hands with them. Butte put our drinks on the large coffee table and went into the kitchen for a couple Snowcaps for Josiah and Oscar. He returned and we all took our seats.

Charlie picked up a whiskey and swirled it before speaking. Then he looked at Huey.

"Wanna start by telling these folks what you and I been up to, Huey?"

Huey, a quiet Norwegian gone to gray, flushed.

"Heard a boom last night," he said. "Woke me up. Went out to the front room, turned on the lights, opened the front door, and there was a body on the porch. Half of his head was all over the brickwork. So I called the sheriff."

He was done.

"*The sheriff*. That would be me, folks. Since some of you have forgotten," Charlie said.

"What's it look like?" Longbeach said.

Charlie cleared his throat.

"He took a .50. Went though his head, though Huey's new brick wall, across the room, though the wall low on the far side, and plowed to a stop in the hardwood floor of the guest room."

Smoke whistled.

"Sniped," Oscar said.

Charlie nodded.

"We rod sighted the hole to the trees across the road. 400+ yards. Easy shot for fifty sniper. Left pod marks but the casing was gone and the body print and foot prints were swept back to where someone had pulled up against the road's plow berm. About one thirty, Huey?"

Huey nodded.

"That's it."

He took a sip.

We all did.

I decided, as soon as the White Horse hit my tongue, that one sip might be plenty that night.

After a moment, "You ID the body yet?" Longbeach said.

Charlie nodded.

"Pulled a negative. Then on a hunch, sent the prints north and the RCMP came through for us."

He set his glass down.

I did the same.

"He was a smalltime punk wannabe gangster out of Kamloops. White guy named Jingles Radcliff. Didn't make his twenty-second birthday."

We considered this. Another Canadian.

Charlie read our minds.

"Our two guests that joined Freddy Stripe at the marina are also Canadians."

He looked at Josiah and Oscar.

"The RCMP said they're from the Neskonlith Indian Band of the Secwepemc (Shuswap) people. One works out of Chase, the other Salmon Arm," he added.

"Just north of the road between Kamloops and Kelowna, I'd say," Oscar Redtail said.

"That's what I'm told."

"And they answer to the Shuswap Nation Tribal Council."

Charlie studied Oscar.

"What's that tell us?"

Longbeach chuckled.

"That it might be our first break," he said. "They're Enforcers."

Butte, who had taken the seat beside Charlie stepped in.

"As in 'law enforcement'?"

Oscar and Josiah nodded and both leaned back, relaxed on the couch. Smiling.

"And Freddy Dickweed Stripe?" Smoke said. "Next you'll be telling us *he's* a Canadian Indian."

"Few are chosen," Oscar said.

"Thank God."

Charlie cleared his throat.

"We don't know a thing about Stripe. Nor do we have a clue where Alex Byrd is. But we do know Byrd's a killer and we're told he's very good at what he does."

I almost raised my hand. Caught myself just in time.

"Do these guys have jurisdiction down here in America?"

"I thought you white people called *everything* over here America. Or was it India?" Oscar said.

"OK. The States."

All but Charlie and I laughed.

"The two guys are Billy Long Gone and Samuel Beauvallon," Charlie said. "And no. They don't."

We were silent. I took a second tentative sip. It was a tiny bit better than the first.

I watched Oscar and Josiah. They were looking at each other very soberly. Reading each other.

We waited.

Smoke reached for a cigarillo, glanced and Butte, and lowered his hand to his glass.

"You know," Longbeach said, "the People in Canada are building tribal casinos too."

"Right," Charlie said.

"Fast."

Charlie nodded.

"And not all Enforcers enforce for the RCMP." This was Oscar. "Unless it's in the best interest of Council."

Charlie nodded. "So, Long Gone and Beauvallon and, say, Freddy Stripe and Alex Byrd might not be good guys."

"We don't know, Charlie," Longbeach said.

"Well, the RCMP does know that Byrd isn't."

"Yup." Then, "I suppose we should track Stripe down and ask him."

Charlie threw the rest of his drink back and got to his feet.

"Well, folks. I've only had four hours sleep. But what I'd like to point out is we have something very dangerous going on here. And I don't know what to do about it."

He hesitated.

"But you four," he said. "If you decided to do anything similar to what Smoke and Paul did yesterday, you better talk to me first. I will call Josiah and Oscar. I will talk to Hammersmith. I will consult with MacAvity here. But if you, Smoke, and you, Paul, don't listen to me, I'll put you behind bars until this thing goes away.

Smoke and I said, "Yes sir," simultaneously.

My mouth had gone dry.

Charlie, Longbeach and Oscar Redtail put on their coats and went out. We could hear their cowboy boots rumble down the stairs, and they were gone.

Huey was as silent as stone. He'd practically gone invisible.

"Well," MacAvity said.

He got to his feet and went over to refresh his drink.

"That was fun."

He looked at Smoke and me.

"Seems he ripped off a few of your stripes."

"Seems like it," Smoke said. "And I think we're fucking lucky we're not in jail. Terrific idea, Butte. Got any more doozies?"

Butte started clearing off the table.

"Wasn't a total loss, Smoke. They found two-hundred grand of crystal meth."

"Seriously?" I said. "Charlie tell you that?"

"No. Charlie told Oscar."

"So Oscar told..."

"Longbeach."

"Who...never mind," I said.

"Like that had anything to do with Paul and me," Smoke said.

MacAvity laughed. "It's not your fault someone is getting all the pie before we get to the table. It's the thought that counts."

Huey had come to life. "So Nelson Yost was distributing it with the hop shipments?"

"Inside the vacuum sealed compressed blocks."

"Clever prick," Smoke said.

We all nodded.

"A dead clever prick," Butte added.

"Unlikely to be both," I said.

MacAvity turned to Huey.

"We're coming home with you, ol' boy. And help clean up the blood and patch the holes before it gets much later."

"I'd appreciate the company," Huey said.

He took the first swallow of his drink since we'd arrived.

Then, "You know when Hammersmith's coming home, Butte?"

"Not for sure. But probably not until he's dropped the hammer once and for all on Spreiter."

Chapter
Sixty

I got home a little after ten. Fed Ollie.

No messages on the answering machine from Lana.

I had a smear of blood on my jeans from scrubbing the blood off Huey's brick wall. I drew a utility tub of cold water in the basement, took the jeans off and left them to soak. The rest of my clothes I left in a pile and jumped into the shower.

The phone rang just as I was toweling off. I trotted back upstairs and grabbed it on the fifth ring.

"Been out partying?" Lana said.

"Hi, sweetie. Where are you?"

"Still at the Saint Maarten. We're flying to San Fran tomorrow morning. Eight-twenty."

"How'd it go?"

"We haven't seen or heard from Joy since we landed. Butte's back and spent practically all night on his cell phone. Ruthie and I ate across the street without him. Thai."

"What's he up to?"

"No good, is my guess," she said.

She was quiet.

"So tell me what Charley wanted."

"I think he wanted to put Smoke and me in jail himself."

She laughed. "He didn't want the Pasco sheriff to have all the fun?"

"But they found a quarter million in crystal meth," I said.

"Well there you go, Paul."

We were silent.

"I miss you," I said.

"Me too."

"When you coming home?"

"Eric wants to visit with Ann for a couple days. I'll probably just walk around Chinatown and Fisherman's Wharf pretending I'm Richard Brautigan."

"So in three days?"

"We'll leave at noon and be in at 4:30. Alaskan."

"Done."

"And Hammersmith wants us to all meet at the pub. We'll be tired."

"Sounds good," I said.

"Says he wants Butte to cook for us in his kitchen and tell us what's happening."

"Butte will love that. Want me to ask him?"

Lana paused. "I think Eric said he was going to."

With the cloud cover gone, the temperature plummeted that night and the house went cold. I woke up with Ollie under all the blankets curled up at my feet, and the bedroom's single paned windows were sheeted with ice half way up. I had slept like the dead. It was nearly eight o'clock and the sun was slanting into the room.

I swung my feet out onto the cold floor and dragged on sweats and slippers. The thermometer outside the window registered minus eight. Not too bad.

I turned up the thermostat on the gas log Jotul to sixty-eight and filled the tea kettle. Ollie came staggering in and stood uncertainly trying to remember what she wanted. I put on a skillet, took out two eggs to fry, and it all came back to her. She managed a half hearted wag to reward me. I broke three more into the pan for myself and added a small pat of Jimmy Dean Hot and sliced some bread and dropped it into the toaster.

By now the sun had filled the kitchen and the house was groaning as its bones began to warm.

So began my day of walking with Ollie and reading and drinking tea. And at three thirty there'd be a pleasant game of cards at the pub.

I only had to fill three days like that before I got to drive to the airport. Wonderful. And after the last two days, my prospects looked delicious. The way things should be when you're sixty-eight, not hung over, not in prison, and not being shot at. Those other things were meant to be left to feckless youth. Let *them* hang their asses out and learn their lessons. Been there.

And even though the thought of bad guys still being out there gnawed at me, I was able to push it to the back of my mind and enjoy myself. I even took time to sweep the house. I knew Lana would be amazed.

MacAvity joined us in the game that afternoon for a bit, filling in for Hammersmith. He played shrewdly and accumulated points just ahead of Huey. Smoke was playing a weak third and I was in the bucket. I acted like I wasn't trying.

"Eric call you yet?" I said.

Butte nodded.

"Wants dinner upstairs for all of us. I phoned Sheila and she's asking Jake to come in to tend bar. I'll rustle up some grub, and Eric can tell us what he and Joy been up to."

"Wow. At his age," Smoke said.

"Must give you hope."

"Maybe she'll give us a table dance."

"She's still in L.A.." Butte said. "Eric doesn't know where she is or when she'll be back."

"But he knows what she's doing?" I said.

"Seems to."

We were able to play for a full hour before Jables Weinman and Don came in, stamping off snow and blowing on their hands. MacAvity dropped his cards, slid out of the booth, and the evening was under way.

I got home at the reasonable hour of six and thought of doing a real meal, not a canned one. I decided to make a feeble showing of culinary skill without poisoning myself and Ollie in the process. So I read the spines of Lana's hundred cookbooks, selected *Recipes for the Pressure Cooker* by Joanna White, and opened it on the counter.

It looked like all I had to do was gather all the recognizable ingredients found in the Master Chef Dinty Moore's stew and put it in the cooker for thirty minutes. So I did. But I had to cube an elk steak first since no beef was in the house. What could be simpler?

I retreated to the living room, had an Anchor Steam to help fill the half hour, listened to NPR, stared at the gas flames, and flinched at the the occasional explosions of steam from the cooker.

When the time came, to be on the safe side, I dished up a small bowl of the resulting glop, cooled it with water, and put it on floor where Ollie slurped it down in moments.

Then I opened another Anchor Steam and went back into the living room to relax and to keep an eye on the dog. After ten minutes the stew was cool enough for me to eat, Ollie seemed fine, and so I tucked in.

And it was even better than Sir Dinty's. Hell, if I'd known cooking was that simple.

Chapter
Sixty-One

The Alaska Airline's turbo prop Grumman landed on time on the sun dried runway. Eight people walked down its lowered stairs and came across the concrete apron under the flood lights. Lana led the way with Hammersmith directly behind her.

On the drive up the grade, I told them about Smoke's and my adventure in Pasco, and as we crossed the Bench I filled them in on the shooting at Huey's.

Eric sat listening, saying nothing.

When I was done I relaxed and waited.

He finally stirred in the crew seat.

"So William Garber tries to kill Wirestone and is killed by we don't know who. Nelson Yost and his men are killed by we don't know who. Now a shooter named Jingles Radcliff tries to kill Huey and is killed by we don't know who."

He studied the road ahead.

"What's MacAvity say?"

"He says someone's beating us to the punch?" I said.

Eric nodded.

"How do they know what's going on?" Lana said. "How could they know there were killers at Wirestone's and Huey's."

"And how did they know Yost was part of the trafficking?" I said.

"These people have some excellent intel going for themselves. That's all I gotta say," Eric mumbled.

I pulled to a stop at the side of the pub and we went up the back stairs.

A large pan was on the tile counter with slabs of white fish marinating. Probably lingcod. There were three long loaves of French bread, two heads of lettuce, a head of cabbage...the counter was filled with food ready to be prepared.

Through the door we could see the others in the living room. We took off our coats and went in to join them.

Charlie, wouldn't you know, was there as well. He put down his beer and got to his feet. He gave Lana a hug and shook Hammersmith's hand.

"I had a call this afternoon concerning you, Eric," Charlie said.

"Who from?"

"From Harley Lappin himself. How do you know the Director of the Federal Bureau of Prisons, Eric?"

Hammersmith nodded towards Huey who was standing by the liquor cabinet.

"I had Huey drop my SEAL team inside Cambodia to get him back. He'd been taken, and one of the Cambodian soldiers, a woman, sent her twelve year old brother on an eighty mile hike into Vietnam to tell us where he was. We got her out too and flew her and her brother back to the states with him. They have three children and eleven grandchildren now, and the brother is a grade school teacher in Saint Paul."

We had taken our seats. Butte mixed us our favorites.

"So what'd he have to say?"

"Lappin a hero?" Charlie said.

"Nope. Very few people even know he was a P.O.W.. He's a private sort of guy. Huey, as we all know, is the hero."

Huey looked at for floor. I could have sworn the old fart was blushing.

"So what'd he have to say, Charlie?"

"His message was to tell you it's a done deal. The move is taking place tonight at one A.M.."

We waited for Hammersmith to explain.

He sipped at the Knob Creek and soda Butte had mixed for him, and was smiling.

Lana was snuggled up against me on the deep couch. She had her hand resting inside my thigh. I draped my arm over her shoulder and held her. Some things never change.

"Well," Hammersmith began, "I met with two of Harley's agents who flew out and were waiting for me at the Intercontinental. I explained our position up here."

He looked at us.

"You ever wonder why we weren't all subpoenaed back when?"

I certainly had.

Charlie answered.

"Because you didn't need to. Spreiter plea bargained."

"Exactly," Hammersmith said.

"And gave up key players in exchange for a low security sentence in Terminal Island."

"Where he started up again," Butte added.

Hammersmith nodded.

"Which I pointed out to them. Which, they agreed, pretty much nullified his bargain with the feds."

"And it is all about to go back into motion," Charlie said.

"That's what I told the agents."

We considered this.

Smoke had on his "let's bomb them" grin.

"OK, Eric," he said. "What'd you do?"

Eric smiled.

"Where did his betrayed pals go to prison?" he said.

Charlie answered. "They are all serving time in the medium security Federal Correctional Institution (FCI) Englewood," he said. "It's a little south and west of Denver in Littleton, Colorado."

"Oh my, oh my," Charlie laughed. "You didn't."

"I did."

Smoke sat back.

"He's being moved there tonight?"

Eric nodded.

"His old crowd is anxious to see him again."

Charlie was shaking his head.

"What?" I said.

"They'll kill him within the week," Smoke explained.

Lana went rigid.

Huey put his head in his hands. A moment passed and then he straightened up and stood. He went to the door, took down his coat, and left, closing the door quietly behind him.

"Tactfully put, Smoke," Lana said.

She got to her feet and hurried after him. We heard her call to him as she rattled down the stairs.

"Are your parties always this much fun, Butte?" Charlie said.

"I try."

He got to his feet as well.

"I'll start getting some grub on."

He went into the kitchen. Smoke went with him and returned with another beer for Charlie. He fixed himself another drink and came over with the Wisers to refresh mine.

He looked at Hammersmith who hadn't stirred.

"How are these people anticipating our every move, Eric?"

"They aren't. They're anticipating the shooter's moves."

"Well they did a piss-poor job beating Yost's shooters to the punch."

Both Charlie and Eric nodded.

I was, as usual, wondering why I didn't see what the hell was going on.

Hammersmith read my mind. Or Smoke's.

Charlie took a large swallow of his Snow Cap.

"What we have here is shooters shooting shooters."

"You're a master of syntax, Charlie," Eric said.

"One group is trying to kill you guys. The other group is killing them. We're trying to eliminate all of them."

Then something occurred to him.

"I think those of you with cell phones should quit using them except for mundane things," he said. "And I think I'm going to make sure my deputies do the same thing. They might be intercepting calls somehow."

"Is it a drug war?" I said.

Eric and Charlie considered that.

We could hear Butte in the kitchen tossing salad in a porcelain bowl.

"Good question," Charlie said.

Eric nodded.

"Well, we do know that Joy Chu is doing something concerning the Furusato gang that Spreiter had on the mainland."

He paused.

"And we know, in the middle, there was Yost Hops. And at the other end, it's the Canadians."

"Shit for brains Freddy Stripe and his two buddies," Smoke said.

"I'm not so sure," Charlie said. "In fact, Oscar and Longbeach have been pretty vague about all that."

"There's also Trent Mazollan," Hammersmith said. "Joy has also been real interested in him. And he's a Kelowna boy too."

"Could Stripe be working for him?" Smoke said.

Eric shrugged.

Charlie crossed his left boot over his knee and ran his hand over the rich tan and black leather.

"I think the key to learning the answer to Paul's question might be to figure out how the people who took out Jingles Radcliff knew he was going to be on Huey's porch when he was. It's uncanny."

"That's a fact," Smoke said. "None of us know stuff like that, cell phones or no cell phones."

It was then that Lana led Huey back into the room.

Smoke stepped forward and wrapped his arms around him.

"Sorry, pardner," he said.

Huey just nodded.

MacAvity called us into dinner.

I was right. It was grilled lingcod. Prepared as only MacAvity could in chili and lemon.

Chapter
Sixty-Two

After fifteen years of admonishment by his doctor, MacAvity took up walking. Religiously. Sherman Vics, who was also the county coroner, had told Butte he was calcifying up in bone and vein like the Carlsbad Caverns. So every morning, early, he walked five miles round trip. He'd been doing it for the past two years.

In the winter he stretched on a pair of postman's treads to give him traction on the shoulder ice and compacted snow and walked the plowed road halfway to the highway and back. When the snows went off, he did circles of Ryback or walked out into the country. Always five miles, two hours every day. The old war horse could be seen pacing along regally under the brim of his Wyatt Earp hat in the growing light.

If he saw Smoke's truck parked at our house, he often came in to visit and watch the three of us eat. He also liked the dark French roast that Lana ground at home and brewed in our Mr. Coffee. He liked it with a teaspoon of sugar and very hot.

That morning, the morning after the lingcod feed, Smoke showed up for flapjacks, and Butte came in the back door about ten minutes later. He stripped off the treads, his coat, hat and gloves and pulled out his usual chair against the back wall.

Lana poured him a cup and brought it over with a spoon.

"Got a Special Forces question for you," Smoke said around a cheek full of pancake.

He chewed twice and swallowed like a dog.

"When did Stripe and his Indian pal get back to the Marina? You hear anything?"

Butte held his cup steady and stirred in sugar.

"Yup. Charlie said they came in about eight in the morning. Were gone for about twelve hours."

Smoke looked at me, eyebrows raised.

"So he had plenty of time to drive to Pasco, whack some guys, and be back the next day in time for lunch."

"Looks like it."

We considered this and ate.

"Charlie say anything about the guy that stayed behind?" I said.

"Good question."

He looked up at Lana.

"Use your phone?"

She reached back and took it off its cradle on the counter behind her and handed it to him.

He dialed and waited. The dispatcher came on. Charlie came on.

We listened to his side of the conversation and were done eating by the time he was done. He handed the phone back to Lana.

"Well, seems the other one was out all night with the Jeep," he said. "What's their names again?"

"Billy Long Gone and Samuel Beauvallon," I said.

"At least you remember names," Smoke said, pushing back.

"Sadly we all remember your real name, too, *Smoke*," I said.

He got up to help himself to more coffee.

"Does Charlie think they did Nelson Yost?"

"Didn't say."

"Jingles Radcliff?"

MacAvity shook his head. "Charlie doesn't know what to think."

He took his first sip of coffee. Carefully.

"'Member he said Oscar Redtail and Josiah Longbeach have grown real vague about Stripe and his pals?"

"Un huh."

"Well he asked Hammersmith last night what's up with his Camas buddies. Eric said he didn't have a clue, but he asked Charlie when they'd started acting like that."

He took a bolder sip of coffee.

"So Charlie said they seemed agitated when he told them the identities of Long Gone and Beauvallon."

"That's understandable, Butte," Lana said. "They're Indians too."

"Maybe now they're thinking we're messing in something that's their business, not ours," I said.

"Maybe."

He looked at Lana.

"You have a good point, but Garber, Yost and now Radcliff are all anglos."

"But anglos who seem to be messing with Indian casinos here and in Canada," Lana said.

We nodded.

"And," she said, "if, in fact, Long Gone and Beauvallon are involved with the bad guys, it's even more their concern."

"This is bullshit," Smoke said. "These guys, Indian or white, are trying to even a score with us Elder Anglos from the U.S. Tribe and are keeping at it even when their fucking leader, Spreiter is behind bars."

"Soon to be dead behind bars," MacAvity reminded him.

"OK. So let's see what happens after that."

"And why has this hot shot hired gun Alex Byrd not shown his hand?"

"I'd like to know where he's hiding," Smoke said. "I'll play my hand for the prick."

"You're going to do what with your hand?" I said.

"Why was Huey so upset last night?" Lana said. "I had to coax him away from the bar to come back upstairs."

MacAvity shook his head.

Smoked leaned forward and put his elbows on the table and crossed his arms.

"Huey and Paul here are not violent like the rest of us, Lana," he said. "And Paul, who is the luckiest shit in the world--he has you after all--has never had terrible things happen to him like Huey has."

He took a deep breath and let it out slowly.

"I guess he's just full up. Can't even stand the thought of Spreiter getting shanked in Englewood."

I sat back and watched Smoke's face. He and Butte had both gone flat-eyed and serious.

"You got to remember," Smoke said, "he was one of the bravest helicopter pilots in Vietnam, his parents are dead, his wife and daughter were killed by a drunk driver, his family home was burned to the ground, he was shot in the face by these same guys we're dealing with here, and the Lutheran mission he established in Vietnam was wiped out and everyone was slaughtered because of what he knew."

He took a breath.

We sat in silence.

"Do you know when Joy Chu's coming back," I finally said.

Lana shook her head.

Butte tapped a finger on the rim of his cup.

"Hmmm. She might be able to tell us what's eating Oscar and Longbeach. Oscar, at least, is on her DEA payroll, is he not?"

"True," Lana said.

"And she did go with you guys to L.A.."

"Also true. But I think it was more to do with the Home Sweet Home gang. The Furusatos. Spreiter's base."

"OK."

He got up. Handed Lana his cup and nodded to us.

At the kitchen archway he stopped.

"I had a thought. Why don't the four of us visit the casino today, ask Longbeach and Oscar for ourselves and drop in some quarters while we're at it?"

"They have any horny widows in their 50s?" Smoke said.

"Dozens, Smoke," Lana said. "And none that will be able to resist your use of the Queen's English."

"Then I'm all over it."

"But you won't be doing the driving," MacAvity said.

"I'll drive," Lana said. "Meet here at five. We'll do supper. It's on Paul."

I looked up at her.

"Oh goodie."

Chapter
Sixty-Three

Butte led the way through the massive oak and glass doors of the Camas Casino and into the lobby. To the left was a gift shop and a tasteful sign over another set of doors that said Smoke Free Gaming. To our right were identical doors identified as Smoking Gaming. In front of us was the entrance to the restaurant.

Smoke veered off to the right and went into the smoking area and stopped just inside the door. We followed.

"Holy shit!" he said. "What a place. This ain't Vegas, kids. This is serious."

The dark room was half again as large as an NBA court and was filled with hundreds of gaudily lit gaming devices. And silent.

Under the towering ceiling and huge trussed beams people sat in front of the machines like automatons watching the displays scroll from one loss to the next. They didn't move. They didn't speak. They didn't sip drinks. Their cigarettes burned in ashtrays untouched. No friendly hostesses came by offering cocktails or snacks. There was no sound of coins rattling out into trays or lights whirling and electronic organ music announcing jackpots. There were no coins at all. Everything was electronic.

We stood and stared.

"Gee, what fun," I said.

"I need a drink. Badly," Smoke said. He stood on his toes trying to see where the bar entrance was.

"This is a reservation, Smoke," Butte said.

"Then we're fucked!"

A short, heavy set Camas lady in her mid-forties wearing tight police style slacks, a white long sleeve shirt and black walking shoes appeared in front of us. Her glossy black hair hung down her back in a braid, and her face was a smooth walnut colored sun. Her gold name plate said Janie Oatman, Security.

"Hi," she said. Not, "Can I help you folks?"

We liked her immediately. Said hi back.

She waited.

"Um, you don't have a bar?" Smoke asked politely.

She shook her head. "But you can buy a beer any day after five in the restaurant."

"OK."

She waited.

MacAvity reached out and shook her hand.

"We'd like to speak with Josiah Longbeach or Oscar Redtail, if we could, please."

"I'm not sure that's possible," she said. "The Assistant Security Director is on from eight 'til four. The Security Director is on now until midnight. Do you know him?"

"We're friends. I'm Butte MacAvity. This is Lana, Paul and Smoke. Could we wait in the restaurant?"

She nodded and walked leisurely to a hallway barely visible in the dark corner to our left.

We went back to the lobby and into the restaurant.

The room was half the size of the gaming rooms. Large. It was filled with small round Corian topped tables, each with two wire backed cafe chairs. The side walls had twelve foot tall windows that looked onto the dirt bank behind the building, and at the back a large buffet stretched from one side of the room to the other. Through two archways a half dozen Camas in white shirts and pants could be seen in a stainless steel kitchen preparing food.

Lana faced Smoke.

"*This* is where you talked with Stripe?"
"Cozy, huh?"
"Military."
Butte nodded.
"Slide a tray down four stainless rails. Hand your plate to a server for meat. To another for mashed potatoes he'll drown with instant gravy. On to the next for string beans. Lovely."
He shook his head sadly.
"I won't touch this stuff. Ate this way nearly my whole life."
"That why you learned to cook?" Lana said.
"Exactly why."
Longbeach came up behind us.
"Haute cuisine, huh?"
"Man, you root eaters never underestimate the White Man's pallet, do you?" Smoke said.
"Can't be done."
He shook our hands.
"So what's up?"
"Nothing we understand," MacAvity said.
Josiah looked around at the tables.
"Well, we can't talk here."
"We did before," Smoke said.
"That was then."
We followed him out. He led us through the non smoking gaming room and down a short unlit hall to a heavy steel door. He inserted a key card and led us up a narrow, dimly lit flight of stairs. At the top he keyed open a second door into a short brightly lit hallway that had four doors on the right and another keyed door at the far end.

He opened the first door on our right and lead us into a windowless office the size of a single car garage. The back wall was faced with colorful LCD security monitors showing the casino's gaming floor. His formica topped desk faced them as if they were a scenic bay window.

He motioned for us to sit in black padded swivel chairs that circled a large round table on our left. A photo of a Camas fishing camp taken in the late 1800s had been blown up to four feet by six and hung on the wall to one side.

He sat down with us.

"So."

MacAvity cleared his throat.

"With all due respect, Josiah, we don't understand something."

"OK."

"OK. Charlie seems to think you and Oscar are holding out on us about Billy Long Gone and Samuel Beauvallon."

Josiah said nothing. He looked at Butte. Expressionless.

MacAvity put his right palm on the table and rubbed its bones and liver spots with his left.

"Why? Is it because they're Canadian?" he said.

Josiah looked at each of us slowly.

Said nothing.

We waited. I had no idea where I should be looking, so I watched the monitors off to my right. Nothing moved in them. Perhaps the players had turned to salt.

Finally, in a relaxed voice Josiah said, "If, say, my daughter fell in love with a boy from the Neskonlith band, I wouldn't be upset or worried she'd move to Canada."

He let us consider this.

"I'd be happy. We will soon have cousins up on the Seymour River and a party to go to."

Butte nodded.

We waited politely.

Then, "Freddy Stripe has his mother living with him. In Kelowna. Her name is Marie Leib. Freddy Stripe's name was Casper Leib. His father was Irish. His mother's maiden name was Marie Beauvallon. Her grandmother was Camas."

"Oh. I see." MacAvity said.

He shook his head. Studied the photograph. Turned back to Josiah.

"Does Hammersmith know this?"

"He's been gone." He looked at Lana and me. "I understand he's back. Micha Wirestone will tell him this morning."

Butte nodded.

"OK." Then, "You worried?"

"We're all worried, Butte."

Butte nodded slightly.

"What about Alex Byrd?"

"No one knows."

Butte took off his hat and swept his fingers through his thin hair. He pulled the hat back on by the brim.

"What do you plan to do, Josiah?"

"Oscar and I will sweat with Wirestone tonight."

"Right. When will we know?"

"Hammersmith will tell you."

"OK."

Longbeach and Butte got to their feet simultaneously. They shook hands, and we followed them out and back down the stairs.

Josiah saw us out the front door.

We started back though the floodlit night towards the Tundra.

"MacAvity," Longbeach said.

Butte turned.

"That's what we know."

"I understand that."

We continued over and got in.

I started the engine, then looked in the rear view mirror at Butte.

"Well, that was brief."

No one said anything.

"I don't understand a thing, here," I said. "Anyone mind explaining?"

Butte messed with his seat belt. Smoke and Lana were staring out the side windows at the front of the casino.

Apparently I was the only one that was confused.

"He was saying we are dealing with family here," Butte said. "Stripe and Samuel Beauvallon are all related to the Camas. Maybe Billy Long Gone as well. They're worried they have become criminals."

"Oh."

"Let's get back to the pub," Butte said. "I'm hungry and I need a drink."

"Ditto that," Smoke said.

Chapter
Sixty-Four

We drove in silence back towards Confluence, skirted the town and started back up the seven percent grade to the Bench. The snow banks on each side of the bare highway were dirty white in the headlights.

I dropped into fourth, settled in at fifty-five, and reran our talk with Longbeach. Wondered what Wirestone would tell Hammersmith.

A pair of headlights slowly gained on us and stayed respectfully behind, waiting for a stretch to pass.

What I had never been able to understand, and probably no one else had either, was how Micha knew so much about practically everything that was going on with everyone on the Bench and on the reservation without even leaving his cabin. Much less his ragged overstuffed chair in front of his wood stove.

At the short straight stretch before the grade made a sweeping turn to the left, the lights pulled out to pass. I dropped back to fifty, then forty-eight to make things easier for them. In my side mirror I could see it was a white 4-Runner with a ski rack on the top. I edged over a bit as it pulled up even with us.

"Paul!" Butte roared.

Out of the corner of my eye I saw the side of the Four-Runner, still coming on strong, sweep over into our lane. I slammed on the brakes and dodged onto the thin line of gravel running along the side of the snow.

It hit us slowly. The sides of both rigs creaked and popped under the pressure. The full weight of the Four-

Runner continued to push against us and the Tundra's right wheels began to lift up on the plowed snow berm. Then over to the far side.

We bottomed out and began to slow. The right wheels hung over the embankment. A gulch was fifty feet below us.

The 4-Runner pulled away. I struggled to keep us going straight until we could stop. Then it swung back and rammed us again, violently.

When our left front tire hit the snow, we slewed to the right, slid sideways, and then dropped down the side of the embankment.

I wrenched the wheel straight downhill so we wouldn't roll, and hung on. A bank of snow plowed over the hood and covered the window, blinding us.

In the background I cold hear Lana and Smoke yelling something. The truck began to buck out of its slide and into the air in great leaps. The wheel spun freely in my hands.

We hit the far side of the gulch in an explosion of air bags and crushing metal. The truck was standing on its nose, then creaked backwards and bounced back on its rear wheels at a forty five degree angle and tipped steeply to the right.

I pushed the airbag down out of my face and looked at Lana. She was draped from her shoulder harness. Her head hung over the transmission hump and she was motionless.

Suddenly the side windows broke over me and the doors began to bang like they were being smashed with framing hammers. My left leg was kicked sideways and went numb. A tremendous flash and explosion roared in the cab behind me deafening me. The ceiling light came on, and over my shoulder I saw Smoke roll out and struggle to gain his footing on the steep snow.

Then a series of explosions let loose. I went totally deaf and my left ear felt like it was being slapped with hot sheet metal.

I fell sideways away from the blows and looked over my left shoulder to see Hammersmith firing up the slope through the back window with his .45 Para Tac-Four. I also saw flashes through the back window. I knew then that Smoke was at the back of the truck firing uphill as well.

Then my vision began to narrow. I lay back on top of Lana and darkness gently drew its black sheet over me.

I remember lots of hands moving me this way and that. I remember the whirling lights, being lifted onto a gurney, being slid into the brightly lit interior of an emergency response vehicle, being rolled down a short hall under blinding florescent light, and a man pushing a needle into the back of my hand and saying something I couldn't hear.

That's what I remember.

A middle aged, white haired nurse was fiddling with a tube and needle on the back of my left hand when I cautiously opened my eyes. I was laying under a thin cotton blanket in a large cold room filled with electronics, tables, cabinets, rolling trays, the works. A couple of young men in green scrubs were leaning casually against a counter across the room killing time.

I rolled my head to the right. Lana and Smoke were beside me seated in gray molded plastic chairs. They were talking quietly.

I realized I was hearing them only from my right ear, and not very well at that.

Then I saw that Lana had her left arm held under her breasts by a blue sling and white cotton straps.

The nurse came around and blocked my view as she bent over and looked into my face. She took out a pen light and shined it into my eyes.

"How do you feel?"

She sounded like she was talking through cotton.

I ran an inventory of my body, starting at my hair, which seemed fine.

Heard myself say, "*Left ear on the blink. Right ear so-so...*"

Lana face appeared beside the nurse's. She was grinning.

I smiled back.

"*You OK?*" I said.

She nodded. Leaned over and kissed me.

I continued my inventory.

Got to my left leg.

"*Left leg seems woody. I feel stoned. I'm cold. And I could use a drink.*"

My vision widened as the nurse and Lana got out of my face. Smoke was standing beside me now, also grinning. Everyone thought I was hilarious.

The two guys in scrubs just looked at me, expressionless.

Then Sherman Vics came into the room and over to the side of the bed. He was in his doctors' uniform, white lab coat, slacks, shined shoes, a stethoscope hanging around his neck. Nice haircut.

He stood and grinned down at me.

"*How you feeling?*"

"*Deaf. Cold. Thirsty. What's with my left leg?*"

"*You took a bunch of door fragments in it along with a bullet,*" he said. He stopped grinning.

"*Feels numb.*"

"*Count your blessings. I'll give you some pills to take when it's no longer numb.*"

He put his stethoscope in his ears, pulled down the blanket, pulled up my backless excuse of a garment and chilled me more listening to my lungs and heart. He pulled my nightie back down, pulled my nearly transparent cotton blanket up, and nodded over his shoulder at Lana.

"Butte ruptured your left eardrum, but it'll be OK. In fact, you're fine. But I'm keeping you here until tomorrow. You've lost a bit of blood."

He took my jaw in his left hand and turned my head sideways. He wiggled his fingers at one of the scrubs who pushed off the counter and brought him a stainless tray. He looked in my left ear with a special light, turned my head to the other side, put down the light and picked up a small hemostat. He pulled a wad of soft gauze from both my ears. The left one was blood stained.

"That better?"

I realized I was a little stoned on something.

"You scared the shit out of me," I said. "Thought I was deaf."

He took a small brown bottle from his lab coat pocket and put drops in both my ears. He recapped the bottle and handed it to Lana. He turned, nodded to the scrubs, then put his hand briefly on my right shoulder.

"I'll see you after lunch," he said, and left the room.

Smoke took his place. He took my blanket and pulled it back like Vics had done, then reached for my backless gown. I grabbed his wrist.

"What the fuck you think your doing?"

"For Lana. See if you still have your dick."

"*You* won't."

One of the scrubs shouldered him aside, pulled the blanket back up and toed off the gurney's wheel brakes.

And away we went. King for a day. Whizzing though halls with my entourage of scrubs, fighter pilots, lovely ladies. People stopping in their tracks in awe. The wounded warrior.

The nice thing about small town hospitals is their rooms are usually empty. Except, of course, nine months after high school graduations when the pregnant graduates are wheeled in.

I had a double room, and once I was settled into bed and the scrubs had left, Lana, Smoke and I had it to ourselves.

Smoke closed the door and sat on the window sill. It was still dark out. Lana sat on the bed beside me.

"MacAvity OK?" I said.

"Home sleeping," Smoke said. "Lana and I haven't had any sleep ourselves. I'm trying to talk her into taking a nap with me. But, you know."

"Nice to know you're there for her."

I smiled at Lana

"What's wrong with your arm?" I said.

"Seat belt turned me sideways and tried to pull my shoulder apart. Then the airbag gave me a knockout punch."

She turned her right cheek towards me. It was faintly purple and swollen.

I pulled her over and kissed it .

"Easy," she said.

Smoke went to the door.

"Shall we?"

"Wait a minute, Smoke," I said. "Weren't we run off the road?"

"We were."

"And shot up?"

"We were."

I raised my eyebrows.

"So? You and Butte kill them?"

"We didn't."

Lana got between Smoke and me.

"He got away, Paul," she said. "One of Charlie's deputies found the 4-Runner at the Confluence Airport. Said it was stolen. Side's all pushed in. Had a bullet hole clear through the cargo area. Charlie said it was from a high powered rifle."

"At the airport? There're no flights that time of night," I said.

Smoke nodded.

"But whatever new car he steals won't be missed until someone arrives from their return flight."

"Wasn't this the same gig we had with that Humvee a couple years ago?"

"Indeed it is."

I considered that.

Then, "Wait a minute. The 4-Runner had a rifle bullet go through it? That wasn't us."

"I know," Smoke said. "Guess we're not the only ones don't like Alex Byrd."

We thought about that.

Then, "How's the new Tundra?"

"Very, very old," Lana said. "She might have to be put down."

"Parted-out," Smoke said. "That's what your insurance will do to recoup some of their losses. Hard to sell a wrecked truck full of bullet holes."

Chapter
Sixty-Five

After Lana and Smoke left, my nurse returned and dimmed my lights so that I could sleep. A good idea. Except that within minutes my leg woke up when pain came to pay a visit. I buzzed the nurse back and she brought me back a single hydrocodone pill nestled in a paper cup the size of a twist off wine cap. Probably was going to cost me a hundred bucks.

And its effects were minimal. My shin bone ached, my calf muscle felt like it was being crushed in a vice, and I decided I would try to divert my thoughts by feeling sorry for myself. It helped. But I couldn't fall asleep.

At eleven thirty Sherman Vics came back with a different nurse who wheeled in a cart.

"Wanna watch?" Vics said.

"Watch what?" I managed.

He pushed a button at the foot of the bed and I was lifted into a semi-sitting position. The nurse pulled the light blanket and sheet to one side revealing my leg and gently lifted my foot onto two firm pillows she took from the cart's bottom shelf. She went to work with a pair of duck billed scissors on the blood stained gauze wrap.

Vics took my temperature and replaced the digital thermometer on the cart without a word.

I looked down as my leg was slowly revealed. It looked like an elongated egg plant that had been practiced on by a ladies' sewing bee. It felt blessedly cool exposed to the air.

"Do I get charged by the foot for the cat gut?" I said.

"We're short on cats these days," Vics said. "We're charging by the knot."

"That's a relief."

"How you feel?"

"OK."

"In the old days they called this a flesh wound. If you don't count the bone being nicked. So you should be up and around in a couple weeks without even a cane. You should feel lucky."

"I do."

"On a scale from one to ten, ten being the most, how much pain you feeling?"

I thought about that.

"Say, five for the muscle, eight for the bone?"

He nodded.

"I'll up the pain killer a little and check with you this afternoon before I head home."

They left, but not before the nurse rolled me slightly over onto my right side and gave me a shot in the left hip.

I was asleep within five minutes.

I dreamed my five Plymouth Rock chickens were trying to teach me how to achieve the state of mind necessary to roost on a closet pole all winter long without getting bored. It was a very complex technique in its simplicity. They were very patient with me. I never quite mastered the technique.

Still in the twilight of consciousness just before I opened my eyes I had the feeling the chickens had put me onto something very profound. My admiration for them was without limit. And then I realized I had to pee more like a horse than a chicken.

I opened my eyes and without thinking threw back the covers and sat up. What little blood I had remaining left my head and I fell back. My leg applauded my efforts with pain similar to the sound of a submarine klaxon.

Lovely.

I groped for the buzzer with my left hand, trying not to move.

Someone, while I slept, had managed to untape my hand, pull out the IV needle, put a band aid over the puncture, and wheel out my IV stand without waking me.

Now how the hell did they manage that?

Oh.

Screw meditation. Chickens need hypodermics.

I found the buzzer. A college age guy in white pants and short sleeve shirt came in.

"Need to go to the bathroom yet?"

"I'd prefer if the bathroom came to me," I said.

He produced a pipe necked pan from inside a cabinet off to the side of my bed and handed it to me.

I knew what to do, did it very carefully and gave it back to him.

He didn't seem terribly grateful.

"You have people here to see you," he said. "You feel up to a visit?"

"Sure."

"There are four of them."

"I'm disappointed," I said.

He left with his treasure.

Moments later Lana came in followed by Hammersmith, MacAvity and Huey. They filed around me like I was a campfire.

Hammersmith took the padded chair, Butte the molded plastic one, Huey the window sill and Lana the bed. I had no idea why I noticed this pecking order, but there it was. Enlightenment. An awareness of the painfully obvious.

When we were done with the how you feeling, did you sleep, does it hurt, and are you hungry, Lana gave me a kiss and took my right hand and held it in her lap.

Then we had nothing more to say.

I groped for a question.

"So, what happened today?"

They seemed relieved.

Hammersmith tried to get comfortable on the padded seat.

"Charlie says when they were dusting for prints they found blood on the 4-Runner's steering wheel."

"So he was hit."

"Looks like it. Or maybe just cut his hand scrambling out of the fusillade Smoke and Butte here threw his way."

Butte nodded.

"I don't think he expected us to still be mobile," he said, "much less armed, dangerous, and pissed."

He paused.

"Good driving by the way. You taking lessons from Smoke?"

"Lana. She drove down to the casino and wanted to see if I could drive back."

"He drove like shit," she said. "You see what he did to our truck?"

"Un huh," Huey said. "Then we went by the marina. Stripe has pulled out."

"Really?"

They all nodded.

"There's more," Lana said. "When I got home early this morning, someone had been in our house. They left an envelope on our kitchen table."

I tried to clear my head.

"How'd they get in?"

She shrugged her shoulders.

The others shook their heads.

I thought about someone walking around in our house in the dark. Thought about Lana being there alone.

Butte was reading my mind.

"Whoever it was must have known the house would be empty. Either you were being watched, or they knew ahead of time."

He paused.

"We looked for tracks around the elevators. Snow is unmarked. No one in town saw anyone hanging around. Looks like they knew we'd be gone and knew for how long."

I felt weak.

"So, what was in the envelope?"

Hammersmith reached inside his long black wool coat and took out a folded sheet of paper. He spread it out and handed it to me.

I took it with my right hand, edged up gingerly on my left elbow and looked at it. It was a picture of an overgrown abandoned two story farm house. Behind it was a half collapsed equipment shed.

"Isn't that on Leaps'?"

"On mine," Huey said. "Leaps' starts across the road."

"Down near the breaks, right?"

"Right."

"This is crazy," I said.

No one said anything for a moment.

"Look closely," Hammersmith said. "What do you see?"

I studied the picture. It was pixilated. So telephotic. Digitally dated yesterday, 14:22. So a digital camera was used and printed out on a quality laser jet. An old farm house falling down. There use to be six farms for every one today. The down side of technology. Dead farm houses. Dead farm towns.

Then I saw it. The equipment shed was three sided like they all are so the combines, grain trucks and tractors can be stored easily. The end of this one, the end closest to the road, was still standing, but barely. Parked just around the edge of its side I could see about five inches of the rear bumper, tailgate and window pillar of a white 4-Runner.

I handed the picture back to Hammersmith.

"Why would a guy trying to kill us tell us where he was hiding out?"

"We don't know it was him," Huey said. "This happened a lot at our mission in Vietnam. People would leave clues where the traffickers were coming over the mountains. Do it so no one knew who they were and come and kill them and their family."

I nodded.

"What Huey's saying is exactly right," MacAvity said. "That's the way things worked over there. Sometimes the clues might be as subtle as two leaves pierced by a sliver of bamboo. You never knew."

"We know this, though," Eric said. "We know that Stripe, Billy Long Gone and Samuel Beauvallon were parked at the marina, not on Huey's place."

He folded the picture back into thirds and returned to his coat.

"And Smoke drove down to the breaks to have a peek. The shed was empty as far as he could see."

Lana was rubbing the back of my hand with the flat of her warm palm.

"You going to tell Charlie about this?" she said.

"I don't know," Hammersmith said. "But I want to see inside that place."

He looked over at Butte.

Butte shrugged.

Huey let his breath out like he'd been holding it.

"Can't we wait until we hear what Joy Chu has to say?"

Eric nodded.

"We can."

"You think we should?"

"I do."

Hammersmith reached into the other side of his coat, took out his cell phone, stood.

"I'll make a call," he said, and went out into the hall. The door shut automatically behind him.

Huey reached and touched the side of his face where the bullet had come out. The forty-two thousand in plastic surgery fees had left it numb but practically scarless. A person had to have known him before the shooting to know his jaw now moved differently when he talked. Seemed to swing minutely to the left.

"Bullets do the job, huh?" he said.

I nodded. "They don't fuck around, that's for sure."

I paused.

"Makes it seem a whole lot different getting the hit than giving the hit, don't you think?"

"Truer words."

We simultaneously looked at MacAvity who had three Purple Hearts and a drawer of what he called other junk.

"What?" he said.

We said nothing.

"You want me to agree it hurts?"

"It won't kill you," Lana said.

Butte gave a short laugh.

"Hurts like a red hot locomotive driving right though your junk, I'd say."

"So it smarts?" she said.

He smiled.

"That's why I like it. In fact, since we're here in a hospital, think I'll just shoot myself in the foot for the fun of it."

Hammersmith continued to talk on the phone.

"What's it really like?" Lana asked us.
"Didn't hurt," I said.
"Don't remember a thing." This was Huey.
"It's like I said, a locomotive," Butte said. "Huge impact. You can't believe the force a bullet transmits to your body. Logical awareness vanishes. Chaos."

He thought a moment. Looked at the far wall.

"It's the after part. The depression. The sense of futility and tragedy. The pity. The bureaucracy and stupidity and medical mistakes and incompetences. The happy realization of who are really your friends and the feeling of betrayal by those you thought were."

He shook his head. Said nothing more.

Eric came back in. "Joy's not going to fly back to her Seattle office," he said. "She's coming directly here to Confluence tomorrow morning on the 11:30."

Then to me, "You getting out tomorrow?"

"Hope so."

"I'll pick Joy up," Huey said. "She can stay at my place, or Smoke's."

"God! Not Smoke's," Lana said. "He'll wear her out chasing her around the living room."

"That a bad thing?" I said.

She looked at me.

"Anyone volunteer to pick up Paul?"

They all shook their heads.

Lana looked back at me.

"Good luck with that."

Chapter
Sixty-Six

Lana spent the afternoon and evening with me. Mostly I rested trying to will my blood count to climb, and she read a James Lee Burke mystery.

At four o'clock Vics and my morning nurse came in. Vics greeted Lana and dropped a folded copy of the Tribune on my chest and stood by as the nurse attacked my dressings again. This time there was only a yellow substance on them. Plasma?

I opened the paper.

SHOOTOUT ON THE GRADE.

There was large picture of our bullet riddled truck half buried in the snow. Smoke's and Hammersmith's .45 brass was scattered about, and the truck doors yawned open.

Lana leaned over to read the article with me. It was brief. Said an unknown assailant drove four Ryback residents (named us) off the "Devil's Elbow" and opened fire with a machine gun. Seems the *elderly* residents (sweet of them to notice), were heavily armed retired military, and drove off the attack. Blah, blah, blah.

I flipped to the continuation on A3. More blah, blah, and then...oh, oh.

"... were members of the same Ryback posse (posse?) that was responsible for the Magruder methamphetamine bust..."

I closed the paper and lowered to my lap.

"That we don't need," I said.

Lana nodded and resumed her seat. "I can feel the thunder of AP hooves headed this way."

But I liked the picture.

"Could we ask for a copy of the picture to hang in the living room?"

"We'd be fools not to," Lana said. "Maybe under a couple crossed .45 automatics?"

"Perfect."

Vics motioned for Lana to come over.

"Want to see?"

She nodded slowly. "Yes and no."

She went around to look. Stared. Covered her mouth with the fingers of her right hand.

"That's got to hurt," she whispered. "My god."

"Lucky there was a door," Vics said. "A portion of the bullet came to rest in the side of his tibia. Had to pull it free with an extractor. Cleaned out the bone chips. The bullet seems to have been designed to fragment. Between it, slivers of door steel and the plastic door panel fabric, he took a hell of hit."

He was bent over helping the nurse rewrap my leg. He explained how they were doing it for Lana's benefit. Wanted her to change it each morning for seven days.

She kept her fingers to her lips and nodded as he went though the steps.

Then he wrote out three prescriptions and dropped several rolls of tape and gauze along with a pile of four by fours into a white plastic bag and handed them to her.

The nurse left.

He looked at us thoughtfully. Made up his mind and reached into the large side pocket of his lab coat.

"MacAvity didn't tell me you were to have this," he said, "so I'm not going to give it to you."

He took out a leather wrapped stainless ten ounce flask.

I took it and put it under the sheets. "Glad you didn't," I said.

"See you in seven days, then. We'll count the knots then and work up a bill. My kid's in college now."

"What could be better?"

And he left.

I kept the flask out of sight. Later Lana and I would spike our dinner coffees. Needed something in order to fully savor that evening's chicken pot pies, red Jell-O, and two inch squares of lemon cake with sugar icing.

But I was hungry and cleaned my pie dish like a good boy. Then pushed the swing-out serving tray as far away against the wall as I could reach.

"Does it get any better than this?" I said.

"I submit it does not," Lana said. She had eaten all of two bites. Seemed plenty.

We spiked our empty coffee cups and added water. Finished those and repeated the process. Lana shook the last drop out and dropped the flask into her messenger bag.

A nurse opened the door and looked in.

"Would you like us to activate your phone?"

"There been calls?" I said.

"No. But there's an insistent reporter from Boise on the line. Says he's an important AP reporter. Said I was to tell you he was the greatest investigative reporter in recorded history."

"He is," I said. "Let me talk to him."

She vanished.

"Billy O'Connor," Lana said.

"I'm hoping."

The phone bing-binged.

First words, "Do I smell scotch on your breath?"

"You talk to Butte before me?"

"Yup."

"What happened to our printer's ink brotherhood?"

He gave a high pitched chuckle as only an Irishman can.

"That rag Confluence calls a paper did say you're in with Sawbones Vics. Had to ask somebody."

"I'm here drinking from Butte's flask with Lana, not Sherm."

"Squeeze something on her for me." Then, "Gonna give me a story?"

I thought.

"It's pretty confusing," I said.

"Bullets make it any less opaque?"

"No. But things are starting to get clearer. Joy Chu is coming in tomorrow on the 11:30. She'll be able to help."

He was silent.

Then, "Where's the meeting going to be?"

I looked at Lana.

"Know where Joy's meeting us?"

She shook her head.

"Oscar Redtail or Charlie might know," I told him.

I could almost hear his mind click.

"I see. I'll call around."

Then, "You get off any shots?"

"Nope. Too busy catching them. Butte and Smoke sounded like they had machine guns of their own."

"I saw the picture. Brass everywhere. I counted it. Nineteen visible. I asked Butte and he said Smoke had his Kimber Ultra. That's seven plus one. And he was carrying his Para Tac-Four, thirteen plus one. That's some heavy firepower there."

"You should consider going into investigative reporting," I said.

"Which reminds me. You guys wing the shooter?"

"Doubt it."

Charlie thought about that.
"Reason I ask--you know where Rice, Washington, is?"
"Never heard of it."
"Gifford?"
"Nope?"
"Huckleberry Mountain Range"
"Negative."
"You ever hear of the Columbia River, Paul?"
"Seems to ring a bell. Why?"
"You heard of Highway 25?"
"Little back road into Canada?" I said.
"Yup."
"This going to be on the mid-term, Billy?"
I could hear labored breathing over the phone.
"As the greatest investigative journalist in the history of the world, after I learned of your shoot-out I did some investigating. There was a car pulled into a turnout along the banks of Roosevelt Lake, aka Columbia River, between Rice and Gifford this morning. Cop pulled over to check it out. There was a dead guy in it sitting in a pool of clotted blood," he said.
"That must be four hours north of here, Billy."
"I know. I did some phoning. Talked to the sheriff. Dropped some credentials and names on him."
I waited.
"The guy was winged in the side. Unfortunately he was carrying around his liver on that side and it got nicked. Leaked like a dripping faucet. He packed a T-shirt over the wound. He rolled up his shirt and tied it around to hold it tight. Still leaked. He apparently didn't want to go to a hospital."
"He ID'd yet?"
"Yup. Stolen car with Idaho plates. Phony Washington driver's license. Phony BC license. Ran his prints. You ever hear of a guy called Alex Byrd?"

I hung my head and shook it. Lana was staring at me.

"That's our shooter, Billy."

He started laughing his head off.

"I knew it!" He laughed. "You owe me, ol' buddy. I want an exclusive."

"You are the best, Billy. No doubt," I said.

"So that's a yes?"

He laughed some more.

"I'll make some calls," he said. "See you tomorrow."

"Tomorrow?"

But he'd hung up.

Lana was reading my prescriptions. "Anti-inflammatory. Antibiotic. Hydrocodon."

She looked up. "Billy want an exclusive?"

"I hope so."

"And he's driving up from Boise as we speak?"

"After phoning Charlie and Oscar," I said.

I took the phone back up and called the front desk.

"Could you turn it back off now?"

"Yes. Anything else?"

"We've dined."

"I'll come and get your chinaware, then."

Chapter
Sixty-Seven

The next morning, well before daylight, I was served a breakfast of a sausage and egg muffin, milk and OJ.

My dressings were changed, and my leg was cushioned in ice gel packs to reduce swelling. I was also given another hydrocodon. An aid brought in a wheel chair, and my belongings were put in a white plastic bag and placed on its seat. My shoes were placed on top of the bag. My left shoe was black with blood.

The male aid, who looked like a married high school dropout, studied the shoes.

"They must have cut your pants off and thrown them away," he said.

I nodded. "You know when I'm being picked up?"

"They said they'd be here now. They ain't. Must be the wind. Got the roads drifting again."

He went out.

I waited.

Ten minutes later the door opened and Lana, Smoke and a muscular orderly filed into the room. The orderly was Camas. His scrubs were stretched tight over rolling muscles on his back and arms.

Lana came over and gave me a sustained morning kiss.

Then Smoke came over puckered up with outstretched arms.

"Call the police," I told the orderly.

He ignored me and went about pulling back my blankets and removing the gel packs and backed the wheelchair to the side of my bed. He pulled a leg extension up and clicked it into place.

Lana helped me into my sweats she'd brought from home. She had cut off the left pant leg so I could get them on.

The orderly stepped behind the wheelchair and motioned for Smoke and Lana to come around in front.

To Lana he said, "Put one hand under his knee and the other under his foot." And to Smoke, "And you, sir, get an arm under his back and a hand under his thigh. I'll take him by the shoulders and we'll lift him in slowly.

And they did.

Not bad.

Smoke and Lana followed behind as I was wheeled down the hall, into an elevator, across the lobby and out into the blowing snow. A drift was forming on the roofed-over apron at the hospital's front.

Smoke went and opened all the doors of a new silver/gray Tundra and moved the seats forward.

The orderly rolled me to the driver's side, turned the wheelchair around, and lifted me out by my armpits. Lana held the chair steady, and Smoke gently lifted my leg. When I was clear, Lana pulled the wheelchair free and the orderly backed into the crew cab lifting my full weight in with him. A normal person would have ruptured every disk he had.

Slick. Just a twinge.

And there I sat, leg outstretched and comfy, on the road for home.

"I assume this pickup is ours?" I finally said.

"The insurance agent told us to go get one," Lana said. "That's what Smoke was doing yesterday while we hung-out."

"Good time of the year to get shot, pardner," he said. "Last year's model. Clearance time."

I considered that.

"So, now a hospital bill and truck payments."

"And your life," Smoke said.

"Don't get sulky," Lana said. "Sherm's working with the hospital on Medicare, our supplemental and our prescription drug coverage. Said not to sweat it. The truck is free and clear."

"Whew."

MacAvity was coming out of our back door and up to the barn as we pulled in. He was carrying a kitchen chair. The snow was blowing sideways off the barn roof, the house and the orchard limbs. It was near whiteout.

They helped me crab from the back seat and lifted me into the chair. Smoke took one side, Butte the other, and with Lana holding my leg, they lifted me and awkwardly maneuvered us through the gate and back door and onto the recliner in the living room. It already had a pillow and wool blanket waiting.

Smoke and Butte were panting from the effort.

"How much do you weigh?" Smoke gasped.

"One seventy."

"Shit. We each carried eighty-five pounds? Didn't your parents teach you how to crawl?"

He and Butte sagged onto the couch.

Lana went and put on coffee. Came back in.

"Joy wants to meet here today," she said. "I'm going to make lunch for everyone. You think you could eat shredded pork enchiladas, Paul?"

"Did I not eat a luke warm pot pie last night?"

"There is that."

Billy O'Connor phoned a little before noon to learn where we were meeting. Said the six hour drive had taken ten. He said the roads were blowing shut and he had to detour around to Walla Walla and old highway twelve, and finally checked into the Best Western in Confluence.

Josiah and Oscar called to check what time, and Charlie called to say he'd make sure he wasn't late but don't start the meeting until he got there. He arrived on time.

By twelve thirty there were ten of us crowded into the living room. The kitchen chairs had been brought in. Lana and my study chairs were added to the circle, and our large square coffee table was loaded down with thirty steaming steaming enchiladas with the trimmings, a large stainless bowl of salad with the trimmings, another stainless bowl filled with refrieds, and Butte had set up a full bar on top of the stereo cabinet. On the floor was a cooler of beer and a bucket of ice.

Seemed everyone, including me, was parched and famished. And not even MacAvity could make enchiladas like Lana could. I doubted if anyone in Mexico could.

Lana made sure Joy, who had come in with Billy, was the understood guest of honor. She was seated in my usual chair. She'd never been in our house before and seemed to like it. Particularly our accumulated artwork. Several graphites had been done by Lana, and I pointed that out to her.

She was dressed in pale gray wool slacks, matching jacket, cream colored silk shirt open at the throat and black riding boots. Her long hair was up in a twist.

"I have good news and bad," she said. She'd made herself a bowl of salad with a dab of refrieds on the side. She talked between small bites.

"We know that the Furusato gang, indeed, are working with Spreiter and his operation. We also know that they have great contempt for him.

"I approached the Azine to see if they could do anything about the situation. They are the political arm of the Asian

American Movement. The YB or Yellow Brotherhood tries to help gang members give up the life. Gangs like the Black Juans, the Dominators, the Koshakas, the Ministers, the Algonquins, the Little Gents...there's tons of them. Some of the shooters are straight A Advanced Placement high school students. Some are working on their MBA's. It's crazy."

She finished off the last bite of her salad.

"And it was a no go. Too much money being made."

She put her empty bowl and fork on the end table. Sat back.

"So we met with the Dub Cs. The Wah Ching. Like the Mafia, only Chinese. It was a high level meeting. There were five of us and five of them. It took two days to just set up the ground rules and the security.

"These guys started as a bunch of picked-on San Francisco nerds that formed a gang in 1966 for mutual protection. Ballooned over night. Today there are three thousand members and another thousand affiliates."

That got some nods of appreciation from us.

Joy smiled.

"So, gentlemen...and Smoke, I'm not at liberty to explain what kind of deal we cut, but within the week, one way or the other, the Furusato will not be an issue."

She was done.

We finished eating and Huey and Smoke helped Lana collect the dishes from everyone and carry them into the kitchen. MacAvity took orders for after dinner drinks, and Oscar went into my bedroom to make a call on his cell phone. He was back out in a couple minutes and nodded to Longbeach.

When everyone was seated again, Charlie leaned forward on his kitchen chair, rested on his knees with his elbows and cleared his throat.

"We all know Mr. O'Connor here," he said, nodding to Billy who sat on his right. "He learned, and I've confirmed, that Alex Byrd, who was undoubtedly hired as a contractor by Spreiter, was found dead along side Highway 25 yesterday morning. He damn near made Canada, but one of Smoke or Butte's .45s winged him."

Apparently Joy was the only one that didn't know this.

"They were talking at the airport about a shooting up on the grade. He the guy?" she said.

Charlie nodded.

Then she smiled at me.

"Feeling good?

"Better all the time."

Hammersmith was sitting on the couch with Josiah and Oscar. He glanced at Huey who was at his elbow in my study chair.

"And last night Harley paid me a social call," he said.

He noticed Joy's frown.

"Harley Lappin," Eric said.

"You know Harley Lappin?" she said, astonished.

"Long story."

She rolled her eyes.

"He informed me that Spreiter remained behind after the inmates finished dinner last night. Had his face in his tray and a sharpened wire protruding from the center of his back."

I glanced at Huey. No change in expression.

Billy, who sat beside Lana and me, was not taking notes. He didn't need to. He had a near perfect photographic memory for details. His eyes shined with energy.

I felt like I was sitting at a round table in a London bunker with Churchill and his cabinet.

"OK," Joy said. "We have Spreiter out of the picture. We're having his end of the trafficking being taken care of. And we have his shooter in the morgue."

She hesitated.

"But how are you sure he's your shooter?"

"That's been confirmed," Charlie said. "The blood on the steering wheel of the stolen 4-Runner driven by the shooter matches the body. The body was identified as Alex Byrd which was confirmed by the RCMP."

"That works," she said. "So we have his shooter in the morgue and another one, William Garber, picked out of a tree."

She looked around the room.

"Am I right so far?"

She saw that she was.

"Who else?"

"Jingles Radcliff," Charlie said. "He was sniped on Huey's front porch."

Joy looked puzzled.

"I didn't hear about that."

We waited.

Then she looked directly at MacAvity, "One of you kill him?"

Butte shook his head. Grinned at her wickedly.

"Do my sniping with a twenty-eight pound Cobb. But I like the .308. A .50 is a wee bit too loud for my old ears."

Joy laughed. We all did.

"You're a dangerous man, Butte," she said. "But I still don't understand. You know anyone that would do it?"

"We don't," Charlie said. "We suspect a guy named Freddy Stripe, who's been hanging around in the area, and his two buddies Billy Long Gone and Samuel Beauvallon. But we don't know where they want to. And we don't have a clue about Trent Mazollan, Spreiter's man in Canada."

Joy nodded.

"Oscar and Josiah have been keeping me up to date on Stripe and his buddies. We're working on it. But something's not fitting here."

I had to move my leg. It was feeling hot. Sat up a bit straighter.

"What'd Micha Wirestone have to say?" I asked Josiah.

Josiah and Oscar were both holding cans of PBR and had hardly moved.

"We sweated. He said the snow is breaking limbs off trees one by one and people were returning to their homes to stay warm."

"Meaning?"

I knew he was messing with us.

"That a bunch of bad guys are getting killed and that Stripe, Billy and Sam made it home OK."

Smoke moaned. "I need a nap."

Oscar and Longbeach bumped shoulders and smiled.

Charlie stood up.

"Gotta get back." Then to Lana, "Thanks for lunch."

"Before you go, Charlie," Lana said, "you figure out yet who came into our house and left the picture?"

He took his Stetson out from under his chair and tugged it on.

"Nope. But I doubt it was Byrd."

He hesitated.

"Anyone up for a drive in this storm to take a look at his hideout with me?" he said. "As long as we're here, you know?"

Smoke, MacAvity and Billy followed him out.

Joy gave Lana a hug, kissed me on my bald head, and followed them with Josiah and Oscar.

Only Huey and Hammersmith remained. They stayed and helped Lana with the dishes. Hammersmith washed, Huey dried, and Lana put the dishes away. They were done in less than ten minutes.

They came back into the living room and helped carry chairs back to their usual places. Then they said their goodbyes and left too.

Lana flopped out on the couch. She turned awkwardly and smiled at me.

"It's so nice to have our friends drop by. The DEA, the sheriff, the press, the cops, our local assassins."

"Hmmmm. Cozy, wasn't it?"

Chapter
Sixty-Eight

The wind continued to blow for the next hour and was joined by heavy horizontal snow.

Lana brought me a glass of water and a hydrocodon, then helped me down onto my hand and knees so I could crawl into my bedroom. I didn't want to hop. We decided crawling with my left foot held off the floor would be the ticket. It was. Ollie helped by licking my face.

I was able to get in the bed single handedly. Lana helped me out of my sweats and then covered me. She buried her face against the side of my neck and kissed me, then handed me Peter Jenkin's book *Across China*, which I was close to finishing. She gave me another kiss and returned to the living room to knit by the front window and gas log stove.

That night the storm mewed and whistled. The old single paned windows rattled in their guides, and those in Lana's room, which were on the windward side, turned white. Only her single side window allowed the outside darkness to show.

The screen door was banging and she got up and latched it. By the time she got the front door shut again, snow had dusted the living room's hardwood floor.

I always enjoy lying in bed listening to a storm. Lana lit a tea candle and placed it on my night stand so I could watched its light dance on the books that cover the wall by my desk. And I enjoy the coldness of the room against my face and the warmth of the blankets piled over me when it storms. It's a good time to dream of summer mountaineering trips and plan which tent, which stove and what food to bring.

I wondered if Charlie and the others had gotten out from inspecting the hideout before the drifts trapped them. If they hadn't, I fantasized, at least they had the equipment shed to burn in the house's old wood stove. So they'd be warm. They also still had Butte's box of booze in the back of Charlie's Expedition. And they could always shoot pheasant, quail and bob whites for food. I also wondered if Joy went to stay at Huey's.

By morning drifts leaned against the side of the house and barn, the wire fence around the chicken yard had been turned solid white, and the roads were sealed off once again.

That morning we listened to NPR, and our portion of Idaho that was pushed up against the Bitterroot Mountains had made national news. Our storm was projected to develop into the worst storm to hit the Pacific Northwest since the winter of 1968-69 when temperature dropped below minus fifty.

That's another advantage of having been born in the thirties and early forties. We still had in our genetic make-up the urge to raise and shoot our own food and put it up in our root cellars, pantries, basements and kitchen shelves. Enough to last six months. Easily.

"I wonder if we'll be able to get out next week?" I said.

Lana was into another book, *Arctic Dreams* by Barry Lopez. Ollie slept on the back of the couch behind her head.

"You mean to have the stitches taken out?"
"Yeah."
"I'll take them out," she said.
I nodded. "Sounds good."
She studied me.

"How you doing?"

"Swelling's better, but the bone is the thing," I said.

"Un huh."

"Doesn't like the weight of my foot trying to bend it. I can't imagine putting weight on it."

She nodded and went back to her book.

I looked around for something to read. Pulled up from a basket under the end table a Cabela's catalog. that was as thick as a dictionary. Sipped tea. Looked at wall tents, wood stoves, and remembered winter elk camps of past hunts.

Lana got to her feet and made us each a bowl of oatmeal with brown sugar and apple sauce. She brought in the bowls, then returned to the kitchen and brought the phone and a copy of *Perish Twice* by Robert B. Parker back in and put them on my end table.

I was set.

By ten o'clock the wind had died to a light blow and thin snow was falling heavily. The temperature had risen to twenty seven degrees.

Lana went to the chicken coop to dig out the door, feed them and bring in three eggs. Then she put elk stew makings in the crock pot and returned to her book.

At noon MacAvity phoned.

"You hear the weather?" he said.

"We're in for it."

"Exactly. An old fashioned winter. You guys doing OK?"

Every year Lonni, our mayor and Grain Growers Union manager, set up a phone tree. Butte had Hammersmith and us on his list, and I had Smoke and Huey. Town folk phoned the farms. If no one answered, someone went out to check on them. The farms were the most likely to lose phone and power lines. Before phones, a hard winter was a serious matter. People died. Now cell phones made living out a lot safer.

"We're set," I said.

"How's the leg?"

"Better. Lana'll remove the stitches if we can't get out."

"Yeah. Lonnie wants folks to stay put. No ripping around on snow mobiles this time. Don't want someone lost out there tipped over or broken down."

"Figgers."

We were quiet a moment.

"You and Lana can't come have a nip with us this afternoon 'cause of your leg, huh?"

"Nope. Think anyone will make it in?"

"Doubt it. Sheila is staying here in her old room at the front. We have a chess tournament going."

That large front room looked down on the street through a wall of windows, and Sheila's grandmother had lived there most of her life.

When Grandma was in her late thirties she had a daughter by one of the passing railroad men who helped put a spur line into Ryback. Butte's grandfather helped raise her. The daughter grew up to live in her mother's room and to become Butte's nanny and his father and mother's only help. She had Sheila as the result of a brief love affair with someone in Magnet, whose identity was suspected but never proved to be the town's dentist.

Butte and Sheila grew up as brother and sister. However, when he would return on leave during his years in the Navy, their friendship took on a new depth, and remained that way for the duration of their lives.

When the present Lutheran minister, now in his mid fifties, first came to town, he made the mistake of saying something one Sunday about Butte and Sheila's atheism and unconventional arrangement. The entire congregation stood and left the church. Only Hammersmith and Ruthie remained seated. They motioned the young minister over and explained things to him. The next Sunday the congregation returned as if nothing had happened. The sermon was about the blessings of contrition.

No one had ever beaten Sheila at chess except for MacAvity, and no one had ever beaten MacAvity except Sheila.

I put my hand over the phone. Got Lana's attention.

"Butte and Sheila for supper?"

She nodded.

"Come over for supper," I said.

He thought a moment.

"I got a damn fine bottle of Krug here."

"Does it go with elk?"

"Let's find out," he said. "And I'll tell you what we found at Byrd's hideout."

"Done."

I put the phone down.

"He's bringing a bottle of Krug."

She raised her eyebrows.

"Champagne? Isn't that stuff in excess of a hundred dollars a bottle?"

"Yup."

"What's he celebrating?"

"He'll tell us," I said.

Chapter
Sixty-Nine

Hammersmith and Sheila arrived just before five o'clock. It was dark out.

They came in without knocking, which was Butte's way, and for some inexplicable reason, Ollie went crazy. Lana had to carry her into the bedroom, put her in her crate, and shut the bedroom door on the din.

Butte and Sheila were blanketed in snow. They were overdressed in matching blue Thinsulite and Goretex hooded overalls suitable for Antarctica. They were hot from the exertion and unzipped and stepped out of their gear with relief.

"Four blocks!" Butte said, breathless. "Might as well been a mile. Three foot drifts to swim through. Headwind. Christ."

Lana helped them.

"And he had me carry the champagne," Shirley said.

She took it from a Powell's Books bag and handed it to Lana.

Sheila was as thin as a cedar rail, narrow faced with mirthful green eyes and hands that looked like powerful hawk feet. Her streaked blond hair was cut very short and tousled, and she was wearing tight blue jeans and a red checked flannel shirt. And she wasn't winded like Butte. She was, as Hammersmith always said, a tough old bird who could kill you with a stare. But under her tough exterior, she was kind and absolutely, unabashedly honest.

"You look like you're milking it, Paul," she said.

She came over and kissed me on top of my head. Just like Joy had done. I wondered, idly, if Smoke had written something on my bald spot with a felt-tip when I was unconscious.

When the champagne had been opened, Lana brought in four flutes and put them on the coffee table and sat in my usual chair. Butte and Sheila were seated on the couch and Butte did the pouring with great care and handed them around.

"One of my men's sons, Terry Coplen, who works in Seattle for Paul Allen, gave this to me," Butte said.

He held the flute to the light and smiled.

"This Krug is a '95 Clos du Mesnil. There were only twelve thousand six hundred bottled."

He smelled it.

"Cheers."

I sipped. It was soft, cool, delicate and vanished thought the tissues of my mouth without being swallowed. It was magic.

Butte watched our faces. Grinning.

"So what do you think?"

"It isn't bad," Sheila said.

Lana had her free hand up to her mouth.

"It's like drinking vapor," she said. "It's fantastic."

I looked carefully at the bubbles easing off the sides of my flute.

"How much does something like this cost, Butte?"

"Glad you were gauche enough to ask," he said. "How much would you guess?"

"$250?"

"Try $750 before appreciation kicked in. Say over a thousand by now."

"My God!" Sheila whispered. "A case of this is a down payment on a mansion."

"Terry likes investing," Butte said.

I took another sip. It was even better. I wondered how much equity we had in our house.

We were quiet for a few minutes.

"You mentioned we were celebrating something?" Lana said.

"Yeah."

He took a swallow and sat the flute on the table by the half empty bottle. He cleared his throat.

"Seems Alex Byrd was a techno sort of modern day assassin. Did his business using a BlackBerry, the greatest invention for the criminal world ever invented. Messages are encrypted to D.O.D. standards, and there's practically nothing it can't do short of microwaving a cat."

"Short of that..." Sheila prompted.

"Joy, Charlie and Oscar went into the house. We had to stay out. Didn't want us to trample the evidence. So we climbed into Charlie's Expedition and passed around a fifth of Smoke's White Horse and waited.

"They didn't come out for nearly a half hour. We figured they found a hot tub or something and Joy was giving back rubs without us."

"And..." Sheila said.

Butte glanced at her.

"And finally Joy came to the door and signaled for us to come in.

"Byrd had swept the mouse shit and debris out of the living room and stretched black plastic over a broken side window and the archway to the kitchen. Behind a door off to the side was a bedroom where he tossed his trash. There were empty packets of instant Quaker Oats and Mountain House dinners with REI price stickers on them. There were also five empty MSR fuel canisters and about a hundred used Stash Tea bags. Apparently ol' Byrd was an outdoorsy sort of killer."

He paused, took another swallow of Krug. We followed his example.

"So it looks like he had been camping there from the time he, Garber and Jingles Radcliff came to pay Ryback a visit. Once here, they split up. Garber parked in the stolen camper truck and Jingles Radcliff went god-knows-where. In a sewer culvert, is my guess."

He thought about that a moment.

We waited.

"He was a smart guy. Seems every time he left the place, he took everything with him. Every time. If anyone happened to check on the place, say Huey, it would be deserted except for the puzzling garbage and the black plastic. So when we winged him, he was already packed for the trip north. Always ready to fold and flee."

He finished his wine. We all did.

"Nice wine, huh?" he said.

He poured refills. Sadly, the bottle was now empty.

"So why, exactly, are we celebrating?" Lana said.

"He's trying for suspense," Sheila said, bumping Butte gently with her pointed shoulder.

"Well," he said. "Seems he left a four gigabyte micro SD card the size of a fingernail on the front window sill. Joy and Oscar think he took it out of his BlackBerry every time he left the house and hid it on his body somewhere. That way, if he was compromised, his BlackBerry wouldn't have anything on it that would incriminate him. Figure he was in a hurry to come and shoot us and left it behind by mistake.

"But we didn't know that. I guess those little flash cards fit cameras and phones as well as Blackberries. So Joy, who has a BlackBerry 8830, pops open this tiny door on the back, takes out an identical card and pops in Byrd's."

MacAvity lifted his flute in a salute.

"And bingo! We have his address book, contacts, banking, the works." Butte laughed. "Some of his employers are going to be very unhappy."

"Joy take it back to Seattle?" I said.

"Nope," Butte said. "Billy went back to the the Best Western, and she drove to Huey's. Probably still there. Anyway, the airport is shut down. But not to worry. She said she'd use her own BlackBerry and zip the data to her people, encripted."

We were nodding like penguins.

"What's Billy going to do with his exclusive?" I said.

"Nothing until things are cleared by the DEA, FBI, and RCMP," Butte said. "Then, once again, he'll have the front page."

Lana was frowning. Butte noticed.

"What is it?" he said.

"I still want to know who was walking around in our house. Who left the picture? It creeps me out," she said.

Butte glance at his drink, then looked steadily at her.

"My guess? Freddy Stripe."

Lana thought about this.

"Why?"

"A gesture. A message."

He hesitated.

"First, I think he wanted us to know he's one of the good guys. He wanted us to know he was on top of things. Knew who was trying to kill us. Even knew where they'd been hiding out."

"But he and his two henchmen took off too." I said.

Butte nodded.

"Because he knew his work was done. William Garber is dead, Jingles Radcliff is dead. Yost is dead. And finally, the worst of the worst, Alex Byrd is dead. No point hanging around. That's what he was saying to us."

"Well shit," Sheila said. The Krug had her eyes shining. "Why didn't he come into the pub like he used to, make Smoke apologize to him, and let us throw him and his two Indian friends a damn party. Hell. I'd give him a damn table dance."

"That might be the reason," Butte said.

"Well Smoke was right about one thing," I said. "Stripe wasn't what he appeared to be."

"That's for damn sure."

MacAvity, who had spent much of his life in the Navy teaching covert operations, thought about this for several minutes.

I finished my second glass of Krug. I felt like Ollie did after finishing breakfast and wanting more. I felt like running around sniffing the corners in case another bottle was hidden somewhere.

"I think," Butte said, "there's a possibility Stripe--with his tricked-out electronic communications center of an luxury RV palace on wheels--is a private contractor."

He took the last swallow of his champagne.

"The question is, though, who is he contracting for. Who's paying him to hit bad guys?"

"Competitors making a takeover?" I said.

"Or some good guys stamping on Spreiter's action," Butte said. "But they'd have to be pretty damn clandestine. It's homicide no matter how you look at it."

He put his empty glass on the coffee table.

"And finally," he said. "I think Josiah Longbeach and Oscar Redtail have known this all along and aren't saying. Don't ask me why."

He looked at Lana.

"So that's what I'm thinking."

Lana smiled.

"So," she said. "Let's have dinner."

They got up and went into the kitchen for bowls of elk stew to bring back in.

I sat silent. I had wanted to ask about Trent Mazollan, the Kelowna land investor. Spreiter's man in Canada.

But I didn't.

Chapter
Seventy

Lana took the stitches out of my leg on day seven and set them one by one on the arm of my chair like insects. She wiped my wounds lightly with alcohol, swept the stitches into her palm, and returned everything to the bathroom and the trash.

The hearing in my left ear was improving as Vics said it would, and I was hobbling around the house like an agile ninety year old pirate with a wooden leg. And grateful for it.

Every afternoon Lana made hors d'oeuvres and every evening one or more friends happened by. Smoke and Butte were regulars, but Hammersmith and Ruthie only managed to get into town once.

It was Huey that concerned us. Joy had caught a flight out, and he had made no effort to come in. He had not phoned. And whenever any of us phoned him his cheerful voice was forced and conversations went nowhere.

Smoke drove out to visit him and came back shaking his head. Then, on the first day of the thaw, he went to visit him again and didn't return until the next morning.

He came in the back door that day in time for lunch looking a little worse for wear.

Lana was making grilled cheese sandwiches in the kitchen. I was sitting in my chair.

"You guys tie one on?" I said.

He fell heavily into the recliner.

"Yup."

From the kitchen Lana said, "Want some lunch?"

"Coffee, thanks."

Then to me, "When was the last time you've seen Huey have more than a couple drinks, pardner?"

"Long time."

"Well," he said, "it ain't because he don't know how. That's for fucking sure."

I laughed quietly.

"We got into it and didn't give it up until two this morning." He hesitated. "I think. Anyway it's that last I remember looking at my watch. Might have been later."

I nodded.

Lana came in with a tall chilled V8 and large mug of coffee Smoke accepted both gratefully. She went back in and returned with two grilled sandwiches wrapped in paper towels.

"Huey have something on his chest?" Lana said.

Smoke drank from the V8 until the glass was empty. He exhaled and sat back with his coffee, blew on it out of habit, and took a sip.

"Sorta," he said finally. "Mostly he just wanted to talk."

"About?"

"Everything. High school, Annapolis, the war, his missionary work...."

He took a swallow.

"Later he took the blame for everything that's been happening for the last two and a half years."

Lana and I worked on our sandwiches and listened.

Smoke glanced at us idly.

"You have any ideas why?" I said.

"Why he's blaming himself?" he said.

I nodded.

"Same-ol', same-ol'. He believes it."

He looked at his cup. "Guys like him can't accept that

they are powerless when it comes to damn near everything in this world. Makes for good missionaries and helicopter pilots, though."

He grinned.

"The wrath of God," he said. "You have total control over a chunk of metal that can fly and lay down death and destruction on evil. Every twitch is obeyed instantly by the controls and the craft."

He paused.

"Then, on base you get a dear-John letter from your girlfriend back home. About something you had nothing to do with. Happened while you were gone. And you can't control it. You can't change the situation. There's nothing you can do about it."

He nodded. Seeing it all.

"Unless you blame yourself. Right?"

We listened.

"So you say, 'It's all my fault. I should never have done and said such-and-so,' and you spend the rest of your fucking tour deciding how you can change yourself and make it all OK and get her to love you again in that special way of hers. So you can take back control."

Smoke drank from his mug and grinned.

"Get home. Go over and her parents say she's married. Expecting a kid."

"You think that's what he's doing?" Lana said.

"There are four things a guy can do when he finds out his girlfriend is now another guy's wife. And as a colonel, I saw it a lot. You can lose it and try to beat the shit out of somebody. You can beat up on yourself with alcohol, drugs or suicide. You can play the martyr card. Or you can do the right thing and just say fuck it, forget it, laugh, and get on with it."

Lana was nodding.

"So what's Huey doing?" I said.

"Well, he's not the pissed off kind. And he's not the martyr. And he's too sensitive to say fuck it and laugh."

Smoke looked at us. "You two know that. So I'd say he's either about to get on with things, or..."

He put his mug down on the arm of the chair.

"...or he's going to ask himself what he has left."

Lana looked grim.

I understood what he was saying.

"So," Smoke said. "We're going to let him know there's a lot. There's *us*. Easy as that."

Lana looked up. She'd gone pale.

"You think he has a time table?" she said quietly.

He shook his head. Picked his mug back up.

"No. Not yet. Depends on if we can get control of this situation we have going here in Ryback. If we can do that and keep him busy in the meantime and get him to take some credit when all the bad guys are taken care of, it will all fade into memory."

"He'll eventually have to learn to deal with it," Lana said.

Smoke nodded.

"Yup. Bring the dragon out of the dark corner and slay it."

He leaned forward.

"Unless there is divine intervention, of course. But right now I'm going home."

He got to his feet.

Lana did as well.

"Hang on a second," she said.

She darted into the kitchen and brought out a third grilled cheese wrapped in paper towel.

"Eat this on your way home," she said.

He grinned.

"I'll try."

He started to leave, stopped, turned back to face us.

"I forgot to tell you. Charlie learned from the RCMP that one by one folks aren't showing up for work at Trent Mazollan's corporate building. Mazollan's not saying a word. His top people are vanishing and he acts like nothing is wrong. And the RCMP says there's not a trace of them. They just up and vanish, leaving everything behind. Five of them."

He winked, shot us both with an index finger, and left.

Lana and I looked at each other.

"They're being taken out?" I said.

Lana stared.

"One by one!" she said.

The thaw became a chinook wind from the southwest. It raged for two days bringing warm air from the Oregon coast. Winds exceeding sixty-five miles an hour left western Oregon a disaster area. And the Bench began to melt in earnest. And then flood. Ryback Valley became a slow moving lake and the town became beach front property.

Great flights of geese heading north to Canada circled to take advantage of this new watery landscape and landed by the hundreds to form large rafts. They chattered back and forth like giddy children at a picnic, and the din filled the days.

Soon the ground and winter wheat began to show in patches, then swaths, and the waters receded slowly. During the third week the geese all left in a single morning and clouded the sky in trumpeting swirls as they took bearings and continued on north. It was spectacular.

It was also that week, Saturday evening, that Lana and I ventured to the Pub for the first time since the shooting.

Chapter
Seventy-One

I hobbled into the pub on Lana's heels. The place was packed. Jake was helping Sheila in the kitchen, and MacAvity, dressed fit to kill in his Wyatt Erp finest, was mixing drinks as fast as he could.

People were standing two deep at the bar, and those lucky enough to have stools were sitting with their backs to the bar so they could carry on conversations.

As fast as Butte placed down drinks, they were taken and passed back to whoever had requested them. Money was dropped on the bar and remained there.

Smoke, Ruthie and Hammersmith spotted us and waved us over to their booth. Lana slid in beside Ruthie and Eric. Smoke moved over for me.

"Huey not with you?" he said.

I shook my head.

Lana got back up.

"I'm going to give him a call," she said. She threaded her way back through the crowd and headed to the phone near the front door.

"Want to go for another ride, pardner?" Smoke said.

I studied him a moment. Shook my head. "Are you out of your mind?"

Hammersmith answered.

"They've been running the data on Byrd's Blackberry card," he said. "There's enough info coming in to obtain search warrants on a number of people stretched from Vancouver, Canada, to Los Angeles."

He sipped his whiskey and soda.

"Where'd you learn all this? Oscar?" I said.

He nodded.

"But there is one number that doesn't fit the pattern, and no one is much interested in it anyway because it's a SEWU agriculture extension lab. It's in that dinky town of Wheatland between Yakima and Othello."

I looked at Smoke.

"So you want to drive to Wheatland?"

He nodded.

I shook my head again.

"This time why don't we just drive directly to some asylum and check ourselves in?"

"So I called SEWU," Eric continued. "Seems it's called Southeast Washington University Columbia Plateau Organic Agricultural Labs. It's run by Dr. Anthony Lark Brockington, Ph.D.."

"Their building large enough to fit the title?" I said.

"And the professor's trying to develop a strain of hops that requires less, if any, spraying."

Smoke winked.

"We're thinking ol' Nelson Yost might have been involved with the good doctor," he said.

Lana slid back in, all grins.

We looked at her.

"What?" Ruthie said.

Leaps, whom Smoke and I drove for each harvest, put two drinks down in front of Lana and me and went back to his conversation.

Lana sipped from hers and looked over the rim mischievously.

"Get this," she said finally. "Our sweet Huey didn't answer his phone."

She looked at Smoke who was frowning.

"But you can put your worries to rest, Smoke," she said. "Joy Chu answered the phone. She came back and has been there for two days."

That got a rise out of us.

Lana grinned wickedly.

"Seems after the night you and Huey got plastered, he gave her a slurred phone call about three in the morning. After that call something clicked between them, and she decided to get ahead in her case loads at the FBI and take a nine day vacation."

She paused.

"With Huey. She has an aunt in Lahaina who owns a cottage they can use."

We raised our glasses and laughed.

"How old is she?" Ruthie said.

Lana shook her head.

"I don't have a clue. In her early fifties?"

That sounded about right. We nodded.

"Well good for him," Ruthie said. "They going to come in?"

"They're on their way here right now," Lana said. "Then they want me to drive them to the airport tomorrow morning. They're already packed."

Half an hour passed before Joy led Huey into the bar and over to our booth. Joy was dressed in tight blue jeans, black heel boots and a black, waist length, soft leather jacket. She was carrying a matching leather messenger bag over her shoulder. She waved when she saw us.

I got up and gave Joy my seat, and Huey and I went into the back room and brought back two folding chairs.

I nudged him off balance on the way.

"Congratulations," I said.

He glanced sideways at me and said nothing.

Joy, Lana and Ruthie weren't in the booth when we got back. I craned my neck and looked over the crowd.

They were standing with their drinks by the front window talking and laughing like school girls.

We propped the unopened chairs against the wall and sat in the booth with Smoke and Hammersmith.

"So," Smoke said.

"So," Huey said, looking at Hammersmith, "Joy has talked with Oscar Redtail who said he's been talking with you. That right?"

"Yup."

"About the lab at Wheatland?"

"She think there's anything to it?"

Huey shook his head.

"She doubts it."

We were silent. He was watching us.

"You three up to something?" he said.

"Among other things, the lab's studying the possibility of developing organically grown hops there, Huey," Eric said.

"And...?"

"The lab's director is particularly keen on that one project over the others."

He watched Smoke light a cigarillo.

"And we're wondering if he might be buddies with the late Nelson Yost," Smoke said.

Huey's eyebrows went up.

"Good idea," he said.

He looked at Smoke and me.

"You going to check it out?"

Smoke nodded.

"We're thinking about driving over there and hearing what he has to say."

Huey nodded.

"Mind if I tell Joy what you're doing?"

"Sure. Go ahead. Can't keep secrets from a sweetheart," Smoke said.

Huey said nothing.

We weren't fooled.

"So Lahaina is on Maui, right?" I said.

"Last I heard," Huey said. "It was a major whaling town at one time."

"Huey and I went down there on R&R one time," Smoke told us. "Had the biggest fucking banyan tree I'd ever seen in the middle of town. Limbs a yard in diameter."

"Joy use to go there with her parents when she was a girl," Huey said. "Stayed with her aunt and uncle who made their fortune wholesaling pineapple."

"Ah, spring love in the islands," Smoke whispered.

Hammersmith pointed his highball glass at him.

"Give it a rest, Smoke."

Ruthie, Lana and Joy eventually returned to our table. Huey and I got up to make room and took our seats in the folding chairs.

Joy handed Huey her messenger bag to hold while she opened it and pulled out a folded newspaper. She took the bag back, wedged it between herself and Lana, and opened the paper, the Los Angeles Times. She held it up for us to read the headlines of a story on the bottom quarter of the front page.

Eighteen Killed in Gang War.

She brushed her hair back with her left hand, lowered the paper and looked around at us. Her face was expressionless.

"It happened under Highway 110 between Carson and Torrance," she said evenly. "About two in the morning two nights ago."

She folded the paper back up and handed it to Huey.

"We suspect the Furusato Gang has been making alliances with the Asian Boyz and the Vietnamese Boyz against the Wah Chings, who have been making inroads on their gang turf over a period of years."

We listened.

Joy smiled.

"But it seems that the Wah Ching Gang has been getting fed high tech intelligence and surveillance equipment from someone. It has given them a decided edge.

"They were able to isolate the Furusatos from their allies and lure their bosses and key soldiers into an ambush under the highway. Every last one of them was gunned down. There were no wounded."

Smoke looked at her. "I wonder how on earth they obtained that intelligence?" he mused.

"Amazing, isn't it?" Joy said.

He nodded.

I reached for the paper.

"Mind if I take this over to Butte?" I said.

"Ask for a round," Hammersmith said. "And ask Butte if Jake can come out from the kitchen and tend bar so he can come over and join us."

Chapter
Seventy-Two

The light on our answering machine was flashing when we got in at eleven. Lana hit the play button. It was Billy. Wanted us to call him as soon as we could.

She flipped open our address book, dialed, and handed the phone to me.

"You do it. I'm getting ready for bed."

Billy answered on the second ring.

"Thought you were an invalid," he said.

"Recovering invalid. What's up?"

I could hear Billy grunt as he took a seat. I pulled over a kitchen chair, sat, and rested my tired leg on another.

"You know about the gang shootings?" he said.

"Yup."

"You know about the killings in Kelowna?"

"Yup. Learned about them recently, and the gang wars just tonight. I was going to call you," I said.

Billy laughed.

"I knew about those things before the victims."

"Well, there's that."

"What I want to ask you is if there is anything going on that my Monday headline might jeopardize."

"What's the headline?" I said.

"How does *Drug Cartel Imploding* sound?"

"Imploding?"

Billy thought.

"*Drug Cartel Dying Off Mysteriously?*"

I had been Billy's editor at the Trib.

"I think you need to work on the headline," I said. "You including Kelowna?"

"And what happened in Ryback, Terminal Island, FCI Englewood, and Los Angeles," he said.

He waited for me to say something.

"You going to run this by our FBI buddies Gibson and Pfeffer?" I finally said.

"Why not Joy Chu?"

"She's here in town, Billy. And she's not going to be available for ten days."

"What'd you guys do--imprison her?" he said.

"She and Huey are taking a vacation to Hawaii. Leaving on tomorrow's morning flight."

"Yikes!" he said. "Who woulda thunk?"

Then, "Where's she staying? I'll give her a call tonight."

"Hard to tell," I said.

He thought a moment.

Then, "Oh. I get it."

"Yup."

"OK. I'll run it by Gibson. He still senior to Pfeffer?"

"But not nearly as smart," I said.

"So, any conflicts with you and your gang of geriatric thugs?"

I adjusted my leg. It was tired and it felt like it was swelling up again.

"What aren't you going to print?" I said.

"I'm not going to print it was Hammersmith who orchestrated Speiter's getting taken out. I'm not going to print that Joy Chu orchestrated the demise of the Furusato Gang. I *am* going to print that the bad guys tried, once again, to take revenge on Ryback and once again failed. And I'm going to print that it's a mystery why they didn't succeed. And it's a mystery who's killing off the Kelowna boys."

"Wait a minute," I said. "They finding them?"
"You didn't know?"
"We're simple farm folk here, Billy. We don't get out much."
He laughed.
"They're showing up here and there. Shot and left in their cars, on the ground, wherever the hit took place."
He hesitated.
"But get this. One was found up in a tree--his head jammed in the fork of two limbs. And he had rocks tied to his feet. Sound familiar?"
"Sounds like the work of pesky redskins," I said.
"Sure does."
"You going to mention the similarities?"
Billy thought a moment.
"No, I'm not. Trent Mazollan is still out there. I don't want to trip up whoever is doing clandestine work for us."
"Any ideas?" I said.
"Yup. I figure it's Freddy Stripe and his two Shuswap cousins," he said.
I moved my leg off the chair and put my foot down flat on the floor. Blood began to throb against my shin bone.
"You could be right. But I'm hurting here Billy," I said. "I'm going to bed with an ice pack."
Then, "You know about the phone traces from Alex Byrd's Blackberry?"
"Yup. They're pulling people in by the handfuls."
I hesitated.
"There's one that Smoke wants to take a look at. It's an SEWU lab in Wheatland. We're driving there tomorrow morning."
I could hear Billy get to his feet.
"Tell me if you learn anything, OK? I'll call Dewayne Gibson now."

There was a pause.
"Give Lana my best."
He hung up.

Smoke and I took highway 95 north over the west end of Cup Hand. He was driving and the black GMC was full of gas and throbbing along almost as if it were delighted to be on the road going somewhere at last.

At the summit, we were able to see the Bench stretch to the western horizon. The sun was low at our backs and highlighted the dune like swells and eyebrows of the rich farmland. The remnants of melting cornices were cupped by the thousands against the north sides of the hills, and the steppe looked like it had rib bones aligned over its entire expanse.

Smoke slowed.

"Hard to get used to this place, isn't it?" he said.

I nodded.

We began to drop down the far side. Smoke renewed our speed.

"I mean," he continued, "we have seasons. It's empty land. There are no fences. The power lines are buried, so there's no wires in the air. We have moose, elk, deer, wolves and cougar wandering around."

I looked at him.

"What's this all about, Smoke?"

He glanced sideways at me. He didn't smile.

We were quiet for several minutes.

I waited.

He cleared his throat and held the speed even.

"After you and Lana and Hammersmiths left the pub last night there were just Butte, Sheila and me there with Joy and Huey," he said. "We went up stairs for a night cap and MacAvity started a fire in the fireplace."

"Good place to build a fire."

"So Sheila is living there with Butte, and Huey and Joy were like lovebirds on the couch, and I started feeling like I ought to start getting my shit back together now."

"Been nearly eight years."

"Yup."

"Don't think she meant you to be a hermit."

"Nope."

He glanced at me again.

"So Joy and Huey were talking. They were saying that Joy will be fifty-five in eight months. Said she's been in the business for thirty-four years. Thirty-five years is the ticket out, and Feebs can retire then with full bennies if they want."

The first vehicle of the day, a cattle truck, came past us from the west and threw sandy road water over our windshield. Smoke turned on the wipers without comment. A first.

"She going to?"

He nodded.

"Yeah. And Huey was sitting there smiling to himself, sipping his whiskey a molecule at a time, and saying nothing."

He turned the wipers back off. We entered Magnet and slowed. The streets were deserted. A Sunday morning. We turned directly west on a narrower road that would soon link with Highway 26 and carry us to Othello.

"They have plans?" I said.

Smoke settled in at sixty and wound through the rolling hills as smoothly as if he were flying between clouds.

"You're not going to like it," he said.

He lit up a cigarillo off the lighter in the dash and opened his wing window.

"They're talking about closing the house and moving back to Vietnam to rebuild the mission."

"Shit," I mumbled.

"Joy speaks Mandarin, Vietnamese, Cantonese, Spanish and English," he said. "A regular UCLA language scholar."

I said nothing.

He looked at me and grinned.

"I know. They're setting it up with people in Hawaii, I guess. Seems between the two of them they have resources mere mortals like you and I can only imagine."

I let out my breath.

"Well," I said, "I guess we should be happy for them."

"If we must."

"Wish they'd stay here with us, though."

We slowed and followed a large tread John Deere tractor for a minute or so, then Smoke pulled around.

"But they can't just sit out their days in a brick farm house," I said.

"That's a fact."

We were silent.

Ten miles slid buy. We passed a group of grain elevators where the town of Grouse Creek had once been.

The sun was up enough now to warm the inside of the cab as it streamed in the back window.

"We've been together our whole lives," I said.

Smoke nodded.

"Except for when we weren't," he said.

"Exactly."

"So should we have a good cry," Smoke said, blowing smoke out the wing window.

"Might as well," I said. "You start. I'll hum taps."

Chapter
Seventy-Three

It was just past noon when we finally arrived in Wheatland. The sun was as high as it was going to get in our northern latitude in early March, but it was warm and the streets were dry and without a trace of plowed snow melting along the sides of the streets.

Wheatland sat on Wahluke Slope on the south side of the Saddle Mountains where the Columbia River cut through and swept north and then south in a pair of dramatic oxbows.

We were hungry. Smoke drove slowly down the main street looking for a burger joint. There were none. The town was the same size as Ryback. And like Ryback it was made of brick and was boarded up. There was one corner store that seemed to function as a grocery, post office, liquor store, hardware and video store, and on the east end of town there were grain elevators and a brightly painted white scales shack. There was also a storefront cafe with a neon beer sign glowing dimly through windows obscured by dozens of potted plants.

A new white Ford 250 crew cab with mud caked halfway up its sides was parked in front of the bar, and beside it was a matching Ford 350 twelve seater Econoline van. Smoke pulled in beside them and killed the engine.

He sat motionless and stared at the front of the building.

"We could eat our shoes," I suggested.

He rolled down his window, took out a cigarillo and lit it. He blew the smoke out into the noon light, leaned back his head and shut his eyes.

"We could die eating in that dive," he said.

He opened his eyes and looked sideways at me.

"Get the map out and see where we can get some food," he said.

I pulled the atlas out from under the seat and opened it to Washington State. I studied it.

"We have the Yakima Firing Center across the river," I said. "That's closed to non-suicidal types. There's the Hanford Reservation south of us if you want to glow in the dark and get shot as a terrorist...."

I shook my head.

"Or we could turn around and drive thirty miles back to Royal City. That's all there is."

He moaned, opened his door and got out. He shut the door and looked through the window at me.

"You had your shots?" he said.

I shut the atlas and slid it back.

"They don't make shots for what's about to happen to us," I said. "Our best bet is to purify ourselves with alcohol as we eat."

He shook his head, flipped his freshly lit cigarillo out into the street and went to the bar's front door. He pushed it open and went in wearing the attitude of a cocked gun.

I got out and went after him, nearly running him down just inside the door. He stood staring.

The three tables in the center of the cafe were filled with college students dressed like farm hands. They were eating thick burgers and heaps of fries with silent determination. They only paused long enough to give us quick glances. There were tall glass pitchers of beer scattered among them.

The counter was empty. We went over to two stools in the narrow slot between the front window and where the bar wrapped around. Smoke edged his way onto the one closest to the wall, and I sat down beside him.

A slender woman in her early thirties with thick black hair pulled back into a pony tail was wiping down the grill with a ball of gauze. She turned, took a frosted pitcher from a tall freezer on her left and held it up to us. Smoke nodded. She put it under the only tap in evidence, a Red Hook tap, and watched it fill.

Red Hook?

When it had topped off, she pulled out two frosted pint glasses from the same freezer, brought them and the beer over and sat them down in front of us.

She smiled brightly. Her teeth were white and slightly crooked. The way teeth should be.

"Lunch?"

"Absolutely," Smoke said.

I nodded.

"We're serving burgers and fries today," she said. "Tomorrow is fried chicken and potato salad if you're still in town then."

Smoke looked at me mischievously, eyebrows lifted. Then he turned back to her.

"What's for supper tonight?"

"I'm roasting a turkey. We'll have it with stuffing, gravy, sweet potato, raspberries and rolls," she said. "Six o'clock."

I looked at the students. At the far table a man in their midst was watching us. He was in his fifties, bald, bearded and fat. He looked like a short brew master who had spent his life drinking the profits.

"Who are these people?" I asked her.

"They're from the labs," she said.

She turned away. "I'll get your lunches started and come right back."

Smoke and I looked at each other.

"I'm in love," he said.

"Right," I said. "She's got to be thirty five years younger than you."

"Perfect."

"I'll say one thing, though," I said. "We found us a gem in the middle of nothing."

He nodded. Poured our beers.

Thirty four degrees. Exactly right. I felt joyful.

Smoke drank deeply and wiped his mouth on the back of his left hand.

"Should call this place, *Take It Or Leave It*. One kind of beer, her kind, and she decides on the..."

She came back.

"...on what's being cooked," she said, and laughed.

"How's that working out for you?" Smoke said.

"Fresh food," she said. "If I give a lot of options, a lot of food sits around waiting for someone to come in and order it. There's no one to come in here except the lab people, a handful of widowers and people that are lost, like you guys are."

"And then I was found," Smoke said. "Breakfast too?"

"That's different. There's a short menu. Oatmeal, flapjacks, eggs, bacon, ham, sausage, granola, juice, mixed fruit bowl, muffins, toast. Order what you want. Every day's the same."

She held her hand out to Smoke.

"I'm Nadine," she said.

"I'm Smitten," Smoke said, shaking her hand lightly.

"He's Smoke," I said. "And I'm Paul."

She had a good handshake.

"Smoke, huh?"

"We call him that because you can see him, but there's really nothing there of substance," I said.

She studied him a moment. Then nodded.

"Yes. I can see that."

That busted Smoke up.

She grinned and went back to finish cooking our lunches.

"Practical, isn't she?" he said.

Students were beginning to push back from their empty plates. They remained seated, waiting for the others to finish. They began to talk quietly among themselves and sneak glances at us from time to time. There were as many girls as guys, and they looked scruffy, fit, and content. The fat man was obviously their boss.

"You think that guy is our Doctor, Professor, Lord Anthony Brockington?" I said.

"Most assuredly," Smoke said. "You wanna be the columnist from the Confluence Tribune seeking an interview with him?"

"I *am* the columnist from the Confluence Tribune seeking an interview with him," I said.

"Oh."

I looked the guy over. He was now intent on not noticing us. Looked like he was doing an abstract in catsup on his plate with a fry.

"I'll ask him when he walks by if we can have a tour of the labs," I said.

"Glad you have a plan," Smoke said.

We were just digging into our burgers when the crew got up and started filing out past us. The brew master came up the rear. He nodded at us without smiling as he came abreast.

"Doctor Brockington?" I said.

He stopped dead in his tracks.

"You know my name?"

I got up from my stool and held out my hand.

"Paul O'Shea. I write a column for the Confluence Tribune."

He smiled and shook my hand.

"I've read your column for years," he said. "You use to do a lot of writing for the Trib. You retired?"

I nodded.

"So you have emeritus status?"

"Something like that."

Smoke stood up. Shook hands.

"I'm with him," he said. "Name's Smoke."

"He's retired as well," I explained. "Annapolis. Ph.D. in Physics. Decorated fighter pilot."

"Ah shucks," Smoke said.

"Can we have a tour of the labs this afternoon, Doctor?" I said.

He nodded.

"Call me Tony. Come out after you finish lunch. Know where we're located?"

We shook our heads.

"Got something to write with?"

Always the reporter, I took my Parker ball point and small tablet from my shirt pocket.

He cleared his throat.

"Keep going through town east for one mile, turn left two miles. We're there."

He laughed.

What a schmuck.

"Could you explain that again?" Smoke said. "I got confused."

The professor went out chortling to himself.

Smoke and I remained standing, looking at each other.

"You bring your pea shooter?" he said.

I nodded.

"You bring your Kimber?"

He nodded.

We resumed our seats.

"Let's eat before we drive out there and kill his pompous ass," Smoke said.

"OK. But I hate waiting," I said.

Chapter
Seventy-Four

Nadine came out from behind the counter and over and sat with us at the corner with a glass of white wine.

Smoke chewed thoughtfully and took a swallow of Red Hook.

"We've been invited to the labs," he said. "You ever been out there?"

"Sure. Everyone has," she said. "They have an open house and summer solstice party there every year. It's OK."

"How long does Doctor Tony stay sober?"

"Not long," she said grimly.

He smiled.

"They have dorms or something for the students?"

"Yeah. They have four custom made double wides with six dorm rooms in each of them. Fleetwood made them."

"Brockington stay there too?" I said.

She shook her head. Sipped her wine.

"He lives here full time. Well, not really *here*. Down on the river. Has a condo in a beach resort there called Desert Sun. Beach, marina, air strip, golf course, lake with a fountain in the center, club house."

"Expensive?" I said.

"Very expensive and very exclusive."

Her wine was almost empty.

"Buy you another?" Smoke said.

"Why not?"

She got up and came back with a half full bottle of Columbia Crest Chardonay, refilled her glass and resumed her seat. She left the bottle on the counter within reach.

Smoke and I were finished with our burgers and were concentrating our efforts on the beer.

After awhile I said, "What's Brockington like?"

"Rich." She paused." And creepy. Has his own Cessna. Stayed after dinner one night after everyone else had left and sat right where you guys are sitting and kept drinking beer and leering at me. Finally told me I should join the Mile High Club. You know, sex at five thousand, two-hundred and eighty feet."

"What'd you say?"

"Told him I already fucked a rock climber in Boulder, Colorado, a mile high city, and *he* was my age and good looking."

We laughed and toasted her.

She wasn't laughing.

"What?" Smoke said.

"He got pissed," she said. "Actually turned purple. Said he knew people who would shut my place down if I didn't shut my fucking mouth. And he walked out without paying his bill."

She took a swallow from her glass. A large one.

"That was last fall. About seven months ago. Still hasn't paid that bill or any others."

Smoke and I stared at her.

Then Smoke. "You mean you keep serving him knowing he won't pay?"

"He just comes for lunch with his students. They pay. He doesn't."

"The students know this?"

She nodded.

We thought about this.

Smoke looked at me. We made eye contact and I nodded.

"You're afraid of him," Smoke said softly.

Her eyes were shiny.

"He came in once with a little guy that had a narrow face and close set eyes. The guy kept looking at my tits and grinning. I was so frightened I nearly passed out. They didn't order anything--just stood in the doorway. Then they left."

She had just described Alex Byrd.

"We knew the guy he brought here," I said. "He's named Alex Byrd."

"You knew *him*?" she said. Her voice squeaked.

"As in *knew*," Smoke said. "He's no longer with us."

She stared at him, and then me.

"As in 'he's dead?'"

Smoke and I both nodded.

"He was leaking," Smoke said. "He had a bullet hole in his liver. Took him a few hours."

She got to her feet.

"Who are you guys?"

She sounded like she was choking.

She suddenly looked terrified of us.

Smoke lifted both his hands slowly so that his palms faced her.

"Easy does it," he said. "We're the good guys. He was trying to kill us and got unlucky. We're just two retired guys from Ryback, Idaho, he didn't like. That's all."

She wasn't the least bit soothed by what Smoke had said.

"So why are you here talking to Brockington?"

    He decided to whisper.

"Because the good professor's phone number was in Byrd's Blackberry," he said. "And we came here to see how come. And you just convinced us that there is a damn good chance that Brockington is dirty."

"You police?"

Now she was whispering. But calmer. I looked over my shoulder nervously to see if there was someone behind me they didn't want eavesdropping. No faces were peering out from the window plants.

"No," he said. "But the police, the FBI and the DEA are interested in all of this. A lot of people are, Nadine."

She seemed to recover a little.

"We're like their point men," he said. He shot her one of his killer smiles.

She eased herself back onto the stool but was still tense. Ready to jump.

Smoke looked at the near empty pitcher, then at his watch.

"I think we'll go out there now. What say, Paul?"

I got carefully to my feet so that Nadine wouldn't bolt.

Smoke gave her another best smile. I worried for her health.

"We'll come back afterwards and fill you in. That OK, Nadine?" he said.

She nodded, still wide-eyed.

We went out and I shut the door softly behind us.

Chapter
Seventy-Five

We drove east from Wheatland and a mile out of town turned left on a paved, single lane road. Yakima Ridge lay ahead of us, and two miles distant across flat sage land we could see the extension labs reflecting the afternoon sun off their fiberglass roofs.

The road ended at a cattle guard that spanned the entrance through a six foot high cyclone fence enclosing the compound. There was a coil of razor wire along its top.

We parked in a gravel lot in front of a flat topped cinder block building with Southeast Washington University Columbia Plateau Organic Agriculture Labs printed in rounded gold letters bolted to its front. There was barely room enough.

We got out.

There was a line of eight greenhouses along the right side of the enclosure. Each one was perhaps thirty feet wide and fifty feet long and large fans hummed in their walls to help stabilize the interior temperatures and humidity. High tech. The best money can buy.

Behind the SEWUCPOAL building were the four doublewide dormitories, and between them and the greenhouses were two, long narrow lab buildings that looked surplused from the second world war. There was also what appeared to be a combination cafeteria and recreation building directly this side of them. Overhead loomed a water tower with the SEWU bobcat logo painted on it. And at the back of the compound was a low, square block building with a large yellow sign. The sign had a black triangle with a skull and crossbones in its center, and below it the word Hazard written in red.

Smoke pointed to it as we headed for the office doors.

"I want to see inside that baby," he whispered.

"Ditto."

The interior of the main building was of standard issue university research decor. There were gray metal military surplus chairs and desks, filing cabinets, glass display cases filled with rip rap and dried plants from the labs, and there was a sulfurous smell of laboratories, bunson burners, test tubes, overheated electrical equipment and poorly functioning air conditioners.

A young brunette girl dressed in a blue denim work shirt looked sideways from her MacIntosh computer and smiled at us.

"Dr. Brockington available?" I said.

"Sure," she said.

This was definitely not an attorney's office.

She took up a Motorola radio, keyed it and said, "Someone here to see you Tony."

Smoke looked at me.

"Formal around here."

"Absolutely rigid," I said.

"He'll be here in a little bit," she said.

She turned back to her work.

Smoke and I went and stood looking out the front windows. There was nothing to see other than white laboratory vehicles, Smoke's sleek GMC, the gravel parking lot, the cyclone fence, and the flat sage land. We could see Wheatland standing alone off in the expanse like an abandoned junk yard.

Brockington came through a side door and down a tiled hallway towards us.

He held out his hand and we shook it.

"Glad you could make it," he said.

Then, "So Paul. What's your idea about an article on our humble enterprise?"

He had remembered my name. I'd attended SEWU for four years in the late fifties and couldn't recall a single professor who even noticed I was in his class.

"Just general," I said. "Nothing special."

"Well, you'll be surprised, then," he said.

He smiled and turned to Smoke.

"You a reporter too?"

"Nope. I'm Tonto, the trusted sidekick."

After that remark, Brockington studied him a moment. Apparently he was no stranger to obstreperous youth and their smart mouths.

Wisely he chose to ignore Smoke completely.

He turned his attention back to me as if Smoke had vanished.

"Let me show you the place."

We followed him out and around the building to the greenhouses.

I decided it was time to be a reporter.

"My editor said you are the world's leading authority on hops," I said.

"Was," he said. "Dr. Noah Hattan's the big gun these days. New Zealand is leading the race in the organic agriculture business now. He's the primary mover for Bio Grow New Zealand Ltd. We're lucky enough to be on his mailing list. He gives us boxes of the stuff from time to time to share the knowledge. It's top rate."

He opened a lightweight aluminum door and we stepped into the first of the greenhouses.

There wasn't a hop vine in sight. Instead, four students were sitting on stools laboriously taking stems of what looked like lawn grass and planting them in flats that were like large egg cartons.

The students looked up at us, smiled, and went back at it.

"In here we're working on developing perennial wheat," he said. He lifted up one of the squares of lawn.

"This is the time of year we get ready for planting."

I nodded like I knew what perennial wheat was.

"You know what perennial wheat is?" he said.

"Comes up every year by itself?"

Smoke was turning around looking the building over and acting about as bored as a person could without falling asleep.

"Exactly." Brockington said.

He turned and lead us back outside and towards the next greenhouse.

"Think of it," he continued. "Perennial wheat doesn't need to be plowed under and replanted but once every seven years. Saves erosion. Saves the enormous fuel costs of plowing. Saves labor costs. It's a gold mine."

"Are hops? They a gold mine?"

"Absolutely. Beer, right? And hops are getting more and more expensive as the choice land is being gobbled up by industrial expansion and subdivisions. And it is one of the most heavily sprayed products out there. And we drink it! Grow it organically and you make yourself a millionaire."

He opened the second greenhouse door and let us look in. It was identical to the first one. Including students planting grass a stem at a time.

"Prairie grass," Brockington said. "Corn is the worst choice for bio fuel there is. Part of the moronic Bush legacy. Pollutes like crazy. Depletes the soil. Takes food out of the mouths of people in developing nations. Takes as much energy to grow as it produces. Prairie grass, on the other hand, is the clean solution."

He closed the door and pointed up the line. "Hops. Peas. Canola. Rape. Barley."

He led us over to the cafeteria.

"Like some coffee?"

We nodded like organ grinder monkeys and followed him in. Like the offices, the cafeteria was standard issue college student union. Only on a smaller scale--eight round tables.

We took up white porcelain cups, filled them from large stainless coffee pot and sat at the windows.

The coffee was good. Which surprised me.

He noticed.

"College kids these days, particularly those from Seattle, will burn this place down if they're given the same coffee we three grew up on."

Smoke flinched. Didn't expect to be included in the remark.

"The kids grind it, brew it, and critique it endlessly."

"So, why do they come into Wheatland to eat?" I said.

"Because we can't find a good cook. We find one, Desert Sun hires them away. The one we got now was a harvest cook up out of Royal City. She drives down here, about now actually, cooks supper, packs lunches for those that sign up for them, puts the lunches in the cooler, then drives home. The students do the dishes, make their own breakfasts, eat their mediocre lunches, or go into town with me to have lunch."

He had a thought.

"You guys want to come to my place and have dinner tonight? I live at Desert Sun. You'll like it."

Smoke and I looked at each other. He winked.

"Sure," I said.

Then, "But before we go, is it OK if we see the labs?" I said.

"And what's in the hazard building," Smoke said.

Brockington chuckled like we were children that wanted to look inside an adults only club.

"Both off limits," he said. "Some of the work we do deals with organic and inorganic materials used to control problems. Hops, for instance, are plagued by powdery mildew, downy mildew, verticillum wilt, hops aphids, and red spider mites. And that's just the hops we're trying to protect organically.

"And several of our lab contracts are with private corporations and are kept safe from industrial espionage. Top secret. Lots of money at stake."

"Thus the razor wire," I said.

"And alarms and motion sensors. The works."

"And all along I thought it was to keep the students from running away," Smoke said.

Brockington sighed patiently.

Looked at me.

"Your friend here always like this?"

"Always," I said. "I find it charming."

"Charming?" Smoke said.

"OK. Endearing."

"That's better."

The doctor watched us passively. Shook his head and stood.

We followed his lead.

"Come on down to the main gate at Desert Sun at six. OK?"

He pushed his chair in.

"The gate guard will be expecting you and tell you how to find my place."

He shook our hands and went back down the hall and out the side door.

Smoke looked into his empty coffee cup, got up, refilled it and headed for the door.

I caught up with him in the lot.

"You stealing that mug?"

"Tax dollar mug, you mean."

He went around and climbed in the pickup. I got in on my side and he fired it up.

"Well," I said. We were passing though the gate. "If Nadine hadn't told us about our friend the professor, I would have assumed we made the trip for nothing."

"Maybe," Smoke said.

He opened it up on the narrow road and the truck surged forwards.

He glanced sideways at me.

"Or maybe not. But I'm going to brace that asshole for the money he owes Nadine. She's good people and shouldn't be pushed around by some arrogant, rich asshole egghead."

"You already used asshole once," I said. "And you're mixing metaphors."

He smiled, eyes slitted against the sun that was getting low in the south west sky. Reached for a cigarillo.

"Try muthafucka," I said.

"It's taken."

"Um. How about flatulent pig."

"Flatulent?"

"It works."

"It does at that," he said.

Chapter
Seventy-Six

Through the window Nadine had seen us pull up and park. When we came in she was putting two frosted pint glasses and a pitcher of Red Hook on the counter where we had sat before. Apparently these were now our privately designated stools. Old regulars. Punch out any stranger from out of town who dared sit in them.

She came around to her corner stool with a fresh glass of Columbia Crest. This girl liked to drink. I would too if I had to live in Wheatland. And she must have considered what we told her because she seemed comfortable with us now. Mostly.

"How'd it go?" she said.

"Delightful," Smoke said. "I'm as giddy as a school girl."

She laughed.

"Brockington has street appeal, doesn't he?"

"For me," I said.

I nodded at Smoke.

"Didn't fool Tonto here, though."

She toasted Smoke.

"Find a good description for Tony yet?" she said.

Smoke nodded.

"We discussed it at length on the way back here."

He took a large swallow of beer.

Looked thoughtful.

"There are so many to choose from. You know?"

"Yes."

"Hard to decide."

"But you did."

He nodded.

"Finally settled on flatulent pig."

She covered her mouth with her fingers and giggled. "That's perfect," she said. She stopped laughing and looked back.

"That's why we chose it," I said.

We were silent for bit.

Smoke was still looking at her. He nodded his head very slightly.

"How much do you think he owes you?" he finally said.

Her face dropped. "I don't know, Smoke."

He looked at me. Studied me without seeing me.

"I want you to work it out and tell us tomorrow when we come in for lunch, Nadine," he said.

He looked back at her and tried to ease the tension by winking at her.

She looked down into her wine glass. Tense.

"OK."

Just that.

I noticed the smell of the turkey baking. I had a pang of homesickness for Lana and Ollie. Kept it to myself.

Nadine looked back up at us.

"So you're staying over?" she said.

Smoke nodded. "Any place to stay here in town?"

She shook her head. "Royal City's the closest. There's a mom 'n pop motel there."

"Brockington has invited us to dinner at his condo," I said.

She nodded.

"We want to check it out. Ask him some names. See what he has to say."

She nodded.

Smoke smiled at her. "Fried chicken tomorrow?"
"Yes."
We said nothing.

Then Smoke got up and put a hand softly on her shoulder as he went behind her. He walked leisurely down the length of the counter and around to open the refrigerator. He took out a fresh bottle of chardonnay, took up a corkscrew from the counter and opened it.

He came back with the bottle, refilled her glass and resumed his seat.

She smiled weakly.

She picked up her glass and took a small sip. Studied the fingers on her right hand. Rubbed them absentmindedly with her left thumb, then looked at the back of the room.

"I live in a small apartment in the back," she said. There's a tiny bedroom and bath, and a living room. When you are done at Desert Sun, come knock at the back door. You can sleep on the floor if you want to."

Smoke didn't move.

He smiled like a wise old grandpa and waited.

"I have a couple old sleeping bags and foam pads left over from my marriage," she said. "I'll get them out for you."

Smoke touched the back of her hand gently with his finger tips.

"You're going to be fine, Nadine," he said.

She nodded. "I know. It's just hard some times."

"Yeah," he said.

I felt like I shouldn't be listening.

Smoke sensed my awkwardness. Looked at me.

"Don't touch me when I'm asleep, Paul."

"Dang."

She smiled.

"What do you guys think Tony's involved in?" she said.

"We're not sure," I said. "He might be involved with some bad people who are responsible for a variety of crimes. We just don't know."

I poured a second pint of beer.

"But we'd like to know. For instance, what did he and Alex Byrd have going? And we want to know who he was obtaining Yakima hops from."

"Oh my God," she said. "You think he might have something to do with the Yost Hops killings? That's still all over the papers. You investigating that?"

Smoke shook his head.

"We're not exactly sure what we're investigating."

"Be nice to know, though," I said.

"Indeed."

She thought about that.

"What do you think? You think he might get killed too?"

"Or he might have been involved in the killing," I said.

She wasn't surprised.

"Because of that creep Alex Byrd?"

"Yup."

Smoke took out a cigarillo, remembered we were in Washington, a smoke-free state, and put it back into his pocket.

"Might not be either one," he said.

She frowned.

"So...what?"

"We're stumped," he said. "You'll be the first to know."

"Which reminds me," I said. "I'm thinking we should call Charlie in on this."

"And get our asses chewed?"

"Exactly."

"Good plan."

"Who's Charlie?" Nadine said.

"Our sheriff," I said.

Then, "And Billy. Get him doing some research on this operation Brockington's got going. And on Desert Sun. And on his income."

"And where he's getting all his loot," Smoke said.

She was watching us like we were a tennis match.

"Do we have a plan forming here?" I said.

"Be a first."

"Wow."

He looked at Nadine.

"And we can be bill collectors tomorrow too."

"Nice to be on the other end of that deal for once," I said.

"Won't it."

We drank.

Nadine sliced some cheese and French bread and cut up some vegetables for the three of us, and tended to her cooking. She let us use her cordless phone with our calling cards.

The afternoon passed slowly.

We were on the phone for well over an hour to Charlie, Bill, Charlie again, and then Lana to say hi. Then we phoned Billy and finally Charlie a third time.

He didn't yell at us. Made me proud.

And we had a plan. And we were going to have help from Gibson, Pfeffer, and Rodney Colton, the local sheriff. Or so Charlie promised.

Chapter
Seventy-Seven

The sun was hard in our eyes the entire way to Brockington's condo. It wasn't until we dropped down from the flats to the Columbia River that we entered the shadows and got some relief.

The Corps of Engineers loves to take majestic rivers and turn them into torpid lakes whose bottoms are littered with drowned peach and apple farms.

Priest Rapids Dam was one such place. It had turned the rapids and Indian fishing grounds of Sentinel Gap into Priest Rapids Lake. And on a bar that extended out along the east banks of this lake, which had once been the Rolling W Ranch's winter grounds, was now a gated community and playground for the filthy rich called Desert Sun.

It was growing dark. We pulled up to the gate, which was fashioned like the entrance to a Spanish mission, and a security guard stepped out of a door in the wall at Smoke's elbow. He was dressed in a starched white shirt with a pseudo police badge clipped to his pocket under a black name tag that said O'Dell. He wore black polyester slacks, shiny black shoes, and was unarmed.

Smoke gave him our names. He checked a clipboard, nodded without saying a word, went back through the door. Shortly after, the pike pole lifted to let us through.

"Just love chatting with officious types. Don't you?" Smoke said.

I said nothing.

Smoke laughed.

Lights were starting to come on by photo switches. On our right, along the beach, floodlights turned on over a dozen empty tennis courts, and along the east side runway, lights began to glow on the private airstrip in the descending darkness. There were three planes with their windows tarped parked at the side of a small hanger.

Smoke slowed to a crawl and studied them.

"Interesting," he said. "A Piper Commanche 250. A PA-18 Super Cub. And a Cessna 182."

"So, which do you think is his?" I said.

We moved forward.

"I'll pick the Cessna. Plus I hope it's his because it's closest to the hanger. Gives me more cover."

I nodded.

Between us and the airstrip were the golf links which opened out at the end of the resort and wrapped around the runway. It was practically the only thing that wasn't illuminated by ground lights.

The condos, which began just past the tennis courts and faced Priest Rapids Lake for a quarter mile, were all lit from the outside by lights which shined up through landscaping against their faux adobe walls. In fact the entire complex looked as if it had been transplanted from Santa Fe.

A summer playground away from the Southwest's heat?

But tasteful.

We entered a roundabout halfway down the line. In the middle was a deserted complex of heated, brightly lit bathing pools. And between them and the golf course, a low hacienda lodge faced the pools and condos. It housed a recreation center, restaurant, bar, and exclusive shopping complex. Everything the idle mind could want.

"My my. Ain't we grand?" I said.

Smoke was leaning forward looking up at the backs of the condos as we slid past them. Each presented triple garage doors set between staggered stuccoed walls three stories high. The walls divided each condo from its neighbors to give a sense of separateness. Above the garages there were round topped windows set close to faux tile roofing, and to the right a single hammered strap hinged plank door. Nothing more. Security.

"Makes me ponder why they built here and not Ryback," Smoke said.

"Much less Wheatland."

"Indeed."

"If they only knew what pleasures still await them," I said.

Smoke pulled onto a short concrete garage apron and up to the doors of condo "N."

We got out, went to the wild west door and pushed a black dime sized button below a small speaker box. We stepped back to wait. Smoke waved. I looked up. A one inch security lens sheltered in a nitch about ten feet over our heads pointed at us.

"Wanted to let him know we're friendlies," he said.

The door opened inwards on bearings and Brockington's voice came over the speaker inviting us up the stairs.

We did so. He was standing at the top, martini glass in hand, smiling broadly. He was dressed in white slacks and an untucked Hawaiian shirt with green parrots and purple flowers printed on it. He was sockless and wore a pair of deck shoes that seemed crushed under his weight.

"Wonderful!" he said welcoming us to the landing. "So glad you made it."

He led us through an archway into an expansive living room with a beam and plank ceiling twenty feet overhead and a wall of windows that looked over the pink waters of the lake and sunset. A lit gas log fireplace faced in flagstone dominated the right hand wall, and a bar/kitchen ran along the left.

White leather upholstered furniture was arranged artfully over a Spanish tile floor. The place looked like it had been taken directly from a southwest issue of Sunset Magazine, arranged by a team of interior decorators, and left to the condos' maid service to maintain.

And it looked expensive.

A slender guy in his late twenties, dressed identically to Brockington but with a shirt that sported fish instead of fowl, appeared behind the kitchen counter. He had long blond hair pulled back in a pony tail. I recognized him as the sullen student I had seen at lunch the day before. Or at least I had assumed he had been a student. Now I wasn't sure.

He put both hands on the counter and smiled for us.

"What will it be?" Brockington asked us. "This is my securities man, Blaine Werneke. He mixes a hell of a martini. Or anything, for that matter."

We told him what we wanted, and Blaine took down glasses, filled them with ice, brought out a bottle of chilled soda and an unopened fifth of Glenfiddich.

Brockington ushered us to the couch and chairs that were facing the fireplace. Smoke and I dropped onto the couch.

Blaine handed us our drinks held in napkins, then vanished again back through the kitchen.

"So, tell me about the article," Brockington said.

I took a sip of Glenfiddich and balanced it on my knee.

"I'm basically interested in the man behind the research," I lied. "You know, where the breakthroughs were. Where the problems are. Where the funding comes in from. That sort of thing."

Smoke, off in his own thoughts, was watching the fire. Brockington nodded.

"Where to begin?"

I took another sip. A larger one.

"Well, let's start with a tour of my humble casa," he said.

We got back to our feet with drinks in hand and followed him. We went to a tiled staircase to the side of the kitchen and went up.

"Downstairs is just the garage and laundry," he said. "Second floor is the bedrooms and baths. But I'll take you to the roof. That's what this place is all about."

We passed a hallway that undoubtedly led off to the bedrooms and switched back up a second flight of stairs through a door. He stopped outside and threw a switch to light the entire area.

We joined him.

The roof was about thirty five by forty and was separated from the condos on both sides by ten foot continuations of the two divider walls. Brockington had landscaped with lawn, evergreen shrubs, dwarfed trees, a ten foot square jacuzzi, an elevated tiled lap pool, and a tiled patio under a vine covered ramada.

It was impressive, but everything was under winter wraps and a chilling wind was coming off the lake.

He hit the lights and led us back to the living room.

"Nice, huh?" he said over his shoulder.

"Great party pad," I said.

He laughed, taking the corner and starting down the last flight of stairs to the living room.

"You have no idea. Imagine those same students you saw yesterday drunk and in thongs."

"Still my beating heart," Smoke said behind us.

"So how does a professor of agriculture afford all this?" I said.

We resumed our seats by the fireplace.

"And is that your Cessna on the tarmac outside?" Smoke said.

Brockington looked into his empty glass, got up and went over and began mixing himself another one.

"Yes. I have a pilot's license. It's a hell of a lot easier getting back and forth to SEWU and down to the hop fields of the Willamette Valley and southern Idaho by private puddle jumper."

No sign of Boy Blaine.

"And no. Not on professors' wages. I'll tell you that much," he said. "And not on an inheritance like one of my colleagues."

He came back. Took a swallow and sighed.

"I love gin," he said.

Then, "I got in on the ground floor of the 1990s real estate boom in Montana's Bitterroot Valley. And I got out before the sub prime fiasco made the market tank."

I looked over at Smoke who had turned his attention back to us.

"You were lucky," I said. "Smoke and I weren't."

Brockington studied us a moment.

"In Montana?"

"We didn't bail quite in time," I said. "Plus the people in Missoula managing our investments got into some trouble."

I stopped.

He was now studying us.

No one said anything.

Then, "What happened?"

I held up a palm as if things were hopeless.

"It's a long story."

"Who were your managers?" he said quietly.

"Some fuckwads called Western Summits Investment Group," Smoke said. "And a sleezeball named Spreiter."

Smoke tossed back a slug of Glenfiddich aggressively and got to his feet.

"Mind if I mix another one?" he said.

Brockington was staring. Shook his head. Waved Smoke over to the bar.

"Sorry to hear about your losses," he said. He had gone pale.

"Anyway," I said, "let's talk about something a bit more cheerful. Tell me where you get your hops from out here in the middle of the sagebrush. Yakima?"

Brockington was trying to regather his thoughts.

"No. I get them from Pasco," he said.

Smoke resumed his seat.

"From Yost Hops? From those guys that got killed?" Smoke said.

Again Brockington was jolted. He looked at Smoke and nodded uneasily.

Smoke looked blankly at the fireplace.

"You know," he said, "I just realized that isn't a real fire."

"No it's not. It's propane," Brockington said quietly. He had forgotten about the martini in his hand. He noticed it now and drank.

"So," I said, "where are you going to get hops after what's happened?"

"Yakima, I guess," he said.

I nodded.

He tossed back the rest of his martini and got ready to stand.

"Look. Let's go over to the lodge. They have excellent filet mignon and lobster and a wine list to die for," he said. "Let's talk over some food."

The restaurant was furnished in heavy furniture, linen, candles--everything to make it appear authentic Southwest.

Smoke and I had the lobster as suggested. It was good. Brockington had hardly touched a char broiled tuna steak he ordered and instead dived into the martinis and talked endlessly about his fame as a renowned scientist.

After an hour, we had quit listening. We had been rendered stupefied and incoherent by his blather.

Which was fine by us.

It was nearly ten o'clock before we left the lodge.

We helped him back to his condo, rang the bell, and Blaine came down and helped lever him inside. He shut the door on us without saying a word.

"Charming help these days, what?" I said.

Smoke turned and grinned evilly at me.

"We owe it to them to go fuck up a Cessna," he said.

We climbed into the Jimmy.

"How you going to do it?" I said.

"I have Duct tape. I'll tape one of my full .45 clips to the back of one of his prop blades. At 1800 rpm that fucking plane will jump around like it's falling apart and ready to explode."

I smiled. "You going to get the clip back?"

"Tomorrow," he said. "Also, we're going to collect that tab he owes Nadine and scare the living shit out of our fat fuck the hop doc."

"Wow. You fighter pilots really have a way with words," I said.

"That we do, pardner."

Chapter
Seventy-Eight

The cafe closed on weeknights at ten o'clock. The lights were out and the blinds were closed. Smoke drove around back and parked. We got out and I knocked lightly on the back door.

Footsteps sounded from inside, and a light came on in the kitchen. The curtain over the door's window pulled back for a moment, and we heard a dead bolt slide back. The door opened.

Nadine was already headed back to her bedroom when we stepped in. She had her hair down over her shoulders, she was barefoot, and she wearing one of the ugliest bathrobes I had ever feared seeing. It was a ragged lime green chenille that reached her ankles and had huge pockets sagging off her hips like jowls.

She turned before closing her bedroom door and pointed to the couch where sleeping bags were rolled up and foam pads had been tossed.

"Make yourselves at home," she said. "And you're supposed to call a guy named Charlie and another named Dewayne Gibson. Their numbers are on the table."

She closed the door quietly. We could hear her bed creak as she lay down.

"You take Gibson," Smoke said.

He shrugged off his leather coat, put it on the kitchen table and stripped off his shoulder holster and Kimber and placed them on top.

He began unrolling our bags.

I took down the wireless phone and sat at the kitchen table.

I dialed my phone card number, waited, and dialed Gibson. He answered on the third ring.

"'Bout fucking time," he said.

"Caller ID, huh?" I said. "You guys have all the high tech gadgets."

"Listen, asshole, I'm tired."

I said nothing.

"We need to work with the locals on this thing," he said. "Rodney Colton...you met him?"

"No."

"He's a good sheriff, Paul. And he's coming to see you guys tomorrow morning to help set this up. He'll have his detective with him. A guy called Todd Kyte who I don't know."

"Whom you don't know," I said.

"What?"

"Nothing."

Gibson was silent for a moment. Probably wanted to call me an asshole again.

"They'll put a wire on Smoke and set up a surveillance camera inside the cafe."

"OK."

"Now, is this Nadine lady up to bracing Brockington for the tab?"

"I'm pretty sure."

He thought about that.

"But if she folds, let Smoke do it. You block the door. Get Nadine out of the room."

"OK."

"Now listen closely. Do not breech this prick's Fourth Amendment rights. Don't lie to him. Don't overtly threaten him. Make sure he decides to talk to you because he feels it is in his best interest, not because he thinks Smoke is going to kill him if he doesn't."

"OK."

He paused.

"Let me talk to Smoke. I'll tell him myself."

I got up and carried the phone over and held it out to Smoke who was unrolling the second bag.

He looked up.

"Fuck."

He took the phone and put it to his ear.

"What."

I went back to the sink, took a glass off the doorless shelves and got myself a drink of water.

Finally Smoke said, "Got it. I will. And you sure know how to fuck up a dog fight, Dewayne."

He ended the call and came over, looked at the phone, and dialed Charlie. He began to bring him up to date on everything we'd learned and done.

I went into a tiny bathroom and washed up. I came back out just as Smoke was hanging up.

"Well, he says it might just work. Thinks it..."

The phone rang. He jerked it up impatiently, hit the answer button, put it to his ear. Listened.

"Yeah. He's here."

He handed the phone to me and went into the bathroom.

It was Billy O'Connor.

"Brockington's investment agent was Justin Stanczak," he said.

"How's he fit in, Billy?"

He laughed.

"Two ways. Three actually. He worked with Spreiter at the Missoula home office as a VP, and he was one of the guys Spreiter rolled on."

He hesitated.

"And get this. He was one of Spreiter's guys that was doing medium security time at Englewood. Had it rough in there. Too much the pretty boy smart mouth. And he's being investigated for Spreiter murder."

"Perfect!" I said.

"So you have the hook," he said. "And my sources say that the additional evidence they were hoping for in Yost's warehouse was nowhere to be found. Canines went nuts on the smell, but no product to match."

"You think Brockington has it?" I said.

"If he does," he said, "and if Gibson gets it tomorrow, do you think he'll crack?"

My turn to laugh.

"The guy's an arrogant pig, Billy. He's a spoiled lush."

He was silent a moment.

"So you think he'll scare into the snare?"

"And you know how to rhyme too?" I said.

"It was a mistake."

"You know Smoke. He even scares me. And I'm a man of steel nerve and resolve."

"And demented."

"When Smoke gets pissed, as I'm sure will happen when we brace Brockington on the tab, Brockington will feel lucky to get out of the cafe alive."

He thought about that.

I waited.

"OK. I'm going to call in an IOU from Senator Eugene Franks and..."

"You know Franks?" I said.

"Eugene was a great admirer of Frank Church, Paul. I PR'd for him when he tried and succeeded establishing the Olympic National Park. Like Frank did in Idaho's wilderness area."

"Which kick-started his career," I said.

"Exactly."

I thought about that.

"So, what's he have to do with what we're talking about here, Billy?"

"He and his wife own one of the condos," he said.

"You're shitting me."

"So I'm going to wake him up, tell him what's going on, ask him if my crew and I can use it."

"So you're coming up?" I said.

"If he will make the call, we'll load up our gear and fly in late in the A.M. on the company's Cessna Caravan turbo prop."

I was silent.

Then, "How you going to do it, Billy, and not queer the deal? Smoke fucked up Brockington's plane. We're counting on the professor using it."

Billy laughed.

"You won't see us, hear us, or smell us."

I didn't doubt him.

"From the roof of the senator's condo?" I said.

"Exactly."

I considered.

"And I'm the only one that will know about this?" I said.

"Yes."

"And you'll come to the cafe with your crew afterwards and tell us what you got?"

"I will."

"OK."

I hung up.

Smoke and I were lounging around at the cafe table nearest the door ignoring our third cups of coffee when Sheriff Colton and Detective Kyte came in and introduced themselves. The handful of farmers and local guys who came in each morning to have coffee and to talk crops had gone. Only Nadine was present. She was scraping dishes and putting them into a washing machine.

"Nadine," Colton said. "You mind giving us a little privacy for a minute?"

"She's in on it," I said.

"That true?" he asked her.

She drew a wet hand across her eyes. "I've had it up to here, Rodney," she said. "He owes me one-thousand, eleven dollars. I'm not counting the cents."

"He say anything more about the one mile high club?"

She shook her head.

He nodded and asked Smoke to lift his shirt.

Smoke eased out of his jacket, revealing the shoulder holster and .45.

Colton and Kyte both laughed.

"Shit. You have a permit for that Kimber, Smoke?"

"Yup."

"Can I see it?"

I pulled back my jacket and exposed my PPK.

They looked at each other and both shook their heads.

"Yours too, Paul."

We got out our permits and handed them over. They barely glanced at them and handed them back.

Smoke had lifted his black T-shirt and waited.

"Well," Kyte said. "You still have a little bit of a six pack there, Smoke."

"Always young and beautiful," he said. He winked at Nadine who had stopped working and was checking him out. She smiled.

Kyte took a roll of athletic tape out of the pocket of his western styled wool dress jacket, and from the other pocket removed a small black button mike and wire that ran to a transmitter the size of a book of matches. He taped the mike to Smoke's sternum, pushed something on the transmitter and taped it to his abdomen.

He nodded and Smoke tucked his shirt back into his jeans and put his holster and coat back on.

Kyte then unhooked a radio from beside his holstered Berretta, and keyed it.

"You copy."

"Clear."

"OK."

"Have fun boys," he said. "Try not to kill anybody."

He started for the door.

Colton placed a simple Casio digital camera the size of a pack of cards at the back of a kitchen shelf at eye level.

He came over to shake our hands.

"That's running now with a four gig SD card in it," he said. "Try not to take longer than four hours."

Then, "I used to work with Dewayne," he said. "Got out to raise a family. He's says there's a bunch of you old timers in Ryback, and that you're all a threat to the twenty-first century. That true?"

"Absolutely, Sheriff," Smoke said.

He nodded. Didn't smile.

He looked over at Nadine who was standing motionless watching us.

He sighed deeply.

I noticed for the first time that he was a clone to Charlie. Short, tough, dressed in jeans, white snap button shirt, cowboy boots, and with a barrel chest that looked the result of years of tough ranch work.

"If this cockeyed plan of yours doesn't work," he said, "don't let anything happen to Nadine. Understand?"

He turned and went to the door.

He pulled it open. Without turning he said, "Christ knows you have enough people pouring in to pull it off."

He stopped just outside and looked back in at me.

"You need to be careful with Brockington's security guy," he said. "He's a weasel with a blond pony tail and a 9mm Glock 26 under his shirt in the back."

"We've met him," I said.

Smoke stepped forward.

"He might queer the deal, Sheriff," he said. "You think you could have a deputy keep him occupied?"

He nodded.

"We'll do better than that," he said. "I'll have Blaine pulled in. We've known him since he dropped out of junior high. There's a dozen things we could sweat him on."

He left.

Nadine still stood.

"I'm scared," she said.

Smoke looked at his feet, then back up at her.

"Stage fright?"

She nodded.

"Me too," he said.

"Likewise," I said.

"But we've done things before."

"That we have," I said.

Chapter
Seventy-Nine

Forty minutes later the lab crew pulled in and parked. We heard the van's door roll back and front doors thump shut. They filed in and headed to their seats at the tables. Blaine Werneke wasn't with them.

Brockington, right on time, came in behind them. He walked over to us.

"Sorry about last night," he said.

He glanced at our plates. Today's fare was lasagna, tossed garden salad and garlic French bread. The fried chicken had been canceled.

"No sweat," Smoke said. "Glad you had fun. We did."

Brockington nodded and smiled.

"You going to be around? Maybe we could do it again some time."

I leaned forward and looked over at Smoke.

"We're shoving off tomorrow," I said.

He nodded.

"Well, maybe I can come in after work today, have a beer with you guys."

"Good plan," Smoke said.

Brockington joined his students. A slender brunette dressed in bibs and a bucket beanie made room for him. Sat close.

Nadine came from around the end of the counter and started loading their plates on the table.

They dug in.

Smoke and I ate slowly.

My stomach was fluttering with adrenaline. I pushed my coffee away and waited to get Nadine's attention.

Eventually she came over. She didn't seem the least bit nervous.

"Can you bring a pitcher, Nadine?" I said.

She smiled and went to the tap.

I leaned back.

She brought the pitcher and cold pint glasses and went to draw dish water.

We drank slowly, trying not to make eye contact with anyone at the tables.

Finally, one by one they finished their lunches and sat talking quietly, waiting for the others.

It was only a matter of minutes.

Then, as if on cue, they counted out bills onto the table, pushed back and got to their feet. They strolled out leisurely one by one.

I got to my feet, edged behind Smoke, and stepped between the last student and Brockington. I shut the door, turned and faced him.

Puzzled, he studied me.

I leaned against the door and slid my hands into my back pockets. The move drew back my jacket exposing the grips of the Walther PPK.

He glanced at them. Then turned and looked at Smoke who was getting to his feet.

"What's going on?" he said. Suddenly alarmed.

He looked back at me. His face flushed. His flesh began to mottle in patches.

I remained passive. Silent.

Nadine came around the counter and held a meal ticket out to him.

He turned, faced her, and took the slip. Looked down at it.

His eyebrows shot up.

"One thousand, eleven dollars?" he croaked. "That's bullshit."

He crumpled the bill in his right hand and flipped it at her. It bounced off her chest and fell to the floor.

She stepped forward. Stopped six inches from him. Eye to eye.

"You're a fucking pig, Tony," she hissed.

His lips began to tremble.

He took a half step back. Stared at her. She held her ground.

He suddenly rolled his shoulder and slapped her heavily on the side of the head. Her hair flew over her face and she spun sideways against the front table.

Smoke was instantly in Brockington's face. He was clucking his tongue like a hen.

Nadine pushed herself upright using the top of the table for leverage. She pushed her hair out of her face and gingerly touched her ear with the fingers of her left hand.

Brockington stood motionless staring at Smoke. He was beginning to realize the peril of his situation.

"Nadine," Smoke said soothingly, "why don't you go out and tell the others to leave the truck here and go back in the van? The good doctor is going to be delayed a bit."

He turned back to Brockington, eyes gone hard. "Give me your fucking wallet, Tony."

I stepped aside to let Nadine by. She gave me a vacant look and edged past and out the door. She pulled it shut behind her.

Smoke had his hands in his back pockets. His shoulder holster and .45 were clearly visible.

Brockington stared. He reached back slowly and came out with his wallet. Said nothing as he handed it over.

Smoke opened the wallet, took out a Mastercard and slid it into a front pocket of his jeans. He handed the wallet back and nodded to the table.

"Take a seat," Smoke said.

Brockington edged away from Smoke and sat down warily. His back was to me.

Smoke pulled out the chair opposite him and sat down. He rocked back on the chair's rear legs and hooked his thumbs in his front pockets. The butt of the Kimber rose and fell against his chest with his easy breathing.

"We killed your side kick Alex Byrd," he said.

Brockington let out his breath and dropped his head into his hands with his elbows on the table top.

We waited.

He shook his head without looking up.

We waited.

"And your pal Nelson Yost is dead," Smoke said.

"I know," he mumbled.

We said nothing.

"Tony," Smoke said.

Brockington looked up.

"You're in deep shit, Tony."

Then, "You still got Trent Mazollan's product?"

"He send you?" Brockington managed.

I'd never seen a man frightened like this before.

"Answer my question, Tony," Smoke said.

Brockington's cheeks were twitching.

"Yes," he said.

Smoke waited.

Brockington's voice trembled.

"Please tell him Blaine and I were going to fly it up Saturday," he said weakly. "But Blaine got picked up this morning."

He put his head back into his hands. He rocked back and forth slightly.

"Spreiter was killed in Englewood by your investment pardner Justin Stanczk," Smoke said. "You know that, don't you?"

Brockington looked up.
"No, I didn't."
Smoke studied him.
"So, let's study your situation here for a minute," Smoke said. "You know Freddy Stripe?"
"No."
Smoke glance up at me, then back at Brockington.
"Billy Long Gone?"
"No."
"Samuel Beauvallon?"
He shook his head.
"I think they know you," Smoke said. "And I think maybe Trent is very, very upset. I think he would like to bury you. I think he's convinced you had his guys killed. I think he figures you're making a move on his operation."
We waited.
Brockington's shoulders were beginning to shake. He was crying.
"You know Alex Byrd?" Smoke said quietly.
"Yes," he whispered.
"He's dead," Smoke said.
"You know William Garber?"
He nodded. Whispered, "Yes."
"He's dead."
Smoke dropped the chair back onto all four legs, crossed his arms on top of the table and leaned forward.
I tapped the door twice with the knuckles of my left hand. Brockington didn't notice.
"You want to live, Tony?" Smoke said softly, inches from Brockington's face.
"Please don't kill me," he mewed.
"You going to get the product and everything else to Mazollan?"
He was crying hard now into his hands.
"Yes."

"Today?"
"Yes."
"And the prod..."
The door opened. I stepped aside and Longbeach and Oscar came in. They were wearing filthy McGregor hats and dusty jeans too big for them, and ragged plaid flannel shirts. They nodded to us and clunked over to the bar in worn cowboy boots and slid onto stools. They rested their elbows on the bar and waited to be served.

We were silent.

Brockington looked up at them. Wiped his face on his left sleeve and tried to compose himself.

We waited.

They sat motionless with their backs to us.

Three minutes. Five minutes.

They got restless.

Finally Oscar turned on his stool, looked the place over and settled on us.

He held his look.

We looked back.

"How's a person get a fucking beer in this place?" he said.

Smoke and I said nothing.

He waited.

He dropped his feet to the floor. Remained seated.

Longbeach turned his head to see what was going on.

Oscar stood upright.

"What are you fuckers looking at?" he said. He was getting angry.

"Cool your jets, Tonto," Smoke said quietly.

Now Longbeach was on his feet.

"Tonto?"

Smoke said nothing.

"He asked you a fucking question," Oscar said, getting loud.

"You're scaring me, Tonto," Smoke said.
I took a step away from the door towards them.
That triggered it.
They started for us and Smoke was on his feet instantly.
We met them in the middle of the room.
Longbeach lunged at me. I cuffed him against his ear knocking off his hat. He got me in a bear hug, lifted me off my feet and ran with me towards the back wall. We crashed though the door, tearing it from the jam, tripped over Smoke's and my sleeping bags and rolled against the kitchen table.

My leg started throbbing where the bone was healing.

We got up quickly, banged the chairs and table around for a bit, and listened to the thuds and grunting coming from the cafe.

It continued.

Longbeach gave me a questioning look and we went into the center of the room so we could look out the splintered doorway.

Brockington was no where to be seen and the front door was standing open.

Smoke and Oscar were behind two overturned tables trying to beat the shit out of each other. They both had blood down their chests. They both had bloody noses. They both had their shirts torn half off.

We ran over the top of the bedroom door into the cafe and tackled them both around their waists and pulled them apart.

Smoke tried to clip me with an elbow and I shrugged it off my shoulder and gripped him as hard as I could. It was like trying to crush a cement pillar.

Longbeach was yelling for them to knock it off.

Nadine, Sheriff Colton and a deputy came in through the front door.

Colton kept saying, "Whoa, boys, whoa. Easy does it."

He and the deputy gave Josiah and me a hand.

Nadine set a table and two chairs upright and stood back.

We finally got Smoke and Oscar separated and both seated.

The deputy and I each had one of Smoke's arms. We let go of him carefully like he was a bear trap.

The Sheriff and Longbeach did the same with Oscar.

Oscar and Smoke continued to pant and glare at one another. Their shirts hung off them in ribbons. Blood dripped from their faces onto their laps.

We waited.

Then they both started to snort through clenched lips, making farting noises. And they busted out laughing.

They howled and hooted. Tears ran down their cheeks. They gasped and tried to gain control then saw each other again and laughed some more.

We stood and watched them patiently.

Nadine brought over four pitchers of beer gripped in two hands and managed to ease them down of the table without dropping them.

Smoke picked one of the pitchers up before Nadine could get glasses, took a huge mouthful, and squirted it at Oscar.

From behind the bar Nadine barked out, "Stop it!"

We froze.

She came back with a tray of glasses and two wet bar towels draped over her left arm.

She slid the glasses onto the table and dropped the towels in front of Smoke and Oscar.

We remained motionless.

Smoke and Oscar began wiping blood off their faces and off the table top.

She stopped and watched them.

Smoke folded his bar towel into a square and held it to his left eye.

"You going to rough house some more or get drunk with me?" she said.

No one said anything.

Smoke lowered the towel. His eye was swelling shut. He reached into his jean pocket and took out Brockington's Mastercard.

He cleared his throat and handed it to her.

"I think Tony wanted to pay his bill and for us to get drunk," he said.

"Smoke," the sheriff said. He was staring at Smoke's bare chest.

"Where's the wire?"

Smoke looked down. He lifted the front of his shirt off his lap. He rummaged around and handed up the transmitter. It had blood drying on it and had the strip of tape still hanging from it. He searched some more and came up empty handed.

"The mike's gone," he said.

Colton shook his head.

"Charlie warned me about you guys," he said. "And if I don't get a call pretty soon to tell me your FBI buddies have pulled this thing off, I'm going to send you both home in cuffs."

Smoke winked at me.

"Can we have a digital copy of our fight, sheriff?"

Colton went over and retrieved the camera. Turned it off, dropped it in his shirt pocket, and stood glaring at him.

Nadine said, "I'll find the mike somewhere, Rod. Relax."

She pulled up a chair for him and another for herself.

He came back over.

She took him by his beefy forearm and made him sit.

"Let's have some beer, folks," she said. "It's on Brockington."

Chapter
Eighty

Sheriff Colton and his deputy didn't stay. As soon as they knew Smoke and Oscar wouldn't start up again and that Nadine was going to be safe, they left for Desert Sun.

Nadine locked the front door behind them and pulled the blinds. She turned and studied the four of us and settled on Smoke.

"Bit of overacting there, Smoke?" she said.

Smoke grinned mischievously. He flipped over the remains of his shirt in his lap, found the pocket and took out a cigarillo.

It was broken in half. He held it up.

"May I?"

"No," she said.

He returned it to the pocket and let the shirt fall back.

She began to smile and then said quietly, "I'll get you brawlers some shirts."

She went behind the bar and took down the phone.

Smoke watched her carefully, then turned to face Oscar.

"Where'd you learn to hit so fucking hard, Redtail? I thought the only thing you Injuns could do was fish."

Oscar put both hands up to the sides of his nose to make sure it was on straight.

"How 'bout you? Grow up fighting with your sisters?"

"Between missions I mixed it up with my buddies in the military police over our poker game disputes," he said.

Longbeach nodded at Oscar.

"My pardner here loves to bounce racists from our casino," he said. "Likes to get them and their friends alone in the parking lot. Teach them about White Bird and all them dead cavalry."

"I look like cavalry?" Smoke said.

They both nodded.

Smoke raised his glass.

We toasted and drank.

Josiah clacked his glass down on the table.

"I hope Sheriff Colton gives us a copy of that camera movie. We'll show it every night on the casino's big screen. Better than bull riding."

Nadine returned and sat down. Smoked poured her a schooner. She took two large swallows and sighed.

"Laureen is bringing over a couple of Rodney's flannel work shirts for you boys," she said. "A bit big, but you'll get used to it."

"His wife?" Smoke asked.

She nodded.

Smoked looked at her.

"And he's your ex," he said quietly.

She nodded.

We drank.

Smoke looked at the back of the room through the shattered jam at the door lying on Nadine's apartment floor.

"They have a True Value or Home Depot or something around here?" he said.

"Yakima," she said.

He nodded. Looked at me.

"Wanna take a trip to Yakima with me tomorrow, Paul?"

Nadine said, "I'd better go with you. Let Paul pour coffee for the old timers. I'll pick it out, and you two can install it."

"Good plan," I said. "Smoke's taste in doors is limited."

It was nearly four o'clock when Gibson and Pfeffer knocked.

Nadine got up and let them in.

They were wearing black baseball caps, black lace-up boots, Levis and dark blue nylon jackets with FBI written in large florescent letters on their backs.

They introduced themselves to Nadine, and she led them over to our table. They snagged two extra chairs on the way. We made room for them, and Nadine went and got more glasses and a fresh pitcher of beer.

"We almost sniped your pal from the Banner," Pfeffer said.

"Thought he and his two side kicks had a fucking cannon pointed at us from a condo roof. Was a huge telephoto lens."

"You take them down?" Josiah said.

Gibson was pouring for Pfeffer and himself.

"The fucker was all set up before we even arrived. Five thirty in the morning for crissake."

He took up his beer and drank.

By now I was drinking coffee. Only the brave can drink beer all afternoon.

"Probably wanted footage from beginning to end," I said.

Pfeffer ignored me.

"So I finally get up there and see who it is. You know what he says? He says, 'About time you bums got to work.'"

He and Gibson looked at me.

"You tipped O'Connor off, didn't you?" Pfeffer said.

"Moi?"

"Yeah, Moi, you pin head," Gibson said. "You could've fucked up the whole thing--you and your paper boy."

Smoke slapped the table with his right hand.

"Look," he said. "Let's be civil here and give Paul a little credit. Or are you pissed because he tore you away from the paperclip chains you were making in your shabby offices?"

Pfeffer looked at Smoke's torn and bloody shirt. Then at Oscar's.

"Matching shirts and all. You two going steady now?"

He checked them out some more.

"And who had the pleasure of beating you guys up?"

"We have a tumultuous relationship," Oscar said.

"Tumultuous?"

"I'm learnin' white speak. Wanna be FBI guy."

It was Nadine's turn to slap the table. A new trend was developing.

"Stop it! Can we stop all this school yard pushing and shoving bullshit for just one fucking minute?"

We were silent.

"Can you two FBI agents please tell us what happened? Please?"

The front door rattled on its dead bolt.

Nadine glared at us, got to her feet, went over and opened it.

It was Billy. He came in looking very proud of himself.

Directly behind him came a strong looking woman in her early thirties with a face tanned by the elements. She had dense wavy auburn hair pulled back into a pony tail and wore Wrangler jeans, rough-out dogger boots, and a ribbon shirt. She looked like someone who had just kicked hay off the back of a truck for a herd of cattle. She stood aside as soon as she was inside the door and took Sheriff Colton's arm as he came in next.

Mrs. Colton.

I glanced at her, at Nadine who was now behind the counter, and back at her. Ol' Rodney had good taste.

They came over on Billy's heels.

"Thanks for waiting," Colton said. "Didn't start without us?"

Then, "This is my wife, Laureen."

He dropped two flannel shirts on the table.

We stood and introduced ourselves. She smiled and shook our hands around the table. Smoke and Oscar shrugged off their rags and put on the shirts.

"Looks like the town population just doubled," she said. "But if you'll excuse me..."

Billy and Colton pulled up another table, and Josiah got chairs for them. We all adjusted.

Laureen went over and joined Nadine behind the counter and had the lid off a large crock pot and was reaching for a wooden spoon. She whispered something in Nadine's ear and I saw Nadine's lips sound "Smoke."

Nadine glanced over her shoulder at him then took the spoon and went to work on dinner.

Billy edged in between Smoke and me.

Colton sat at the head of our double table.

"So whadda we got?"

Nadine sat another pitcher on the table and a half gallon of Wild Turkey.

"Hang on a minute," she said.

She returned with a tray of tumblers and two schooners, and resumed her seat on Smoke's left.

"What we have," Gibson said, "is Brockington's laptop and five boxes marked "Yost Hops" weighing in the neighborhood of ten pounds each. Brockington hustled these out to his plane in his golf cart while we all," he nodded to Billy," watched."

Billy nodded.

"Each box held exactly five kilos of crystal meth shrink wrapped with the same markings we had on the Magruder bust. So we know it's from Mayanmar and we know it came through either Thailand or Hong Kong. And, thanks to Joy Chu and Hammersmith, we know it landed in L.A.."

Smoke poured the Wild Turkey into a tumbler, took one, and left the rest in the middle of the table.

Colton and Billy both reached for one.

Billy took a cautious sip.

Gibson waited.

"What's the meth worth?" Nadine said.

He looked at her.

"Despite the fact meth is losing popularity in the states to our old friend cocaine, it still sells for a hundred bucks a gram.

Josiah did the math. He whistled though his teeth.

"Twenty-five kilos. Shit. That's twenty five thousand grams. Same amount as last time. Two and a half million dollars."

"Josiah did well in fifth grade math," I explained.

Billy apparently decided Wild Turkey wouldn't kill him and took a decent sip. He was wearing a leather jacket and reached into a side pocket and handed Smoke's .45 clip over to him.

"I couldn't believe my eyes," he said. "Brockington left his golf cart right there on the tarmac, climbed into the Cessna and fired it up."

"We thought we were about to lose him," Colton said.

Billy nodded.

"So he gives it the juice, and just as it starts to roll forward, the whole damn plane gives kind of a shiver and then it starts shaking like wet dog with a duck in its mouth."

"With a duck in its mouth?" Oscar said.

"Then all these FBI guys in black boots and assault rifles charge the plane and drag him out onto the ground."

He laughed.

"Great footage."

"So you're sharing your royalties with Dewayne and me," Pfeffer said.

"Just when you're getting adjusted to life in a trailer court?" Smoke said. "Don't do it, Billy."

Smoke suddenly winced. Looked at Nadine and grinned.

I suspected she had abused him under the table.

"You guys want Blaine?" Colton asked Gibson.

Both Gibson and Pfeffer shook their heads.

Gibson reached for one of the tumblers.

"You can keep that piece of shit. He's your boy, not ours."

He took a substantial swallow. His eyes watered and he put the glass down.

Colton nodded.

Gibson was having trouble swallowing.

Then, in a whisper, "This whole hair-assed bust is so unorthodox and fucked-up we're going to bless you with the credit."

"Thanks," Colton said.

"OK with you Billy?" Pfeffer said.

"If you don't mention these Ryback Rest Home Renegades and our Camas chums in any of your press releases," Billy said. "They shouldn't be provoked further."

"We might need to depose them," Colton said.

Billy shook his head.

"I can spin this several ways, gentlemen."

He scanned the three of them.

"The headlines can read that a local sheriff sleuths out a major link in a west coast drug trafficking cartel and delivers it to the Federal Bureau of Investigation..."

Billy gave his watch-your-next-comment smile.

"Or...college professor...entrapment..."

"OK. OK. We get your point," Gibson said.

"Can we do it without them?" Colton asked.

"Yes."

"What about me?" Nadine said.

We all looked at her.

She scanned all our faces. Settled on Smoke's.

He held up his palms.

"Don't look at *me*."

We were quiet for a bit.

"You could have your door fixed," Colton said.

"Rod," Laureen said from behind the bar, "you know what she's asking."

Sheriff Colton nodded.

"He paid what he owed you, so I guess it doesn't need to go any further than that."

He hesitated.

"Unless you want to bring assault charges against the bastard."

Smoke jumped in.

"He in one of your cells?" he said.

"Yeah."

Smoke grinned and glanced at Gibson. Gibson gave a slight nod.

"So sheriff," Smoke said, "you ever have a prisoner go crazy and attack you inside his cell?"

"Not until now," Colton said.

He smiled. "I just hope he doesn't resist when I come in to turn him over to Gibson and Pfeffer here.

"Could get ugly," Pfeffer said.

"Line of duty." This was Gibson.

Nadine took a deep swallow and lifted a pitcher to refill her glass.

"I guess there's really no need then to file assault charges," she said.

She looked over her shoulder.

We followed her gaze.

Laureen had set the counter up cafeteria style. A stack of plates, a tray of flatware, the crock pot filled with what proved to be boston baked beans. A smoke cured ham. A large bowl of tossed salad. And two pans of cornbread.

Laureen came around the end of the counter and over behind Colton. She put one hand on his shoulder, kissed him on the ear and reached past him for one of the whiskeys.

"Well?" she said. "I ain't dishin', so you'd better get your asses up before it gets cold."

Chapter
Eighty-One

We finished our dinners, followed Colton's lead, and bussed our own dishes ranch-hand style. We took them into the kitchen, washed them in the large sink tubs and put them in a rack to dry.

Josiah Longbeach and Oscar Redtail were the last to leave. It was nine o'clock. They said the Yakima Rez was only a half hour away and they had cousins at White Swan they wanted to visit.

That left Billy, Smoke, Nadine and me.

We were enjoying the silence that descends after a large group of people leaves. Comfortably.

Billy, a professional Irish whiskey drinker, didn't look ill from the low grade Wild Turkey he had been nursing. Maybe it had grown on him.

Smoke could drink turpentine.

Nadine sat with her right shoulder resting lightly against Smoke and was ignoring her fourth whiskey. She didn't slur her words. Didn't seem to show fatigue from the day's events. And she hadn't touched the side of her face again after Brockington had hit her.

Tough gal.

As long as it was on my mind, I said quietly, "How's the ear?"

"Oh, fine," she said.

She didn't look at me. Didn't seem to be looking at anything.

But Smoke was. He was studying her right hand resting beside his on the table. She had long fingers, nails trimmed short, and smooth tanned skin.

"You roll with that hit he gave you?" he said.

"Probably."

He nodded.

"Where'd you learn to do that?"

She looked at him. Held it.

"My older brother was kind of crazy when he drank."

She looked back at her glass.

"He was eight years older than me and came back from the Gulf War kinda unhappy. Just hung around the house."

She thought about it.

"Then one day Dad decided he'd had enough and he and Colton loaded him in the back of a cruiser, and Colton drove him over to Fort Lewis. Signed him in to the hospital there. He gave them paperwork to keep him in there until they were satisfied."

She looked at the cafe wall and a Remington print of a mounted cowboy shooting a carbine over his shoulder at a band of Indians in hot pursuit.

Then, "He's married now, living in Shasta, California. The two of them own a little bakery and espresso place on a corner. They're teaching their little girl how to ski."

"Sounds OK," Smoke said.

"It is. Colton's a good man for doing that for him."

"Plus you know how to take a hit."

"Exactly."

We were silent for awhile.

"Well," Billy said, "I'm blowing this joint. Tired."

He scraped back his chair and got to his feet. He shook Nadine's hand and thanked her for everything. He dropped two hundred-dollar bills on the table.

"For repairs," he said, and looked at me.

"Why don't you and Smoke come join me at the Senator's digs tonight," he said.

I glanced at Nadine.

She acted hurt.

"And give up my splinter covered living room floor, Paul?" she said. "I'm crushed."

I stretched my stiff neck, sore back, and injured leg and got to my feet.

"Sounds good, Billy."

Smoke remained seated.

Nadine looked at him. Put her face inches from his.

"Well?" she said.

I leaned on the back of my chair with my arms straight and waited.

He studied her.

"You going to be OK?" he said.

She put an elbow on the table and titled her head as she looked at him.

"Hard to say," she said slowly.

I waiting a moment then straightened up.

I turned and nodded for Billy to follow me. We went to the front door and I opened it for us.

He started though.

"You have a ride?" I said.

"Nope. Came in with Pfeffer and Gibson. Street's too narrow for the Cessna."

I nodded, turned back to Smoke and held out my hand.

He dug in his jeans and tossed me the keys for the Jimmy. They landed on the floor three feet to my right. I picked them up and followed Billy out.

"Be sure to lock up," I said over my shoulder.

I shut the door behind us and we stepped out into the street. The air was cold and sweet with the smell of new spring grass.

We drove on out of town.

Senator Franks' condo was exactly like Brockington's, but unlike Brockington's it was cozy and lived in. The furniture was a mix of refurnishing leftovers from his 1930s mansion on Seattle's Queen Ann Hill. The majority was mission style with an assortment of overstuffed 40s pieces mixed in.

And there were framed photos scattered everywhere. Photos of him and his wife, their friends, their three daughters, three sons and their spouses, and dozens more of their grandchildren at play. A rabbit hutch couldn't have had more photos.

The two bedrooms behind the kitchen were suited for adults and both were modestly furnished with twin beds and private baths. The three bedrooms down the hall from the upstairs master bedroom were filled with bunk beds, two pairs per room, posters, a computer and study desk in each, and a clutter of plastic stack bins overflowing with whatever it was kids thrive on these days.

The patio roof had a ten foot in diameter, stand alone, four foot deep kids' pool, a smattering of plastic toys, and under the ramada a sanctuary for parents that included a barbecue, large round glass topped table, deep lawn chairs and a wet bar.

Not bad.

We returned to the kitchen.

Billy switched on the recessed ceiling lights and began opening the walnut cabinets until he found the Glenfiddich. He took down two heavy glasses and poured.

"Where's your crew?" I said.

"Probably at the lodge celebrating. They must have spent all afternoon editing our footage before uploading it to the Banner with my story."

"You've already done the story?" I said.

He nodded.

"Didn't I tell you I'm the..."
"...best investigative journalist? Yes," I said.
"Well?"
"Was it like you negotiated at the cafe?"
"Of course."

I shook my head.

He handed me my glass. There was a scant half inch of scotch in it.

I hadn't had anything but coffee and water since three that afternoon. The scotch smelled like a burning peat fire in a shepherd's stone cottage and warmed me like a mother's love.

We both let out our breath simultaneously.

"It sure the fuck isn't Wild Turkey," Billy said. "But I'm too damn tired to enjoy it."

I nodded.

We swirled our Glenfiddich, leaned against the counter and sipped until our glasses were empty. We washed them, put everything away, and headed down the hall for bed.

I stopped.

"Billy," I said. "Footage? It just dawned on me. You doing TV *and* newspaper now?"

"You gotta get out more, Paul. I've been doing both since you gave me the Spreiter exclusive," he said.

He went into the bedroom.

"You made me famous," he said back through the door. "And now you've done it again."

"How famous?" I said.

"Hundreds of thousands, Paul."

I stood staring after him. Then shook it off and returned to the living room to call Lana. To tell her about the day. To tell her I missed her and Ollie and that Smoke had a thing going. And to tell her I was going to ask Billy to

drop me off tomorrow at the Magnet airport on his way home to Boise.
   And I did.

Chapter
Eighty-Two

Ground fog bright with sun and thin as linen blanketed the valley that morning. The air smelled of river and sage, and Smoke's Jimmy was blanketed with dew. I turned on the wipers, fired the engine up and held it at a throbbing idle as Billy got situated and shut the door.

"Mercy!" Billy said. "Am I hung over or just getting old?"

"Yes," I said.

We broke into a cloudless royal blue morning up on the plateau, accelerated to seventy and headed back to Wheatland.

"Your two-man crew show up last night?" I said.

"Beats me. They're night owls. They try not to sleep before two o'clock or wake up before eleven."

"How's that working out?"

"A lot of the flying and filming happens in the afternoons and evenings, so just fine."

I crossed the highway. Wheatland was in sight now.

"So, who's the pilot?"

"Sam. The heavier of the two. The Banner hired him away from the Air Force, and on the ground he's trained as our sound man. You don't have to know much to hold a boom mike. But in the air he's about as good as they get. Smoke excluded."

We pulled up and parked in front of the cafe. It was past seven-thirty and the sidewalk steamed in the sun.

A group of perhaps ten farmers seated around two tables turned as one to look Billy and me over as we came in. They ranged from their twenties to sixties and were dressed for hard work and long hours. One of the oldsters got to his feet, pulled over two more chairs, and made room for us. Billy nodded and sat down heavily.

Smoke and Nadine were working at the grill with their backs to us. Smoke looked over his shoulder with his good eye and nodded for me to come over. His other eye was open a slit, and the yellow and purple swelling had flattened and spread to his forehead and jaws.

He was stirring a two gallon pot of sausage gravy with a large stainless spoon. Nadine was lifting biscuits off cookie sheets and placing them in a stainless warming bin she had lifted onto the far right side of the grill. Plates, glasses, coffee mugs, two cartons of orange juice and cutlery sat on the counter. Again, buffet style.

"You roll the truck?" Smoke said.

He lifted the pot of gravy and sat it on an electric hot plate at one end by the flatware.

"Only once," I said. "So what's the plan?"

Nadine filled a bamboo basket with steaming biscuits and placed it beside the gravy.

She looked over at the farmers.

"Dig in, men," she said.

The group stood in a racket of chair legs scraping the wood floor and came over casually. They formed up and began loading their plates with biscuits, ladling the thick sausage gravy over them.

Smoke wiped his palms on a white towel tied around his waist.

"Nadine and I are headed into Yakima right about now," he said. "We'll get a pre-hung solid wood door."

He leaned over and said quietly, "And I'm going to buy her a sofa-bed to replace that piece of shit she's passing off as a couch."

"Tired of the floor, Smoke?" I said.

"Once was enough."

I thought this over.

"So you didn't sleep on the floor a second time? Like, say, last night?"

He ignored me. "How about you playing cafe owner for a couple hours or so?"

"Sure. I'll have Billy be my waitress."

Billy was dishing up.

"Can't," he said. "Sheriff Colton, Gibson and Pfeffer invited me along on this morning's nine o'clock search of the mysterious Brockington labs. A couple of mucky mucks from the university will be accompanying us."

He poured a ten ounce glass of orange juice and turned with his breakfast back to the table.

"Should be interesting. But they decided I couldn't bring in my camera crew. Bad PR."

Nadine wedged in between Smoke and me. Her hair carried the smell of fresh baking. She put a hand on my elbow.

"You don't mind tending the store, Paul?"

I smiled and shook my head.

"When you think you'll be back?"

"Three hours. Eleven o'clock at the latest," she said. "In time to prepare pizzas for lunch."

I nodded.

She took off her cook's apron and tossed it into a hamper under the counter.

"I'll put a cigar box out on the counter with change money in it. Folks can pay their own bills. There's only about five more that come in--the old guys, and they'll sit up front and visit."

She stood on her toes and kissed me lightly on the cheek.

"Grab something to eat," she said.

They headed for the door as I dished up. Nadine stopped at the tables on her way and said something to the men that made them laugh. She caught up with Smoke and they went out into the sun.

I took my plate over to the table, came back for my cup of coffee and glass of juice, and sat in the empty seat beside Billy. Nadine had added a hint of red pepper to the gravy for a little zip. I dug in happily.

No one said anything.

One of the middle aged men got up and went for seconds. He was wearing White boots and a McGregors cap and was built like a whiskey barrel. Wide black suspenders held up his tan Carhartt carpenter's pants and his powerful shoulders flexed under a long sleeve cotton shirt that had black labs and ducks printed all over it.

One by one we finished eating and sat back with our coffees.

"So, you boys are reporters?" Whisky Barrel said. His voice was surprisingly high. Irish?

Billy nodded. "We use to work together at the Confluence Tribune,"

The old guy sitting at Billy's left who had pulled over chairs for us sat his cup on the table and looked at the other men.

"These are those guys from Ryback that keep getting shot up," he said.

"That ain't so," a young guy across from us said. "They's the ones that done the shootin'."

Several men nodded.

The big guy was studying us thoughtfully.

"Well," he said, "I'm glad you're in one piece. That was some serious business you found yourselves in."

Then he smiled.

"But I understand the DEA agents and you staged a fight yesterday that kinda got out of hand."

"Just a fraction," I said.

"Damn clever."

He pondered his own statement.

Then, "That professor has had it coming a long time around here. Glad you could help out."

He looked at his watch. Sucked on his teeth, pushed back his chair and got to his feet.

"Nice meeting you," he said. He went over to the counter and dropped a five dollar bill in the cigar box. The others followed his lead, some making change, and filed out one at a time.

The old guy got up last. He put his hand on Billy's shoulder as he edged past.

"Keep up that column you write, Mr. O'Conner. We get it in our Yakima rag, and it's damn interesting."

"Thank you," Billy said. He sat looking as the door closed behind him.

"Talkative bunch, weren't they?"

"Thought they'd never stop," I said.

Billy looked at me.

"Want to jump on board the Cessna after the labs are shaken down?"

"I was going to ask," I said. "I'll phone Lana to pick me up."

Billy shook his head.

"I'm not heading that way just yet," he said. "We've filed flight plans for Kelowna today. All we need to do is radio an established time of arrival and hope to be there within fifteen minutes of it."

I sat my half finished coffee down on the table. Studied him for several moments. Then nodded.

"You're going to confront Trent Mazollan, right?"

He shook his head.

I held up my palms.

"So tell me."

"You and I are going to go pay Freddy Stripe, aka Casper Leib, and his mother a visit," he said.

Before I could respond, a car horn sounded outside.

Billy grinned and got to his feet.

"That's my ride, ol' chum."

Chapter
Eighty-Three

The morning dragged by. I washed dishes, put the leftover biscuits in a gallon ziploc, and poured the last bit of sausage gravy into a tupperware and set it out behind the cafe for any stray dogs the town might have.

The old timers nodded to me politely as they trickled in one by one. They poured themselves coffee and took seats at the front table. Other than that, I was on my own.

They left a little after nine. I wiped their table, washed their cups, and took a chair out onto the sidewalk. I sat in the sun with my back against the door jam, sipped coffee and read the Yakima News. From time to time a farm truck drove by and the drivers gave me a nod or finger wave, and I returned the greetings.

I had no idea life as a small town cafe owner could be so relaxing.

Smoke and Nadine returned from Yakima fifteen minutes before eleven o'clock, and I helped carry in a white prehung door and a heavy beige sofa bed.

I told Smoke I was flying out with Billy and that Billy wanted to drop in on Freddy Stripe.

Smoke laughed sarcastically.

"Fine," he said. "Maybe you'll learn what a phony that asshole is."

I studied him a moment.

"Why don't you jump on board too? Maybe broaden your horizons a bit. Make you into a loving, forgiving, accepting and genuinely sweet retired fighter pilot."

"I need that about as much as a fish needs a bicycle," he said.

I laughed.

"Isn't that a feminist's expression?"

He shook his head hopelessly.

"I'll get the door installed and head back this afternoon, Paul. Meet you at MacAvity's tonight."

"And not try out the sofa-bed?" I said.

Nadine was rolling out pizza dough and ignoring us.

There was going to be an interesting topic for the lab crew to discuss over lunch. Unless the FBI placed them all in leg irons.

The Banner's Cessna Caravan was either a huge private plane or a tiny passenger plane. It had originally seated eight, four lining each side with an aisle down the middle. There were two tables between the forward pairs, and the Banner had taken out the four seats at the back and installed a flying communications center and news room.

A wide work counter spanned the rear bulkhead. It sported two keyboards and 20" MacIntosh displays and all the makings for satellite internet and phone links. Every spare inch of the back wall was faced with gadgets and gizmos that glowed with red, blue and green LED lights like the operations center of a miniature nuclear submarine.

Billy and I sat opposite each other in plush leather seats. I was facing the back of the plane and Sam was piloting at my back on the other side of a privacy screen. Billy's cameraman was seated at one of the computers working a QuarkXPress layout.

"There was nothing unusual going on in the off-limits building," Billy said. "It was exactly what it was designed to be--a clean room and bio chem hazard area."

We were drinking Guinness long necks. He set his down and wiped foam from his upper lip with a thumb.

"But the canine got interested in one of the shipping tables at the back of an end greenhouse. So one of the Feeb techs vacuumed the area for a lab work-up. Gibson is certain it'll be a positive. And Rodney is going to lean all over that punk of Brockington's and turn him."

I could see the Okanogan Valley slide by five thousand feet beneath us.

"So tell me," I said. "Why are we going to visit Stripe instead of Mazollan. You think he's the mastermind behind all this?"

"No. Mazollan is."

"So my question stands."

"Because I have insights you and I will share with our boy Freddy that will be hugely entertaining for both of us," he said. "But I want to talk to the RCMP first."

I nodded. I knew from past experience that when Billy was on a scent, he was loathe to discuss it. Better for me just to trot along and observe.

"Well tell me this, O master of the printed page, how did Stripe get his men and his arsenal across our border what with all our formidable national security gum shoes trotting around?"

Billy adjusted his bulk in the seat and picked his Guinness back up.

"That's a damn good question. And it's not like a person can smuggle a RV the size of the Queen Mary past border guards."

He took a large swallow and burped politely.

"My guess is that he had permission from higher ups."

"How high is that?" I said.

"Damn high. And get this, our good buddies Longbeach and Redtail--and now that I think about it, Pfeffer and

Gibson--who should have been highly concerned about that, never said a thing any of the times I interviewed them."

He paused. Studied me.

"They ever discuss that around you?"

I shook my head.

"Kind of implies they don't like to share intel with us paper boys, doesn't it?" I said.

"Indeed it does."

We both looked out the window. We were passing over the small city of Penticton and the beginning of the hundred mile long, one mile wide Okanogan Lake. The scene looked more like a village on the banks of a Norwegian fjord than a scene from the Canadian wilderness.

Sam eased back on the throttle and we began to lose altitude. Kelowna was less than fifty miles away. He was already in contact with the airport's tower and was discussing the approach.

"John," Billy said over his shoulder, "connect me with the RCMP in Kelowna, will ya?"

Billy turned back to me.

"Good cameraman. Even better mandolin player," he said softly.

Within moments John got up from his seat and handed a sleek narrow black phone to Billy and went back to work without saying a word.

Billy put it to his ear and winked at me.

"O'Conner here....Thanks....Yes....We're on the approach....I understand."

Billy continued to listen for several minutes. From time to time he made concurrencies and acknowledgments but said nothing.

"I understand....Yes. Thank you very much."

And he pushed a button on the phone and reached back.

John took the phone and Billy grinned at me.

"We are to go directly to Freddy Stripe's house," he said. "He's expecting us."

I stared at him.

"He's expecting us?"

"Apparently."

I shook my head.

"Well, I suppose you know where he lives."

"Just learned." He tapped his temple with a finger. "Got it right here. But no matter. We're being met on the strip."

We could feel and hear the landing gears thump down and lock into place. The Cessna wobbled twice to adjust angle and the pitch of the turbo props whined louder.

"What's going on, here, Billy? Why are we being met?" I said.

He shrugged.

"Like I said. This is going to be an unusually entertaining day, ol' friend. And it's about to begin."

Chapter
Eighty-Four

A pewter colored Lincoln limo met us at the airport and drove us five miles south along the lake shore to the outskirts of Kelowna. We turned east into the older residential section between downtown and timber covered hills. Here cottages gave way to broad streets lined with massive hardwoods and homes that sat back from the streets on one or more acres of meticulously landscaped yards and gardens. Had this been in the states, it would have been a gated community. In fact, Kelowna itself was so clean and tastefully prosperous the whole town should have been gated. Apparently the American dream the Bush administration had killed was still alive in Canada.

The Stripe residence was a large, two story, brick 1920s Arts and Crafts bungalow trimmed tastefully in white and clothed in ivy. The circular drive was of granite pavers, and as we pulled in, we saw that Stripe was already standing on the porch waiting for us, coffee cup in hand. Beside him stood an ancient Indian woman with perfectly white hair hanging down to her waist in two long thin braids. She couldn't have stood any taller than five feet and was dressed in an ankle length, dark blue velvet dress with stitching on the sleeves, and her feet, covered by blue felt scuffs, peeked out from under its hem.

Stripe was wearing tasseled loafers, thin black wool slacks, and a gray silk dress shirt open at the collar. He came down the steps as we came to a stop and opened the rear door for Billy. The driver came around, opened mine.

I swung out and walked around the rear of the car as he drove off.

Billy and Stripe were shaking hands.

"Glad you could make it, Mr. O'Conner, he said. "We've been expecting you for some time now."

He turned and shook my hand as well.

"But I'm sorry Smoke couldn't have joined us, Paul," he said.

I nodded.

He reached back and gently presented his mother to us.

"This is my mother, Marie Leib," he said.

She smiled and motioned with one hand for us to follow. We filed into the house behind her. Stripe came up the rear.

We were led through a plaster and beam living room heavy with dark oak upholstered furniture and recessed glass doored bookcases jammed with books and periodicals. We went into a long formal dining room. Billy and I were motioned to take seats at a linen covered table. We sat with our backs to a bay window topped with a line of rectangular panes that looked over a formal English garden

"So," Stripe said, still standing, "I apologize for not having Starbucks or Seattle Best coffees for you, Mr. O'Connor..."

"Billy is fine."

"...Billy, but a gentleman imports and roasts our own beans here in Kelowna, and I must say they make your corporate coffees seem inadequate, somehow. I also know you like a splash of Irish whiskey in yours, so I have an unopened bottle of Black Bush, if you'd like."

He waited with his hands clasped lightly in front of him.

Billy was looking up at him carefully.

"That would be fine," he managed.

"Mother loves tea," Stripe said. "And isn't that your choice for a late morning pick-me-up, Paul?"

"Yes, thanks."

He nodded.

"A blend? I could do a lovely pot for you and Mother with peppery Royal Golden Yunnan blended with Mangalam Assam," he said. "It was Sir Edmund Hillary's drink. Joked it got him up Everest."

"Sounds good," I said.

He turned and went into the kitchen. Billy and I looked at each other and then at Marie. She smiled and brought her hands up from her lap and folded them on the table. Her bones showed through their backs and were covered with shiny skin that resembled crumpled, walnut colored tissue paper. She looked like a wizened lady leprechaun.

She said nothing.

I wondered if she spoke English. Or if she spoke at all. Perhaps she had decided it was a frivolous pastime that only created problems.

We sat in silence.

A tea pot began to whistle in the kitchen. We heard ceramic being moved and opened, and shortly Stripe returned balancing a large silver tray. He lifted off a bottle of Bushmill Black Label Irish Whiskey, a French press with coffee grounds swirling in its hot water, and a Brown Betty tea pot. He put the emptied tray on the china cabinet behind him and pulled up beside his mother across from us.

He examined the coffee, and satisfied, pressed the plunger and poured coffee for Billy and himself.

"The tea has a few more minutes to go, Paul," he said.

Then, "So tell me, what brings you to our lake side village?"

He opened the Irish whiskey and handed the bottle to Billy. Billy took it and poured a healthy slug into his coffee. The resulting smell, which immediately filled the room, was deliciously smoky and rich.

"Seems a shame to pour Black Bush into coffee, Mr. Stripe," Billy said.

"Freddy."

"Freddy. And how did you come by a bottle of it?"

"A friend brought it back. I've had it in the cabinet for several months. But it's available here in Canada now. I'm glad to share it with you."

Billy took a sip and nodded, smiling.

"You remind me quite of bit of Butte MacAvity," I told Stripe.

He stood slightly out of his chair and poured his mother's tea and then mine.

"Thank you," he said.

"But you're not the Freddy Stripe that hung out at the pub with us. When you were visiting us you were impersonating a rednecked racist," I said.

He grinned.

"Wanted to fit in," he said.

I shook my head.

"That's not an accurate assessment of Ryback," I said.

He nodded. "I know. I was being ironic. But I suppose I didn't want to stand out. I wanted to look like a typical Snow Bird in an RV."

I glanced out the window behind me.

"Where do you park that monster, anyway?"

"It's not mine, Paul," he said. "It was loaned to me."

Billy was recovering from his Black Bush reverie.

"By your old pals in the CSIS?" he said.

Stripe's stopped smiling and looked at Billy carefully.

"Indirectly, I suppose," he said.

Billy considered this, then took a surprisingly different slant.

"Is Marie related to Micha Wirestone, Freddy?"

"Cousins."

Billy smiled.

"Like you and Samuel Beauvallon?

"Exactly."

Stripe was smiling now as well. He took a sip of his coffee and waited.

Billy nodded.

"And Samuel and Billy Long Gone are Shuswap Enforcers?"

"Yes."

Billy took another sip of his coffee.

"Umm. This is excellent."

He sat the cup back on its saucer.

"As an operative for the Canadian Security Intelligence Service for over two decades, and as a highly trained RCMP, you bring a lot of expertise with your retirement back to your people, Freddy," he said.

"Yes, I suppose I do."

I guessed my tea was cool enough to taste without slurping. I lifted the thin walled china cup to my lips and took a small sip. The tea sat a moment on my tongue. I swallowed. It was a serious tea. I knew I was in for an experience only a truly special-fine-tippy full-leaf tea can induce. A euphoria, in fact.

I sat the cup back down and glanced over at Marie. She had been watching me and her eyes were bright and pleased. She nodded slightly and lifted her own cup to her lips and took a sip, still watching me over the rim.

Billy cleared his throat and leaned towards Stripe. I braced for what he might say next. When Billy cleared his throat, it usually meant the next question would either tank the conversation completely, or get it going somewhere. Or not.

"Did Micha Wirestone contact you?" he said.

"He dropped in last fall, actually," Stripe said. "Invited me to come and pay a visit."

"Micha came here?" I said.

"Yes."

"I didn't think he ever left his cabin anymore."

"He doesn't," Stripe said. "But he did last fall."

"Must have been something on his mind," Billy said.

Stripe reached out for the Black Bush and poured a small amount into his own coffee. He held his cup up to Billy and they toasted.

They put their cups back down and Billy rested both elbows on the edge of the table and waited.

Stripe leaned back in his chair and folded his hands over the ends of the chair arms and relaxed.

"Billy, you are, indeed, the world's greatest investigative journalist as I have been told, and I am, you could agree, a decent sort of spook."

"There is that," Billy said.

"And you want to know if my cousins and I culled members of Spreiter's renewed drug cartel, am I right?"

"You are."

"And you have a hunch we did it to keep our People and our People's children safe from the drugs of the underworld."

"Indeed I do," Billy said.

"And you plan to pay Trent Mazollan a visit as soon as you have completed your visit with my mother and me."

"That was my hope."

Stripe sighed and leaned forward again. He took a swallow of his Irish coffee. He shook his head slightly, looked into his cup and then looked at his mother. They retained eye contact without expression for several moments.

Stripe turned back, glanced at me and then focused again on Billy.

"You have a fine mind, Billy, and you, indeed, know how to earn money as a journalist. And you deserve a great deal of respect for your penchant for the truth and your courage to present it to your readership.

"But that, and a fine taste in whiskey, do not complete you as a gentleman."

Billy went totally passive. His body seemed to settle in on itself. I had a bad feeling this was not going to turn out well.

"My mother and I would have enjoyed a letter or call from you requesting to visit us at our home. We would have been glad to welcome you in and tell you anything you needed to know about our People and our relatives the Camas.

"You did not need to file a flight plan into Canada and arrange a meeting with my old friends at the RCMP in hopes of gaining entrance through our front door. Our door is open."

He nodded at me.

"Paul and his friends had one of the most powerful drug cartels in the western United States fall on them two years ago because of good deeds Huey and Hammersmith did thirty some years earlier in Vietnam. And relief work Huey continued to do during those thirty years and now is going to continue doing through his mission work on the Mekong."

"He is?" I said.

"And Billy," he said, "you helped prevent Huey and his friends from getting killed. You also helped all of us put Spreiter in prison and knock back his organization."

He hesitated.

"And now you want to know if this time around the Shuswap People helped. You want to know if I helped. You want to know if Wirestone helped and if Josiah and Oscar helped. You might even want to know if Mother helped."

He paused for several moments, watching Billy carefully. Billy looked back without expression.

Freddy Stripe, aka Casper Leib, CSIS, continued.

"And, perhaps, you feel knowing those things now will make a difference. And how is that? Will knowing those things allow you to unmask Trent Mazollan?"

Billy said nothing.

"Well it won't. Trent Mazollan is dead. You should know that. So--help me here. How do you think knowing who did what and for what reasons will change a thing? How will it help? I want to know."

I had had enough.

"I resent the direction you're taking here," I said. "Are you implying that Mr. O'Conner is self-serving?"

He looked from me back to Billy.

"*Are* you vainglorious and self-serving, Mr. O'Conner?" he said.

"Probably," Billy said, after a moment. "Are you at least willing to share how Mazollan died?"

Stripe came close to chuckling. Sounded like a cough.

"The RCMP concluded that he jumped from his fifth floor office balcony to the sidewalk," he said. "They've decided to ignore the fact that one of his shoes was still behind his desk ten feet from the sliding glass doors."

"Did Mazollan like to walk around with one shoe off?" Billy said.

"Apparently."

Billy drank the rest of his coffee and sat his cup down gently.

Stripe stood, opened a frosted glass door at the top of the china cabinet, and placed two small heavy glasses between them. He poured each of them half full of whiskey and resumed his seat.

Marie got to her feet carefully and went into the living room. She eased into a small mission style rocker and sat looking out the front window at the distant street.

"As a truly vainglorious, self serving man," Billy said, "I should have barged in here with my camera crew. As things stand, I am requesting, for my own personal edification, your take on the role you have played that impacted my Ryback and Camas friends."

He paused.

"If you'd be so kind."

They picked up their glasses simultaneously and drank.

After a moment's consideration Stripe nodded.

"I suppose the big picture is the Canadian-American border," he said. "I'm only speaking as a Shuswap, here."

Billy nodded.

"White people, which I am too, drew a line dividing our People. They love to do that. They drew a line through Vietnam. They drew a line through Korea. They drew a line through the Kurds. They draw lines between Protestants and Catholics, between Christians, Jews, Muslims and Atheists. Between Whites, Blacks, Asians, and Indigenous Peoples. And it always ends in hatred and war and makes everyone sick in their hearts and souls."

He tossed back the rest of his Black Bush.

"The thing is, Billy, and you too, Paul, it's not just that the Shuswap People see the land's treasures emptied on wars--they don't see it feeding the poor and curing the sick. And they don't see it enforcing the law."

I wasn't sure what he was driving at.

Stripe noticed my look.

"When it's clear, in our culture, that there is a snake in the village, the elders meet and discuss what to do about the threat it poses. Then we discuss their conclusions with the snake. If the snake strikes anyway, we kill it. If it's a large snake, we start at the tail and work our way forwards, and when we reach the head, the snake can't strike anymore because it no longer has a spine. Then we kill the head."

Lana had said basically the same thing.

Billy nodded.

"Did you speak with Mazollan?"

"Several times. And Spreiter as well. And because they were snakes in our villages, we felt no need to consult with a culture that recently came to our land and started drawing lines and imposing their own laws. We are our own nation, and the Canadian-American border has no meaning for us."

He picked up the whiskey and motioned if Billy would like more. I held out my tea cup.

He poured all around.

"Well," Billy said, "there goes the fame and fortune I was counting on, Freddy."

We drank. The whiskey immediately reacted with the Mount Everest tea I had imbibed, and within two swallows I knew I was doomed.

"Listen," I said, "you could have been more forthcoming. But despite the fact you are only half right about Billy's motives, and not right at all about his character, I'd like to tell you that even Smoke had a hunch that you have been the one behind the snake hunt, and I can say we're all extremely grateful."

"Hear, hear," Billy said.

"In that case," Stripe said, "I'll go gather Mother and take us all downtown to lunch. Billy Long Gone and

Samuel Beauvallon are waiting for us at an excellent seafood grill on the top floor of the Okanogan Hotel."

"Are they all spiffed up like you?" Billy said.

"Absolutely. Silk shirts all around," he said. "And if we sit here much longer, I run the risk of impairing myself on this wicked malt."

"How the hell do you know ahead of time our every move?" I said.

Stripe got to his feet.

"Because I am a half decent retired CSIS spook, Paul," he said.

"Oh."

Chapter
Eighty-Five

Billy called Lana on the Cessna's satellite phone. She said she'd meet us at the Magnet Air strip in an hour. He didn't bother handing the phone to me--he said okay, clicked off, and handed it back to Sam.

He hadn't said much since we'd left the Okanogan Hotel in another limo, this one white. Lunching with Stripe, his mother, Marie, and Stripe's two enforcers, Billy Long Gone and Samuel Beauvallon, had been polite but fruitless.

Billy had sat without comment across the aisle from me scribbling lines on a yellow legal pad with a ball point and scratching them out again. I couldn't tell if he was pissed at me or in a dour mood because the Canadian project had jammed up.

I didn't care to know which, either.

Instead I felt my own exhaustion from the past three days push on me like a headwind. I shifted my mind into neutral and focused on the Salmo Priest Wilderness mountains that swept slowly under us. And then the Kaniksu National Forest edged on the east by the enormous length of Priest Lake.

John, a permanent fixture at the back of the plane, made me jump by saying, "It's up, Billy."

He pointed to the display to his right. It showed the front page of this afternoon's Boise Banner.

Billy got slowly to his feet and went back to take a look. He eased onto a padded computer chair and with a few keystrokes converted the pages to single fourteen point columns. Billy's article was headed, SEWU PROFESSOR ARRESTED IN DRUG BUST. He read the article slowly, scrolling as he did. It was at least a twenty four inch article and had a photo of the labs.

I shut my eyes and focused on the smooth rush of the Cessna's turboprop. I knew Billy would spend ten minutes or more mulling over what he had written. I had done the very same thing a thousand times when I was doing active journalism for the Trib. I still did it with my puny six inch column that came out each week, always looking for an error or some oversight that would make my heart drop.

Billy eventually came back to his seat and picked up his legal pad. He noticed me stir and looked over.

"You all right?" he said.

"How'd the article look?"

"Like shit," he said. "Good for a crime beat, but didn't have the metal I was hoping for. I was holding back the big picture--you know, "crime syndicate finally has balls cut off," that sort of thing--until I'd got something out of Trent Mazollan. So the inconsiderate fuck gets himself tossed off his office balcony and kills the story."

He shook his head hopelessly.

"Stripe and apparently all of the Indian Nations came and did the job and left all the rooms empty. Nothing left to write about except horse shit and feathers. Hopeless."

"Maybe this?" John said. He waited as six pages spooled from an HP laser printer. He gathered them up and swiveled around so that he could hand them to Billy without getting up.

Billy took them, put them flat on the table and read carefully, turning each page as he did.

We started losing altitude quickly. Magnet's air strip was short and surrounded by rolling hills. Landing there closely resembled *hitting* there, and we were obviously making our approach. The landing gears whined down, locked into place with thumps, and rushed with noise as they cut through the air.

Billy finished reading, picked the pages up, squared them against the table top and laid them flat.

"Bingo!" he said. "Now I can do my job."

The plane began to bob and yaw as it lined up through the turbulent surface air for the landing.

"What?" I said.

Billy held up his hand like a traffic cop.

"Let's land first," he said. I'll tell you then."

I nodded.

"You want to lay over and enjoy a little of MacAvity's pub food tonight?" I said. "Introduce your crew to a bunch of old farmer types that enjoy shooting drug thugs?"

He shook his head.

"I gotta get back. It's going to be a late night. I finally got something to justify the expenses of this junket. And I gotta figure what I can print that doesn't compromise Stripe, the Shuswap People, the CSIS, the RCMP, the Camas, and Stripe's mother. The mother alone, with a single nod of her head as she sits in her living room rocker, probably has enough influence to have me and and my entire family hung in ghost trees."

"You don't have an entire family, Billy," I said.

"Then dammit, I'll get one for them to kill. Marry me a sweet little fat lady and live in a townhouse off Boise Park."

"You should," I said.

We touched down with a jolt and a howling of brakes and engine. Within seconds we were rolling softly off the runway to the hanger.

"You sure Sam's not a drunken bush pilot, Billy?" I said.

"I heard that!" Sam said from the cockpit.

There was a buzz and a light on the panel facing John came on. He lifted the receiver again, listened and handed it to Billy.

We rolled to a stop and the engine whined down and grew silent. I looked out the side window and saw Lana step away from the terminal door and walk across the concrete apron towards us. She was dressed in faded jeans and a white long sleeved shirt.

John cracked the togs and lowered the stairs. He got out first and stretched his back in the sunshine. I edged down the three narrow steps behind him and met Lana at the tip of the wing. She wrapped both arms around my neck and we kissed and rocked back and forth.

"Paul!" Billy behind us.

He was holding out the six pages John had given him.

"Take these. Everything's in them you need to know."

I went back to the steps and he folded the pages up and handed them to me.

"That was the boss. I gotta boogie. I'll call you at home tonight," he said. "We'll talk about it."

"Home or at MacAvitys, OK?" I said.

Lana drove us back quickly. I kept my left hand on her thigh and I filled her in on everything that had happened. Then I removed my hand and unfolded the pages Billy had given to me. I read them aloud, and for the rest of the drive we discussed their implications and the jam Billy must be in.

Smoke and I had only been gone three days but there were only a smattering of snowdrifts still under the brows of the hills, and the winter wheat had taken on the deep green of Irish turf. I rolled down my side window and breathed in the sweet warmth of the late afternoon air.

Lana and I were sitting at the bar less than an hour later.

Smoke hadn't shown yet. Huey and Joy weren't due back from Hawaii. Ruthie had returned from San Francisco, and she and Hammersmith had phoned Lana to say they were spending the night at home and would be in touch tomorrow.

Everyone else, it seemed, was taking advantage of the warm weather to get as much planting and spraying done as possible and would work into the night with flood lights.

The pub was empty and blessedly silent. Butte mixed us Sapphire gin martinis.

Sheila came out of the kitchen and set four filet mignons in front of us and slid onto a stool at Lana's right. The grilled filets shined with juice. They were two inches thick, bacon wrapped, and Sheila served them with a single small yellow fin potato and a ladle of buttered baby peas. With eight ounce cuts like these, I knew nothing else was needed.

Butte sat on a stool opposite us studying the pages Billy had given me. He moved them aside to make room for his plate, but didn't stop reading.

I pulled my plate closer and picked up my fork and one of the razor sharp German steak knives Butte insisted on providing for his diners. I gently pressed the blade through the meat and took a bit.

Butte gave a *humph* and pushed the pages aside and pulled his plate up as well.

"I bet that makes Billy happy," he said.

Sheila looked up from eating.

"So what's this about? Something to do with that professor?"

"Yeah," Butte said. "Brockington spilled his guts this morning after Sheriff Rodney Colton arranged for him to spend a frightening night in the slam with a very drunk local rodeo clown."

He took a bit of his steak and with raised eyebrows nodded at her, chewed thoughtfully, and winked his approval.

"Seems the clown wanted more than light conversation," he said.

Sheila slit her potato and dropped a spoonful of sour cream into it.

She looked up at Butte.

"So?"

Butte continued to eat.

"So," I said, stepping in, "every year the professor would begin grooming a female Ph.D. candidate. He would pay her student debts, offer them back to her interest free, and as chair he would make certain her orals went smoothly and her dissertation was accepted. Finally, he'd use his influence to get her a assistant professorship at a major university somewhere.

"And along the way, the candidate would become more and more obliged to him. First sex, then turning a blind eye to little incongruities that were going on at the lab...that sort of thing.

"Until, finally, after she was all situated and happily at work at, say, University of California Davis, or University of Oregon, or some other agricultural research university, he would show up at her office and set the hook."

Sheila listened without moving. Full eye contact.

I tried to get it right.

"So all she now had to do for Brockington was set aside certain samples among those he sent her from his labs. The selected few could be recognized by a code number printed on the boxes.

"Then this young associate professor was to allow a particular visitor to take the marked samples away. The code numbers of the samples and the code name of the pickup man she'd get e-mailed to her the day before they arrived. Simple."

I took another bit, chewed and swallowed. Sheila had marinated the meat in something that was both peppery and hinting of garlic.

"And if everything went as planned," I said, "the student debts she owed Brockington would slowly be canceled. And if she didn't go along, she would be exposed, have her career smashed, and have her loans sold to unsavory mobbed-up types."

Butte chipped in. "And she'd know she'd never be able to make the vig. She thought she was working for tenure but would end up a perfect candidate for a different and older line of work."

Sheila nodded. "That's fucked up," she said.

I nodded.

"Brockington gave these poor women up, and Gibson and Pfeffer are having him make one last dummy shipment so they can set up a sting and catch the pickups and their distributors as well."

I cut open my potato, pressed out the steaming yellow meat with the back of my fork and spread sweet salted butter over it.

"If a person were to research which agricultural universities and their attached communities have a meth problem," I said, "you'll know which five Brockington said he had been successful at."

Sheila was tapping a finger.

"What was Yost doing then besides samples for the labs? Doesn't seem the university distribution thing would involve much volume."

"Brockington was just a branch of Yost's trafficking," I said. "All the others have been nailed, thanks to Alex Byrd's micro chip."

It was at that moment Smoke came through the door. He was momentarily silhouetted against the pink light of the fading sun reflecting off the brick wall of the fire station across the street.

He looked totally exhausted. But happy.

Chapter
Eighty-Six

I was nearly asleep that night when Lana pushed open my door and looked in. The soft glow from the grain elevator's yard light coming through the front window reflected off her right side. At age sixty five she still had the slender body and smooth skin of a woman in her thirties.

I held up my blankets and she came into the room and slid in beside me. She hooked one knee over my thigh, placed a hand on my chest, and snuggled down with her head on my shoulder.

"Paul," she said, "is all this stuff over now?"

"I think it is," I whispered. I placed my hand on the hollow of her waist.

"And we can just be happy?"

"I'm sure of it."

We lay quietly for some time.

Then Lana stirred and tipped her head upwards a fraction.

"I forgot to tell you something," she said softly.

"That you love me a little?"

"You know I love you a little," she said.

Our oldest joke.

I waited.

Her fingers moved over my chest.

"Huey called from Maui while you guys were gone," she said. "Joy was on the cottage's other phone and they took turns talking."

She settled in more snugly.

"They're going on to Vietnam and the burned-out ruins of his mission."

I nodded, rocking her head as I did. How the hell did Stripe learn this? CSIS monitoring international phone calls of Chinese peoples? Probably.

"Joy's aunt flew to Honolulu yesterday," Lana said, "She called a meeting with her large extended Chinese-American family. They came from several of the islands for the gathering."

"What about?" I whispered.

"They're very wealthy. They are going to give Huey and Joy the money they'll need to rebuild the mission and build themselves a home there."

I nodded.

"I'm gone three days and everything goes to hell."

"Which is why you should leave more often," she said. She pressed her chin painfully into my chest.

"And they want us to all fly to Lahaina next month for a good old fashioned Chinese/Occidental wedding ceremony," Lana said.

She waiting for my response.

I pulled her over on top of me and kissed her hair.

"That's the best news I've heard in years," I said.

"So you're excited?"

I rubbed my hands down her back and wrapped my arms around her slender waist.

"Can't you tell?"

"That too," she said.

Then, "You think there's anything between Smoke and Nadine?"

I shook my head. "No--I think they've both found new best friends in each other," I said.

"Smoke bought her a sofa bed. Something to sleep on when he comes to visit?"

"Right. Not a queen sized bed."

Lana dropped her legs down each side of me and scooted lower on my stomach.

"You think they have sex?" she whispered.

"Probably."

She kissed my chest.

"Like good friends?"

"The best of friends," I managed.

end